WHERE'S KOJAK WHEN YOU NEED HIM?

The captain glared at me. Here I was a potential murder victim and he was showing as much concern for my welfare as he would for Public Enemy Number One. "Why haven't I been given police protection?" I demanded. "That stuff was sent to *me*, not to Rudy."

"Was it? The sample that came in the mail could have been exactly what the label said. We don't know when the cyanide was substituted. It's an old ploy, claiming to be the intended victim. Lots of killers use it."

That made me see red. To come off a rotten day like the one I'd just had and listen to some fat cop hinting that I'd deliberately given Rudy cyanide. "You can't be serious..."

Captain Michaels leaned over me, all muscle and authority and don't-mess-with-me, the bully. His breath stank. "I'm dead serious, lady, and don't you forget it."

Bantam Books offers the finest in classic and modern American murder mysteries. Ask your bookseller for the books you have missed.

Stuart Palmer

THE PUZZLE OF THE SILVER PERSIAN
THE PUZZLE OF THE HAPPY HOOLIGAN

Craig Rice

MY KINGDOM FOR A HEARSE
THE LUCKY STIFF

Rex Stout

AND FOUR TO GO
BAD FOR BUSINESS
THE BROKEN VASE
DEATH OF A DUDE
DEATH TIMES THREE
DOUBLE FOR DEATH
A FAMILY AFFAIR
THE FATHER HUNT
FER-DE-LANCE
THE FINAL DEDUCTION
GAMBIT
THE LEAGUE OF FRIGHTENED MEN
MURDER BY THE BOOK
NOT QUITE DEAD ENOUGH
PLOT IT YOURSELF
THE RED BOX
THE RUBBER BAND
SOME BURIED CAESAR
THE SOUND OF MURDER
THREE DOORS TO DEATH
THREE FOR THE CHAIR
TOO MANY CLIENTS

Victoria Silver

DEATH OF A HARVARD FRESHMAN
DEATH OF A RADCLIFFE ROOMMATE

Max Byrd

CALIFORNIA THRILLER
FINDERS WEEPERS
FLY AWAY, JILL

R. D. Brown

HAZZARD

Sue Grafton

"B" IS FOR BURGLAR

Robert Goldsborough

MURDER IN E MINOR

Ross MacDonald

BLUE CITY
THE BLUE HAMMER
GOODBYE LOOK
THE MOVING TARGET

A. E. Maxwell

JUST ANOTHER DAY IN PARADISE

Rob Kantner

THE BACK-DOOR MAN

Joseph Telushkin

THE UNORTHODOX MURDER OF RABBI WAHL

Ted Wood

LIVE BAIT

Barbara Paul

KILL FEE
THE RENEWABLE VIRGIN

THE RENEWABLE VIRGIN

VIRGIN

Barbara Paul

BANTAM BOOKS
TORONTO · NEW YORK · LONDON · SYDNEY · AUCKLAND

This low-priced Bantam Book
has been completely resent in a type face
designed for easy reading, and was printed
from new plates. It contains the complete
text of the original hard-cover edition.
NOT ONE WORD HAS BEEN OMITTED.

THE RENEWABLE VIRGIN
A Bantam Book / published by arrangement with
Charles Scribner's Sons

PRINTING HISTORY
Charles Scribner's Sons edition published April 1985
Bantam edition / November 1986

ISBN 0-55-26234-3

PRINTED IN THE UNITED STATES OF AMERICA

KR   0 9 8 7 6 5 4 3 2 1

1
Kelly Ingram

Rudy Benedict and I were just beginning to get something going when I found out he saw himself as David ready to take on the giant. What Rudy didn't know was I'd always been on Goliath's side.

"What is there to fear?" he said, puffing away on his pipe in that writerish way of his. (Anybody else would have said *What's to be afraid of?*) "The networks are composed of mere human beings motivated by the same fears and ambitions that drive the rest of us. There are no superpowers involved."

Except that those mere human beings controlled budgets in the millions while good folks like Rudy and me or I had to scrabble for a piece of the pie. "What are you up to? You're cranking yourself up for something."

He gave that smug little smile of his that was *just* beginning to irritate me and didn't answer right away. Making me wait for it. "I'm writing a play. I'm returning to the theater—where I really belong."

I didn't see how anybody could return to where he'd never been, but I was being polite that night and didn't say so. "Well, congratulations, Rudy. That's good to hear."

"I'm not telling everybody, Kelly. But I wanted you to know."

I nodded. "Thanks for the confidence. It's important for Leonard and I to keep track." Leonard Zoff was my agent.

"Me. For Leonard and me."

Guessed wrong. "Me, then. What's your play about?"

Rudy took a long draw on his pipe and said, slowly, "I'm writing about television. So of course there's no chance of getting it produced *on* television. And the movies aren't any better, not any more. You can't beat that system either."

So it was theater by default. "Exposé sort of thing, you mean?"

He looked pained. "Please, Kelly. I don't write sleaze. All I want to do is show that television is merely one fingernail of the multi-armed corporate powers that control our lives."

I took a moment to work my way through that metaphor and then said, "Didn't Paddy Chayefsky already do that?"

Rudy waved his pipe dismissively. "Merely as one episode in an ongoing David-and-Goliath confrontation. Chayefsky always wrote about the little guy fighting the good but futile fight. One small man failing to topple the giant. That's not what I'm interested in. I want to probe more deeply into the nature of the beast."

"So you're not interested in giant-toppling?"

He smiled in that charming way that reminded me why I'd been attracted to him in the first place. "I didn't say that, Kelly. But I'm not such a fool as to think my one play will miraculously open everybody's eyes. This country is so addicted to television that people simply *refuse* to believe their attitudes are manipulated every time they turn on the set."

I thought it more likely they just didn't care. "So you do want to topple the giant."

His charming smile eased into his smug one. "My goals are more modest. Just shake him up a bit."

So there it was. Rudy Benedict saw himself as a giant-killer, no matter how modest he claimed his goals were. Like David, standing in a place of safety with his long-distance weapon, taking pot shots at the giant with impunity. (Impugnity?) Only Rudy's weapon would be a play instead of a sling. "Got a part for me?" I asked automatically.

"Maybe," he answered just as automatically. "The *dramatis personae* isn't complete yet. Ever acted on the stage?"

"No." Ever written for the stage? "Should I do Off-Broadway, Rudy? I keep getting contradictory advice."

He shrugged. "Good showcase. Wouldn't hurt. The kind of stage training you get depends on the director you get. Wouldn't hurt, Kelly."

I nodded, as if thinking it over. I had no intention of committing myself to a not-completely-professional production that would tie me up all summer on the million-to-one shot that some Big Producer would turn up in the audience one night. I had better irons in the fire.

Rudy had already turned the talk back to his play. I'd flattered him by asking his advice and he hadn't noticed. If he'd needled me for trying to stroke him, I'd have respected him for it. If he'd preened himself on being consulted as a figure of superior experience, I'd have accepted it. But when he didn't even *notice* . . . sometimes I think writers are the most unobservant people in the world.

I'd met Rudy three years earlier, in California, when I was still in my second-generation Barbie doll phase. Slit skirts, sprayed-on plastic face, the whole shtick. I hated looking exactly like everybody else but it was the only way to get roles. Rudy Benedict was one of a trio of writers grinding out unfunny scripts for a show in which the actors mostly rolled their eyes suggestively while the laughtrack man punched the button marked "Dirty Snickers." The script called for a Playboy-bunny type who for some reason agrees to go out with one of the show's yokel heroes. My agent's West Coast rep happened to be sucking up to the right people that week so I got the part. I appeared in two scenes and had a total of seven lines, one of which was "Yes." Rudy swore he didn't write that one. Then I kind of lost track of him for a while, until we ran into each other in New York.

Just then he was lighting his pipe again, the seventeenth time in the past hour. Rudy was a good guy, but his putting on egghead airs was beginning to get on my nerves. I understood he needed those props to help him make the transition from TV hack to Serious Dramatist. Rudy wasn't forty yet; he'd just scheduled his mid-life crisis a little early, that was all. I wished he'd go on and get the damned play written so he could forget about all the posturing he thought was supposed to go with it.

Finally he gave up on the pipe and decided to nuzzle my neck instead.

"Rudy, you ought to stop smoking that pipe," I told him. "It's given you another headache, hasn't it? You've got that pinched look again."

He rubbed his forehead with the tip of his middle finger. "Now that you mention it . . ."

He left soon after that. Sometimes it works.

After a good night's sleep I allowed myself the luxury of feeling a little guilty about Rudy. I didn't want to dump him;

he was good fun when he was thinking about something other than himself. Besides, there was always the chance that he might turn out to be a Big Talent after all. I resolved to be nicer to Rudy Benedict.

But I never got a chance to put my good intentions into practice, because about then somebody came along and murdered him.

When Rudy Benedict decided it would be easier to be a Serious Writer on the East Coast than on the West, he'd moved into an apartment in Chelsea and hated it. He'd told me he'd been looking for a better place to live for almost a year but couldn't find what he wanted; welcome to the club. I'd been to the place once and it was crowded and littered-looking, nothing special. Rudy had taken it only because someone had told him a lot of writers lived in the area.

Rudy hadn't completely broken his ties with the West Coast, however, and that's how I happened to run into him again. I'd moved back east myself because I'd gotten a small continuing part in a series about a private investigator, to be shot entirely in New York City. ("Pea eyes are making a comeback," my agent, Leonard Zoff, had said.) This one was a sort of Harry O in the Big Apple, and I had the Farah Fawcett role, the Sex Object Next Door. ("Play it sweet," Leonard told me when I went in for my interview. "Make it like 'Who, me—sexy?' We're in a *conservative* period, darling. Play it real sweet and make sure they know you're not wearing a bra.") So I'd been all bright-eyed innocence, seemingly unaware that my clothing and movements were come-ons. That'd been just what they were looking for and I had my first continuing role in a series.

At first I didn't have any great hopes for it except as a way to get myself seen; I mean, I didn't have much expectation for the *show*. For one thing, it was a Nathan Pinking production ("If it's stinking, it's by Pinking")—and even if it did hit, that was no guarantee I'd be remembered as anything other than the broad in *LeFever* or by some equally unflattering label. That was the name of the show, *LeFever*, just the one word. Hot stuff, you see. One of the writers soberly explained to me the word had been chosen because of its "rhythmic compatibility"—a three-syllable word with the stress on the middle syllable, like "McMillan." Also, "LeFever" was elegant-sounding, easy to remember, and not too ethnic.

So I'd moved back to New York, right where I'd started out making whee-look-at-me shampoo commercials until I was told at age twenty-three I'd gotten too old for the image. After that had come five frustrating years in Hollywood, taking every shlock TV role and movie bit I could get. Then along came *LeFever* and it was back east again. I was pushing thirty and fully intended to go on pushing it as long as *LeFever* played. ("Stay young," Leonard had told me. "Forget Shakespeare, they're still buying youth.")

The initial feedback from the network had been good. They said the mail indicated the viewers wanted to see more of me. Nathan Pinking wasn't sure whether that meant they wanted to see me in more scenes or whether they wanted to see more of me physically, of my own personal bod. So we did it both ways; my role got larger and my costumes smaller. I even did one scene nude. But the network censor wouldn't let it pass, even though I'd played it sweet.

That's where Rudy Benedict came into the picture. Nathan Pinking had signed him some time ago as part of his stable of writers (you're *supposed* to think of horses), and the contract still had a year to run. But this last year Nathan wasn't using Rudy as a regular but instead kept bringing him in to do rewrite work and to fill in on this series or that as needed. Nathan had four series in production, two of them shooting in New York, so Rudy had been able to make the move back east without violating his contract. He told me he liked doing rewrite work—at least it suited him just then. He didn't have the responsibility of a weekly grind, and it was always fun to walk in at the eleventh hour and point out to the other writers what they'd done wrong. Didn't win him a lot of friends, but he said it felt *so good*. Nathan Pinking called him in on *LeFever* when one of our regular writers had to go into the hospital for prostate trouble.

I asked Rudy to give me some comedy lines and godblesshim he came through with some good ones. The ass playing LeFever was so dumb he didn't even know the scene was supposed to be funny until someone showed him a notice in the *Daily News* that said I'd revealed an "unexpected flair" for comedy. So he'd come in the next morning mad as hell 'cause I'd gotten the good lines and demanding to know why he'd been left out of the fun. But our regular writer was back then and Rudy was long gone, Nathan Pinking had turned invisible, and so I took the heat. Ass.

Thus Rudy Benedict was doing oddjob rewrites for Nathan Pinking while all of what he called his true creative energies went into the Great American Mellydrammer about television, a subject on which everybody in the world considers themselves, ah, himself or herself, or whatever, an expert. But Rudy really was an expert, or as close to being one as anyone who works *for* the medium can be. As opposed to those who make the medium work for them, owners and execs and such. Rudy'd been around almost since the day he'd left college, fifteen, sixteen years maybe. That's a lot of television scripts. Rudy had survived writer burn-out by working only half of each year.

The night after I'd sent him home with a headache, Rudy had failed to show up for a poker game in the same building where he lived. Since Rudy was supposed to bring the chips, an annoyed host had gone up and pounded on the door. There'd been no answer, but the host could hear the radio playing in Rudy's apartment. So he got the super to open up, and the two of them found Rudy crumpled up on the floor.

Rudy Benedict was dead, and he'd been poisoned—the police weren't saying what kind of poison or how it had been administered. It was a hell of a shock. Rudy wasn't what you'd call a threatening man—he was more like, well, like a *supplicant*, a petitioner. Trying to crash the inner circles, you know, that kind of person. He was a moderately successful man within his own field of expertise, but the field was kind of narrow and Rudy was beginning to feel squeezed. That's one reason he wanted to write a real honest-to-God play, I think. Not to get into the theater so much as to get out of television. Although theater has its own inner circle Rudy would have loved to crash. Not the money and muscle you find in TV and the movies, but there were compensations in belonging to that particular club. Poor Rudy never even got close.

Shock's funny, everybody doesn't react the same. For me it was like pulling back to a kind of platform and looking at the world from that slight distance. Things were a different color, too, a kind of yellow around the edges, I don't know why. That faded after a couple of days. Rudy Benedict and I were not close, had never been close. But the potential for *getting* close had come up and that made all the difference.

* * *

LeFever was shooting exteriors at the UN Building when the police came around to talk to me. I was waiting for a new camera set-up when the questions started.

"He was writing an exposé of the television industry," I told the policewoman who was questioning me. "A play."

"Gawdalmighty," she groaned. "That's the first thing everybody says." I let my surprise show, so she dropped the other shoe. "And it wasn't even true."

"Whoa, wait a minute." I thought a moment. "First of all, who's 'everybody'? Rudy didn't tell *everybody.*"

"He might have missed a few people in Manhattan," she said sardonically, "but not many." The policewoman was Detective Second Grade M. Larch, her ID had said; she had a gray potato face and was tired and fed-up-looking. Either a long day or a frustrating one, probably both. "Rudy Benedict told everybody he knew—in strictest confidence, of course— that he was writing a play about television."

"But he wasn't?"

"Not really—just piddling around. He'd made some notes about the story, but he hadn't gotten very far. He didn't even have names for his characters yet. Just called them A and B and C and like that."

"Maybe that's all you found . . ."

Detective Larch shook her head. "That's all there *was*. He did more talking about that play than he did writing. Writer's block, maybe?"

I shrugged. "Maybe. I thought he really was working on it. How can you be sure there wasn't anything else? Research notes, incriminating letters, all that stuff? Maybe somebody stole them. The same somebody who killed him."

She smiled, the first time. "You want it to be an exposé, don't you? All you folks in television, everyone I've talked to wants it to be an exposé. Sorry to disappoint you, but what notes Rudy Benedict left indicate his play was going to be one of those crisis-of-conscience things. Moment-of-truth stuff for the hero. The hero was to be a television writer who was afraid something he'd written might be harmful to young viewers. Autobiographical?"

I answered with a question of my own. "Something the hero had written? Like what? Maybe that—"

"Benedict hadn't even figured out *what* yet. He was just doodling. He was writing no exposé, Ms. Ingram, believe me."

"Call me Kelly," I said absently. "So he wasn't killed because of his play?"

"Doesn't look like it, although we're keeping that door open. Who were his enemies, Ms. Ingram?"

Okay, if she didn't want to call me Kelly, that was her business, what did I care. "I don't really know, *Detective Larch*, ma'am. I hadn't seen Rudy for a couple of years until I ran into him again a few weeks ago."

She sniffed at me. "You've got to have an idea or two. Give me some names."

"You want me to *guess*?"

Detective Larch looked tireder than ever. "Yes, Miss Kelly Ingram, guess, if you have to. Give me some names. I've got to have something to report."

She didn't give a damn what I said, just so I said *something*. Terrific police work. "His ex-wife, maybe," I said reluctantly—not out of concern for the former Mrs. Benedict (didn't even know her) but because I hate being bullied. "But I understood she and Rudy were on good terms. But then, *I* thought Rudy was writing an exposé of television, so what do I know. She's remarried, living in Connecticut. I don't think Rudy ever told me her married name—pretty sure he never mentioned it."

"Turrell, Mrs. Roger Turrell. She was home in bed with Mr. Roger Turrell the night Benedict was killed. Guess somebody else. Somebody he might have been on *bad* terms with."

I lifted my shoulders. "Just about any producer or director he worked with. Writers are always crying about how their scripts are butchered."

"Name one."

I looked around; nobody within earshot. "Start with the one who's running this show. Nathan Pinking."

"Pinking was a bad enemy of Benedict's? Ruined his scripts, did he?"

"I don't know if Nathan Pinking was any kind of enemy. You said name somebody and I did. Nathan's no worse, no better than other producers. Maybe a little better than most because he's so careless."

Bloodshot eyes in a potato face, blinking at me. "How's that?"

"Nathan's always in a hurry, which makes him careless, which keeps him from interfering too much. He's not even here most of the time—just shows up once in a while to make sure we aren't all off playing hookey on his time."

"Is he here now?"

"No. Just a couple of his lackeys."

"Who are they?"

I was pointing them out to her when the word came the cameras were ready. All I had to do in the scene was get out of a cab, run up some steps, and hand an envelope to the actor named Nick Quinlan who played LeFever. The first time we did it he dropped the envelope.

Nick Quinlan was a big, hunk-style male with the right haircut and the right mustache. He looked as if he was showing off his bare chest even when he was dressed to the teeth—really gorgeous to look at, if you didn't mind obviousness. But he couldn't talk. "Hey, make sure I got aholt fore y'leggo, woncha?"

"Ask for some stickum for your fingertips," I smiled.

I'd only recently got to the point where I'd started complaining out loud about Nick. When we first started shooting *LeFever*, that ox had stepped on just about every line I had. If I had a speech made up of more than one sentence, I had to run them together in a breathy attempt to get everything said before Nick came butting in with his line. But when he did interrupt before I'd finished, I didn't say anything to the director. I just smiled and kept a stiff upper lip and refused to complain. I was being professional, I was being a trouper, blah blah blah. Until I realized that nobody cared. Nobody even *noticed*. So from then on, every time Nick cut off one of my lines, I hollered. I hollered loud.

Right then the director was doing some hollering of his own, so I went back and got in the cab. Out the door, up the steps, hand over the envelope. Look concerned.

Nick had a line. It was supposed to be, "You'd think he'd know better than to write something like this, wouldn't you?" It came out, "Y'd thank he'd write sumpin bettern this, wooden chew?"

Flubbed lines are redone in television only if they are flagrantly wrong, like changing the meaning as Nick's misreading had just done. By then the director had worked with Nick enough to know that once his leading man started out blowing a line in that particular fashion, he'd never get it right. So right then and there the line was changed to read,

"I wish he hadn't written this." Nick could handle that. In television, everybody was used to disposable writing.

The next time we tried it somebody who wasn't supposed to be there wandered into the scene. The fourth attempt was ruined when Nick stumbled as he stepped forward to take the envelope and grabbed my arm to keep from falling—making me fall instead. But the fifth time we got it. Five tries to get what should have been a one-take sequence. Normal for *LeFever*.

It was the last shot of the day, so we were free to go. Detective Larch was waiting where I'd left her, leaning against one of the camera vans. She was staring at Nick Quinlan as he stood talking to the director. "What's wrong with him today?"

"Nothing. He's always like that."

She shook her head disbelievingly but made no comment. She started asking me about the last time I saw Rudy Benedict, the night before he died.

"He went home early, with a headache," I fudged a little.

"You didn't see him the next day at all?"

"No. Detective Larch, when did he die exactly? The papers didn't say."

"About an hour before his poker buddy found him. You're sure you didn't see him that day at all?"

"Of course I'm sure. The last I saw of him was about ten o'clock the night before."

"What did he talk about?"

"His play. The one you say he wasn't writing."

She sighed. "I gave you the wrong impression, didn't I? I meant he hadn't really got started on it, he was still doodling around. But he was planning a play, getting ready to write."

"And you know for a fact that it wasn't going to be an exposé of any sort. You're *really* sure of that, are you?"

"The Captain is sure. He's told us to look elsewhere for a motive."

The Captain, as if there was only one in the entire world. "Captain who?"

"Captain Michaels. He's in charge of the investigation. How did Benedict seem that last time? Upset, nervous...?"

"Just a little headachy. And that wasn't bad. He'd recently

started smoking a pipe, and I think that sometimes bothered him."

Detective Larch's bloodshot eyes stared straight into mine. "Headache. You said that before. My God, I must be tireder than I thought. Did he take anything for it?"

I thought back. "No, he—wait a minute. I gave him some, ah, Bromo-Seltzer."

At that the policewoman's entire appearance changed—her face came to life, her body woke up. "Bromo-Seltzer. You're sure it was Bromo-Seltzer?"

I stared at her, horrified. "You mean the stuff I gave him . . . you're saying I gave him the poison?" I could hear my voice rising.

"Take it easy, take it easy," Detective Larch said hastily, her own voice rising. "Let's get it straight first. Are you absolutely positive it was Bromo-Seltzer you gave him? Take your time. Think back."

I took my time and I thought back. I remembered the sample coming in the mail, in a box that was . . . *yellow*, not blue. "No, it wasn't Bromo-Seltzer! It was some new product, something for headache and upset stomach. I don't remember what it's called, it was just something that came in the mail. A sample."

"Did you take any of it?"

"No, it just came that day. Was that it? Was—"

"Ms. Ingram, try to remember the brand name. Take your time."

I looked at her closely. She knew the brand but was being very careful not to tell me. Trying not to damage her evidence by putting words in my mouth, I suppose. Evidence for what?

"Think," the detective said.

It came to me. "Lysco-Seltzer," I said. "Rhymes with disco. Detective Larch. Give me a straight answer—please. Was that what killed Rudy?"

The expression on her face told me the answer before she could say anything. She reached out and touched my arm. "I'm sorry. You all right?"

"No, I am not all right," I said numbly. "*I* was the one who gave Rudy . . . somebody wanted *me* to take that . . ." I just stood there and shuddered. "My God, it's like the Tylenol murders all over again! Some nut out to poison the whole world—"

"No, wait a minute, it can't be the same as that," she scowled. "The Tylenol killer substituted capsules full of poison for the headache medicine and then put the bottles back on drugstore shelves. That's entirely different from getting hold of sample bottles going through the mail. Besides, we've got all these new safety packaging regulations now. Your Lysco-Seltzer—there was a seal over the mouth of the bottle, wasn't there?"

"I don't know, I never opened it. It just came in the mail."

"Well, did it have a—what do they call it—a film-sealed cap? Or one of those plastic envelope-type things around the whole bottle?"

I visualized the bottle. "No. No, it didn't have anything like that. But if there wasn't any seal inside, Rudy would have noticed, he must have."

"He could have noticed and not thought anything about it. The bottle came from *you*, not from a drugstore. He probably just thought you'd already opened it yourself."

"Oh Jeez." The camera van had packed up and gone, and Detective Larch and I were left standing on a public sidewalk—not the best place in the world to find out someone had mailed you some poison and you'd passed it on to a friend. "I need a drink. In fact I need two drinks."

"So do I," the policewoman muttered. "Come on." She grabbed my arm and steered me down the street toward a welcoming watering place.

By the time we'd finished our second drink the detective and I were calling each other by our first names (hers was Marian). She told me a half-empty bottle of Lysco-Seltzer had been found on Rudy's kitchen cabinet. But instead of headache medicine the small plastic bottle had held cyanide crystals.

"That's the part that doesn't make sense," Marian Larch said. "Cyanide is fast-acting, damned fast. Matter of minutes. Yet he didn't die until nearly twenty-four hours later. Did you actually see him take it?"

"No, he said he'd wait until he got home. He just dropped the bottle in his pocket and left."

"Ah." She nodded her head. "Then when he got home . . . perhaps he forgot he had the stuff and took a medicine of his own. Or . . ." She must have seen a giveaway expression on my face because she said, "You know something you're not telling, Kelly."

On the whole I am more truthful than your average person. Out of necessity. I don't seem to be able to get away with much when it comes to fabricating off-camera. I know people who lie as easily as they breathe and nobody ever calls them on it. But me—the least little fib I tell catches up with me. Like now.

"I don't think he really had a headache the night he was with me," I admitted, feeling sheepish. "I just told him he did."

Marian's eyebrows rose. "How's that?"

"Rudy was either in a suggestible mood or else he was looking for an excuse to split. I just said don't you have a headache, and he said yes I do, and that was it."

"You wanted to get rid of him?"

"Well, not really get rid of him, I just wanted him to go home, you know."

"What's the difference?"

"I didn't want him to stay that night, that's all."

She smiled wryly. "Gotta ask you this, Kelly. Were you sleeping with him?"

I shook my head. "Not yet. But that's where we were heading, kind of. That night, the last time I saw him—well, I had a long, tight shooting schedule the next day and I just wanted to get to bed and *sleep*. I didn't want to have to say no to Rudy if he decided to make his move then. Besides, I like to say when myself, not wait to be asked. It was no big deal, I was only trying to avoid hurt feelings. Just not *that* night."

Marian nodded, understanding. "So by the time he got back to his own place he may have decided his headache had cleared up by itself or whatever. But then the *next* night, right before his poker game—yes, that would do it. The next night he did have a headache, a real one. So he opened the Lysco-Seltzer . . ."

"And it killed him."

The next day was Friday, which meant we had to wrap the week's episode by six o'clock or else go into overtime and Nathan Pinking simply did not *believe* in overtime. He would put a mystery on the air with the mystery unsolved rather than go into overtime. He would tape "The End" after only four acts of *Hamlet* rather than go into overtime. We'd finished all the indoor shots, so the whole day was spent rushing from one outdoor location to another. I had to make one wardrobe change on the run, in the back seat of a taxi, while the make-up woman frantically tried to restore order to my face and hair—all because that ass Nick Quinlan had taken the only limo the budget provided that week. The cab-driver loved it.

But I was damned grateful for the frantic pace because it kept me from thinking about that weirdo out there who'd sent me cyanide crystals disguised as Lysco-Seltzer, rhymes with disco. But I wasn't going to let it get to me, I wasn't even going to think about it until the day's work was finished, not even then, not until tomorrow when I was rested and more up to tangling with the notion that I was somebody's intended murder victim.

"Go home!" the director screeched joyfully, and we were finished. My feet hurt and my shoulders ached and I was really dragging, and I couldn't even draw any satisfaction from thoughts of a job well done, thenkyew. It had all been mechanical stuff, concentrate on getting it right the first time, the director had said, just don't make mistakes, leave the Emmy performances for next week. That idiot Nick made several flubs of the sort that should have been reshot but we didn't have time. So that week's episode was going to go out even shaggier-looking than usual.

I was turning down the associate producer's invitation to dinner (pleading exhaustion and wondering why he couldn't tell I was dead just by looking at me) when Detective Marian Larch materialized in front of me. The Captain wanted to see me, she said.

"Can't it wait until tomorrow?" I complained. "I'm bushed, Marian. What does he want to see me about?"

"I don't know," she said, perhaps truthfully. "He just told me to bring you in."

"*Bring me in!*" I shouted, outraged. "Am I so desperate a character your Captain had to send a police detective to *bring me in*?!"

She stared at me, amused. "God, you're prickly tonight. It's just a phrase, Kelly. Doesn't mean a thing."

"I told you I was bushed," I muttered.

"Yes, you did, and I'm sorry about this. But it has to be done. Look, I checked out this nice, shiny police car to come get you. Tell you what. I'll wait for you, and when Captain Michaels is finished I'll drive you home. Deal?"

"No, it's not a 'deal'—it's *coercion*," I grumbled but started to climb into the front seat. Then I remembered the man whose dinner invitation I'd been declining when Marian Larch showed up and turned to say goodbye. He'd disappeared.

Marian and I didn't talk during the drive to the Headquarters building at Police Plaza. She took me up to Captain Michael's office in the Detective Bureau and did a fast vanishing act. Michaels was sitting behind what looked like a brand new desk. He was an overweight, fiftyish man who looked first at my breasts and then at my face. "Siddown, Ms. Ingram."

Why, thank you for your gracious invitation, sir. I sat. "What is it you want, Captain?"

"That story you told Detective Larch last night," he said. "I want you to tell it to me."

That *story*? "What's wrong?"

"I'll ask the questions. Start with the last time you saw Rudy Benedict." He was actually looking down his nose at me.

I couldn't believe this guy. His body posture, his tone of voice—he was behaving as if he thought that was the way tough guys were *supposed* to act. Jimmy Cagney nasty. I did what he said; I told the "story" again.

"And your sample of Lysco-Seltzer came in the mail when?" Captain Michaels asked.

"The same day I gave it to Rudy. I hadn't even taken it out of the mailing box yet."

"There was no mailing box in Benedict's apartment—just the sample bottle. How do you account for that?"

"I don't think I have to account for it," I protested. "Come on, Captain, what is this? I probably threw the box away myself, when I gave Rudy the sample bottle."

"*Probably*. Don't you remember?"

"No, I don't remember. Why should I? Do you remember every box and envelope you throw away?"

"I'm asking the questions." He sounded like a man afraid of losing the initiative. "How do you dispose of your trash?"

"My trash?"

"Yes, lady, your trash. How do you get rid of it?"

"I throw it down the waste chute in the apartment building."

"How often?"

"As often as I need to. I don't have a *schedule*."

"You throw out your own trash, do you?"

"Sometimes. The cleaning service takes care of most of it."

"What about the Lysco-Seltzer mailing box? When did you put that down the chute?"

"You mean the one I don't remember throwing away at all? Gee, Captain, I really couldn't say."

He glared at me coldly for a few moments, doing nothing to relieve the tension. Here I was a potential murder victim and he was showing about as much concern for my welfare as he would for Public Enemy Number One. "Why haven't I been given police protection?" I demanded abruptly. "That stuff was sent to *me*, not to Rudy. It was sheer accident that he took it instead of me."

"Was it?"

"What do you mean, was it? Of course it was! Somebody mails you poison, they don't expect you to pass it on to somebody else."

"If it was sent to you."

"What 'if'? What are you talking about?"

"The stuff that came in the mail could have been exactly what the sample label said it was—Lysco-Seltzer, a patent medicine. We don't know when the cyanide was substituted. It's an old ploy, claiming to be the intended victim. Lots of killers have used it."

That made me see red. That really made me see red. To come off a rotten day like the one I'd just had and have to sit there and listen to some fat cop hinting that I'd deliberately given Rudy cyanide—then it suddenly hit me what I was being accused of and I was scared. I mean I was *scared*. "You can't be serious . . . why would I want to . . . and where would I get the . . . you can't be *serious*!"

Captain Michaels came around from behind his new desk and leaned over me, all muscle and authority and don't-mess-with-me, the bully. His breath stank. "I'm dead serious, lady, and don't you forget it. You could be the intended victim or you could just be putting on an act. I gotta know a hell of a lot more before I can say which. So why don't you start by telling me about *your* enemies? Who would want to kill you? Why are you such a threat?"

Right then I felt more threatened than threatening, but

at least Michaels was asking the kind of question I thought he should have started off asking. So I did my best to tell him what he wanted to know. I named all the people who might have a grudge against me, such as a couple of dozen actresses I had beat out for the role I was playing in *LeFever*. It all sounded kind of superficial in that place, full of gun-toting men and women who dealt with professional criminals every day of their lives. But I had to admit Captain Michaels didn't make me feel dumb; he listened carefully, taking notes and asking questions once in a while. Had he deliberately set out to scare me at first just to make sure I'd cooperate later? It went on and on and on.

Finally Michaels decided he'd heard all he needed to hear, and he did something I'd never have expected. He apologized. "Sorry to put you through this when you're obviously tired. We wanted to talk to you first thing this morning." He grinned. "We couldn't find you."

Couldn't find me? Oh, sure. I'd spent the day rushing from one part of town to another. I made one of those subverbal sounds that can mean anything.

"I'll get someone to drive you home," the Captain said.

"Detective Larch said she'd wait for me."

He nodded and thanked me for coming in. So was he a good guy or a bad guy? I was too tired to decide.

Marian Larch tried to talk me into stopping and getting something to eat. "It's nine o'clock and you haven't eaten since noon. How about it?"

"All I want is to get home and soak in the tub. I'm so tired dinner would just make me sick."

"A sandwich, then. You need something in your stomach. It'll pick you up, Kelly."

"I can make a sandwich at home. *I wanna go home*, dammit."

Her potato face crinkled into a smile. "Okay. Home it is."

I wasn't too tired to notice I didn't have to tell her where I lived; she'd looked my address up or read it out of my police file or something. My police file! Christ.

Before long Marian pulled up to the curb in front of my building. "I'll wait until you're inside."

The apartment building where I lived didn't have a doorman and depended solely on an electronic security system. We had to unlock two sets of doors just to get into the lobby, and the exterior of the building was always kept brightly lighted.

Well, almost always. Tonight one of the lights was out.

I was fumbling with the first key when a figure stepped out of the shadow. I jumped and started to yell until I saw it was a woman.

"Kelly Ingram?" she asked.

I relaxed. She was an older lady, gray and tired-looking, as tired-looking as I felt. "Yes?"

"My name is Fiona Benedict. I'm Rudy Benedict's mother. I just wanted to see the woman in whose place my son died."

2

Fiona Benedict

I hadn't heard from Rudy for almost three months, but that wasn't unusual. Rudy often went for long stretches of time without communicating, and then suddenly would telephone every night for a week. Or write long, single-spaced letters about everything under the sun or sometimes about nothing at all, writing for the sheer pleasure of writing. He did sometimes tend toward excess. In the meantime I kept sending my regular letter every other week, providing what stability I could. Washburn, Ohio, had not been "home" to Rudy for a long time, neither the town nor the university. Nevertheless I kept him informed about our comings and goings. Whether he acknowledged it or not, Rudy needed a touchstone outside the world of commercial illusion he lived in.

I was in class lecturing on the Crimean War when the call came from the New York police. I remember being annoyed at the interruption and had no foreboding of bad news. When the man on the telephone, a Captain Michaels, told me about Rudy, I made him repeat what he'd said, twice.

Then I hung up on him. Later when I'd collected myself, I called him back and asked for details. Poisoned? How?

At that point all the police knew was that Rudy had ingested cyanide crystals under the mistaken notion he was taking medicine. Who had substituted the cyanide for the medicine was not known. "I'm sorry to have to tell you this, Dr. Benedict," Captain Michaels had said, "but it looks like murder."

I arranged for someone to take my classes, got through the night somehow, and flew to New York the next morning. When I got to Police Plaza Captain Michaels was out on a case or too busy to talk to me or perhaps just didn't want to be bothered. But finally a nice young man whose name I'm sorry to say I've forgotten helped me find what I needed to know. Rudy's body wouldn't be released until the autopsy report was received from the medical examiner's office; the young man said it was expected late that afternoon. I spent the intervening hours arranging for the cremation of my son's body, in accordance with Rudy's frequently expressed wishes. The process for making such arrangements consisted primarily of proving my ability to pay for the service.

As it turned out the autopsy report didn't come through that afternoon after all—some delay or other. I finally did meet Captain Michaels, though, a florid-faced, overweight man headed for a coronary. By then I'd had enough time to adjust to the idea that someone had hated Rudy enough to want him dead, incredible though that seemed. But I'd no sooner reached that point than I had to make a complete reversal.

"We learned something new just last night," Captain Michaels told me. "It looks like the cyanide wasn't meant for your son at all. Seems he took it by accident."

He couldn't have stunned me more if he'd slapped me.

"His girlfriend gave it to him," the Captain went on. "He was complaining of a headache and she gave him a sample bottle of a new remedy that turned out to be cyanide instead. We're checking her out, but it looks like she was the one meant to get it, not your son."

Looks *as if,* I thought numbly. "What's her name?"

He hesitated, guessing what I was feeling. "Look, Dr. Benedict, you can't really blame her. She—"

"I'll find out eventually, Captain," I said mildly.

He shrugged. "Kelly Ingram. She's a TV actress."

I didn't know the name. "Do you have her address?"

"Dr. Benedict, I know how you must be feeling, but try looking at it this way. It was an accident. Same as if he'd died in a car crash. Crazy and stupid and no reason behind it, but happens just the same. Try thinking of it like he'd died in a traffic accident."

I'm certain his intentions were good but I loathe being patronized. "You have the wrong idea, Captain. You say this Kelly Ingram was my son's girlfriend. I want to meet her—she's the one Rudy was spending his time with before he died. I simply want to meet her. Is that an unreasonable request?"

Still he was reluctant. "I don't like giving out addresses, ma'am, you understand. But I can fix it for you to meet her here . . . maybe tomorrow. Let's see, tomorrow's Saturday, yeah, that'll be all right. Where you staying?"

I gave him the name of my hotel and had to settle for his assurance that he'd contact me as soon as he could arrange a meeting.

It had been a long, horrible day and I should have been glad to go back to the hotel and collapse. But I was plagued by a sense of something left unresolved, something more I should do. Visitors at Police Plaza all wear badges which are to be turned in at the time of departure. Captain Michaels had assumed I was on my way out, but I didn't want to leave, not just yet. I didn't feel satisfied, somehow. So instead of checking out I found a chair in a waiting area near the Captain's office and sat there.

I wasn't even sure what I was looking for—reassurance, possibly. Rudy had died by accident, the Captain had said. Part of me rejoiced that my son had not turned out to be the sort of man who could provoke murderous hatred in another person. But another part of me said *Are you sure?* What if the Ingram woman hadn't been the intended victim at all? What if she had deliberately poisoned Rudy and simply pretended the rest of it?

A dismaying thought, and probably a calumnious one. It had undoubtedly occurred just as Captain Michaels indicated: someone had aimed at Kelly Ingram and hit Rudy by mistake.

A low snicker brought me out of my musings. Two uniformed police officers nearby were talking *sotto voce* with the kind of snide look on their faces that meant they were making sexual remarks about a woman. I followed their glance to see an absolutely stunning young woman following a policewoman into the Captain's office. Could it be . . . ?

I stood up and walked over to the two officers, watching their faces turn carefully blank. "Excuse me, could you tell me who that was? The woman who just went into Captain Michaels's office?"

"That was Kelly Ingram," one of the officers said. "She's on that show *LeFever*."

Aha. So she was right here, and Captain Michaels must have known she was coming, and yet he'd put me off with promises of a meeting tomorrow. Why didn't he want me to see her tonight? Probably he had other matters to take care of first; police are supposed to be sticklers for procedure, I understand.

I'd never heard of *LeFever*. The officer had said she was *on* the show, not *in* it. Television instead of Broadway, then. The Captain had said she was a TV actress.

The policewoman who'd taken Kelly Ingram into the Captain's office came back out, a doughfaced woman in her thirties who looked as if she knew her way around. She and the glamour girl she'd escorted into the office were just about as different as any two women could be. The policewoman was homely and tough-looking and undoubtedly could take care of herself. Kelly Ingram was glamorous an soft-looking and probably would never have to take care of herself her entire life. She looked like the kind of woman whose beauty was so extraordinary she'd simply rely on that to carry her through life, never developing any other aspect of herself, not her mind or her personality or any possible talent she might have.

And this was the sort of woman my son had chosen.

If Rudy had been younger, it would have been understandable. But he'd reached the age where seasoned judgment was supposed to have taken over. Rudy would have been forty next month, early middle age. And he was keeping company with this sensual *child*—early twenties at most, barely out of her teens. Not quite Lolita, but too close for comfort. It would appear my son had become conscious enough of his own advancing years to begin hankering after young flesh. It was later than I thought.

Was it Kelly Ingram's beauty that made someone want to murder her? Was it envy? Sexual treachery? Why was I standing there guessing?

The doughfaced policewoman started down the hall, reading from a manila folder as she walked. Without even thinking about it I fell in behind her. At the back of my mind was the idea of waiting until Captain Michaels was through with Kelly Ingram and then catching her as she left. But still I followed the policewoman; I followed her straight into the ladies' room.

She'd been carrying several folders other than the one she'd been reading from, plus a stack of official forms of some sort. All in all they made too big an armful to juggle in the small stall, so the policewoman had piled them on the shelf over the washbasins. She'd already gone into the stall before I entered the restroom and so she thought the place was empty; but it was still rather careless of her. The top folder was marked *Ingram, Kelly*.

There were her home address, several business addresses, physical description, age—I was surprised to learn she was twenty-nine. Not the child I'd thought, then, but I'd had only a brief glimpse of her. I had no time to read further as a flush from the stall told me not to linger. I was standing in the hall wondering what to do next when the police officer who'd identified Kelly Ingram for me came up and pointedly asked if I was looking for somebody. It was time to leave.

Once I was outside, waiting for the Ingram woman in the vicinity of Police Plaza suddenly seemed a less than brilliant idea. Besides, I had her address now. I stepped off the curb and held my right arm in the air until a cab squealed up to me.

Kelly Ingram lived in a new-looking highrise in midtown. The building had no doorman; that meant I couldn't wait in the lobby. My plane had left Ohio at 7:10 that morning and I'd been on the go ever since. I was not a young woman, and the day had finally caught up with me. My legs were trembling as I sat down on that part of the steps that was not in direct light.

I think I actually fell asleep. I know she was at the door unlocking it before I realized she had come. I called her name and stepped into the light so she could see me.

And when I told her I wanted to see the woman in whose place my son had died, she attacked me.

I sat in the kitchen of Kelly Ingram's expensive apartment drinking instant Sanka while the doughfaced policewoman made sandwiches, talking nonstop as she worked. Her name was Detective Marian Larch, and it was she who had prevented the Ingram woman from shaking my head right off my shoulders. The glamour girl herself was soaking in the tub.

"She's had a gawdawful day," Detective Larch was saying. " 'Course, yours couldn't have been all that great either. But your showing up like that, when you did—well, it was the proverbial straw that broke the camel's back. She was depressed about Rudy to start with, and then she's scared because it sure does look like somebody wants to see her dead—that would throw anybody. She had this long, rotten work day where nothing went right. Then Captain Michaels keeps her in that office for a couple of hours, and he makes it clear she's not off the hook as a suspect herself. She was tired and she hadn't eaten and she was wanting a bath, and then you step out of the shadow and point out your son would still be alive if it wasn't for her. No wonder she went a little crazy."

"Yes, I should never have said that." I did regret saying it. It was senseless and self-indulgent and could have accomplished nothing under the best of circumstances. "I think I was a little crazy myself. I'm glad you were there, Ms. Larch. I could never have stopped her." The shaking had given me a terrible headache, but I wasn't too eager to take something for it. Not in that apartment.

Among Detective Larch's other talents seemed to be an ability to read minds. She opened her bag and took out a sealed packet containing two headache tablets. "Straight from the dispensary—I took some earlier today. Go on, they're safe."

I thanked her and swallowed the tablets. Detective Larch placed a platter piled high with aromatic sandwiches on the table. My stomach turned over at the odor; but it had been nine hours since I'd last eaten and I needed something. I found one sandwich containing nothing but a bland cheese and took that one.

Our hostess came in wearing a robe, her hair still damp. With her make-up washed off she looked closer to the thirtyish person she was, but she was still one of the most astonishingly beautiful women I'd ever seen. I found myself staring; she noticed, and had to grace to pretend not to.

She sat down next to Detective Larch and reached for a sandwich. "*Now* I'm hungry. Thanks for making these."

The policewoman said something unintelligible, her mouth full.

The Ingram woman and I eyed each other warily. We'd both apologized, once we'd come to our senses, but there was still tension between us. I was still blaming her for Rudy's death, and she knew I was. I should have been blaming the murderer—but I didn't know who the murderer was, and I *did* know who should have died instead of Rudy and she was sitting right there across from me. I was offended by the casualness of the scene, by the ordinariness of her sitting there in a mundane domestic setting, eating pastrami on rye. I kept telling myself I should be feeling compassion for this woman who could still be murdered at any time, who might be dead by this time tomorrow. I kept telling myself that, but I couldn't make myself listen.

She'd finished her first sandwich and was half-way through her second with no sign of stopping. Detective Larch said, "How can you eat like that and stay thin?"

"Chose my grandparents carefully," the Ingram woman said.

That surprised me. Most of the slender people I knew liked to credit their good figures to their own self-discipline. Yet this woman whose very livelihood depended upon her appearance had casually admitted it was none of her doing; she just happened to get born with the right genes. So the glamour girl could afford to be a big eater, while poor Marian Larch looked like someone who'd put on five pounds if you so much as said the word *chocolate* in her presence.

"When did you get in, Mrs. Benedict?" the police detective asked.

"This morning."

"Talked to the Captain yet?"

"Captain Michaels? Yes. He said he'd set up a meeting with you, Ms. Ingram. He wouldn't give me your address."

"Call me Kelly," she said. "He didn't say anything to me about any meeting."

"He must have forgotten," Detective Larch offered. "Mrs. Benedict—if the Captain wouldn't give you Kelly's address, how'd you find out where she lived?"

Oh-oh. "Why, I just asked someone else," I said innocently.

Detective Larch shrugged. "Okay, if you don't want to

tell me. You're here now." She changed the subject. "Are you having your son's body shipped back to Ohio?"

"No, Rudy wanted to be cremated. I'm having it done here. But his body hasn't been released yet. The autopsy report hasn't come through."

"Probably tomorrow," the detective said.

"I was wondering why the delay."

"Medical examiner sometimes has a backlog. They get the reports out as fast as they can. It's nothing to worry about, Mrs. Benedict, it happens a lot." She seemed to hesitate. "Excuse me if I seem insensitive—but do you plan on taking your son's ashes back with you?"

What a gruesome thought. "No, I don't."

"Then be sure to tell the people at the crematorium ahead of time. Otherwise they'll hand you this little box—"

"Oh, good heavens!" I shuddered. "Thank you for warning me." Just then Kelly Ingram surprised me for the second time in five minutes; she reached out and touched my arm in sympathy. "You're a history professor, aren't you?" Getting my mind off Rudy.

I nodded, and wondered what else she knew.

"That's all Rudy told me," she said. "That you were a history professor and you lived in Ohio."

"Is it Dr. Benedict then?" Marian Larch wanted to know.

I said it was, but did not tell them to call me Fiona. Both of these women were part of an alien, violent world that I did not care to be on a first-name basis with. I stared at the table and said nothing. There was one sandwich left on the platter, exuding a spicy odor impossible to ignore. It was an association I have resented ever since, remembering the smell of garlic every time I think of that period of my life when I was arranging for the disposal of my son's body.

Detective Larch said, "Is there somebody back in Ohio who can help you with all this—the arrangements, I mean?"

"I can manage, thank you."

"But a little help would make it go easier. Isn't there someone—"

"There is no Mr. Benedict, if that's what you're fishing for," I said calmly. "He deserted Rudy and me when the boy was eight."

The Ingram woman looked surprised at my mentioning so personal a matter but Marian Larch didn't bat an eye. "No,

I meant a neighbor or friend. Or one of your colleagues. Can *I* help?"

I shook my head. "Thank you for your offer, though. I have to go through Rudy's apartment tomorrow and decide what to do about his belongings, the things I won't want to keep. I won't know what I'll need to do until I see what's there."

Kelly Ingram said, "That'll be a big job. I was there once, and the place is crammed with files and papers and stuff. It'll take you a while."

I'd expected the files and papers, but I hadn't expected that other thing she'd said. "You were there *once*? Only once?"

She raised one graceful eyebrow. "That's right."

"Captain Michaels said you were Rudy's girlfriend. I'd have thought . . ." I trailed off, not really knowing how to finish.

She sighed. "I was Rudy's *friend*, Dr. Benedict. Not 'girlfriend'—did the Captain really use that word? Rudy and I weren't lovers."

And still another surprise. "Oh," I said, trying not to show I was flustered. "Captain Michaels led me to believe, ah . . ."

"I can't help what Captain Michaels thinks," she said, an edge to her voice. "Rudy and I hadn't seen each other for a couple of years, not until just a few weeks ago. We were only getting reacquainted. We weren't lovers."

She didn't say *yet*, but she might as well have. But she'd made one other thing quite clear: whether they would eventually have become lovers or not, Kelly Ingram quite clearly had not been *in love* with Rudy. She was not crushed by his death. Upset, yes—even horrified, perhaps, but in that distanced way one reacts to the misfortune of someone who is an acquaintance rather than an intimate part of one's personal life. Kelly Ingram was an actress, but I didn't think she was that good an actress. She had not been in love with Rudy.

I accepted Marian Larch's offer of a ride to my hotel.

The next morning the medical examiner's report came through and Rudy's body was released. I notified the crematorium.

Rudy's apartment in Chelsea was what in my younger days would have been called bohemian—arty and cheap. It was the sort of place I could see Rudy living in fifteen or twenty years ago, when he was just starting out. It was a *sophomoric* apartment.

Rudy had five or six pieces of original artwork, but he'd hung none of them. Instead, what wallspace wasn't taken up with bookshelves was covered with posters, most of them advertising theatrical events. Rudy had said he didn't like the apartment and was looking for a better place to live; perhaps that was why he'd never bothered hanging the paintings. I found them in a small pantry off the kitchen that Rudy had used as an all-purpose storage room; they were still in the movers' crates from the time they'd made the trip from California, almost a year ago.

I'd already decided to box up all of Rudy's papers and ship them to Ohio; there I could go through them without rushing, taking as much time as I wanted. The clothes could go to Goodwill Industries or the Salvation Army. Rudy had quite a few pieces of good furniture; I'd ask the Ingram woman if she wanted any of them. I'd need to get the phone disconnected, notify the utility companies—I decided to make a list.

I was sitting at Rudy's desk trying to think of everything that needed to be done when the door buzzer sounded. As soon as I figured out how the intercom worked, I heard a voice saying, "It's Kelly. May we come up?"

My heart sank; it was hard enough going through Rudy's things, but having to be polite to that . . . yet I could think of no reason to refuse and buzzed her in. The other part of "we" turned out to be a successful-looking man whom she introduced as Howard somebody. Each of them was carrying a stack of flattened cardboard cartons.

"The shippers can pack most of what you'll want to send back," the Ingram woman said, "but there are always some things you have to take care of yourself. Now, we'll help or we'll get out of your way, whichever you say. Just tell us."

It was a little thing, showing up with some boxes, but it made me realize that on the whole she'd been behaving better than I had. "I'd like you to stay," I said as pleasantly as I could. "Right now I'm trying to make a list of all the things that need to be done."

"Did your son have a safe-deposit box, Dr. Benedict?" Howard the mystery man said.

"I have no idea."

"Have you gone through the desk yet?"

"Not yet."

"Then that's the place to start. Was there insurance, a will?"

"Howard's a lawyer," Kelly Ingram explained.

"A will ... I don't know," I said. "I do know there was insurance."

"He probably had a safe-deposit box, then," Howard said. "Look for a key and his bank statements. Then we'll get a court order to open the box."

"The key might be in the bedroom," the Ingram woman said and went to look.

I looked at the man named Howard. "Are you Ms. Ingram's lawyer?"

"Personal friend."

One of her men, then.

"Mind if I take a look?" he said.

I yielded the desk to him, and watched as he quickly and methodically went through the papers. Kelly Ingram came back in from the bedroom waving a key just as Howard held up a bank statement. "Barclays Bank," he said. "This is Saturday, Dr. Benedict. I won't be able to get an order to open the box until Monday. If you want my help, that is."

"I would like your help very much, Mr. ... ?"

"Call me Howard. Let's see what else we have here." He took a ledger out of a middle drawer, opened it, and said, surprisingly, "Glorioski!"

The Ingram woman laughed. "Glorioski, Howard?"

"The inner child speaks. Do you know what this is?" He meant the ledger. "It's an inventory of his belongings—location, cost, and so on. Thank the Lord—a careful record-keeper! This will simplify things enormously. And look here. Will, two insurance policies, some stock, title papers to various things like his car and some paintings—the papers are all in the Barclays box. Great. Kelly, do you know where he kept his car?"

"In a garage on Eighth Avenue. I don't remember the name, but I know where it is. What paintings?"

"What's that?"

"Didn't you say paintings were listed there? I don't see any paintings." She gestured at the postered walls.

"I know where they are," I said, and led them to the pantry.

"Yup, there they are," Howard said. "One, two, three, four, uh, five? That's all? There're supposed to be six. Where's the other one?"

"Perhaps he sold it," I suggested. "Although that doesn't seem likely. I don't think they were worth very much."

"Not a whole lot," Howard agreed. "The most expensive was twenty-five hundred. All six together cost less than what he paid for his car. One of them he paid only five hundred bucks for. Who are these people? The artists, I mean." He held the ledger out to me. "Do you know any of these names?"

I glanced at Rudy's carefully printed list and shook my head. "I'm not a good one to ask. I know very little about contemporary art."

"Don't look at me," the Ingram woman said.

"Well, let's see which one is missing," Howard said. Rudy had taken a black felt-tip marker and printed the title of each painting on the crate it was in. The missing painting turned out to be one called *Man and Shadow*, and the artist was someone named Mary Rendell. I'd heard of neither painting nor painter. *Man and Shadow* had cost Rudy only eight hundred dollars.

Howard said, "If the safety deposit box has ownership papers for just the other five, then I think we can assume he sold the painting. Or maybe gave it away, birthday or Christmas present or the like."

"And what if the papers are there for all six paintings?" I asked.

He shrugged. "Cross that bridge when we come to it."

It went on like that for a while, until we reached a point where only I could make decisions about the disposal of Rudy's personal belongings. I thanked Kelly Ingram as graciously as I could manage for bringing a lawyer to help out. After all, she was doing the best she could to atone for having caused Rudy's death.

The will in Rudy's safe-deposit box listed me as sole heir, and the two insurance policies both named me as beneficiary. One had originally been taken out to benefit Rudy's wife, but even when they divorced he hadn't changed the policy. Only when she remarried did Rudy substitute my name for hers on the second policy. I learned from Detective Larch that Rudy's ex-wife had been notified of his death soon after his body was discovered, almost twenty-four hours before Captain Michaels had contacted me. It was just like her not to call me. Impossible woman.

Howard the lawyer found a buyer for Rudy's car. The offer was low but I accepted just to be done with it. Marian Larch was intrigued by the fact that the deposit box had contained bills of sale for six paintings but only five were in the apartment. I think she had visions of *Man and Shadow*'s turning out to be a priceless American primitive and that there was some sort of crime-within-a-crime just waiting to be discovered. I made it clear I was not sympathetic to her supersleuth ambitions; at a time like that I couldn't be bothered with what happened to be an eight-hundred-dollar painting.

Nevertheless Marian Larch had taken Rudy's inventory list and contacted several galleries and museums, trying to "get a line on the artists," she said. The experts she consulted hadn't even heard of most of them; none had heard of Mary Rendell, the artist who'd painted *Man and Shadow*. She'd tried to track down the California dealer whose name appeared on the bill of sale, but his gallery had gone out of business several years ago. So Marian Larch asked permission to make one final search of Rudy's apartment before the packers and shippers took over. I told her yes just to get her to stop bothering me.

She found nothing, of course. "It's odd," she said, as we waited for the men from the shipping company. "The first thing you think of in the case of a missing painting that everybody says isn't worth anything is that it *is* worth something. If not for itself, then maybe somebody painted over an old painting that *is* valuable. A Corot or a Manet or something like that."

"It's the first thing *you* think of," I pointed out to her. "The first thing I think of is that the movers lost the painting when Rudy came here from California. Or he did give it away but didn't bother passing on the bill of sale. Or he got tired of looking at it and threw it out. Rudy wasn't a collector. He'd just buy something now and then to hang on a bare wall."

"Did you ever see the painting?"

"I've been trying to remember. The last time I visited Rudy—let's see, I spent most of last year in London, and . . . it must be close to five years, the last time I was in California. And I just don't know whether I saw *Man and Shadow* then or not. I didn't pay much attention to the paintings, I'm afraid. I know I didn't ask Rudy their titles."

"Do you remember seeing one of, well, a man and his shadow?"

I didn't. "To tell you the truth, Ms. Larch, I don't really remember any of them."

Just then the shippers showed up, to finish the packing and clear the apartment. They were rough and noisy and couldn't seem to work without a transistor radio blaring away, but they were fast. I appreciated their being fast.

At last it was done. Marian Larch drove me back to my hotel. She told me that when I got back home if I thought of something I'd forgotten to do, just give her a call and she'd take care of it. Belatedly it occurred to me the police detective had shown a lot more consideration than her job required her to, so I tried to thank her but she wouldn't let me. Strange woman, Marian Larch. But nice.

In my hotel room I'd just finished locking my suitcase when there was a knock on the door. It was Captain Michaels—whom I'd thought I'd seen the last of.

"Could we sit down, Dr. Benedict?" he said. "I have something to tell you."

I didn't like the sound of that and said so.

He plunged right in. "We've just had the final report from the crime lab. They go over the scene of the crime pretty thoroughly, you know."

Scene of the crime—Rudy's apartment, which I'd just closed. "And?"

"And they found some undissolved Lysco-Seltzer crystals caught under the surface rim of the drain. The drain in your son's kitchen sink."

I failed to see the significance. "And?" I repeated.

"Don't you see what that means, Dr. Benedict? Somebody dumped out the Lysco-Seltzer right there in Rudy's sink. That bottle hadn't been tampered with before it went through the postal service and ended up in Kelly Ingram's mailbox."

I began to see—dear God, I began to see.

"What probably happened was, your son came home from visiting Kelly, put the Lysco-Seltzer on the kitchen cabinet, and just left it there. He may have taken part of the bottle that night or he may not have, the medical examiner can't tell us that. But some time the next day somebody emptied out whatever medicine was left in the bottle and substituted cyanide crystals."

"So the poison wasn't meant for Kelly Ingram at all," I said woodenly.

Captain Michael's florid face was drawn into a scowl. "'Fraid not. It seems your son was the intended victim all along."

3

Kelly Ingram

I was so relieved when Rudy's mother went back to Ohio I felt like celebrating. I know that sounds callous and I can't help it, but I was glad she was g-o-n-e, *gone*. She'd had one bad shock after another, enough to flatten most people, she'd handled it all with considerable aplomb, I think I'm using that word right, and she'd been courteous to me after that first meeting when I went off my head and flew at her. *Stiflingly* courteous. She drove me nuts.

And I'm not going to say how sorry I was to hear poor old Rudy was the "right" victim after all, because for starters nobody would believe me. I was truly sorry Rudy was dead and I hated the idea that his murderer hadn't been caught, but I still liked that scenario better than the one that cast *me* as the body on the floor. So I'm thick-skinned and unfeeling— okay, that's too bad, I'm sorry. But I'm also alive and likely to stay that way, and I'm happy about that part of it.

Now that I've got that out of my system, I can say I did feel sorry for Dr. Benedict, in fits and spurts. (Starts?) She made it hard for you to feel sorry for her, being so formal and remote like that. She did it on purpose, that *don't-touch-me* bit. I don't like people getting too close either, unless I say so, but I'm no ice lady like Dr. Mrs. Fiona Benedict. No wonder Rudy didn't talk about her much. I tried to help; I even took Howard Chesney along to handle the legal details for her. She thanked me, but it was obviously killing her to make the effort.

She was still blaming me for Rudy's death, right up to the time Captain Michaels told her about the Lysco-Seltzer in the sink. I saw her only once after that; she stayed on for a few more days to answer what questions she could about Rudy, but then she had to get back to her classes. That couldn't have been easy for her, going back home with all those questions about Rudy's death still not answered. And then having to stand up in front of a classroom with all those students knowing—well now, wait a minute, maybe they didn't know. Would the murder have made the Ohio papers? Dr. Benedict sure as hell wasn't going to make a public announcement if she didn't have to.

Marian Larch seemed to think Rudy's death was somehow tied up with a cheap painting that was missing from his apartment, but she admitted nobody else at Police Headquarters thought so. Captain Michaels had told her to stop wasting time on it. *I* still thought the play Rudy'd been going to write had something to do with it, but I couldn't get Marian interested in that at all. I kept trying to tell her the whole thing seemed wrong, somehow. Rudy Benedict just wasn't the *type* of person to get himself murdered, it seemed to me.

That amused Marian, in a morbid sort of way. "Oh?" she'd said. "Tell me, Professor Ingram, what do you consider the right *type* to get murdered?"

"Don't get smart, I'm serious," I told her. We were on a break in shooting *LeFever*; Marian Larch had gotten into the habit of dropping in—continuing her investigation, she said. I think she just liked to watch what was going on. Or maybe she liked watching Nick Quinlan; lots of women did, Lord help us. "Rudy wasn't a threatening person," I said. "Aren't people who get murdered supposed to be a threat of some sort?"

"You'd be surprised," Marian said. "Some of the people who get killed were so mousy when they were alive you could forget they were there at all."

"I didn't say Rudy was *mousy*—"

"I know, I know, that was just an example. Don't be so loose and easy with that word *type*. Kelly, there just aren't any murder victim *types*—not really. A guy overhears something by accident that makes him a danger to the mob so they put out a contract on him..."

"Yecch," I said.

"...so what does this guy's 'type' have to do with anything? He just happened to be in the wrong place at the wrong time so they kill him for it. It happens like that, you know, more often than you'd imagine. Couple of months ago an old woman was fished out of the East River, a landlady from Lois Aida—"

"From where?"

"Lower East Side, that's the way they say it. One of her tenants was a pusher and she stumbled on his cache and he killed her. She probably would have kept her mouth shut, but it was easier for him to kill her than worry about her talking. We got the pusher, but that didn't help the landlady any."

"You know, I was beginning to feel safe again until we started this conversation."

"And what do you really know about Rudy Benedict?" she plowed on. "You hadn't seen him for two years, Kelly. You don't know what kind of enemies he might have made in that time. He could have changed completely from the last time you knew him."

"No, he was the same old Rudy." I was on firm ground there. "Putting on the dog a little because of that play he was going to write, but he was still Rudy. Wanting more than he had, but not really knowing how to go about getting it. Trying to change, but not really making any big break from what he'd always done."

"Well, there—what about that? *Trying to change.* Doesn't that indicate things weren't the same for him as they used to be, that he wanted something different?"

"Aw, no. Rudy was always complaining—even when I knew him in California. He grumbled all the time about the tripe he 'had to write every week. But the money was good and Rudy wasn't about to throw that away. He didn't really like what he was doing, but he didn't know how to get out of it without giving up the comfortable way of living he was used to."

"But he had decided to go ahead and write a play. He must have been giving something up for that," she mused.

"Not really," I said. "He was still getting a salary from Nathan Pinking—his contract hadn't quite run out yet. He wasn't taking any risks. Rudy just wasn't the daring type, Marian. If you'll pardon the four-letter word."

"You mean 'type'? I'll pardon it. But there had to be something out of the ordinary in Rudy Benedict's life or else—Kelly, is that man trying to get your attention?"

I glanced across the set of LeFever's office to see a familiar figure jumping up and down and waving his arms. "That's Leonard Zoff, my agent. He doesn't like coming here—something must be up. Come on."

We picked our way around the set, Leonard helping us by pumping his arms faster. He wouldn't have dreamed of working his way over to us; too many things to trip over.

"Hello, Leonard, why didn't you just yell, the way you usually do?"

"Laryngitis," he whispered, and peered suspiciously at Marian. "Whozis?"

"Marian Larch, of the Detective Bureau. Marian, this is Leonard Zoff."

"Oh—okay," Leonard rasped before Marian could say anything. "Kelly, we gotta talk. We—"

Sometimes he really bugs me. "Not *Oh, okay*, Leonard. *How do you do* or *Pleased to meet you* or just plain *Hello*. But not *Oh, okay*."

Leonard had a standard response for that kind of situation. He slipped an arm around Marian Larch's waist, leered into her face, and whispered, "Don't mind me, darling. No offense intended—I'm just in kind of a rush, y'know?"

She stared at him. "I think I liked *Oh, okay* better."

Rolled right off him. "Kelly, we got a biggie coming. You ready for this? The Miss America people are considering you for one of the judges. Whaddaya say to that?"

Me, I didn't say anything; I was speechless. But Marian snorted, "That meat parade!"

"Meat, schmeat, it's *exposure*, darling." Leonard's eyes were dancing and his lived-in face was one huge grin; he was angling a big one, all right. "Every year they have one professional beauty among the judges to show the little girls how it's done, and I been telling them how next year it's gotta be Kelly Ingram."

"This is for next year?" I asked.

"Oh yeah, these things gotta be settled way ahead—you got your foot in the door now because the broad, 'scuse me, the *lady* they had lined up went and got herself preggie.

You're still on the pill, aren't you, darling? Anyway, they were thinking Bo Derek but I talked them out of it. By the end of the season, I told them, Kelly Ingram's going to be the biggest thing on the tube. I said you want somebody visible, don't you? Shit, I got other clients, I said, but I'm telling you Kelly's the one you want. How do you like that—I'm in there pitching for you, Kel. You got that?"

"I got it, Leonard."

"Right. So now all I got to do is persuade Nathan Shithead that it's just what the *LeFever* image needs. And it **is**, it is!"

Marian was looking puzzled. "If this other woman is pregnant now and this contest isn't until *next* year . . . ?"

"Why can't she go ahead and do it?" Leonard rasped. "Because this is her first baby and some women lose their looks when they become mommas. Sorry, darling, but that's the way it is. The Miss America people just can't take the risk." Leonard's grin had disappeared; he swallowed, painfully—his throat must really have been hurting. "Nathan Shithead has graciously granted me an appointment, ain't that generous of him? The Miss America Apple Pie folks want a guarantee there's no contractual problems before they'll even negotiate."

"Why didn't you tell me this was in the works, Leonard?" I asked. "You know I like to be kept posted."

"I didn't want to get your hopes up."

"Meaning you didn't think the pageant people would go for it."

"Now, darling, don't go putting yourself down like that—you've got to have faith!"

"In myself, I got faith. It's you I'm not so sure about."

"Don't be so hard on a sick old man," he rasped. "Call my office later—I'll leave word. Glad to've met you, uh, Marilyn." His grin flashed back on for a tenth of a second and he was gone.

"Whew," Marian said, looking after him. "Is he always like that?"

"Usually he's noisier."

Just then they called me to do my half of a telephone scene. The assistant director stood off-camera and read LeFever's lines to me with far more expression than Nick Quinlan would ever be able to manage. When I finished the story editor's secretary came up and handed me some green pages. I groaned.

"Only two lines in your part, Kelly," she smiled. "Easy changes."

I managed to smile back, but I didn't mean it. I hate it when we get as far as green pages.

"What's the matter?" Marian Larch wanted to know.

"Script changes," I told her. "Every new set of changes comes through on a different color paper. This week's script already looks like a rainbow and now—well, I guess these aren't so bad." I read through the new dialogue quickly. Two new lines for me, I already knew them. Trouble was, I still knew the old ones as well. The trick was remembering which set to say when you were in front of the camera.

"Kelly—"

"Come into my dressing room, they're getting ready to shoot."

With the door to the dressing room closed we could talk, if we kept our voices low; the soundproofing wasn't all it was supposed to be. Marian was worrying about what Leonard Zoff had said. "Is that true about the pregnant woman? That the Miss America people won't take a chance on her keeping her looks after she gives birth?"

"No," I laughed. "There's not a word of truth in it. In fact, I'm pretty sure there wasn't any pregnant woman at all—Leonard just made her up."

Marian Larch's eyebrows climbed. "But why?"

"To keep me in my place, grateful and grovelling. Notice how Leonard supposedly slipped and said *broad*—and then made a big production of correcting the word to *lady*? Well, that was deliberate, that was. Good old subtle Leonard, reminding me I'm just a package to be sold but *he's* the salesman. Then he came on with this story about the pregnant woman—to make me think I was the pageant officials' *second* choice. And then they only came around to considering me because of Mr. Leonard Zoff's superior powers of persuasion."

"You mean you might have been their first choice?"

"I mean I'll never know—which is exactly what Leonard had in mind. He knows I don't swallow most of that guff he dishes out, but he likes to keep me off-balance. Figures he has more control that way."

She just looked at me. Then: "Why do you stay with an agent like that?"

"Find me a better one and I'll change."

"You mean he's so good at getting results you're willing to put up with all that other stuff?"

"I mean he's no worse than the rest of them. And Leonard does know everybody. Right now he's in the office whispering in Nathan Pinking's ear about how this Miss America gig will be just what *LeFever* needs next year. And Nathan will loll there in his big leather chair, letting himself be convinced. He likes to see Leonard sweat."

"Why Nathan Pinking? What does he have to say about it anyway?"

"It's in my contract—it's a personal contract Nathan had me sign before he'd give me the role in *LeFever*. I can't do anything outside *LeFever* without his say-so. He vetoed a greeting card commercial I'd been offered because he said down-home wholesomeness wasn't exactly the image he had in mind for me. Nathan told me to try to get one of those pantyhose commercials—you know, the ones where the models sit down without *quite* putting their knees together."

"I know the ones," Marian said sourly. "Your Nathan Pinking must be a real prince. Kelly, are you really going to do it? Be one of the Miss America judges, I mean."

"Sure, if Leonard can arrange it."

"And it doesn't bother you at all?"

Oh boy. "Look, Marian. A beauty contest is sort of like an audition, you know? It's a recognized way of getting started on a career."

She snorted. "It's a *meat* parade. All those young girls offering their bodies for inspection—like prize cows at the county fair. And you sanction that?"

"Hey, wait a minute—nobody's forcing those girls to take part. Hell, that's what they *want*, a chance at the spotlight."

"Sure, they *want* it—because they're young and just beginning to feel their power and flushed with new success. And because they're taught every day of their lives that girls are supposed to be ornamental. They want it because they don't know what else to want."

I snorted at that. "Well, I'm going to do it, and that's that. *If* Nathan Pinking doesn't decide to say no just to bug Leonard."

"Why would he do that?"

"Notice how Leonard always calls him Nathan Shithead?"

"Could I miss it?"

"Leonard hates Nathan Pinking's guts. And Nathan returns the compliment. Yet each of them is the other's best customer. When Nathan's putting a new show together, he doesn't call a casting office until after he's talked to Leonard. And whenever Leonard manages to sign up an established star who's just fired his old agent, Leonard makes sure Nathan gets first crack at him. They can't stand each other, but they always find a way to do business."

"A love-hate relationship?"

"More like a hate-hate relationship. They really do loathe each other. But money's money, so they'll keep doing business as long as it's profitable for both of them. But if one of them ever starts to slip, the other one will drop him like hot potato."

"What if Leonard's the one to slip? Where will that leave you?"

"With a new agent. I'm not going down with anybody's ship but my own, may it never come to pass. Here, check me on my new lines—read me my cues."

"Ah, it's time I was getting—"

"It'll take you twenty seconds, for crying out loud. There are only two lines. Come on, read me my cues."

She grumbled, but she did it.

I didn't see Marian Larch for a while after that. I couldn't tell whether the investigation of Rudy's death was easing off or just heading in a different direction. Or maybe Marian had run out of excuses for dropping in on the *LeFever* set.

When he had a show taping in New York, Nathan Pinking rented space at a converted movie soundstage on West Fifty-fourth Street. We had a few permanent sets, but mostly we shot exteriors. New York wasn't like California, where everything you needed to make a movie or a television series was all right there together in the same studio—the crews, the commissaries, the costume shop, the print shop, the scenery docks, the prop shop, everything. Like a factory. In New York you had to go hunting for all the things you needed in a hundred different places. So, nobody came to New York to make a series *indoors*. You came because of what the city had to offer in the way of location shots. The place was an inexhaustible backdrop. *And* a good filler—for those weeks when the script was a mite on the skimpy side and you had to fill in those empty spots with pretty pictures. That happened on *LeFever* every week, by the way. We never ran long, never went into overtime. Nathan Pinking didn't believe in overtime.

I had a week off from the show. I yelled bloody murder but they wrote me out of the script just the same. The episode was being shot in London and the writers explained in this overpatient way they had of talking to dumb broads that there was no way to justify LeFever's taking a girlfriend along with him on an overseas business trip. *Oh yeah?* I said. *What about all those Congressional junkets?*

But the answer was still no, and the real reason, as always, was money. The episode was being financed by a British production company that wanted to use *LeFever* to introduce the hero of a new series they were making. The British were going to try for a direct sale to American television instead of playing it in England first and then selling it to Masterpiece Theatre fifteen years later. So the deal Nathan Pinking had worked out was that the British would pick up the tab for an episode showing LeFever in London cooperating with *their* hero—but the funds were not limitless. Certain things had to go, and the character I played was still on the expendable list. I wasn't exactly overloaded with job security just then.

I called Leonard Zoff and demanded he do something about it, but he wouldn't even try. "These things are decided long in advance," he said. "I know what the Brits budgeted for and there just ain't no traveling money for little Kelly. Accept it, darling—there's nothing to be done."

"I'll pay my own way."

"Like hell you will!" he exploded, causing me to jerk the receiver away from my ear. "Once you start that, Nathan Shithead'll have you paying through the nose until the very *second* your contract runs out! Don't you suggest it, don't you even *think* it—do you hear me?"

I told him I heard him but he went on hollering until I said okay *okay* and hung up. So I was to be the Invisible Woman that week.

I had a special reason for wanting to be in that episode. Their hero was a hell of a lot more attractive than our hero. I'd seen their leading man in one movie and almost wrote the guy a fan letter. I wanted to meet him, that's all there was to it. And then when Nathan Pinking pretended to be doing me this big favor by giving me a week's vacation in midseason, I almost poked him one.

Nathan had said okay to my being a judge at the Miss America contest, so Leonard Zoff was trying to arrange it. If Leonard could bring it off, I'd go through with it, no question. I know what side my bread's buttered on. It was easy for Marian Larch to sneer at the "meat parade" side of it. She didn't have to worry about the right exposure at the right time in order to earn a living. So a lot of women didn't like the contest, so that was too bad.

Not my problem.

My problem was a bad case of the fidgets. I could use the time off, though. I had my hair done by somebody other than the *LeFever* people, checked my wardrobe, watched the cleaning service people do their weekly thing in my apartment, read some of my mail, and went dancing. That took care of Monday.

The man I went dancing with also took care of Tuesday and Wednesday, but Thursday he felt he should go back to work. He was an architect, and his boss was quote the most demanding, most unreasonable man in the universe unquote. (He worked for his father.) So on Thursday morning I was thinking of getting on a plane and going somewhere for the weekend when the mail arrived, containing a little something I wasn't expecting at all.

It was a yellow box and it had black and white letters that said "Sample—Not for Sale" and its name was Lysco-Seltzer.

Now, there's no need to panic, I told myself in the calmest and most rational way imaginable. Somebody intent on murder wouldn't use a Lysco-Seltzer bottle *again*, surely. Would he? No—it was exactly what it appeared to be, it had to be. Thousands and thousands of other New York mailboxes were holding little yellow boxes that morning, *and they were all exactly alike*. There was absolutely no need to panic.

I called Police Headquarters and screamed for Marian Larch.

One thing about Marian, she never tried to brush your anxieties aside as something you just imagined. She always took *me* seriously, anyway, and while I expected her to say things like *You're making a fuss over nothing* or the like, she never did.

What she did do was take one look at the Lysco-Seltzer box and drop it in her shoulder-bag. "It's been tampered with," she said.

After one look she could tell that? "How do you know?"

"The address label. That address was typed individually— it didn't come out of a machine like an Addressograph or some sort of dry-process addressing machine. In mass mailings they use a master list and print from that. This box goes straight to the lab. Why are you home?"

It took me a second to figure out what she meant. "I'm not in the episode they're taping now. I have the week off."

"Oh, that's nice," she said dubiously.

"No, that's not nice."

"No, that's not nice," she agreed. "Look, just sit tight until the crime lab gets finished. Don't go out, keep your door locked."

"Count on it," I said grimly.

Marian didn't get back with an answer until the next morning—that was one very anxious day and night I spent, I can tell you. I'd almost talked myself into thinking there was nothing to worry about when she'd pulled that label stunt on me. Well, *she* didn't pull the stunt, of course, but it was the kind of news I could have lived without knowing. Or maybe I couldn't. *Live* without knowing it, I mean. Jesus.

I was sitting and staring at a big cardboard carton that United Parcel had just delivered when Marian showed up around ten Friday morning.

"What's that?" she asked.

"A bomb, no doubt," I said fatalistically.

"Nonsense." All brisk efficiency. "Too big for a bomb. Besides, you'll be happy to learn nobody mailed you any cyanide in a Lysco-Seltzer bottle."

I perked up at that. "You mean the bottle wasn't tampered with after all?"

"Didn't say that—it *was* tampered with, all right. But whoever did the tampering didn't substitute cyanide this time. The lab boys said it didn't even look like cyanide crystals—*or* Lysco-Seltzer. Yellow instead of white, for one thing. So maybe the guy who sent it didn't really intend for you to take it at all. Maybe it was just a joke."

"Joke? What do you mean, *joke*?" I looked at her closely, but that potato face wasn't giving much away; I've got to stop thinking *potato face*. "Marian, what was in that bottle?"

"Phenolphthalein. Ever heard of it?"

"Spell it."

She spelled it. "It's not hard to get hold of, the way cyanide is. Anybody can buy it in a drugstore—you don't even need a prescription. Kelly, phenolphthalein is used mostly as a laxative."

I just stared at her. "Somebody sent me a laxative?"

She nodded soberly, but I suspected she was trying not to laugh. "Somebody sent you a laxative."

I was absolutely dumfounded or even dumbfounded, I'm not going to look it up. "A laxative." I was at such a loss I went over and kicked the United Parcel carton, I didn't know what else to do.

"Hey," Marian said uneasily.

"You said it wasn't a bomb. Nobody's out to kill me. They're just out to give me diarrhea. Isn't that wonderful? What a glamorous ailment to come down with! *Why would anybody send me a laxative?*"

"Maybe simply to get a rise out of you—to make you react the way you are reacting."

"And they just happened to pick the same means that was used to kill Rudy? A Lysco-Seltzer bottle? Come *on*. That's no coincidence."

"No—I don't think it is. It certainly could be Rudy Benedict's murderer who sent you the phenolphthalein. Or somebody else who found out it was your Lysco-Seltzer that had been doctored in Benedict's apartment and decided to give you a little scare just for the fun of it. A sadistic practical joker."

"Great idea of fun, isn't it?"

"Whoever sent you the laxative would have to get pleasure out of what he was doing—there's nothing else to be gained. Do you know anybody with that kind of personality? The kind that would get a kick out of embarrassing you?"

"A couple of hundred," I said without hesitation. "Nathan Pinking, Leonard Zoff, Nick Quinlan—"

It was Marian's turn to say, "Oh, come *on*."

"Come on, nothing. Most of the people I know would think it was funny to put somebody out of commission that particular way. Using the same kind of bottle that killed Rudy is ghoulish, sure, but that just puts an edge on it. It's the kind of thing Nathan Pinking especially would get a kick out of. He's not exactly nice people."

"But why would he want to put you out of action for even a day? Wouldn't that cost him—oh, that's right. You're not in this week's episode."

I said, "Nathan's always doing things just to show you what he can get away with. Do you remember Christopher Clive?"

"An actor, sure."

"Not just *an* actor. He used to be somebody, a Shakespearean actor primarily. An Englishman, same kind of training as Gielgud and Richardson and the rest of them. But he went on the skids, stopped acting for years. You know, one of those alcoholics who have to stop drinking altogether because one more swallow will kill them? Well, he's trying to make a comeback. He takes any role he can get."

"That's it," Marian said. "He was on *LeFever*, wasn't he? Small part. Thought I'd seen him recently."

"Remember the scene in Central Park where he lost his trousers? That wasn't in the script. Nathan Pinking wanted him to drop his pants for a cheap laugh. Christopher Clive is a man of enormous dignity, even as a reformed drunk. It was painful for him. But he did it—he needed the job. Nathan just stood there and snickered. He humiliated that man just to prove he could. Now, do you think somebody like that would hesitate to send me a laxative disguised as something else?"

Marian shook her head. "I got to admit, he sounds like a good candidate. But those others you mentioned—what about your agent, Leonard Zoff? How would hurting you benefit him?"

I shrugged. "Leonard sometimes calls himself a flesh-peddler. I think he dislikes women. His speech is just full of little put-downs—well, you met him, you know what he's like. I don't really know what goes on in Leonard's head. But I take it back about Nick Quinlan. On second thought, I know he didn't do it. He's too dumb. Nick couldn't even manage typing the address label much less all the rest of it."

"I'm glad you eliminated one suspect," Marian said dryly. "Do you really spend your life surrounded by so much ill will?"

"Absolutely. You mean you don't? You're a cop, you should know what it's like. Look what's happened here. Somebody just told me they think I'm shit. How am I supposed to feel about that? What am I supposed to do—take it in stride?"

"Kelly—"

"I can't even hit back! Oh, how I'd love to hit back!" Something occurred to me. "I wouldn't mind slipping little of that phenolwhatsit to Nick Quinlan. Is the crime lab finished with that bottle? Do you suppose—"

"No, you may not have it back," Marian said disapprovingly. "You shouldn't mess around with chemicals you don't know anything about. What's a safe dosage? Don't even consider it."

I muttered something at her. She was right, of course. I just didn't want her to be right, not just then; I wasn't in the mood for it. I went over to the United Parcel carton and thought about kicking it again.

"Why don't you open it?" Marian asked. Then, when I hesitated: "Would you like me to open it for you?"

"No, I'll do it." I couldn't spend the rest of my life being afraid of *boxes*. The carton was taped shut and I had to get a knife from the kitchen to cut it open.

"You'd think the crown jewels were in there," Marian said as I sawed away at the tape. But it wasn't the crown jewels inside.

It was toilet paper. Seventy-two rolls of White Cloud toilet paper, three hundred double-ply sheets to the roll.

4

Fiona Benedict

When I got back to Washburn, Ohio, I "confided" in a few people that Rudy had died of an allergic reaction to a new medicine he was taking for high blood pressure. Some of my high-minded colleagues immediately assumed *overdose*, I'm sure, but I couldn't help that. It was better than putting up with the kind of stares that were bound to come my way if it were known I was even remotely connected with a murder.

Washburn, Ohio, was where I intended to live out my retirement, starting in three years' time. I did not intend to live there as an object of curiosity.

Poor Rudy. How hard he'd tried, how much boasting he'd done. He was too bright for that world of flash and glitter he'd moved in, but not really inventive enough for any enduring work. In the beginning I'd thought television would be good for him, mature him a little. By constant exposure to the perfectly horrible example television offered, he'd learn how *not* to write, I'd hoped. Eventually, I thought, he'd move on to better things.

But no, he never did. At first I'd assumed Rudy had been seduced by the easy success he'd found, but later I came to understand it was fear that kept him from venturing farther afield. He never took any real risks in his life, and for that I blame his father. All of Rudy's confidence in himself evaporated the day that cowardly man left us to cope on our own. Rudy was supposed to have been planning a play when he died, and there's always the possibility that he would actually have gone ahead and written it. But I didn't think so; it was all talk. Rudy was a big talker. That New York police detective, the doughfaced woman named Larch—she'd brought up the subject of Rudy's play every time she could. I suppose she was trying to give me a good final memory of him: the serious writer embarking on a major work. But it was a false picture; I knew my son.

Rudy had started rebelling against me soon after his father left us and never quite grew out of it. He blamed me for his father's going; and by the time he was old enough to understand what had happened, it was too late. The pattern was set—he needed to blame me. In the last letter I had from him, he was still telling me (in a disguised manner, of course) how important he was in the world he had chosen—as distinguished from the one I inhabited. His father had also been a historian, but in college Rudy had taken courses exclusively in the soft disciplines, art and literature and music appreciation, the sort of thing in which the student's opinions of works of art are treated as more important than the works themselves. And then midway through his senior year, he quit. One semester away from graduation, and he walked out. Rudy had taken a perverse pleasure in leaving school before getting a degree; it was his way of thumbing his nose at the academic life that he identified with me.

At least, that's what I was supposed to believe. On the surface Rudy and I were always on good terms; the rebelling was more in the nature of needles in the side. And I did believe his walking out of college was basically a defiant gesture directed at me. But not completely. By rejecting the academic world, Rudy would never have to live up to its standards—which weren't all that high even then. But the way he systematically avoided the hard disciplines was revealing. By avoiding them, Rudy never had to risk failing. Rudy didn't like taking risks.

When he first started selling scripts to the various series, I watched every show he wrote for. But even on television Rudy rarely missed a chance to get in his digs at the academic life. Repeatedly he pictured it as a retreat, a hiding out from "real" life—which on television was always assumed to be violent and exhibitionistic and loud and vulgar. That was "real" living? Being "street wise" was the epitome of human achievement?

It's an attitude that has always amazed me. Rudy frequently had his heroes sneer at teachers as head-in-the-sand milksops, people who never really knew what was going on *out there* in the "real" world. Rudy wasn't alone in claiming that, of course; it's a favorite excuse of dropouts, failures, those too lazy or too afraid to use their brains. But it seemed to me *they* were the ones with their heads in the sand. I know perfectly well that the polite life led by a small, self-contained academic community in the "safe" state of Ohio is not typical of all human life. I have never claimed that it was. But it's a way of life that does exist and it isn't going to go away, no matter how loudly the outsiders proclaim it isn't *real*.

And what did Rudy know of street life? He loved to write about wise-cracking private eyes and fast-talking con men and dedicated social workers and crime-busting lawyers and world-weary police officers. None of that Rudy had any direct experience of; his knowledge of his subject matter was second-hand and even his attitudes were borrowed—from other writers, other shows. He was my son, but I'm afraid there wasn't one spark of originality in Rudy. Even when he was writing comedy his protagonists were usually unlettered but "savvy" people who consistently triumphed over their better-educated adversaries. And that, I think, was the secret of Rudy's success. He was a populist writer. He repeatedly gave voice to enduring folk ideals, such as the one that celebrates getting something for nothing. Or the one about the simple soul who wins out not through superior intelligence or skill but just by being his own wonderful self.

There must be a frighteningly large number of people in this country who need to believe that kind of thing; otherwise Rudy's particular brand of dramatized exculpation wouldn't have been so much in demand. This is the way he'd spent his life, telling TV audiences the self-flattering things they wanted to believe. Rudy did not pretend he was doing great work; he affected a certain cynical nonchalance that said this was the only way to survive in the "real" world.

So Rudy deceived himself as well as his audiences. He always wrote safe stories, ones that could be counted on not to disturb, not to challenge. He took no risks. And yet he looked down his nose at me for hiding in a safe environment. He never saw that he was doing the same thing himself.

And in the end, it hadn't protected him after all.

The semester would be over in another few weeks, and I had plans to make. I notified the dean I wouldn't be available for either summer session after all, and asked him to find someone to take the two courses I'd agreed to teach. It was late notice and rather put him on the spot, but he told me he'd take care of it and not to worry. A considerate man, and a friend.

I had made up my mind that if the police hadn't caught Rudy's murderer by the end of the school term, I'd go back to New York long enough to hire my own detectives. I was concerned that I might be leaving it too late, that whatever trail the murderer had left might have grown cold. But there were too many obligations keeping me in Washburn just then; the end of the term meant final exams and term papers to grade. Also, I had to finish correcting the proofs of my book, and that was something I simply could not rush. After spending eleven years on research and three more on the writing, I wasn't going to allow hasty proofreading to mar the finished product.

So I really had no time to spare when Captain Michaels called me from New York and told me he wanted to send Marian Larch to look through Rudy's papers.

"Why didn't you do that before I had them all shipped here?" I asked in exasperation.

"We didn't want to delay your departure," he said blandly. (I translated that to mean he hadn't thought it necessary then.) "She'll take nothing without your permission—she won't even photocopy anything without your permission. We have no authority in Ohio, but I'm hoping you'll cooperate. I'd like to send her, Dr. Benedict."

"It'll be a waste of time, Captain. Rudy's papers are mostly writing notes, business correspondence, copies of his scripts. The paperwork any writer accumulates over a period of years."

"Have you read it all?"

"No, I just sorted through it to see what was there, I haven't had time to read it yet."

"What about personal correspondence? Do you have his personal letters too?"

"There weren't any. Rudy never kept personal letters." He certainly didn't keep any of mine.

"Still, there might be something. Dr. Benedict, we've got to consider everything."

"That means your investigation has reached a dead end, I take it."

A brief silence from the other end. "We aren't getting very far here," he admitted. "Let me send Detective Larch. It won't hurt for her to take a look."

In the end I agreed, on condition that she stay at my house and pass herself off as a personal friend of Rudy's here for a visit. I didn't want to have to explain a New York police detective's poking through my son's papers. So now I had a house guest to concern myself with.

I prepared the way by telling a few people she was coming, friends such as the Morrisseys. Drew Morrissey's field was the American Civil War, and Roberta taught in the English Department—Victorian period, mostly.

"I don't remember your ever mentioning a Marian Larch," Roberta Morrissey said in that annoyingly straightforward way she had.

"I just met her, when I was in New York," I said truthfully. "She was a friend of Rudy's," not truthfully at all.

We were in the faculty lounge of Cuthbert Hall, going through the morning coffee break ritual. Drew cleared his throat. "Fiona, I don't mean to be nosy—but did you invite her here?"

"She invited herself."

"Then why, Fiona?" That was Roberta. "Why are you letting her come? Intruding on you at a time like this!"

I liked her honest indignation, but I went on with the lie just the same. "Ostensibly she's coming here to console me, but I think she's really looking for consolation herself." How glibly it came out. The Morrisseys were my closest friends, and I didn't like deceiving them. But the true story was so unpalatable I couldn't tell even them.

Drew was looking especially concerned. He'd turned almost completely gray this past year, something I'd not realized until I got back from New York; I'd watched it happen, little by little, without seeing it. Drew glanced at Roberta. "Dinner?" She nodded. "Bring her over to dinner one night," he said. "That'll take up some of the time. When is she getting here?"

That seemed a little risky to me; I didn't know how good Marian Larch was at acting a part. But I could think of no reason to refuse, so we agreed on a time. I was sure I could count on the detective's willingness to go through with the charade; she'd shown herself to be a considerate woman in New York.

"You'll have to call me Marian," was the first thing she said. "Although I'll go on calling you Dr. Benedict, of course." She'd rented a car at the airport and found my house on her own; I didn't even have to meet her.

"Yes, that's probably best, Marian," I agreed. I don't like calling near-strangers by their first names but it would have looked odd not to, this time.

"Just so we'll be telling the same story," she went on, "am I right in assuming you haven't told the people here your son was murdered?"

"You assume correctly."

She kept her face expressionless. "Now, if you'll show me where the papers are? The sooner I get started, the quicker I'll be out of here."

I took her up to the attic where I'd had Rudy's things carried. I'd put up a table and chair near one of the dormer windows; I planned to work there myself when I got around to reading the papers.

She was appalled when she saw how many there were. Fourteen good-sized cartons plus three filing cabinets. She opened one of the cartons. "I had no idea—so many scripts! And all these other folders—what are they?"

"Notes, outlines. Works he never completed, probably meant to get back to eventually. Some research work—background material, mostly. Rudy rarely threw anything away."

"You've read all this?" Her dough face plainly said she didn't believe it.

"No, I'd planned to give the summer over to it."

She scowled down at the carton she'd opened. "Well, I can't read everything here—I'd be here all summer myself. Where's his business correspondence?"

I indicated one of the filing cabinets. "By the way, we're invited out to dinner tonight. The Morrisseys, friends of mine."

She nodded absently as she lifted an armful of folders out of the file cabinet. Then as I started to leave, she said, "Oh—will we be back by ten?"

I lifted my shoulders. "I doubt it. Why?"

"This is Thursday—*LeFever*'s on at ten. They're into re-runs now—you did know the episode your son worked on is showing tonight, didn't you?"

"No, I didn't know—and I would like to see it. Thank you for mentioning it."

"Did you miss it the first time?"

"I don't have a television set. We'll watch at the Morrisseys." I saw her eyes grow large and hurried to cut her off. "When my set broke down a few years back, I somehow never got around to having it repaired. I'll call you in time to get ready for dinner."

I left before she could answer. I knew what she was thinking: *Her son was a TV writer and she didn't even bother to watch?*

Roberta Morrissey had cooked her usual roast beef and Yorkshire pudding, although the weather was getting too warm for so heavy a meal. But Marian Larch loved it; she ate with gusto, murmuring compliments between bites that had Roberta beaming. Both the Morrisseys accepted her without question, although I think Drew had been expecting someone more glamorous.

Marian told them she did secretarial work for Nathan Pinking's production company. "I read audience mail, type

up script changes, things like that." She told how each new
script change was typed on a different color paper to help
keep them straight. Color-coded script changes! The kinder-
garten approach to records-keeping. I'm sure Marian was
making it all up as she went along, but on the whole she told
a convincing story.

After dinner Roberta took my guest off to show her
where the bathroom was while Drew and I cleared the table.
"When is your book due out?" he asked.

"Publication date is November fourteenth. But it will
probably be available before then. You know how that goes."

Drew nodded. His last book—about the Battle of Shiloh—
had been published almost four years earlier, but he was
through with all that now; he'd said at the time it would be
his last book. Since then Drew had published a couple of
short follow-up articles, unable to leave it alone—but that was
all. Roberta liked to say Drew and I were both unabashedly
drawn to violence, since we confined our efforts to military
history. We were still talking publications when Roberta came
back with Marian Larch, who wanted to know what my book
was about.

"It's a biography of Lord Lucan," I told her, "not the
present one but the Lord Lucan who fought in the Crimean
War." Silence. "Nineteenth Century?" I wasn't particularly
surprised at the blank look she gave me. "He was one of the
four men responsible for that bloody mistake known as the
Charge of the Light Brigade."

"Aha," Marian said, her face lighting up. "The raglan
sleeve!"

"Very good," Drew laughed. "And the cardigan sweater."

She didn't know that one, so I said, "Lord Raglan gave
the order to charge and Lord Cardigan carried it out. Except
that the order Raglan gave wasn't the one Cardigan followed—
it was so vaguely worded it was misunderstood. Lucan was
the man in the middle. He was in a position to stop the
slaughter but didn't."

"Lord Look-on," Drew said.

"That's what his men called him," I told Marian, "even
before that infamous charge. A very cautious, unimaginative
man who would do nothing without direct orders."

"That makes three," Marian said. "You said four men
were responsible."

"Primarily. The fourth was a young officer named Lewis

Nolan. Undoubtedly the most intelligent of the four, but he behaved stupidly at the moment of crisis. He was an impatient young man—full of contempt for the slow-moving, incompetent type of British officer that infested Victoria's army during the entire Crimean campaign. Men such as Lord Raglan, Lord Lucan, and Lord Cardigan."

Marian smiled and shook her head. "How could Lucan have stopped it?"

"Chain of command. Lord Raglan was up on a ridge overlooking a long valley, and he could see along the ridge to his right where some Russian troops were capturing the few British cannon lined up there. Raglan wanted the Light Brigade to charge up the slope and scatter the Russians. That's what light cavalry was for—quick, darting action. So Raglan dictated an order saying the Light Brigade was to prevent the enemy from carrying away 'the guns.' What he neglected to say was *which* guns. Ragland forgot that people down at the bottom of a hill can't see the same things that people on top of a hill can see."

"Or read minds," Roberta smiled.

"Lewis Nolan carried the message," I went on. "He delivered it to Lord Lucan, the commander of the Cavalry Division, who was to pass the order on to the commander of the Light Brigade under him. A confused Lucan asked what guns did Raglan mean. And hot-headed young Lewis Nolan flung out his arm and pointed down the valley to the *Russian* guns, the enemy cannon. '*There* are your guns!' he answered quite insolently."

That was the crux of the whole affair—that moment between Lucan and Nolan. "It's been well over a century since that young man flung out his arm and pointed to the wrong guns," I said, "and we're still trying to figure out why he did it. But whatever the reason, Lord Lucan passed on the order that the Light Brigade, designed only for quick skirmishes, remember, was expected to charge Russian cannon. Lucan should have demanded a confirming order."

"*Cardigan* should have demanded a confirming order," Drew muttered. "What an ass. Leading his men into so obvious a death trap."

"Lord Cardigan was the commander of the Light Brigade," I told Marian Larch, who kept nodding her head through all this. "He was the one who actually had to carry out the order, and I don't think there was a more stupid man in the whole British army than Lord Cardigan. The man had the brain of a bird."

"A peacock," Drew said.

"So that birdbrain actually led men armed only with sabres in a charge against cannon. Nearly seven hundred men rode into that valley. Fewer than two hundred rode back out. Cardigan himself survived the charge, but the entire light cavalry was virtually wiped out in less than twenty minutes. And the whole thing was a mistake."

"Responsibility ultimately lies with the commanding officer," Drew said sententiously.

"Of course," I said. "Besides, it was Raglan's vague wording that caused the misunderstanding in the first place. But that's the odd thing about this battle. Everyone who writes about it feels compelled to take sides—it's intriguing the way so many reputable historians forget they are supposed to be disinterested analysts and instead become passionate partisans once they start writing about the Charge of the Light Brigade. Excepting Cecil Woodham-Smith, of course. She just states flatly they were *all* a passel of fools."

"Why do you write about English history?" Marian Larch wanted to know.

I smiled. "Why not leave English history to the English, you mean? It used to be that way, but the invention of the airplane changed all that."

"And the foundations," Drew added. "Don't forget the foundations."

"Lord, no," I said. "I'd never have been able to write my *Life of Lucan* without grants to pay for all those trips to London. But national origins aren't important to historians, not really. The English have turned out to be the best French historians. And the Germans are doing good work in Soviet history."

Roberta leaned toward Marian. "Did you know Fiona's book is the first full biography of Lord Lucan ever written?"

Marian looked at me in surprise. "Really?"

"That's right," I said. "Millions and millions of words written about the Crimean War, and nobody ever got around to doing a study of Lucan's life." I laughed. "Probably because he was such a stodgy, predictable man." I stopped; I'd been going to mention something Lucan had done in Ireland but an expression had appeared on Marian Larch's face that I recognized. It was the glazed-eye look of those who don't really care what happened before they were born.

We talked desultorily of other things until ten o'clock, the hour of *LeFever*. The Morrisseys had an elaborate, big-screen television console, purchased at Roberta's insistence back when the BBC first announced plans to produce all of Shakespeare's plays. The set tended to dominate the room.

Rudy was one of three writers listed in *LeFever*'s credits. I'd once thought that meant a big budget, but Rudy had told me the script fees were fixed by the Screen Writers' Guild and more than one writer simply meant the money had to be split. I listened carefully, but I couldn't hear any lines that sounded more like Rudy than any others. That was good from the show's viewpoint, I suppose, that kind of homogeneity. But this episode was of the sort that had caused me to drift away from watching television in the first place.

It was the kind of story in which the viewer quickly learned to stop listening and just watch. The lines were dull, the plot slow and disconnected. There was no meaning to be found; the script discouraged active participation, it discouraged thinking. It was as bland as oatmeal. The people and the settings, on the other hand, were *beautiful*. Envy-arousing beautiful. The hero, LeFever, was a vain, muscular young man who posed his attractive body against a variety of luxurious backgrounds. No scenes took place on dirty streets or in slum buildings. The fad for picturing New York as a sewer must have passed; these things probably went in cycles.

And then there was Kelly Ingram. Her role was a lot smaller than LeFever's, but when she was in a scene with the hero, *she* was the one you looked at. I wondered if the actor playing LeFever knew that; he didn't strike me as being particularly bright.

"What a *beautiful* woman," Roberta murmured. Drew, who'd been in danger of falling asleep, opened one eye.

"That's Kelly Ingram," Marian Larch said. "She's even more beautiful in person."

"Oh, that's right—you know all these people, don't you? Do you know her, Fiona?"

I said I'd met her. There *was* something about Kelly Ingram; if appearance was all it took, she was bound to become a star. Her movements were graceful and unstudied. She walked like a dancer—no, that's wrong; dancers waddle like ducks when they walk. Kelly Ingram walked *as if she were dancing;* that was better.

Her role was that of an adjective describing the noun hero. She was the sexually available but eternally fresh female, experienced innocence personified, the kind of woman whose virginity is renewable upon demand. We were supposed to think that if LeFever could have a woman like that gazing upon him adoringly, then he must be one hell of a man. The same little-boy notion of manhood that has always kept women prone in a male society. I wasn't too surprised to find the Ingram woman helping perpetuate the notion.

The show came to its bland conclusion. Marian Larch and I thanked the Morrisseys and took our leave. On the way home my guest started to say something but stopped. I think she was going to ask me what I thought of the show but then changed her mind.

Marian winnowed a few letters out of Rudy's business correspondence that she wanted to take back with her. They were all concerned with details about scripts Rudy had contracted to write and didn't seem especially significant to me—but historians never give up papers without a fight, so I told Marian I'd take them to school with me and get them photocopied. That was agreeable to her.

She was making plans to leave early Saturday when I asked her to tell me honestly what progress had been made in finding Rudy's killers. I told her I was considering hiring detectives.

"That's your privilege, of course," she said. "But it's my opinion you'd just be wasting your money, Dr. Benedict. This isn't one of those cases where a private operative can go in and do things the police can't. In fact, we have resources private agencies don't. It's the lack of motive that has us stumped. We can't find even a hint of a reason why anyone would want your son dead."

"Then you are stumped."

A pause. "Yes. We are. I'm sorry. Rudy had the usual number of people in his life who didn't particularly like him, but nobody hated him—which I'm told is unusual in television. Of all the people he knew, there's not one you could call a real enemy. There was no woman in his life at the moment— he and Kelly Ingram were just beginning to get together. He wasn't engaged in any illegal money-making scheme we could find out about. The medical examiner said he wasn't a user. There's nothing. That's why Captain Michaels sent me here—in the hope there might be something to give us a lead."

"What about those letters I had photocopied? Anything there?"

She sighed. "Not really, just a sort of side issue. Look—you can help. There's no way the Captain is going to let me sit in your attic for the next few months. You said you were going to give the summer over to reading Rudy's papers?"

"Yes, that's what I plan to do."

"Then how about reading for anything specifically out of the ordinary? Help us out."

"But it's all fiction, Marian—television scripts, plot outlines, something the industry calls story treatments . . ."

"I know. But maybe one of those plot outlines will tell you something. Or maybe a letter got misfiled. You never know. Will you do it? Will you watch for anything the least bit unusual?"

"Well, of course I'll do it. It's just that I don't think anything will come of it."

We left it at that. Friday had been a hectic day for me; I didn't even have a chance to read my mail until breakfast early Saturday morning before Marian's flight. Once again I had no premonition, no anticipation of disaster. The letter was from my publisher.

We have just learned that Walter Cullingham, Ltd., plans to publish Richard Ormsby's biography of Lord Lucan on October tenth, a month before we will be ready to release your *Life of Lucan*. Cullingham plans simultaneous British and American editions; and our source informs us that while the book is not quite in the coffee-table mode, it is lavishly illustrated and written in Ormsby's usual breezy style.

While Ormsby's book will undoubtedly cut into our immediate sales, we feel there is no long-range need for concern. We expect your *Life of Lucan* to be a steady seller over the years that will outlast the initial impact of Ormsby's version. We were surprised that no word of his work-in-progress had reached us; but we understand Ormsby had once planned a BBC television series about the Crimean War which he had to abandon as unfeasible. Then rather than waste the research he'd had done, he put together a hasty biography of one of the participants. The fact that Ormsby calls his book *Lord Look-on* should give us a fair indication of the profundity of his work.

These things happen, unfortunately. But let me repeat that we feel the long-range reception will be in our favor.

The next thing I knew I was on my knees on the floor fighting for breath. I heard Marian Larch's voice as from a great distance, demanding to know what was wrong. She forced me to lie on the sofa, although I didn't feel faint. It was just that *breathing* had suddenly become so difficult.

Some time evidently passed, because the next time I was fully aware of my surroundings, the Morrisseys were there; Marian must have called them. Drew stood around looking helpless, but Roberta was fussily taking over, apparently under the impression that lowering my body temperature was the thing to do: ice cubes on my wrists, cool wet wash cloths on the back of my neck. Oddly, it did seem to help.

I sat up and apologized for creating such a fuss. When they all wanted to know what had caused it, I just pointed to the letter I'd dropped on the floor.

The Morrisseys understood immediately. Marian Larch had some notion of what it meant; but not being a scholar herself, she couldn't quite appreciate the way fourteen years' work on my part had been neatly undercut by a pop historian whose specialty was providing simplistic explanations of complex matters. Through his use of television, Richard Ormsby had made his face and name familiar to people who hadn't looked at a history book since high school. How could I compete with that?

Drew, the eternal optimist, jumped on the one bright note in my publisher's letter. "He doesn't seem at all worried about the long-range sales, Fiona," he said. "You and Ormsby won't be selling to the same market—he writes for the dabblers, the amateurs. Yours is the study that will become the standard—perhaps even the definitive work. In the long run you won't have anything to worry about."

"Drew," I said, "I'm sixty-two years old. I may not be around for the long run."

He didn't have anything to say to that.

Marian Larch missed her flight because of my little fit; that meant she had to stay over until Monday, as there were only two flights a day out of Washburn—one eastward, one west—and none on Sundays. She kept watching me the whole weekend, trying to get me to eat when I didn't want to eat, or talk when I wanted silence.

"You just had an anxiety attack," she said kindly. "Like a pressure valve letting off steam. It'll be all right."

Anxiety attack—a fancy name for getting news so shocking it literally takes your breath away.

Richard Ormsby was a youngish, blond, upper-class Englishman who was carefully articulate and consciously charming. He was one of those "popularizers" who have sprung up in just about every discipline lately. I'd watched him several times at the Morrisseys', always on BBC mini-series (horrid neologism). At first Ormsby had won cautious praise from historians for creating a new interest in a subject that usually evoked nothing but groans from the non-readers around us. But then it became clear that Ormsby was marketing *himself*, and even that faint praise disappeared.

He'd followed the usual procedure in such matters—first the TV series, then the book based on it. All ballyhooed by means of press interviews and frequent appearances on television and radio talk shows. Ormsby was more a media personality than a historian, but his efforts were well-funded. He did virtually none of his own research, hiring professionals rather than depend upon graduate students whose work would have to be checked. Both television series and book were then written up in a chatty, informal style that reduced momentous decisions and actions to one-dimensional matters that could be understood with a minimum of effort. My publisher had said that Ormsby's proposed series on the Crimean War hadn't worked out and rather than waste the research, he'd tossed off a book about Lord Lucan. I was certain the only reason he'd chosen Lucan was the lack of competition. In well over a hundred years no one had yet published a biography of the man; maybe Ormsby had heard about the woman in Ohio who'd just finished a study of Lucan's life, maybe he hadn't. Somehow I didn't think it would have made any difference.

You spend years learning and working toward a goal and doing your best to create something of quality—and some glib, pretty, young person comes along and with a laugh and a

wave of his hand *dismisses your life*. And not only is he
allowed to get away with it, he's rewarded for doing so.
Richard Ormsby was everything I hated about contemporary
life—the cheapening, cashing-in quality that polluted everything it touched.

Some of this I tried to explain to Marian Larch. There
were rivalries in all fields, of course; but I could think of a lot
of people I'd rather be in competition with instead of Richard
Ormsby. I didn't doubt for one minute that mine was the
superior book; but hustle and hype had invaded the study of
history, and I could be hurt by it.

Marian caught the one eastbound flight Monday morning. Tuesday's mail brought another letter from my publisher,
this one gently informing me that the History Book Club had
decided to distribute Ormsby's book instead of mine.

5

Marian Larch

Captain Michaels had a standard way of dealing with lack
of progress in a case, and that was to yell at people who
couldn't yell back. The day after Fiona Benedict went back to
Ohio, he let us have it with both barrels. He called in those
of us assigned to the Rudy Benedict murder and gave us a
dressing-down that I stopped listening to after the first ten
seconds because it was so foolish. Abusive language wouldn't
create new leads for us.

He ended with his usual unhelpful instruction: *Get out
there and scrounge*. I did what I usually did in such instances—I
swapped interviewees with another investigator. Ivan Malecki
would go talk to Kelly Ingram while I gave Nathan Pinking a
try. Ivan allowed as how he wouldn't mind too much.

Pinking had just got back from London and quickly let
me know he was doing me a big favor by fitting me into his
busy, busy schedule. We were in his office on West Fifty-
fourth, a suite that was smaller than I'd expected. A framed

photograph on his desk showed a woman and three teenaged girls. All four looked happy.

Pinking's file said he was fifty-one, but he looked a lot younger. I'd never seen the man before and his face startled me a little. It was the eyebrows you noticed first. The right one was straight and ordinary, just an eyebrow. But the left one was bushy and greatly arched. It made the eye under it look larger—no, the left eye *was* larger than the right. The nose also had that same kind of lopsidedness; the right nostril looked normal, the left one was fleshy and flared. Same difference in the two sides of the mouth. The left side of the upper lip lifted and seemed more curved than the right; the lower lip was full only on the left, and it drooped a little. Nathan Pinking had two halves of two perfectly good faces that just happened not to fit together. I resisted drawing conclusions about the proper Dr. Jekyll right side and the sensuous Mr. Hyde left.

"I don't know what this is for," Pinking said. "I've already told everything I know to that other detective, Ivan somebody."

"Ivan Malecki. Just a couple of questions, Mr. Pinking. How long had you been buying scripts from Rudy Benedict?"

"Oh God, years."

"Can you be more precise?"

He looked annoyed, but jabbed a finger at the box on his desk. "Tansy, bring in Rudy Benedict's file."

A voice said it would and I had to smile. "Tansy?"

Pinking grinned mechanically. "They're all called Tansy or Tawny or Silky these days."

Or Kelly. "Benedict was on the last year of his contract with you, is that right?"

"Yeah, but I would have renewed. Benedict was a good reliable dialogue man."

"But would *he* have renewed? He was planning to write a play."

He snorted. "Look, Detective, uh—"

"Larch."

"Yeah, well, Benedict had been threatening to quit television and write for the stage almost as long as I knew him. Ten, twelve years. But it was all talk. He'd never have gone through with it."

"He'd started. Notes, some plot outlines."

Pinking shook his head. "Security blanket. He was always making notes for things he never got around to writing."

"You sound as if you knew him pretty well."

"I did."

Just then pretty blonde Tansy came in looking perplexed. "Mr. Pinking, the Rudy Benedict folder isn't in the filing cabinet."

"Bull. Look again."

Tansy faded out of the room with a whispered *Yes, sir* and I said, "How long have you known Leonard Zoff, Mr. Pinking?"

His eyes narrowed. "Too long. Twenty-five years at least. Why do you ask?"

"Did Zoff ever represent Rudy Benedict in his negotiations with you?"

"Zoff doesn't handle writers. He's an actors' agent."

"Who was Benedict's agent?"

But Pinking had quickly had his fill of answering questions. "Funny thing—I forget. You'll have to see your friend Ivan for that. He asked the same question."

Tansy came back in. "Mr. Pinking, the Rudy Benedict file just isn't there. And Mr. Cameron is here to see you."

Pinking gave her a look that would have melted a steel girder. "You're just full of good news, aren't you? Tell Cameron to wait." He waved her out. "Now look, Ms, uh, I don't know anything about Benedict's murder. I can't even think of a reason why anyone would want him dead. It was probably a mistake—that stuff must have been meant for Kelly Ingram. She's a much more logical target."

I explained about the Lysco-Seltzer crystals in Rudy Benedict's sink and emphasized that Benedict was the "right" victim. "Why do you say Kelly is a more logical target?"

"Because of who she is. A very sexy, very visible young woman about that far away from being a star." He held thumb and forefinger a centimeter apart. "Women like that are natural magnets. It's a special quality they have."

And men like Pinking were always there to cash in on that quality. "Still, the cyanide was not meant for her. It—"

I was interrupted by the door bursting open. An angry man I'd never seen before came shooting into the room as if fired from a slingshot. "Goddamn it, Pinking, I will not sit there cooling my heels awaiting your pleasure! You go too far. You—" He broke off, seeing me for the first time.

He was a lean, black-haired man in his forties with the strangest eyes I'd ever seen. The blue of the irises was so faint as to be virtually colorless, making him appear from a certain angle as if he had no irises at all. It gave him an outer-space look. Not spaced out—just other-worldly.

"I'm sorry, Mr. Pinking, I couldn't keep him out," came Tansy's faint voice. She was waved out again.

Pinking obviously wasn't going to introduce us so I said, "I'm Marian Larch, with the New York Detective Bureau."

Pinking's laugh had a needling edge to it. "That's right, Cameron. I'm being grilled by the police."

Good manners struggled with anger, and manners won. "Ted Cameron," he said, offering a hand. "Sorry I burst in on you."

I shook his hand and said, "That's all right, Mr. Cameron, I was about finished anyway." Pinking had already made that clear. "Are you in television?"

"I advertise on television." He didn't sound particularly proud of it.

"Cameron is *LeFever*'s new sponsor," Pinking said with a barely concealed smugness I didn't quite understand. "Or rather his company is. Cameron Enterprises."

Oho, one of *those* Camerons. Sportswear, sporting goods, radios, other things I couldn't remember. Cosmetics. "Then this isn't your maiden voyage?"

"God, no," Pinking laughed before Ted Cameron could answer. "But this is the first time Cameron Enterprises has deigned to associate itself with a Nathan Pinking production. Ah well, Teddy old boy, we have to take the rough with the smooth."

"So they say," the man with the invisible irises said. He'd decided to hold it in until I was gone.

"You're in for an education," Pinking went on. "Watch what happens to your profits once Kelly Ingram starts wearing your swimsuits. Through the ceiling! And you'll owe it all to me. Think you can stand it?"

I wasn't too crazy about Leonard Zoff, but I was beginning to understand why he hated Nathan Pinking so. The man was deliberately abrasive, going out of his way to offend just to show you he could get away with it. I stood up. "You'll get in touch with me when you locate that missing file?"

"Sure, sure," Pinking said dismissively. He wouldn't.

I said goodbye to Cameron and left through the outer office. Tansy was sitting disconsolately at her desk looking at a magazine. She lifted her head and said, distinctly and puzzlingly, "Julia Child doesn't like sauerkraut."

I nodded and went on out. Sometimes it's best not to ask.

At Police Plaza, Ivan Malecki hadn't yet got back from interviewing Kelly Ingram; somehow that failed to surprise me. I called a few contacts in industry and did some checking. Cameron Enterprises had been started three generations ago by Henry W. Cameron, a haberdasher with big ideas. What was originally a small family business had grown rapidly, acquiring smaller companies along the way until now it was a fairly large conglomerate. Various family members were involved in the conglomerate's operation; old Henry's great-grandson, Ted Cameron, currently sat in the president's chair.

What was the president of a company that large doing *personally* overseeing a television series the company was sponsoring? Wouldn't that be a job for the advertising department? Or at least for someone lower down in the hierarchy. And why all that animosity between Cameron and Nathan Pinking? Perhaps the man with the invisible eyes didn't have absolute powers; maybe his board of directors had forced him into sponsoring a show he didn't want. Strange thing for a board of directors to be concerning itself with. Or maybe not; they'd want to use their advertising dollars to reach the highest number of customers possible, and *LeFever*'s ratings had been climbing steadily.

I went in and told Captain Michaels about Rudy Benedict's file that was suddenly missing from Nathan Pinking's office, perhaps conveniently so.

He made a vulgar noise. "Benedict's papers. We should have gone through them."

We'd been through this before. "A writer's papers, Captain. Big job—time-consuming."

"Got any other suggestions?" he came close to snarling. "I tell you to go out and scrounge and you come back and tell me a file folder is missing. So what does that mean—our answer is written down on a piece of paper? We got nothing else." He picked up the phone and started punching out a number he read from a folder on his desk. "Go home and pack, Larch. I have to get the old doll's permission, but she won't say no."

*   *   *

I'd never associated Ohio with anything in particular, so the community of Washburn made me revise a few of my ideas about smalltown America. I'd halfway expected a wide place in the road that had no reason for being there except for the university it served. But Washburn smelled of prosperity, and of *taking care*. I don't mean the place was a hotbed of millionaires; but the people who lived there were fussy about their surroundings. Manhattan's Fourteenth Street would have driven them crazy.

Washburn was pretty, in an unremarkable way, and clean. Fiona Benedict lived in a conventional red brick house, white trim, single story plus basement and attic, attached garage, nice yard. She'd taken me up to the attic where Rudy's things were stored—and one look was all I needed to tell me I'd never get through all those papers in the two or three days Captain Michaels had told me to take. So I settled for just the business papers, trusting Dr. Benedict to search through the rest of it for us.

Fiona Benedict was a strange woman. She'd told no one in Washburn that her only child had been murdered. She'd made up some story about accidental death that I agreed to go along with. But I couldn't imagine someone keeping a thing like that to herself. It wasn't that she didn't have any friends; she was liked and respected in Washburn. But the murder of her son was just too painful or too private or too something; she wouldn't or couldn't tell anybody. And the odd thing about it was that I got the impression before I left that she didn't really like Rudy very much.

My first night there was a revealing one; I learned several interesting new things. We went to dinner at the home of two of Dr. Benedict's friends, Roberta and Drew Morrissey. After a marvelous dinner, Roberta Morrissey showed me the way to the bathroom—and displayed a rather disconcerting curiosity about me. She had a very direct way of talking, and we were no sooner out of the dining room than she started pumping me about my supposed friendship with Rudy.

The best way to avoid answering personal questions is to ask questions yourself. "Rudy never talked to me about his father," I said. "I'm sure he remembers him—Rudy was eight when his father left. Did his parents ever divorce, or what?"

Roberta Morrissey shot me a funny look. "Is that what Rudy told you?"

"That they divorced?"

"No, that his father deserted his family when Rudy was eight."

Since I'd never spoken to Rudy Benedict in my life, I wasn't sure what I should say. But there was something funny about that question and the way she asked it. "No, it was his mother who told me that. Rudy never talked about his father."

Roberta Morrissey looked at me a minute, and then said, "Rudy's father committed suicide." I stared at her open-mouthed, and she said, "Here's the bathroom."

She was waiting when I came back out. I said, "You mean Dr. Benedict has rationalized his suicide away? That she calls it desertion to keep from facing up to what really happened?"

Dr. Mrs. Morrissey sighed. "No, she really does see his suicide as desertion. As an inexcusable abandoning of Rudy and herself. She's never forgiven him."

"Why did he kill himself?"

I don't think she wanted to talk to me about it, but she felt obligated to finish what she'd started. "Shame, humiliation. Depression. Evidently Philip Benedict wasn't a very good historian. He'd been taken to task rather severely for some inaccurate translations he'd done—he was a medievalist and he had to deal with archaic language a lot. But then he fabricated some evidence for a book he'd written and was found out. It was pretty much the end of his career. His department head asked for his resignation. Publishers wouldn't take a chance on him after that, and the best teaching position he could ever hope for would be in some small community college somewhere that would consider itself lucky just to get a Ph.D. I never knew Philip Benedict, but from what Drew's told me, I'd say he was just trying to keep up with Fiona. Which was foolish—that need to compete. Fiona is rather special."

"And you never met Philip Benedict at all?"

"I didn't even know Fiona when all that happened—they were teaching in Indiana at the time. Drew knew them both, from history conventions they all attended. But when Philip killed himself, Fiona wanted to take the boy and start over someplace else. Drew called and told her there was an opening at Washburn, and she's been here ever since."

So father and son were both murder victims, one by his

own hand and the other by a hand still unknown. I began to see why Fiona Benedict hadn't wanted her peers to know how her son had died. Poor woman.

Then that "poor woman" displayed a side I'd never seen before. The personality she'd always shown me was cool, composed, withdrawn, plainly inaccessible. She had a very good defense system. But then in the Morrisseys' living room she started talking about a new book she'd just finished that had taken her fourteen years to research and write—and the change in that woman was downright spooky. When she spoke of the Crimean War and the Charge of the Light Brigade and idiotic lords and misunderstood orders and fatally foolish actions—well, she was a different person entirely. Her face lit up and her voice became musical and her body was animated—she looked a good fifteen years younger. She was happy and even a little bit excited, but it wasn't a gushing kind of enthusiasm she showed. The lady was simply in her element.

Then we turned on the TV to watch *LeFever* and she changed again, this time into the Bride of Frankenstein—all hiss and sparks and disapproval. The only thing missing was the Elsa-Lanchester-electrocuted hairdo. It was a dumb show, true, but it didn't seem to be Rudy's script that made her so mad; she acted as if she hadn't expected anything better on that score. No, it was Kelly Ingram that got her so riled.

It was easy to see why. I couldn't think of two women more different from each other than Kelly Ingram and Fiona Benedict. Kelly was extroverted glamour and sparkle and good times; Dr. Benedict was privacy and quiet, a thinker. Of course the serious woman would have no respect for the frivolous one.

Yet I thought Dr. Benedict underestimated Kelly Ingram. People see a face as beautiful as Kelly's and they tend to assume there can't be a brain behind it. Kelly wasn't an educated woman by Fiona Benedict's standards, but that didn't mean she was stupid. In fact, she was rather shrewd in her own way. Kelly never kidded herself about what she was doing for a living or tried to pretend it was anything more significant than it was. She never put on airs or played the great actress. I liked Kelly—I liked her energy and her style and her upbeat personality. What Dr. Benedict saw was a useless woman who was getting a free ride through life because she happened to be born beautiful. I thought there was more to Kelly than that.

Kelly struck me as being a halfway woman—no, that's not the right way to put it. Kelly was a woman stuck between time zones, getting messages from the past and from the present at the same time. She was sure-footed in a highly competitive profession where you have to be able to take care of yourself if you intend to survive. But she'd gotten where she was by playing the men's game, by catering to male fantasies. Sure, she did it all tongue-in-cheek—but she still *did* it. I don't think Kelly would ever claim women's only function was to serve as objects of male desire. But her extraordinary beauty had singled her out from birth for just that very role. It's what she knew, it's what she understood—of course it directed her behavior. But she wasn't particularly impressed by any of it.

And, well, to tell the truth, there was another reason I liked her. She'd flattered me. When Kelly got that second Lysco-Seltzer bottle in the mail and was scared half out of her skull, it was me she turned to for help. Not Captain Michaels, *me*. Women don't generally look to other women for help. Men are the protectors, the capable ones, right? We're taught from childhood that women are supposed to be helpless. I mean, women are *supposed* to be helpless; it's expected of us. But when Kelly felt threatened and decided she needed help, I was the one she called. Think that didn't make me feel good?

On the way back to Dr. Benedict's house I'd wanted to talk to her about Kelly, but the look on her face said *No Trespassing* so I didn't.

There was a repetitiousness about Rudy Benedict's business papers that soon had me nodding. I forced myself to pay attention to letter after letter detailing percentages, residuals, kill fees, on and on. Reams of paper spent on correspondence about details of scripts in progress—should the villain be kind to animals, how about discovering the body inside a case of peat moss in the greenhouse, etc. Rudy Benedict had spent so much time writing and reading letters I wondered how he ever got anything else done.

The only thing of interest had to do with satisfying my personal curiosity instead of helping to solve a murder. It was a series of four letters concerning a script Benedict had written twelve years earlier. The contents of the correspondence were about the same as all the others; it was the letterhead I found so interesting. It read: "Pinking and Zoff Productions, Inc."

So those two had been partners once—the source of their present mutual hatred? Somehow I couldn't see Leonard Zoff as a producer; he seemed so right in his role of huckster, wheeling and dealing and selling his human products for all he could get. I decided to take copies of the letters back with me; I had to have something to show Captain Michaels for my trip to Ohio.

Then right before I left, Fiona Benedict got some really nasty news: Channel 13 idol Richard Ormsby was publishing a book called *Lord Look-on*. The news hit her so hard I was worried about her; at first I thought she was having a heart attack. I stayed on until Monday, and over that weekend she opened up more than I'd yet seen her do. The *pain* that woman was feeling was overwhelming—I was hurting for her myself. By the time I left Monday morning, she'd withdrawn into herself again; her mouth was bitter.

It was a peculiar thing, and maybe I wasn't being fair in thinking it, but it seemed to me Fiona Benedict was mourning what happened to her book the way you'd have thought she'd mourn what happened to her son. Not that her book was dead, far from it. But what she was feeling was pure and simple grief, no question of that. Yet all the time she'd been in New York seeing about Rudy's cremation and closing his apartment and disposing of his things—she'd been icily calm and collected, never displaying anything of what she was feeling. She was a very private woman.

Perhaps she could handle one horrible thing happening to her, but not two so close together. Or perhaps it was the order in which they happened. If she'd heard about *Lord Look-on* first, then it might have been Rudy's death that caused her to grieve. Or perhaps it was exactly what it appeared to be: the murder was an attack on a son to whom she'd not been close for decades, but the book was an attack on her personally.

Back in New York I made one more visit to the *LeFever* set. They were shooting their last episode and I wanted to find out where Kelly Ingram and Nathan Pinking would be during the rest of the summer. And to see if Nick Quinlan had learned anything about acting yet.

There was a last-day-of-school sort of gaiety on the set, but the laughter was a little too loud and a bit edgy. I guess doing a weekly series does get to be a strain after a while. There were visitors on the set, mostly young women clustered around Nick Quinlan. The director looked harried, but determined to keep his temper.

"Well, there she is, the missing policewoman!" Kelly Ingram's voice bubbled behind me. "Where've you been lately? I thought you'd deserted us."

"Blame Captain Michaels," I told her. "He decided I wasn't working hard enough."

"Come along, I've got to do some pickups," she said, not really listening. "They might even use one of them, who knows?"

An assistant director fussily positioned Kelly in front of a neutral-colored wall. "Give us some choice, love," he said. "Yes-no-maybe should do it."

Kelly stood in front of the camera and registered three facial expressions, each one lasting about ten seconds—a smile, a worried frown, and a perfectly blank look that could be anything at all. If the episode ran a few seconds short that week, a shot of Kelly "reacting" could be inserted.

"Harder than it looks," Kelly said to me in mock seriousness. "Have you tried holding a smile without moving for a full ten seconds? Your face starts twitching."

"What terrible things you're called on to do," I murmured.

She smiled her big smile, not the one she used for the camera. "It's those little things that sometimes mean the difference between working and not working. Once I got a role because I was the only woman interviewed who could run down a flight of stairs without looking at her feet, *my* feet. And once when we were..." She trailed off without finishing. Then Kelly did an odd thing: she ducked her head in a curiously childlike and vulnerable-looking gesture I'd never seen her make before.

"Kelly?"

She raised her head and peered over my shoulder. "Who," she whispered, "is *that?*"

I turned to see Nathan Pinking introducing the man with the invisible eyes to Nick Quinlan. "You mean Ted Cameron? That's your new sponsor—haven't you met him yet?"

A barely perceptible shake of the head. "*That's* Ted

Cameron?" She seemed surprised. "My God, what eyes!
They do have irises, don't they?" she half-laughed.

"Pale blue ones. *Very* pale. You have to stand at a certain
angle to see them."

"How come you know him, Marian?"

"Met him in Nathan Pinking's office. Last week."

"Ladies, you're going to have to move," a tense male
voice told us. We moved; a camera was rolled past us,
followed by two men arguing quietly.

"Poor Harry," Kelly smiled.

"Poor Harry" was the director, who looked as if he
wanted to lie on the floor and kick his heels and scream a lot.
Here he was trying to keep to a tight schedule when the boss
showed up with the new money man, wasting valuable
shooting time.

"Do something!" Poor Harry hissed to an underling.
"Get them off the set!"

"How can I get them off the set?" the underling hissed
back. "You do it!" I wondered how long *he* would last.

I turned back to Kelly, but she was no longer there.
She'd moved off by herself. She stood quietly, watching Ted
Cameron.

And then slowly, gradually, he became aware of her
attention. Cameron kept on talking to Pinking and Nick
Quinlan, but his eyes slid over to where Kelly stood silently
watching. Then looking at her became the main thing and the
talking with the others slipped to second place. Finally he
excused himself and walked over to her.

"Yeah, she can do that all right," a voice behind me said.
It was Poor Harry. "Make men come to her just by standing
still. It's her most marketable commodity."

I whirled on him angrily. "What a *vile* thing to say."

He looked honestly surprised. "What? I didn't mean
anything."

He probably didn't at that. I muttered something concil-
iatory and moved over to where Nathan Pinking and Nick
Quinlan were standing watching their new sponsor and their
leading lady.

"She sure doesn't waste any time," Pinking snickered.
"Go for the bucks, babe." Both halves of his mismatched face
were busy grinning in their separate ways.

I made my presence known. Strange thing, in all the
times I'd come around while *LeFever* was shooting, I'd never

yet met Nick Quinlan. But Nathan Pinking assumed I had—and so did Nick Quinlan.

"Hiya," he said, casually draping an arm over my shoulders. The familiarity was only slightly offensive, because with this man it had about as much meaning as a handshake did with other people. He probably remembered seeing me around the set and thought we were old friends.

I asked Nathan Pinking where he'd be for the next couple of months.

"Here, California, London, goddamned Cairo. You ever been in Egypt this time of year? And someplace cool, if I can squeeze in a vacation."

"Sorry to push, but I have to have dates and addresses. We need to keep track of where everybody goes once *LeFever* finishes."

"Hell, I don't remember all that. Ask my secretary—she'll give you a list."

"Tansy?"

The right side of his face grinned. "Mimsy. Tansy left."

Surprise attack. "When did you dissolve your partnership with Leonard Zoff?"

Surprise defense. "What partnership? I was never partners with that worm."

I didn't bother hiding my surprise. "Well, isn't that interesting. And here I found some correspondence from Pinking and Zoff Productions, Incorporated—right there among Rudy Benedict's papers."

"Oh, that." He shrugged. "Must have been dated twelve, fourteen years ago, right? In a moment of weakness I actually considered going into business with Leonard Zoff. But sanity returned in time. He must have had the stationery printed up—I don't remember it. Whose signature was on the letters?"

"Zoff's." On all four letters.

"There you are," Pinking said dismissively. "Zoff is such a tightwad he'd use the stationery even if the business didn't exist." Then, with no attempt at subtlety at all, he switched the subject back to what we'd been talking about before. "See Mimsy. She'll give you my itinerary. I'll be going a lot of places in the next few months."

"I'm goan' to Wes' Germany," Nick said helpfully. "Man, y'looka that? They just' glommed onna each other."

I stood there in the quasi-embrace of a TV star watching Kelly Ingram and Ted Cameron discovering each other. I couldn't hear what they were saying, but their talk didn't have the flirtatious look to it you might have expected. Instead it was intense, almost urgent. And private—oh boy was it private, in this very public place. The rest of us just weren't there.

Even Nathan Pinking sensed something unusual going on. "I never saw two people take to each other quite like that."

"'S fast," Nick nodded.

It was more than just fast. It was *meant*. I realized I wouldn't be talking to Kelly any more that day, so I said goodbye to the two men.

"Y'take care y'self, promise?" Nick called after me.

I promised and left, faintly bemused by what I'd seen. I knew Kelly Ingram was no nun, yet I was still a little surprised by the swiftness with which she'd acted. She'd taken one look at Ted Cameron, decided that was what she wanted, and made her move. I was willing to bet next month's salary it had *not* been like that with Rudy Benedict. Suddenly it became important to know more about Ted Cameron. The one time I'd talked to him, I'd seen only a man restraining his anger in order to be polite—which made me think well of him.

Captain Michaels had been only mildly interested in the Pinking and Zoff letterhead stationery I'd found in Ohio. He'd been disappointed I hadn't uncovered the entire solution to Rudy Benedict's murder in the writer's papers, and he'd even hinted it was my fault the crime was still unsolved. But Nathan Pinking's explanation of the stationery as a leftover from a partnership that had never materialized was peculiar, to say the least. I decided to check with the other "partner."

Leonard Zoff's office was on Seventh Avenue, and I had to get past no fewer than three Tansys (or Mimsys). There were four or five young hopefuls waiting to see the agent, but my gold shield got me in ahead of them.

To my surprise Leonard Zoff remembered me. "Hello, Marilyn, how's the policing business? Sorry, darling, I can't recall your last name."

"Larch. And my first name's Marian."

"Sure, sure, Kelly's friend, I remember. Have a seat and what can I do you for." The only other time I'd seen Leonard Zoff he'd had laryngitis and had barely been able to whisper.

Now he talked in a voice so loud it made me wince. I hate loud voices. I'm surrounded by them constantly—screaming, abrasive voices, and I hate them.

I sat down and said, "I want to ask you about Pinking and Zoff Productions."

At that he threw up both hands, palms facing me, fingers spread—as if I'd said *Stick 'em up.* "Temporary insanity," he said in an incongruous attempt at wistfulness. "That's the only possible explanation. I hadda be mad to go into business with Nathan Shithead."

"Then you *were* in business together?"

"Whaddaya mean 'were'? Shit, we're still in business together. I can't get rid of the sonuvabitch. He won't sell me his forty-nine, so I sure as hell ain't gonna sell him mine."

I couldn't make heads or tails out of that. "What are you talking about?"

"I'm talking about Nathan Shithead refusing to let go," he shouted at me. "'Pinking and Zoff'—what a laugh. It was Pinking and Pinking and Have Some More Pinking and Who the Hell's Zoff? I stuck it out for two years and when I wanted to sell that shithead knew he had me."

Just thinking about it made him boil, but eventually I got the story out of him. Zoff had wanted out of the partnership about ten years ago; Pinking wouldn't buy him out. Their contract said neither partner could sell to a third party without the consent of the other partner, a consent Pinking had steadfastly withheld. According to Zoff, their production company was more than slightly wobbly at the time, and Pinking had wanted a little insurance. So eventually they worked out a deal. Zoff would start his own theatrical agency, which Pinking would help underwrite in exchange for forty-nine percent ownership. In return, Zoff would retain forty-nine percent of the production company. That way if either enterprise failed, the losing partner would have something to fall back on. It certainly explained why they continued to do business in spite of hating each other; it was to their mutual benefit to do so.

But things had changed in the ten years since Pinking and Zoff had become Nathan Pinking Productions. Both the producer and the agent had succeeded on their own, and that insurance policy didn't look quite as attractive now as it did back in the earlier days. At least not to Zoff. "I've offered to buy him out a hundred times," Leonard Zoff told me. "But he won't give up his piece of my agency. The shithead."

"Pinking told me less than an hour ago that he and you had never been in business together. Why did he say that?"

Zoff snorted. "Instinct. Sonuvabitch *never* tells the truth. He lies on principle. How do you think he got to be such a successful producer? He talks shit. Don't you believe anything he tells you."

"So when he tells me he's going to Egypt next month..."

"You can be damned sure he's headed for Australia, darling. Don't believe *any*thing that shithead tells you. How did you know about Pinking and Zoff? It ain't something *I* talk about."

I told him about finding the letters among Rudy Benedict's papers.

"You went through his papers? I thought his momma took everything back to Michigan."

"Ohio. I made a special trip there just to read the papers. But I couldn't go through all of them—there are just too many. I had to skip his scripts and story treatments and so forth."

Zoff was nodding thoughtfully. "Think there might be anything there? Some clue, I mean. In his scripts?"

I shrugged. "Long shot at best."

"Nobody's going to read 'em and see?" He looked mildly shocked. "Seems to me you oughta check everything. Rudy shouldn't have died—he was a sweet, harmless guy. Who'da needed to kill *him*? You oughta check everything."

"Dr. Benedict is checking for us. She's giving the entire summer over to reading through all his papers. She gave me her word she'd let me know if she found anything the least bit out of the ordinary."

That seemed to satisfy him; we both stood up, and he made a production out of shaking my hand. "Good to see you again, Mary Ann. Any time I can help, you just lemme know."

This time I didn't correct him, because I'd finally caught on. This important, successful man had so many things on his mind he couldn't be expected to get my name quite right, yet he'd courteously made time for me to ask my little questions. If Nathan Pinking lied as a matter of principle, then Leonard Zoff played one-upmanship games for the same reason.

I should have stopped off in Pinking's office before

leaving the *LeFever* set, but I hadn't. So when I got back to my desk at Police Plaza, I dialed Nathan Pinking's number and got this low, velvet voice that assured me I was indeed talking to none other than Mimsy herself. The owner of the voice claimed there was nothing she'd rather do than type up a copy of Mr. Pinking's itinerary for me—and made me believe it. I sure would like to have a secretary like that.

I'd just hung up when Ivan Malecki came over and perched his butt on the corner of my desk. "Did you hear about your Ohio hostess—our murder victim's mother?"

"Fiona Benedict? What about her?"

"She's here in New York, and—are you ready? She's just been arrested for attempted murder."

"*What?*"

"She tried to shoot a guy. Some Englishman who's in town to publicize a new book or something."

"Richard Ormsby? She tried to shoot Richard Ormsby?"

"Yeah, that's the name—hey, how'd you know that?"

But I didn't answer, because I was already out the door.

6

Kelly Ingram

I came out of the shower wearing a towel and my dewy-fresh look.

Nick Quinlan looked me up and down with his x-ray eyes and then with a masterful gesture of his head commanded me to come closer. Eagerly I obeyed.

He placed one hand on my hip, leaned down so our faces were almost touching, and whispered softly, "Doncha got summon more uh uh cum, cumfable more'n 'at?"

"That was fine, Nick," the director said through clenched teeth. "But we're running long and we're going to have to cut the line. Just say, 'Comfortable?'"

"Cumfable."

"That's it. Kelly? From the shower, please."

The next time Nick was concentrating on his change of
line and didn't pay enough attention to what his hands were
doing and I lost my towel—nevertheless disappointing all the
drooling letches on the set who were hoping for a juicy
outtake, because I'd had the foresight to wear a bikini underneath. I'd been working with Nick Quinlan long enough to
know better than go on to an open set with nothing on under
my towel.

I ruined the next take myself. By laughing at the wrong
time. Most of the two-shot close-ups you see on television
have the two actors impossibly close to each other, their
noses sometimes only a couple of inches apart. It's awfully
hard not to get tickled when you are supposed to be saying
serious lines with your face shoved up into somebody else's
face like that. Besides, when Nick is really concentrating, his
eyes tend to cross.

The next time we got it. Four takes. We were getting
better.

I just realized I've never said one nice thing about Nick
Quinlan. I've given the impression that he was beautiful but
dumb—a clumsy, slow-witted peacock who liked admiration
so long as he didn't have to do anything strenuous to get it. I
probably gave that impression because it's true. Oh sure, I
know, there are always two sides to everybody, two or more
they say, and I'm not going to argue about that, that's okay.
But if you want to see something other than Nick's dumb
side, you really have to go looking for it. I mean, that's a wild
goose chase, why kid ourselves? But still, it doesn't make me
look very good when I go around badmouthing the star of the
series, the creep.

Therefore I am going to say something nice about Nick
Quinlan. Right now.

I'm thinking, I'm thinking.

Ha—got it. He did not smell bad.

I've been rattling on about Nick Quinlan like this because he's the kind of man most people admire and I don't
really understand why. A good ole boy with the rest of the
boys (accent on *boy*) whose proof of maleness lay (laid?
—grammar, not sex)—whose maleness *depended on* the number of women he had at his feet, urf, what a sentence. And he
looked and talked and acted just like everybody else, but

maybe a little prettier. Yet when somebody really special like Ted Cameron comes along—nobody notices!

The first time I saw Ted I was talking to Marian Larch on the *LeFever* set and honest to God I had to look away. I could not *look* at him, he took my breath away so; excuse the cliché but that's what happened. He was just too good to be true and I was afraid if I looked too closely too soon, he'd melt or turn into the Hulk or something. But when I could look again he was better instead of worse, better even than I'd hoped.

When I'd gotten over my astonishment at those eyes of his, I shot a quick look around the set. There were some visitors, girls mostly, and they were standing and gawking at Nick Quinlan. Ted was only a couple of feet away but they didn't even *see* him, the idiots. I'd had trouble looking at him at first but then I couldn't take my eyes off him. He was slim and together-looking and leaned slightly forward as if ready to take on whatever came next. He wasn't a big man, just medium, and you could tell at one look he wasn't the kind who went around pumping up his chest all the time. His clothes were part of him, not just something hanging on his body. My hands began to itch, I wanted to touch him so much. Then he turned those way-out eyes on me and looked at me. I mean really looked at me. Windows to the soul? Ha. Signals from outer space.

The first thing he said to me was, "Are you real?"

It didn't take us long to figure out neither one of us was the victim of a one-sided attraction; that's what I was most afraid of. I touched his face, once, for reassurance, then put my hands behind my back. Saving it. He lived in Tuxedo Park and neither one of us wanted to make the drive so we stayed at my place that first night.

In retrospect, I guess it was just glands calling to glands, but never in my life had I wanted a man the way I wanted Ted Cameron. The pressure was unbearable; I ached from wanting him even in the very act of making love. It was not altogether a pleasurable experience. You want contact with the other person so much, you try to get through each other's skin. I wanted Ted with me every minute of the day, I wanted constant physical contact, his body right there next to mine *all* the time. Which of course was impossible. It was very frustrating.

Those first few days were especially troublesome. *LeFever* still had a couple of more days to go, and Ted and I didn't really have time to get to know each other. What I knew at that point was a lover who seemed to have been made just for me. I spent my time on the set thinking of Ted and bed; I just sleepwalked through my role. And there were complications. Ted had a business to run, and I had some ugly news to deal with.

The very day after Ted and I had met, I went on to the *LeFever* set and learned Rudy's mother had been arrested for attempted murder. I called Howard Chesney and asked him to make sure she had legal representation, send the bill to me.

Ted was with me, concerned and wanting to help. "Do you want to go see her?"

I shook my head. "She wouldn't want to see *me*. She doesn't really approve of me, Ted."

"I thought you said a friend . . ."

"She's the mother of a friend. Rudy Benedict's mother. Rudy was a writer who, oh damn, he was murdered."

Ted knew about Rudy, but he hadn't known he'd been a friend of mine. Ted slipped an arm around me and said, "I'm sorry. This can't be easy for you. Who was it she tried to kill? Somebody she thought murdered her son?"

"No, it was Richard Ormsby—you've seen him on Channel 13, haven't you?"

He looked puzzled. "Why would she want to kill Richard Ormsby?"

"Well, they're both historians—that's the only connection I can see. But historians don't go around shooting guns at each other, do they?"

In the end all I could do was leave it to Howard Chesney. I didn't really want to see her, either. Part of it was I was so absorbed in Ted I didn't have room in my life for anybody else, even people in trouble—yes, I was that selfish about it. But part of it was I just didn't *want* to see her.

Then we finished *LeFever*, and I had some time before I had to start work on a project Nathan Pinking and Leonard Zoff had lined up for me. Time for nothing but Ted Cameron, and he finally began to emerge as a personality instead of this irresistible force looming over my life.

What I saw was a man in thorough, easy-riding control of his life. He was in the driver's seat and he was comfortable there. A man of authority ruling over a kind of kingdom, making decisions, giving orders. And doing it all with such ease and grace that you'd think he was to the manor or manner born. As I guess he was, come to think of it. His personal life was under that same kind of unfussy control; he'd had two not-very-successful marriages that he'd ended, neatly and amicably. Ted's entire life was *neat*.

Little by little I learned more of him. Ted Cameron turned out to be kind, courteous, decisive, intelligent, sexy, generous, knowledgeable, gentle, self-aware, courageous, worldly, reliable, determined, considerate, amusing, resilient, adventurous, playful, straightforward, upright, and steadfast. I liked him a lot.

In spite of what you're thinking, Ted was very human; he did have one serious flaw. He didn't like to dance. (Imagine!) He was so out of it I even had to explain that disco had been passé for some time now. A man whose whole life was a stately dance, a minuet maybe—and he didn't like to dance. Incredible.

But when that first bone-aching obsession with each other began to ease up, we found we had something better, at least I thought I had. I had a partner, a companion. I had somebody to share with.

7

Fiona Benedict

The lump in my stomach did not start small and gradually grow larger. It was just suddenly *there*. Solid stone.

What the romantics call fate and the frightened call God's will, historians call pattern—mundane, earth-generated pattern, responding to the human need for connections. My pattern: the result of wanting to fill in a gap in our knowledge. The fourteen years of studying the life of George Charles Bingham, third Earl of Lucan. *He* called *his* book *Lord Look-on*. Cute. Dismissive. Cashing in.

The stone grew heavier.

Personal artifacts tell a history. In a box in a drawer in a bureau in my bedroom: one loaded gun. A gift from Rudy; *for protection*, he'd said. Prompted by some feeling of guilt, belatedly being The Good Son. A California gun, he'd said, laughing to make a joke of it. I'd never needed to fire it. Before now.

They must be stopped, the invaders. My life had been violated by a profane Englishman who in all likelihood would go on to rape again. No one would stop him. No one would object. What did it matter, what he'd done to me?

It isn't a matter of loneliness; if the work is good, the cocoon is warm. But when the cocoon is ripped away, the only consolation is the perfunctory sympathy of one's peers. Of *some* of one's peers. Others betray. Garfield of Columbia, in *The New York Times Review of Books*, cashing in on the casher-in. Jumping on the pop history bandwagon, survival of the flightiest. Elsewhere in the out-of-town edition, an announcement of his arrival in New York, spreading the good news about the wonderful thing he's done, how he's saved everyone the trouble of having to read Fiona Benedict's *Life of Lucan*. We are being invaded and we must defend ourselves.

The young woman at the airline counter seemed most concerned over my lack of luggage. Why would I need luggage? But I didn't even get near the airplane; I had to turn back. I'd forgotten about those detection devices they use to keep people from carrying guns on to airplanes. The stone in my stomach and I rode the bus all the way into New York City.

No sleep, no food—how long? Doesn't matter; time seems to have lost its divisions. Uptown is which way? We *are* being invaded, you know.

A talk show at CBS: how to breach the Black Rock? As a member of the audience. Polite words but still pushing and shoving, a man's elbow just missing my eye, *I'll shoot you if you do that again*, I have the means. A woman's high heel on the arch of my foot, not even noticing, too busy showing off for the accompanying man. Pain and dizziness and finally a place to sit down. A seat in the last row.

Then they were all screaming and a light popped out and the pain and dizziness were too much for me and I went down, down. A hand pressing the back of my neck, forcing my head between my knees and consciousness returning. A voice saying *There's the gun*, another voice saying *Don't touch it*. A woman's face peering anxiously into mine, asking if I was all right.

"Is he dead?" I whispered.

"No, that maniac missed him. I *think* he's all right."

That maniac?

A man's horrified face. "Hey, lady, you better watch out! She's the one who tried to kill him!"

"Are you crazy?" the woman said. "It was a man."

"It was her!"

"It was a man—I'm pretty sure."

A third voice: "I thought it was a boy."

More noise, arguing. My stone and I wanted to lie down, but there was no place. Then a policeman was asking me, all of us, for identification. As a result, one question was answered, at least: he did know who I was, he did know about my *Life of Lucan*.

He stared wide-eyed at me and said in that theatrical English voice, "*You* are Fiona Benedict?" Then he took one of the policemen aside and explained something, earnestly and at great length. I wanted to, I *had* to lie down.

"She's the one, I tell you!" the man with the horrified face kept insisting. "I saw her!"

A hundred years later I was arrested and charged with attempted murder.

But still they wouldn't let me lie down. They took me to the nearest precinct station, and asked questions, questions, questions. I couldn't think, I couldn't see straight. I said nothing, nothing at all. Fingerprints, photographs with a number, other indignities. No, I did not want to call anyone.

At last they let me lie down.

8

Marian Larch

Captain Michaels had said, "Bullshit. Nobody tries to kill another person over a *book*." He'd been in the business long enough to know that people do dreadful things to each other for far flimsier reasons than that, but he just couldn't bring himself to believe Fiona Benedict had tried to shoot Richard Ormsby. "Not her. You, me, anybody else—but not her."

But then he hadn't been there in Ohio when she first learned about *Lord Look-on*. I knew she could do it, and I understood why. But Ivan Malecki agreed with the Captain; both men were uneasy about the arrest. And with reason.

There was only one positive eyewitness in that small studio audience, a loud-voiced man who kept insisting that he'd seen Fiona Benedict firing a gun at the stage area. Unfortunately, there were half a dozen other people who sort of thought it was a small man or maybe a teenaged boy, they weren't sure. The man who'd fingered Dr. Benedict was the one positive one, but there was only one of him and six of the other kind.

Fiona Benedict was a lousy shot. She'd emptied the gun, executing a lighting instrument and wounding a camera but missing all the people. I wondered if she'd ever fired a pistol before. The gun itself was no help. It was not registered in New York; it was either purchased elsewhere or acquired illegally here. There were no fingerprints, but then there almost never are. Guns don't take fingerprints at all well, despite what the movies and TV say.

The arresting officer had made a really dumb mistake of the sort that occurs more frequently than we like to admit. Whether a suspect has fired a gun or not is determined by performing a test for powder and/or primer residue on the hand *within two hours* of the shooting. After a couple of hours, the residue is absorbed naturally into the skin. And before that, it can be washed off with plain old soap and water. The most reliable method of testing is atomic absorption spectrophotometry or by using scanning electron micrographs linked to an x-ray analyzer. But ordinary precinct stations don't have that kind of fancy equipment; and what with the delay caused by checking everybody in the TV audience, they were getting awfully close to the two-hour limit for testing.

So rather than risk passing that time limit by moving Fiona Benedict to a crime lab, the police decided to perform the nitric acid test for primer residue only, right there in the precinct station. And that's where the dumb mistake came in—not in procedure, which was routine. The nitric acid test reveals the presence of barium nitrate and antimony sulfide and a few other chemicals present in the primer, a residue of which is left on the thumb web and the back of the hand when a gun is fired. But the arresting officer neglected to tell the people performing the test that the weapon in question was a .22 caliber pistol—an evidence-destroying oversight, as it turned out. *Because the nitric acid test doesn't work on .22 caliber residue*. The .22 primer doesn't contain any barium or antimony.

So the nitric acid test was performed and proved negative, Fiona Benedict washed her hands with soap and water, and everyone started wondering if they'd arrested the wrong person. By the time they figured out what had happened, the one piece of hard evidence they might have got had already gone floating down the drain of a washbasin in the precinct station house. If they'd taken her to the lab straight off, there'd have been at least a chance of getting something.

But Fiona Benedict was the only one in the studio audience with a grudge against Richard Ormsby, and the police believed the one insistent witness who claimed Dr. Benedict was the lady with the gun. It was a none-too-sturdy case, but it *was* a case. The DA's office decided to prosecute.

Since the intended victim was a celebrity, the story of the attempted shooting was picked up by the wire services and also broadcast by all three networks. Two of the networks also included the news that Richard Ormsby's attacker was the mother of a victim of an unsolved murder. And one of them aired a hastily scheduled symposium called *What's Happening to America?*—in which the participants all argued about the changes taking place in this country that could lead even civilized people such as college professors to try solving their problems with violence.

All that coverage meant Washburn, Ohio, now knew its quiet and erudite Crimean War specialist was in fact a dangerous woman capable of pointing a loaded gun at someone and pulling the trigger. They also knew that Rudy Benedict had not died by accident, as his mother had led them to believe. Fiona Benedict's carefully constructed safe world had collapsed around her, just as earlier Rudy's had collapsed around him. Even as Rudy's father's had, too, I suppose. You could almost think the Benedicts were cursed—that family certainly seemed marked for tragedy. The father a suicide, the son a murder victim, the mother a murderer—a failed murderer, true, but there was murder in her heart. Fiona Benedict had stood at the back of that studio and fired her pistol over the heads of the seated audience, endangering all those people, in an attempt to destroy another person's life. She was guilty as hell.

She was also sick—she hadn't been eating or sleeping and what with the nervous strain and all she was on the verge of collapse. When she was arrested she'd made no statement to the police, had said nothing whatsoever, she hadn't even told anyone her name. She'd offered identification when asked for it, but she just hadn't talked at all—much to the delight of her high-powered lawyer who had suddenly appeared out of nowhere. But the woman was declining visibly. All the fight had gone out of her.

So, once again, I called her friends the Morrisseys.

Drew Morrissey's shock and disbelief were audible all the way from Ohio. "I couldn't believe it when I heard it on the news," he said. "I still don't believe it. There must be some mistake."

"There's no mistake. She was there and she tried to kill Richard Ormsby. We have evidence."

" 'We'?"

"Dr. Morrissey, I'm afraid I deceived you. I'm a police detective, and I was in Washburn on police business. Dr. Benedict didn't want you to know." There was a silence. "Dr. Morrissey?"

"Yes, I'm here. Just one new revelation after another, I'm not too . . . well, I'm stunned."

"Yes, of course you are. Look, the reason I called is that Dr. Benedict isn't in very good shape, frankly. She's deteriorating physically, and her morale is shot to hell. She's all alone here. The presence of a couple of friends would help, I'm sure of it."

"Well, ah, that might prove difficult. Ah, I have meetings scheduled all next week, you see, and—"

"I'll be there tomorrow morning," Roberta Morrissey said on the extension.

I went to the detention cells on Sixty-seventh Street where Fiona Benedict was being held, to let her know Roberta was coming. I had to wait a few minutes as she was talking to her lawyer. When he came bustling out, I heard her call him Howard; Howard looked cheerful. He probably had a good chance of winning this one.

I sat down opposite her at the table in the interview room. "Hello, Marian," she said sadly. "Howard says I'm not to talk to you. He's my lawyer."

I nodded. "I saw him leave. What's his last name?"

She dropped her forehead into one hand and laughed shortly. "I don't know."

It turned out that Howard the Nameless was a gift from Kelly Ingram—who herself had not been in to see Dr. Benedict. "She's involved with something right now," I said, thinking of Ted Cameron.

"Good," she said with something of her old asperity. "I hope she stays that way." Here she was in jail for having tried to kill a man and she still disapproved of Kelly Ingram. But she would have said the two things didn't have anything to do with each other, and perhaps they didn't. I told her Roberta Morrissey was coming to New York and watched her look of astonishment turn into one of gratitude.

"I'm surprised she's still willing to acknowledge me as a friend," she said. "But then friends are the ones who come when you need them, aren't they?"

I didn't mention Drew Morrissey's suddenly remembered busy schedule or his continued presence in Ohio. That would occur to her soon enough.

An answer came to a request for information I'd put in with the Securities and Exchange Commission. I'd asked for a disclosure of all listed owners of Nathan Pinking's production company and Leonard Zoff's theatrical agency. Those two men had told me directly conflicting stories and I wanted to know which (if either) was telling the truth.

Leonard Zoff was. Both he and Pinking owned forty-nine percent of the other's business, just as Zoff had said. So Nathan Pinking had lied, and he must have done so knowing full well he'd be found out. The itinerary Mimsy had sent me said Pinking would be out of town until the end of the week, so I'd have to wait to confront him with it.

But at last Captain Michaels was interested. "A power struggle, a potential take-over?" he mused. "What's Benedict's connection? Did he learn something he wasn't supposed to know? You may be on to something there, Larch. Keep on it."

I intended to.

9

Kelly Ingram

Ted Cameron was being blackmailed, I was sure of it.

I was staying with him at his estate in Tuxedo Park until it was time for me to go to California to start work on a TV movie I was scheduled to do. Ted played hooky as often as he could, bless him, but he did have to drive into Manhattan now and then to take care of business. I always went along— hah, I guess I did at that. I just wanted him with me all the time but if that couldn't be, then I wanted me with him, if you see the difference. Truth was, I couldn't get enough of him. I was a Ted Cameron junkie.

We eventually passed our hiding-from-the-world phase and started going places—a show and late supper, usually. Ted was just bored by dancing, a shock I was still recovering from. We went to see Abigail James's new play—talk, talk, talk; I'm afraid I drifted off.

But you see, that's all we had—in time, I mean. We'd gotten just that far when this other business took over. Three things made me think Ted was being blackmailed.

Once I'd gone to my apartment to take care of some things while Ted went to a meeting. He came in about the middle of the afternoon, and he was seething with anger. But he didn't want me to know! I felt a sinking feeling when he tried to pretend he wasn't angry, tried to make me think everything was fine. Now I'm not one of those who believe the truth shall *always* make you free, I think everybody ought to have a secret or two. But it's still a blow when a man you're *that* close to deliberately lies to you for the first time—no matter what his motives are. And it didn't make much sense anyway, because what he told me sounded like good news at first.

"You're going to Barbados in October," he said. "Nathan

Pinking got a commitment from the network for an additional three original episodes of *LeFever*."

"Additional?" I said. "You mean plus, also, too? In addition to the regular twenty already in the can?"

"That's right. Plus, also, too."

"And did you say *Barbados*?"

He smiled naturally for the first time since he'd come in. "Thought you'd like that. The scheduling is a bit close, but the three episodes will be inserted towards the end of the season."

"And the network went for it?"

"Sure, why not? A producer goes in with a sponsor already in his pocket, the network isn't going to say no." He must have heard the bitter tone of his own voice, because he made a conscious attempt to speak more lightly. "I decided it would be a good opportunity to show our new line of swimwear—as modeled on the show by none other than Kelly Ingram and Nick Quinlan."

I didn't believe it; he sounded to me like a man backed into a corner. "Ted? Why are you really doing this?"

His eyes slid away from me and turned invisible. "I told you, to show our new line of swimwear."

So he wasn't ready to talk to me about it. He considered himself in Nathan Pinking's pocket, did he—how had that come about? And he didn't want to talk about it. All right, I could live with that, for a while. I put my arms around his waist and hugged hard enough to make him grunt. "You're coming to Barbados too, aren't you?"

"I have to," he said with mock resignation. "Somebody has to make sure Nick Quinlan doesn't put his trunks on backwards."

That was the first thing. The second thing was a snatch of conversation I overheard in Tuxedo Park.

I'd just opened a door to go out on the patio when I heard a man out there saying, "We can't do it, Ted! Why do you keep insisting? That damned show would take our entire advertising budget. What are we supposed to do, forget about newspapers, magazines—"

"Maybe I can get Lorelei Cosmetics to share the cost in exchange for a few spots," Ted said worriedly. "If I can't, then you'll just have to use your whole budget."

"For a hick sitcom that's never once made the Nielsen top twenty? That's crazy! *Why*, Ted?"

Then they both became aware of me and one of those *horrible* silences developed that go on and on and on and you think are never going to end. For the very first time, I felt like an intruder in Ted's world and I didn't like the feeling at all. The other man turned out to be Roger Cameron, Ted's cousin and the president of Watercraft, Inc., one of Cameron Enterprises' ancillary companies, that's the term Ted used. I was beginning to feel a bit ancillary myself.

The third thing was more roundabout. Ted was thinking out loud, making plans. "I should be able to take a few weeks off before long—we can go to Scotland. Would you like to go to Scotland?" He laughed, happy at the thought of getting away for a while. "They say July and August are the best months for spotting the Loch Ness Monster. We can go to Inverness and join the monster-hunt."

"If we can schedule around my television movie," I reminded him.

He looked surprised. "Time for that already? I thought it was later. How long will it take?"

I smiled. "A Big Production like this one? Nathan has scheduled three whole weeks." Three weeks to make a movie. And it was important to me because it wasn't *just* a movie—it was also a pilot. "It can mean my own series, remember."

He knew; we'd talked about it. "Make the movie," he said firmly. "You should have your own series. I don't like seeing you as a bit of fluff for Nick Quinlan to play with."

"Yes, sir," I said, straight-faced.

He grinned, his eyes looking blue instead of invisible for a change. "Sorry, didn't mean to sound bossy. Kelly—do you like working for Nathan Pinking?"

Strange question. "Nobody *likes* working for Nathan. Except maybe Nick—they get along."

He looked dissatisfied. "You could do better than Nathan Pinking schlock."

"*You* do business with him," I pointed out.

"That's different. There are other things involved."

I decided to take the plunge; this had gone on long enough. "Ted, it's obvious you can't stand Nathan Pinking and it's equally obvious you don't want to sponsor *LeFever*. So why don't you just cut out? Why are you putting your company's money into a show you don't really want to have anything to do with?"

"Sometimes these decisions are automatic," he said in a tight voice, and refused to discuss it. He absolutely *refused* to talk about it.

Now, there was only one way I could read all that, and that was that Ted was being blackmailed and it sure as hell looked as if it was Nathan Pinking who was doing the blackmailing. Nathan was clearly forcing Ted to sponsor *LeFever*, and it probably went farther than that. Ted wanted his cousin Roger to put *his* company's money into what Roger called a hick sitcom. One of Nathan Pinking's other shows was titled *Down the Pike* and could be fairly described as a hick sitcom, I think.

There are few things I can think of that would be worse than knowing someone like Nathan Pinking had a stranglehold on your life. I got along with the man by telling myself *constantly* that other producers were worse, whether it was true or not—but Nathan was one of those people you just knew you could never trust. He liked being ugly merely to show you he could do anything he wanted. And if he controlled Ted, that meant he had Cameron Enterprises' assets to draw on, and *that* meant he had somebody to pick up the tab for whatever he wanted to do on television. What a guarantee against failure! An insurance policy to end all insurance policies, the deadbeat creep.

I was sorry about the company, but I couldn't get real worked up about that when I knew what this had to be doing to Ted. My God, it must be eating him up inside! And all this time I'd thought Ted was so in control of his life—the decision-maker, the man who gave orders. I'd just plain misread the signs. It was all a façade, a brave face Ted was showing to the world. How could he stand it? Must be like living in a torture chamber.

I was trying to think of something to do to help. How do you get rid of a blackmailer? Other than, well, *get rid* of him, I mean. The only thing I could think of was to get something on *him*, and then blackmail the blackmailer. But Nathan Pinking had a reputation for being able to protect himself in the clinches, and he wasn't just going to leave weapons laying around you could use against him. (Yes, I got it—*lying* around.) So could I hire a detective to dig up some dirt on Nathan? There *was* dirt; I don't think there could be any doubt of that. But how do you find the right kind of detective? I thought Marian Larch could probably tell me, but how did I go about getting the information out of her without letting it slip that Ted was being blackmailed? Oh, what a mess.

And still . . . and still no matter how I fought it, there was one nasty question that just kept on coming back to me: What

did Ted *do* that was so awful he had to give in to Nathan
Pinking in order to keep it quiet?

10

Marian Larch

Roberta Morrissey looked shaken when she came out of
the interview room.

"What is it? Did she say something?" I asked.

Roberta shook her head. "It's just seeing Fiona in a place
like this . . . it takes some getting used to, that's all."

I understood. Poor lady, she really looked upset. "Let's
go somewhere for, ah, coffee?"

"I'd rather have a drink."

I took her to a place on Fifth that was fairly quiet. When
she started looking steady again, I said, "There's something
I'd like to ask you about. This isn't official, it's only to satisfy
my own curiosity. Dr. Benedict was carrying a *Times* review
of her book with her. Do you know about that?"

She smiled sadly. "The infamous *Times* review. Yes, indeed, I know about it. It was probably what tipped her over."

"But why? I read it. The reviewer said a lot of nice
things about her book."

"He said even nicer things about Ormsby's. That's the
trouble with these double reviews—one book always ends up
looking inferior. The reviewer acknowledged Fiona's book as
the more scholarly piece of work, but it was *Lord Look-on*
that got the nod of approval in the final analysis. Ormsby's
version was "more fun" to read, he said. He actually said
that—'more fun.' As if entertainment value were *the* ulti-
mate criterion."

It still didn't seem that bad to me and I said so.

Roberta looked at me a moment and then asked, "Marian,
when was the last time you bought a history book?"

I grinned sheepishly.

"Did you *ever* buy a history book?" she persisted. "In

fact, have you even read any history since you finished school? Don't look like that, you're in the majority. I write a book about the Brontë sisters and I can count on some slight general interest outside academic circles. Historians don't have even that. Barbara Tuchman's work always sells—but she's an exception. Oh, occasionally a book of contemporary history will be highly touted and have respectable sales, but Drew is convinced most of them are never read beyond the first fifty pages."

"Not even Richard Ormsby's books?"

"Well, Ormsby has an advantage over people like Fiona and Drew. He has no scruples about oversimplifying things that perhaps ought not to be made simple at all. And that jazzy writing style helps sell his books to the popular market. But the legitimate historians can't write for that kind of market."

"So they end up writing for . . . each other?"

"For the record, say—for libraries, in a way. You know it's sustained library sales over the years that justifies the publisher's investment. But the way library budgets have been cut to the bone the last few years, librarians aren't going to order two new biographies of Lord Lucan when the world has been happily bumbling along with none at all for over a century and a quarter now. Know how many books are published in this country every year? Almost fifty thousand."

"Every *year*?" I'd had no idea.

"Every year. So library purchasing departments have to depend on publications like *Library Journal* or *Publishers Weekly* to help them decide what to buy. Both those periodicals gave brief, equally favorable reviews to Fiona's book and to Ormsby's. That means the librarians have to turn to other reviews." She finished her drink.

I held up two fingers to the waiter. "So the *Times* review will affect library sales."

"Undoubtedly." Roberta Morrissey looked depressed as she thought about her friend's book. "Do you understand what that means? It means that all over this country *and* in England history students will be consulting Ormsby's book when they're studying the Crimean War. *He* will be the authority, not Fiona. Oh, the large universities with strong history departments will know the difference and they'll order Fiona's book. But the kids won't know. In most schools that assign papers on the war the students will consult Ormsby and maybe never even know about Fiona's work."

So it was more than just professional jealousy; it was a matter of professional responsibility. Fiona Benedict must have felt her whole life was under siege when *Lord Look-on* started shooting the foundations out from under her own book. So she'd picked up a gun and started shooting back.

I drove Roberta to her hotel and thought about having another go at Nathan Pinking, but decided against it. I'd talked to him once right after he got back to town. When I confronted him with his lie about never having been in business with Leonard Zoff—he simply claimed he'd never said any such thing. I'd misunderstood him, he said, both sides of his mismatched face equally bland. Leonard Zoff must have been right; Pinking lied automatically. He didn't even care that I knew he was lying.

At Headquarters I found Kelly Ingram waiting for me. She was sitting quietly by my desk, seemingly oblivious of all the attention directed her way. It was the first time I'd seen her since the advent of Ted Cameron.

She seemed nervous about something. "Marian, I . . . I wanted to ask you, uh, I wanted to, uh . . ."

"Yes?" I put as much encouragement into the one syllable as I could.

"I wanted to ask you . . . could I go see Dr. Benedict?" she finished in a rush.

You're lying, I thought. That wasn't why she'd come in.

But before I could say anything Ivan Malecki came up to the desk and cleared his throat. "Hello, Kelly, remember me?"

Kelly glanced up. "Oh hello, Ivan, how are you?" She'd not only remembered him, she'd remembered his name as well. After a minute's worth of inane dialogue, Ivan strutted away, his existence justified.

"You don't really want to see Dr. Benedict," I said.

"But I do!" she protested. "I should have been in before this but I, uh . . ."

"Kelly. You once told me you couldn't get away with telling lies off camera. You were right. Now why did you come in?"

"I told you—I want to see Dr. Benedict."

"Your nose just grew another inch."

She looked at me disconsolately a moment and then

made up her mind. "All right, here it is. I need a private detective, and don't ask me why because I'm not going to tell you. The yellow pages are full of names, but they don't tell me what I need to know."

"Which is?"

"The ones that are legit and the ones that are a smidge on the shady side."

"Uh-huh. And which kind do you want?"

It was hard for her to say it. "The shady kind."

Oh my! Now what did this pretty doll-woman want with a shady detective? What had gone so wrong in her glamorous, successful life that she should need expert help from someone who wasn't averse to bending the law a little if the pay was right? There was only one new element in her life that I knew of.

So I said: "What's Ted Cameron done?"

"Oh, *Marian!*" She looked hurt and exasperated at the same time. "Are you going to give me a name or not?"

"No, I am not going to give you a name. At least not the kind you want. I'm a policewoman, remember? Sworn to uphold the law? I will give you the names of a few reputable people, if you like."

"I thought you'd help."

"I'm trying to. But I can't read minds. Why don't you tell me what's wrong?"

"I can't do that. Damn it, Marian! Just one lousy stinking name."

"Forget it. Why do you want to have your boyfriend investigated?"

"I don't! Oh, you've got it all wrong."

"Then set me straight. Tell me what's going on."

She thought about it a few minutes, but ended up shaking her head. "I can't tell you. I can't tell anybody." She sighed. "As long as I'm here—I might as well go see Dr. Benedict. I'm allowed, aren't I?"

It would be my second trip to the detention cells that day. "I'll have to take you. This isn't a regular visiting day."

"Oh—I didn't think of that. Marian, I don't want to put you out—"

"It's okay," I said. And it was. I was thinking that on the drive over I might get a little more out of her about why she wanted a shady detective.

But what I got was a new lie she'd had time to think up. "I might as well tell you," she said. "I want somebody to find out who sent me the laxative and the toilet paper. You remember that time, don't you?"

I stopped at a red light and just looked at her. The lie was so blatant she had the good grace to laugh at her own clumsiness.

"Won't do, Kelly," I said.

"Won't do," she agreed. "Especially between you and I." She frowned. "I?"

"Me, I think. Besides, it's easier to tell the truth."

But mentioning the laxative had started her thinking. "I probably never will know who sent it, will I?"

"There's no way of proving it," I said carefully. "You can make a reasonable assumption, however."

"You think you know? Who?"

"Laxative and toilet paper," I said. "Who is it among your acquaintance that can't get through a conversation without using the word *shit* over and over again?"

Her eyes grew large. "Leonard Zoff? Leonard sent me the laxative?"

"He'd be my guess." The light turned green; I eased the car forward. "Didn't you once tell me you thought he didn't like women? And here you are, extremely female, one of his brightest prospects for success if not *the* brightest. Maybe sending you that laxative was a way of relieving his own tensions a little—oh dear, bad word choice. But all that's just speculation, Kelly. I may be maligning the man."

"If he sent *me* a doctored bottle of Lysco-Seltzer..." She didn't finish.

"Did he send one to Rudy Benedict too? We don't think so. Whoever substituted the cyanide had to do it the same day Benedict died. Zoff had an alibi for almost the entire day. He was on the go, had a lot of appointments. But we checked all the people he met with, and there just doesn't seem to have been time for him to slip down to Chelsea, make the substitution when Rudy wasn't looking, and keep to his schedule. It's not airtight, so he *could* have found a way of doing it. But it doesn't look likely."

Kelly accepted that. "Besides, Leonard would have no reason to kill Rudy. They were friendly. They weren't even working together—they never did, so far as I know."

"Yes, they did—about a dozen years ago," I told her. "When Rudy was writing scripts for that well-known production team, Pinking and Zoff."

Her head swiveled towards me. "Pinking and Zoff? You mean Leonard was a *producer*? Wow. And in business with Nathan Pinking?"

"That's right." The news so surprised her that she was quiet the rest of the way to the detention cells.

Inside the building, we waited in the interview room while Fiona Benedict was being brought up. Kelly began to have second thoughts. "I'm not sure this was such a good idea."

"Too late now," I said as the door opened and a matron escorted Dr. Benedict in.

She stopped cold when she saw Kelly. "What do you want?" Not a very auspicious beginning.

Kelly stood up, hesitated. "I, ah, I wanted to see if you were all right. If you needed anything."

"Nothing." Fiona Benedict's eyes narrowed and she forced herself to say, "I suppose I should thank you for sending Howard."

Well, yes, I suppose you should, I was thinking, but Kelly said quickly, "That's all right, glad to help. Is there anything else? Anything you want that I can bring?"

The dislike on Dr. Benedict's face was so naked that I wasn't surprised when Kelly flinched. I doubted that she'd ever been looked at like that before in her entire life. "The role of Lady Bountiful doesn't suit you," Dr. Benedict said contemptuously. "Not convincing, not convincing at all."

"Wh-what do you mean?" Kelly stammered.

"Little Miss Innocence. You forgot to bat your eyes."

Kelly looked as if she didn't believe what she was hearing. "Why are you talking to me like this?"

"What are you doing here?" the older woman snapped out. "Did you come to crow? Go away, Kelly Ingram, go away and don't come back. I don't want to see you or your kind ever again. You and your flashy looks and your cheap obviousness—"

"Now, wait a minute!" Kelly said hotly, stung into defending herself. "Who the hell are you to call me *cheap*?"

"Oh, I'm sure you put a high price on yourself," the older woman said heavily. Her shoulders slumped. "You sell yourself and then you sell out the rest of us."

Kelly glanced at me; I shook my head—I didn't know what she was talking about either. "What are you saying, Dr. Benedict?" I asked.

"Look at her, Marian," she said bitterly in reply. "So pleased with herself. So willing to adjust to whatever demands a man might make of her. But she's never tarnished and she's always fresh and ready for more. The ideal woman—a renewable virgin. What a role model for young girls!" She took a couple of steps towards Kelly. "We're *all* teachers—don't you understand that? You go on that asinine show and teach schoolgirls to be exhibitionists. You teach them that their function in life is to display their bodies and never think at all. You're telling them the only worthwhile goal in life is to attract male attention. Yes, I call that *cheap*."

Kelly was outraged. "It's only a *role* I'm playing, for crying out loud!"

"And if you don't do it, somebody else will? That's the rest of the argument, isn't it? The same rationalizations women have always used. You made your choice long ago—you're selling yourself, and there's no way you can pretend you're not."

Kelly looked as if she'd been slapped in the face; you could almost see the fingermarks on her cheek. I decided to interfere. I stepped between the two of them and said, "Fiona, that's enough. You're being unfair. Don't take it out on her."

She looked me straight in the eye for a long moment and then without speaking turned on her heel. The matron opened the door and they were gone.

Kelly sank weakly into the nearest chair. "How can she hate me that much? I never did anything to her."

"It wasn't really you she was telling off. It was Richard Ormsby."

"Ormsby? But I don't even know him!"

"You're both attractive, successful television personalities. Dr. Benedict attacked you because you were the handiest representative of a world she feels threatened by. And it's the world her son chose to live in, don't forget—that's mixed up in it too."

"But all that business about selling myself—"

"Well, she couldn't very well blast you for writing bad history, could she? That's really what's bugging her. She sees it as a form of prostitution."

"Marian, do you think I'm selling myself?" While I was floundering for an answer, she went on, "I am going to judge the Miss America contest. It's all set. I'm going to do it."

I started to say *Oh, Kelly* in exasperation when I realized what she was telling me. Any other woman in her place—myself included—would have been furious, striking out at her accuser, indulging in a long process of self-justification. But Fiona Benedict had said *selling yourself* and Kelly Ingram had thought *Miss America*. A natural link. I always knew Kelly was more self-aware than most glitter girls. She understood the prostitutional aspect of meat parades.

Now if she would only turn her back on it.

But right then she didn't look up to making any decisions at all. "Come on, let's get out of this place," I said. "It's beginning to depress me."

In the car Kelly asked me to come home with her. "You're through for the day, aren't you?"

I said I was. "Where's Ted Cameron?"

"Los Angeles. Soothing his Aunt Augusta. Wouldn't you know he'd have an aunt named Augusta?"

I knew of Augusta Cameron; she was the head of Lorelei Cosmetics—one of those *grandes dames* who seem to be the natural rulers in the realm of fashion and cosmetics. "Why does Aunt Augusta need soothing?" I asked.

"Oh, Ted says every couple of years she gets it into her head she could do a better job of running Cameron Enterprises than Ted and he has to go out and calm her down."

I was hungry and announced the fact. When we got to her apartment, Kelly called the restaurant at the top of the building and ordered dinner to be sent down. While we were waiting I turned on the news and heard something that made me forget all about food.

And that was that Richard Ormsby had been shot.

It had happened while the Englishman was leaving the NBC studios in Rockefeller Center. His assailant had stood behind a barely open stairwell door and fired at Ormsby from there. No one saw his face. His aim had been perfect: his victim died on the spot. The killer had done his damage and made his escape before witnesses were fully able to realize what was happening.

Richard Ormsby was as dead as they come. And all the time Fiona Benedict had been locked up in a detention cell on Sixty-seventh Street, where we'd left her not more than forty-five minutes earlier.

11
Kelly Ingram

Ted gave me the news on Thursday, just after noon. I always knew the end of the world would come on a Thursday.

Look at me, making jokes, ha ha ha. I don't know what else to do so I make a joke about it, how else do you stay away from the funny farm when the sky falls on your head? And it fell, all right, oh *wow* did it fall. Crash, bang, BOOM, noisier than the sound track of a science fiction movie, jokes again. *It has to be this way*, he'd said. Sez who? *Why* does it have to be this way? Where's that written down?

No explanation, no answer, no real reason. Just *we're going to have to stop seeing each other, Kelly*. Stop *seeing* each other? Good God, I'm not a character in a 1940s movie, wasn't even born then. And the worst part was he didn't mean it, I mean he *meant* it, we *would* have to stop "seeing" each other, but he didn't want to mean it, he didn't want to say it. Ted did not choose to end the affair. He was being forced to end it.

Doesn't that sound stupid? Paranoid, even. Woman gets dumped, thinks up elaborate explanation to save face. *Are you going back to your wife*, I said. *I don't have a wife*, he said. *You've got two*, I said. *Ex-wives*, he said, *and I'm not going back to either one of them*, he said. Then *why*, Ted? Why?

But he had no reason. Just: *It has to be this way*. It was as if he wanted me to know something was wrong, otherwise he'd have made up a believable excuse or tried to make me think he wasn't interested any more or *something*. But there was nothing like that; just *Goodbye, Kelly*, like that. Was he really saying *Help me*? Am I looking for excuses?

He made sure we were in my apartment when he told

me—so *he* could leave, I guess, rather than put himself in the
spot of having to tell me to go. After he'd gone, I just sat
there and stared at the wall until I realized I couldn't see
anymore, it had gotten so dark. Wednesday he ordered the
tickets for our trip to Scotland, Thursday morning he went to
a meeting, Thursday afternoon we were through. So all right,
Sherlock, figure out where the change came. I didn't know
who or whom his meeting was with; he always told me when
I asked but this time I hadn't, damn it. But something had
happened that Thursday morning to make me *persona non
whatever*, and of course I had to wonder if it had anything to
do with the blackmail. Damn Marian Larch, if she'd given me
a name when I asked for one maybe all this could have been
avoided.

I refused to accept it. It was a temporary separation,
that's all, forced on Ted by a villainous blackmailer, Nathan
Pinking or somebody else, somebody hateful. *Why* was utterly beyond me, I couldn't even begin to guess. But what was
happening now was only an interruption of the normal state
of things, an obstacle to be overcome, a thing-in-the-way to
be removed, the course of true love never did run on
well-oiled wheels or however. It was up to me to do something.

Big talk. Do what? Two little words, floating on top:
Marian Larch. That'd do it—sic the police on them. That
would do *something* all right, maybe put Ted in jail? (What
did he *do*?) Didn't really mean it, I was just thinking nasty
things—I was hurt and I wanted to hurt back. Yes, Ted, I
wanted to hurt *you*. Why hadn't you managed better? You are
a *professional* manager, you should have managed your personal business better.

But I didn't want to call in Marian Larch or Ivan Whatsit
or Captain Whoosit for another reason, the best reason in the
world, and that was it was too embarrassing. I'd be damned if
I'd play a woman-scorned role. Because that's what I'd look
like if I went to the police for help, a woman scorned who was
getting even—with Ted, with whoever was blackmailing him.
With the *world*. And I *wasn't* scorned, dammit! Ted was
almost crying when he told me it was all over.

But still he did tell me.

Oh Christ, what a mess. Somebody had Ted's life on a
string; all he had to do was pull the string and Ted jumped.
Was it Nathan Pinking? Whoever it was, he'd come between
me and Ted—for what reason? For kicks? Just to prove he

could do it? *That* sounded like Nathan Pinking, all right. Nathan didn't particularly dislike me, and that Fiona Benedict was the only person I knew who outright hated me. (I think.) But Nathan had invested money in me, I was one of his more promising "properties"—why would he want to hurt me? Maybe he didn't; maybe he was just using me to get at Ted; maybe it wasn't Nathan Pinking at all; and maybe I should stop making up fairy tales.

Wish I hadn't thought of that woman. The way she lit into me—my God, so much resentment! Rudy's mother, I mean. As if she'd been storing up grudges against me for *years*, and we'd only known each other a couple of months. The very first time I saw her she accused me of having caused Rudy's death, the old bitch, God, listen to me. I felt like killing her, completely forgot myself. If it hadn't been for Marian Larch—

I don't think I've ever known two women more unalike than Fiona Benedict and Marian Larch. Rudy's mother is awful, just awful—arrogant and disapproving and always looking down her nose at me. At *me*! But Marian Larch doesn't judge everybody by herself, she's friendly and helpful and in her own way a very cool lady, she doesn't get rattled and she always knows what to do. She agrees with Fiona Benedict about one thing, though, the Miss America kind of thing, but she never makes me feel like some kind of worm from under a rock because I don't agree with *her*. But Dr. Benedict makes me feel I could never never never do anything that would please her, not that I want to, please her, that is.

Older people are *always* doing that, it makes them feel superior. If they don't have anything else going for them, they claim *age* automatically gives them answers that are withheld from undeveloped ignoramuses like me. They specialize in being right. No matter what happens, they say in their smug little voices: "You don't know yet, wait until you're older." God, is that infuriating! They can tell you *any*thing, anything at all, and then stop you from disagreeing with them by saying you're not old enough to know. You mean you believe that ridiculous story about the world being *round*? Oh dear, tee hee. *You don't know yet, wait until you're older.* Fiona Benedict had done something like that to me. She'd taken one look at me and decided *no*. Who the hell is she to set herself up as my judge?

I'll tell you who she is. She's a dried-up old prune who's

past it, that's who she is. These women who are always saying *Stop making yourself a sex object*, they're always old or ugly or both. I hate to say it, but if Marian Larch was even a little bit pretty, she might not be so quick to turn up her nose at the Miss America contest. I *like* looking the way I look, damn it, and why should I have to apologize for it? Why is it so wrong to be pretty?

It's not wrong. It's just jealousy, homely women have always been jealous of pretty women, that's all it is, plain jealousy. Well, they didn't actually say it was wrong—she said, Dr. Benedict said, she meant what I was doing with my looks was wrong. Hair-splitting. What does she know about it? What does she *know*? With all her college degrees and her easy life, she never had to put herself on display like some prize cow at a county fair, hoping to God some fat-cat producer would see her and like her. She never had to do that. But Marian had said she wasn't really yelling at me anyway, she was just using me as a substitute for Richard Ormsby. Well, maybe.

Would Ted have tuned in to me like that if I'd been homely? No. He would not have. Would *I* have tuned in to him if *he* was homely? Maybe. I don't really know. Men don't have to be beautiful.

But now one beautiful man by the name of Richard Ormsby was dead, and Fiona Benedict *couldn't* have killed him because she was locked up at the time it happened. In a way that was too bad, I *liked* thinking of that know-it-all woman as a villain. But that must have been why she was so cranky and nasty, because she was in jail for something she didn't do. But Marian said she *did* try to kill Ormsby in the CBS studio, so who did kill him in Rockefeller Center, an accomplice? What was this, a conspiracy of historians? Oh, come *on*.

Dear Mom, nothing much happening here, two murders and a little blackmail, write soon. The more scared I am, the worse the joke. I was scared of what was happening to Ted, and I was scared I wouldn't be able to do anything about it. I was terrified that two murderers were running around out there whose paths had crossed mine and could do so again. Or was it only one murderer? Did the same guy who killed Rudy also shoot down Ormsby? Richard Ormsby—a stranger with whom I had no connection at all, yeah, *whom*. Except that a woman who had tried to kill him also hated me. I was even scared of Fiona Benedict.

Now wait a minute, wait a minute, don't go lumping everything together like that. Three different things had happened. Thing number one was that Rudy Benedict had been murdered. Thing number two was that Richard Ormsby had been murdered. And thing number three was that Ted Cameron was being blackmailed, probably by Nathan Pinking but maybe by someone else. There was no reason to think things number one, two, and three were connected with one another. Trouble was, there was no reason to think they were *not* connected, either.

The only link between the two murders that I could see was Rudy's mother. But Rudy's death didn't have anything to do with the competition between two books about some British officer way back in Queen Victoria's day. (I think it was Victoria.) And what did Ted's blackmailer have to do with either death? Nothing that I could see. Ted didn't even know Rudy Benedict; he knew about his murder, but then he didn't know Richard Ormsby either. Was Marian Larch wrong about Fiona Benedict? Maybe she hadn't tried to kill the Englishman at all. But whether she did or not, that was one set of problems and they had nothing to do with me, thank God. The sooner I saw the last of Fiona Benedict the better.

I couldn't make any sense of it. Best leave it to the police to figure out, don't try to second guess the professionals. Marian and Ivan and Captain—what *is* his name?—Michaels, Captain Michaels, that's it; they were the ones to figure out the mess.

Except that I knew something they didn't know. I knew that Ted Cameron was being blackmailed.

But that wasn't connected to the murders, right? That meant there'd be no real danger to Ted if I told Marian he was being blackmailed, right? I was damned sure of that, right? I was willing to risk Ted's neck on my certainty that he had no connection with either murder. Right?

Well, not *wrong*. But not exactly right either. Could the police investigate a case of blackmail without uncovering what it was the victim had done that made him blackmailable in the first place? What did Ted *do*?—it always came back to that. How much did I trust him?

How much did he trust me? He wanted me to know something was wrong, I was sure of it. It wasn't just business problems either, although things were going bad for him there too. Aunt Augusta and Cousin Roger and Nephew Somebody and a few more sisters and cousins whom he reckoned by the dozens were all ganging up on him, he said, making a bigger fuss than usual in their periodic tries to take the presidency of Cameron Enterprises away from him. But if Ted was kicked out as president, that meant he wouldn't be able to keep on paying off his blackmailer and then what? And Thursday morning something had happened to make him break up with me. Why? To protect me? Was something so horrible going to happen to Ted that he wanted to make sure I was in the clear before it all blew up?

I was still trying to decide what to do when I got a call from someone who identified herself only as Mimsy and who asked me to come to a meeting in Nathan Pinking's office. I hadn't seen Nathan for a while—I was nervous about facing him. I don't know how to talk to *blackmailers*. But when I got to Nathan's office, I stopped worrying about blackmail because something else had come along, something in the person of Leonard Zoff—who'd probably sent me laxative and toilet paper. Besides, Nathan Pinking and Leonard Zoff in the same room at the same time is not my favorite way to spend an afternoon.

Oh yes incidentally and by the way, there was one other little matter that kept me from feeling on top of the world at that particular moment. It was my birthday. Yep, I'd actually done it—I'd turned thirty. I didn't, tell, a, *soul*.

So there I was, feeling elderly, in a room with two men I didn't trust, not sure how I should act toward either of them—because they were in the middle of grandiose plans to make me rich and famous. That's right, rich and famous: *Kid, I'm gonna make you a star*. They were planning a campaign to put me in the public eye, everything from presenting awards at a boat show on the West Coast to narrating a pop documentary about women's hairstyles.

"Your so-called agent has been holding out on you," Nathan snickered to me. "Buncha junk lined up for you he didn't tell you about. Afraid you'd kick him out. Guest announcer at a ladies' wrestling match? Haw! Zoff, you've got as much class as a garbage collector."

"Don't listen to that shithead, darling," Leonard said loudly around a cigar in his mouth. "As usual, he don't know what he's talking about. I always have something in the works, but I don't tell you about it till it starts to firm up."

"Lady wrestlers?" I said dubiously, while Nathan laughed haw-haw-haw.

Leonard gave a long martyred sigh, something he was good at. "No, not lady wrestlers. I told you not to listen to that shithead. A new series of specials about women's sports, different host every week, different *sports* every week. The network wants you for one of the segment hosts, nothing to do with *announcing* a wrestling match. Might not even be on your segment. See how that shithead twists everything? Couldn't tell it straight if his life depended on it."

It made no impression on Nathan, who kept right on haw-hawing. "You watch, you'll end up ringside calling the blows," he told me between guffaws.

Supposedly I'd been summoned so my agent and my producer and I could talk over plans for my future, but after a while it became clear I could just as well have stayed home. *They* were making the decisions, and I would do what I was told. Somehow those two enemies had agreed that one more year of *LeFever* would be my last, whether the show was renewed or not. By then they hoped to have a new series ready for me, if not the result of the TV movie I was scheduled to make, then something else.

Almost casually Nathan Pinking informed me that re-write work was being done on the script. It seemed the setting was to be changed, damn it. The original plan was to show me as a bright young thing fresh out of law school who's taken into a big, tradition-bound firm where my unorthodox ways stirred things up a bit. The stirring-things-up-a-bit episodes were to alternate with ones in which I benefited from the experience and advice of older, wiser heads. Some-thing for everybody, you see? Rebellion for the young, triumph over rebellion for the old. With a fair sprinkling of steamy love scenes for everybody.

As shallow as it sounded, I was still looking forward to the role because it would give me a chance to do something other than show off the bod. Being ornamental is okay but not if it's the *only* thing you get to do. There are only so many ways you can pose prettily for the camera. I was always asking the *LeFever* director for things to do, sharpening a pencil, piloting a space ship, anything.

So I was sorry to hear the law office setting had been

scrapped. The series format would be kept, but the whole thing would be transferred to a hospital setting. ("Hospitals are back," Nathan Pinking had announced.) Now Nathan and Leonard were arguing about what my role should be. Nathan suggested brain surgeon.

Leonard's mouth dropped open and he almost lost his cigar. "I swear to God, Pinking, you must be taking stupid pills," he said. "We've been selling her as a piece of tail for two years and all of a sudden everybody's gonna accept her as a *brain surgeon*? I've spent the last twenty-five years listening to your shit, but that's the biggest piece you ever came up with!"

"A *sexy* brain surgeon, you Neanderthal asshole, that's the difference—is that too much for you to grasp? Underneath all that brainy efficiency she's still all woman, she's still a garden of delights for the right man. Got that? No matter how intimidating she is during the day, at night in bed things are like always. You think *that* won't go over, hah? Top of the ratings."

"We've got a problem," I said. "I can't control what you two say to each other when I'm not here, but I cannot sit here and allow you to talk about me like this." I turned to Leonard. "Do you realize you just called me a piece of tail?"

He was instantly and unconvincingly contrite. "Darling, what can I say? You know talking to this shithead always makes me vulgar. You know you're no piece of tail and I know it, don't hold a slip of the tongue against a harried old man. Okay?"

"Right, right," Nathan said impatiently. He had more important things to concern him than my thin skin.

So they went on with their arguing, quickly forgetting all about my objection to being spoken of as if I were a whore. Four or five years ago I'd have given my eyeteeth to be where I was now, sitting in the office of an important producer while he and my agent worked out the specifics of my career for me. But there was no good feeling to it, there was nothing good about any of it. I felt like a piece of meat.

A piece of tail, Leonard Zoff had said.

You're selling yourself, Fiona Benedict had said.

A prize cow at the county fair, Marian Larch had said.

Nathan gave in on the brain surgeon, and they eventually settled on resident psychiatrist. By then I didn't really much care. How did I get myself involved with these two? I was legally bound to both of them for another few years, and they were giving me the full star build-up. So what the hell was I complaining about? I'd never had to do any of the things a lot of women had had to do in this business. Leonard had never handed me a list of producers with instructions to sleep with as many as I could. And Nathan had never called on me to put in appearances at *that* kind of party. Strictly speaking, they had both left me alone.

So why was I feeling sick to my stomach? I knew Leonard looked on his women clients as so much meat, why was I so surprised? And Nathan had the same kind of respect for his actors that Sherman had had for Georgia. I was a big girl now, what did I expect—soft music and flowers? Girl Scout cookies?

When it was time to go, I was still caught up in my own thoughts and wasn't aware of the fancy footwork going on until it was over—Nathan had maneuvered Leonard out of the office while I was still inside and had quickly locked the door. Leonard pounded on the door and yelled at me not to sign anything, I yelled back that I wouldn't, and I turned to Nathan Pinking to see what it was all about.

He waited until Leonard had given up and gone away, and then said, "I want you to sign an exclusive management contract with me. Dump Zoff, Kelly. The man has no vision, no class. He thinks small time, he can't help it. That business about calling you a piece of tail—that was no one-time thing. He calls you that all the time. You're just not around to hear it. Why stay with a man who thinks of you like that?"

So there it was; Nathan saw Leonard's slip of the tongue as a chance to undercut his old enemy. Marian Larch had said the two men had once been partners; how could they ever have stood each other? Nathan would have signed a trained seal act away from Leonard if he thought it would cause Leonard trouble.

"Leonard and I have a contract," I said noncommittally.

"Contracts can be broken. And where has it got you anyway?" he sneered. "Lady wrestlers! You're too classy for that kind of action, Kelly, but that's something Zoff will never see. You sign with me and you'll never have to do those schlock bits again. You won't have to do anything just for the exposure."

"Leonard isn't just going to roll over and play dead, you know," I stalled.

"There are ways of handling these things," Nathan said with a knowing smirk. "And I'll tell you something in confidence, Kelly—Leonard Zoff is holding on by his fingernails. He talks a good game and brags about all his successful clients, but he's in hock up to his ears. He's gambling on *you* to hit it big and pull him out of his mess."

"So if I sign with you, Leonard will go bankrupt?" Nathan grinned, but didn't say anything. Nathan lied a lot, so I didn't completely believe that story about Leonard hanging on by his fingernails. But if it were true, Nathan would be quite willing to lure me away from Leonard *just* to bankrupt him, not because he had any big plans for me. In that case I'd be better off staying with Leonard.

Not to mention the fact that this man hustling me now was probably a blackmailer. I thought of poor Christopher Clive, the Shakespearean actor Nathan had made drop his trousers for a cheap laugh—just to prove who was boss. Had Nathan come between Ted and me for the same reason? Did he want to humiliate me, the way he'd humiliated Christopher Clive? And this was the man I was supposed to trust, the one I was to allow to make *all* the decisions concerning my career! Leonard Zoff sometimes drove me nuts, but he was still a thousand times better than a sadistic creep like Nathan Pinking.

I wanted Nathan's plans for me—the movie, the series—but without Nathan attached to them. How unlucky the two came together, package deals stink. From where I was standing I could see the framed photograph on the desk, the one showing Nathan's wife and daughters. How could they look so happy with an ogre like Nathan Pinking for a husband and father? "I'll think it over," I told him.

"I have a whole campaign in mind for you, Kelly. It's keyed to climax during the first season of your new series."

"You seem pretty certain there'll be a new series," I said. "You can't be sure the network will buy it."

"Oh, they'll buy it," he said, "if we go in with a sponsor already sewed up. And don't you worry, we'll have a sponsor."

Sure. Cameron Enterprises.

"Anyway, the way it works is like this," Nathan went on. "All next season, we do this big publicity putsch about your new show, how excited you are to have your own series, the usual gaff. Maybe something about getting Nick Quinlan to do a guest role on your show. But here's where we pull a

switch. When the new show starts, you begin dropping hints
in interviews and on talk shows that somehow it's not quite as
satisfying as you thought it would be."

"The show is not as satisfying?"

"Not the show—the show's great, the cast is great, the
writers are great, you've got a terrific crew, the whole schmeer.
But *being a big television star* isn't the rewarding thing you'd
thought it would be, and you're feeling a little disappointed.
Then along about renewal time, you confide to Johnny Carson
that what you really want is a home and family. That if the
right man came along you'd give it all up like a shot. You
see?"

"I see I'm going to throw up in about two minutes." I
turned to leave.

"No, wait, wait—look, Kelly, it's perfect. Every man in
America will feel a little bigger when you say you're willing to
give it all up for a man. And every one of them will have a
sneaking suspicion that *he's* the man you're waiting for. And
housewives all over the country will nod their heads in
approval, because the famous, beautiful Kelly Ingram is at
last catching on to what they knew all along. They'll be
thinking here is this big TV star who wants to be just like *me*.
It can't miss! You'll get the men and the women both, and the
show'll be good for a long run, Kelly, much longer than
LeFever. And I can make it all happen. What do you say?"

I said again that I'd think it over and left before I lost
control of myself and kicked him in the teeth.

So I was to act out the male fantasy that what a woman
really wants is a Strong Man to protect her, was I? Same old
con. When I was growing up the style was unwed mother-
hood à la Vanessa Redgrave. But I remember looking at my
mother's old movie magazines, *Modern Screen* and *Silver
Screen* and *Photoplay* and a couple of others, and they all had
articles about movie actresses who "really" just wanted to be
wives and mothers, all sorts of different people like Lana
Turner and Jeanne Crain and Rita Hayworth and even Bette
Davis, I think. Even back then it was what people wanted to
hear, how celebrities longed to be ordinary and just like
everybody else. And here was Nathan Pinking proposing the
same slop for me—and acting as if nobody had ever thought
of it before. Nathan had never had an original idea in his life
and he sure as hell wasn't going to start now.

Stupid part about it, though—before Ted Cameron I

probably would have gone along without thinking twice about it. But this man who had thought up my new persona for me was the same thug who had Ted by the balls. And Nathan's little proposal had told me something, that little conference convinced me. Nathan was indeed Ted's blackmailer.

All I want is a home and family, that was to be my line. But it wouldn't be very convincing if I was already married, would it? And Nathan Pinking, watching how much time Ted and I were spending together, had started to see his whole campaign for the new series going straight down the toilet. So one Thursday morning he calls Ted in and tells him to kiss Kelly goodbye.

It had gone too far. Nathan Pinking was controlling lives and money and television shows and indirectly even Cameron Enterprises—and he was getting away with it. The man had no *right* to that kind of power. He was sure to misuse it; Nathan wasn't really a very smart man. He was a *ruthless* man, and self-defensive—that's why he'd gotten as far as he had. Now he had to be stopped. It was clear the only thing for me to do was go to Marian Larch and tell her everything I knew.

And in doing so throw away my chance at my own TV series. My own series. Based on a pilot produced by Nathan Pinking. A chance I might not ever get again.

My own series.

Maybe I should wait until after the movie pilot was made.

12

Marian Larch

Captain Michaels was openly relieved when he got word from the DA's office to let Fiona Benedict go. The case against her had been shaky to begin with and she never had admitted shooting at Richard Ormsby. Now that it was clearly somebody else who killed Ormsby, the prosecutors knew they'd never make the charge of *attempted* murder stick. Especially since the earlier murder method had been repeated—a public shooting at a television station. "I always had a feeling she was innocent," the Captain said.

"Innocent my foot," I said. "Innocent of Ormsby's murder, yes, but guilty of trying to kill him earlier. Two different events."

"Hey, what you got against little old ladies?" the Captain grinned. He was in a good mood since things were working out the way he wanted them to.

"Surely she's not old enough for the little-old-lady label," I said. "Early sixties. That's too young." I refrained from pointing out that Fiona Benedict was only about ten years older than Captain Michaels himself. "She fired that gun at Ormsby—six times she fired it. The fact that somebody else came along and did the job right later on doesn't change what she did in that CBS studio."

"Bull," said Michaels bluntly. "She should never have been arrested in the first place. That woman's no killer. You're the only one here who thinks she's guilty."

"Because I was the only one *there* when she first learned about Ormsby's book. It literally put her on her knees, Captain—it hit her that hard." I didn't particularly want Fiona Benedict behind bars; there were far worse criminals roaming the streets. But any investigation of Ormsby's murder would have to take into account the earlier, unsuccessful attempt by Dr. Benedict. Whoever investigated mustn't make the mistake of assuming the same person shot at Ormsby both times. "I want to be assigned to the Ormsby investigation," I told Captain Michaels.

"You and every other gold shield in Manhattan," he grunted. "No, you stay put on the Rudy Benedict case—I'm pulling everybody else off, I need the men. Anything new on the Pinking and Zoff power struggle?"

I thought *power struggle* too fancy a term for the sniping going on but didn't say so. "Only that Nathan Pinking is now indicating his willingness to sell his share of Leonard Zoff's agency. If the price is right."

"Why the change of mind?"

"Zoff isn't taking the offer seriously. I think it's all part of the same game of cat and mouse those two have been playing for twenty-five years. That's how long they've known each other, a quarter of a century. And they've hated each other every minute of it."

"So why is Rudy Benedict the one who's dead?" Captain Michaels scowled. "Pinking bought scripts from him, period. That's the only connection, the whole relationship? And not even that much a one between Benedict and Zoff. There's some other connection we don't know about. Larch, I want you to find it. No more excuses, no more fiddling around. Find that connection."

"What if there isn't any?"

"Find it anyway."

Get out there and scrounge. I left the Captain's office and went back to my desk. It was going to take some doing to concentrate; I kept thinking about the Richard Ormsby killing. Whoever had shot the Englishman had certainly done Fiona Benedict a favor. Two favors. Killed her enemy for her and got her out of jail at the same time. Two big favors.

Just exactly how good a friend *was* Roberta Morrissey anyhow?

Feeling an absolute fool, I called one of the investigators assigned to the Ormsby case and asked him about Roberta. He said she'd been talking long distance to her husband at the time Ormsby had been shot; the hotel switchboard records bore her out. I thanked him and hung up, feeling an even bigger fool. Was anyone in the world a more unlikely murder suspect than Roberta Morrissey? Well, maybe on the face of it Fiona Benedict was more unlikely—but look what *she'd* done. Little old ladies just weren't what they used to be.

I forced my attention back to Rudy Benedict. To Pinking and Zoff. Leonard Zoff and Nathan Pinking were involved in a one-upmanship contest that just kept accelerating and accelerating, with no real resolution in sight. Right now it looked as if Pinking was ahead in the success race, but I supposed that could easily change. I wondered if that was what really drove these two—the desire to outdo the other.

I thought about talking to both of them again, but there wasn't any point. Pinking would tell me some new lies and Zoff would call me Miriam and I'd be no further along than I already was. Kelly Ingram was making a TV movie and wouldn't be back in town for another week. Nick Quinlan was making a movie too, in Munich—in German, no less; his part was to be dubbed, fortunately. Fiona Benedict would soon be on her way back to Ohio, and Roberta Morrissey with her.

This might be a good time to go talk to Ted Cameron.

Homework first, though. I called Bill Sewell at Heilveil, Huddleston, and Tippet and invited him to lunch. He accepted; he always did.

Heilveil, Huddleston, and Tippet was a firm of stockbrokers, and Bill Sewell was a very junior partner there. He was a reliable source of useful information, if we didn't tap him too often. I think Bill enjoyed being a police contact, although he said he did it for all the free lunches he got. We met at a restaurant on St. Mark's Place, and I waited until we'd ordered to ask him about Cameron Enterprises.

"Good time to buy in—shares are dropping a little," he said. "But that's not what you want to know, is it?"

"It might be. Why are the shares dropping?"

"We're getting rumors of internal dissent. Happens a lot in these third- or fourth-generation family businesses. One small business grown into a conglomerate, squabbling among the descendants of the founder, family unity merely a fond memory from the good old days."

"Ted Cameron's in danger of losing control?"

"That's about it. Way I hear it, Augusta Cameron and a few of the others haven't been too happy with the way Ted's been running things for some time now. But recently something's brought it all to a head."

"What?"

"That I can't tell you—the rumors stop there. Haven't really tried to find out, though. But the shares go on dropping, a point or two a week—good indicator of how fast the rumors are spreading. Ted's been challenged before, and he's managed to pull out of it. But this time I think it might be different."

"Will it hurt the company?"

"Depends on who ends up in charge."

"Do you know Cameron?"

"Met him. Weird eyes."

The food came then. I gave Bill a chance to take the edge off his hunger and then asked how the decisions for spending the advertising budget were made at Cameron Enterprises, but he didn't know anything about that.

"Why the interest in Cameron Enterprises?" he asked. The rules of the game were that you gave something for something—but the something you gave should always be less than the something you got. "They're sponsoring a television show next season, and we're investigating the death of a TV writer."

"Sounds pretty thin. Any connection between Ted Cameron and your dead writer?"

"None that I can see. Frankly, we're reaching."

He grinned. "I knew that when you invited me to lunch."

I paid the tab; Bill waved a cheery goodbye and headed back downtown to his office. I went back to Headquarters and did the paperwork for other things I was working on; the Rudy Benedict investigation was no longer a full-time job. At four o'clock I had an appointment with Ted Cameron that had taken me a couple of days to get; Kelly's boyfriend was a busy man.

The corporate headquarters of Cameron Enterprises were on Lexington. The reception area was curiously undistinctive, but the receptionist was expecting me and led me to Ted Cameron's suite—where it took two secretaries working in relay to conduct me into the inner sanctum.

Cameron himself looked *besieged*, that's the only word for it. He made an effort at appearing calm, but his physical mannerisms revealed a lot of inner tension. When he turned from the window to greet me, the movement had a clearly self-protective posture to it.

I reminded him we'd met before, in Nathan Pinking's office. I don't think he remembered me, but he pretended to; whatever his problems, he hadn't lost his manners. "What can I do for you, Detective Larch? My secretary said you were investigating a murder?"

"Rudy Benedict's murder. Did you know him?"

"I know who he was. We never met."

"Have you had much contact with television people? I know *LeFever* isn't your first venture into TV advertising."

"We've done mostly spot advertising up to now. We've sponsored a few specials, but we've never undertaken a series before. So to answer your question—no, I haven't had much contact with television personnel before now. Rudy Benedict's path and mine just never crossed."

"Who made that decision, Mr. Cameron? To sponsor a series, I mean." I was looking straight at him and I swear his irises turned invisible as I watched. He didn't move his head or anything, but the blue just vanished.

"A great number of people contribute to a decision like that. Our advertising manager, the budget director, a demographics consultant—"

"But ultimately somebody has to say yes or no. Whose responsibility is that?"

"Mine, of course. Why do you ask?"

Flank attack. "Why is there so much hostility between you and Nathan Pinking?"

His jaw clenched; one of those giveaway signs. *Too* giveaway, it seemed to me. A successful businessman would have to hide his reactions better than that, wouldn't he? Ted Cameron made me think of a dam about to break. "I have difficulty in working with a man for whom I have no respect," he said in answer to my question about Pinking. "But it's something I often have to do."

"Then why sponsor *LeFever* if you think so little of Pinking?"

"It's the show we wanted, not its producer. We can reach millions of potential customers through *LeFever*. That's all we're interested in."

Sounded reasonable. Okay, try the other flank. "What are your chances for retaining control of Cameron Enterprises? Is Augusta Cameron likely to win this one?"

I had to admire the way he took it. He didn't pretend not to know what I was talking about or stall for time or anything like that. "So even the police know about it." He smiled wryly and stood up and began to pace. "May I ask how you found out?" Still polite.

"One of our sources on Wall Street."

He nodded, continued pacing. He was harried-looking and obviously under pressure, but he still managed to look, well, *graceful* as he paced the room. I could see why Kelly was so taken with him—the man had style. He was attractive in such a subtle way—nothing obvious or overstated about him. Ted Cameron had a quiet kind of magnetism I'd missed completely when I first met him. But Kelly Ingram had spotted it. She'd spotted it the first time she laid eyes on him.

Finally Cameron decided on an answer he wanted to give me. "For some time now, Aunt Augusta has been challenging me over the presidency. She does this periodically—

about every two years, I'd say. You know she runs Lorelei Cosmetics, don't you?"

"Yes."

"Well, that's not enough for her. She wants to run the parent company instead of just one of its subsidiaries. At first she was content to try to wheel and deal her way into power—she didn't resort to frontal attack until I moved the corporate headquarters to New York. She—"

"Excuse me—when was that?"

"Ah, thirteen . . . twelve or thirteen years ago. Formerly we were headquartered in Los Angeles, where Lorelei Cosmetics is located. Aunt Augusta felt threatened when I took the business offices to the other side of the country. She changed her tactics."

"And this time?"

He was silent a moment. "This time she has new allies. Some other members of the family."

"Why? Why would they side with her against you this time?"

"Because of certain matters of policy—and that, Detective Larch, is in the nature of being a company secret. Don't ask me to reveal business decisions to someone outside the firm because I won't do it. Besides, what does all this have to do with Rudy Benedict's death? It looks as if you're investigating *me* instead of him. I don't see the connection."

Neither did I. "Just a standard procedure of police work, Mr. Cameron. We check everything, even things that don't seem to have any connection at all." He didn't quite believe me, but that was all right. I made one more try. "This matter of company policy you don't want to talk about—it wouldn't have anything to do with the way you spend your advertising money, would it?"

"I'm sorry, I'm just not going to talk about it." His words were calm, but his voice was tight and pinched. He opened the office door and stood waiting for me. Our brief interview was over.

I left wondering if we could get the Los Angeles police to go after Augusta Cameron. Since she was the one who was so bothered by the "secret" company policy, maybe she'd be more willing to talk about it than her beleaguered nephew.

*　　*　　*

A few days later I found a note on my desk saying Kelly Ingram was back in town and wanted to see me immediately on a matter that was urgent and important.

Urgent *and* important? Well, certainly mustn't delay, then. On the way over to her place I tried to guess what might be so urgent. (And important.) Another bottle of Lysco-Seltzer? Not likely, not again. Hate mail from Fiona Benedict? Silly.

When Kelly opened the door, the first thing she said was, "Nathan Pinking is interfering with my sex life and I want you to make him stop."

Well, *that* was something I certainly hadn't thought of. I invited myself to sit down and waited.

"Nathan's blackmailing Ted," she said bitterly. "He's forcing him to sponsor *LeFever*, and he's forcing him to stay away from me."

I asked her how she knew, and she launched into a long story of improbable events and overheard conversations, all neatly wrapped up with some cause-and-effect deductions on her part that I had to admit sounded pretty plausible.

"So he's afraid I might marry Ted," Kelly said, still talking about Pinking. "He busted us up because I'd be no good to his smarmy little promo scheme if I was married. I have to stay fresh and available."

A renewable virgin? "What's Pinking got on Ted Cameron?"

"I don't *know,*" she said with real despair. "Marian, this is just making me sick! Can you nail Nathan for blackmail without . . . without . . ."

"Without exposing what Ted Cameron's done that's made him vulnerable to blackmail?" I sighed. "If he's committed a felony and that comes out in the investigation, we can't just look the other way, you know that."

"But if what he's done isn't illegal, if it's just, oh, personal, or something he doesn't want the rest of the family to know about or something like that—you wouldn't have to hassle him then, would you?"

"No, we'd have no reason to." I couldn't quite figure Kelly. Surely she knew if she blew the whistle on Nathan Pinking the chances were that Ted Cameron would get caught in the blast too. She sounded just a touch angry when she talked about him, I thought. Because he'd allowed himself to be outmaneuvered by someone like Nathan Pinking? "You must be awfully sure Ted hasn't broken the law."

"Well, yes." She didn't sound sure. "He's a *good* man, Marian. He's not like Nathan Pinking."

"So what's to keep *him* from blabbing—Pinking, that is? Even if the police do keep quiet."

"Well, I was thinking maybe plea bargaining. You know, you could promise him a lighter sentence if he'd keep his mouth shut?"

In her own way Kelly was a rather worldly woman, but sometimes she could be so naïve I wanted to scream. "In the first place," I said, "would you trust him to keep his word? I wouldn't. Second, I don't have the authority to agree to plea bargaining, that's up to the prosecutor. Third, we have no evidence of blackmail yet and may not be able to get any. Don't worry, don't worry—we'll give it our best shot." She'd looked panicky there for a moment. "But you've got to realize there's a big difference between knowing somebody is a blackmailer and finding evidence that will stand up in court. I believe you're right about Pinking—I already thought his relationship with Ted Cameron had a strong odor of fish about it. That two-sided face of Pinking's should have warned me," I said facetiously, in a weak attempt at lightening the mood.

All it did was puzzle Kelly. "Two-sided face? What are you talking about? You mean two-faced?"

"No, I mean his face has two sides to it."

"Hasn't everybody's?"

Why had I started this? "Nathan Pinking has halves of two different faces, and they don't fit together. Hadn't you noticed?"

She stared at me. "No." Translation: *What are you, a crazy lady?*

"Okay, forget Nathan Pinking's face," I sighed, pulling out my notebook. "Now I want you to go over it again, and this time give me all the names you can. Like that cousin who came to Tuxedo Park—which Cameron was that?"

"Roger. He runs Watercraft."

We kept going over it until I had everything she could give me. Kelly had been suspicious for some time; there'd been a number of incidents stretched out over several weeks that had led her to conclude blackmail was the name of the game. So she'd had plenty of time to think about it. Yet I couldn't help but notice she'd put off calling me until after she'd finished her TV pilot movie. If the Cameron-Pinking-

LeFever world was about to collapse, Kelly Ingram would not be one of its casualties.

I promised to keep her posted and left.

13
Fiona Benedict

Eventually I learned to ignore the ringing of the telephone, and I stopped answering the door almost entirely. The solicitous expressions of concern proclaimed, no, *de*claimed by acquaintances who spoke too loudly, too brightly—it got to be more than I could bear. Their intentions were good, of course, but they were embarrassed, ill at ease. And why not? Who among them had prior experience of such a situation? What do you say to a colleague who has just been released from jail after having been charged with attempted murder? Most of them said, *Oh, Fiona, I knew it was a mistake all along!* That's what their mouths said. But their eyes weren't so sure.

Drew Morrissey was the worst. Roberta Morrissey had been the Rock of Gibraltar when I needed her, but Drew acted as if he wished he'd never met me. He mumbled and stuttered and shifted his weight from foot to foot and managed never quite to look me in the eye. He didn't have the foggiest notion of what to say to me. I knew what to say to him. *Goodbye*.

Howard—I never will know his last name now—Howard had given me good advice. *Say nothing at all*, he'd told me. *Not even "I didn't do it"—we don't have to enter a plea yet. Say nothing.* So I'd said nothing; and when Richard Ormsby was murdered, my immediate release was not complicated by any statement I might otherwise have signed. Howard would accept no money; the Ingram woman's doing again, no doubt.

I'd submitted my resignation the day after Roberta and I returned to Washburn. The dean said he would just hold my letter for a while, in case I wanted more time to think it over.

My future was in limbo; it depended upon decisions I had yet to make. But I didn't see how I could just pick up and go on at Washburn as if nothing had happened. The administration and my colleagues were all being "understanding"—but I'd still be pointed out to newcomers as the local criminal. I can't stand being stared at.

Too much had happened; I couldn't have remained unchanged by it. I felt a need to take my time, to wait to find out, to discover what I had left of my old self. I was plagued by feelings of uncertainty that I either had to dispel or else accustom myself to living with. There were too many unanswered questions; I was having difficulty maintaining my sense of balance.

For instance, I had no idea why Richard Ormsby had been killed. Whoever had shot him couldn't have had the same reason for wanting him dead that I'd had. If I'd just waited—oh, that's even more cynical, more reprehensible. Wanting someone else to do my murderous dirty work for me. I *had* tried; I had done my very best to remove that academic trash from the face of the earth, but I'd failed. It needed someone with a steadier hand and a more accurate eye than mine to get the job done.

And I didn't even know who. But whoever it was, he had acted as my surrogate. Some mysterious someone had appeared out of nowhere and had done for me what I'd been too inept to do for myself. I had fired Rudy's gun at that man six times—and I missed six times. Missing doesn't make me innocent; it merely makes me a bad shot. Nothing will ever make me innocent.

I was taking a bath and two showers every day. Roberta Morrissey kept insisting that I was imagining the smell. She was undoubtedly right, but that didn't make it any the less real. I'd heard of the strong disinfectant used in jails but I'd had no idea how astringent and overpowering it was. It stung my mucous membrane and made my eyes water. It permeated everything—my hair, my skin, that rough clothing I was made to wear. Roberta said the odor was long since gone, that I was the only one who still smelled it. I will always smell it.

I wondered if someone had followed Richard Ormsby to New York from London, if his death was the result of some old enmity in his home country. What kind of enmity—personal, professional? Or had my bootless attempt at murder inspired some unstable occupant of the lunatic zone into an act of emulation? An attack upon a public figure breeds further attacks. Even the self-inflicted death of a celebrity stimulates imitations—two hundred suicides in the month following Marilyn Monroe's death, I once read. Had my firing at Ormsby made him suddenly appear a desirable target to some deranged soul in search of an outlet? Where does my responsibility end?

Another remembered smell: garlic. From a sandwich on the Ingram woman's table, the night I first met her. She and Marian Larch sitting there, offering uninvited sympathy for the death of my son. My refusing to tell them to call me by my first name, my resisting an intimacy with them—because they belonged to a harsh and violent world! Something was wrong with me. Something was very much wrong with me. I was not reacting right. The only thing I truly regretted was that someone other than I had had the pleasure of killing Richard Ormsby.

In the meantime I needed something to occupy my mind, or at least distract my attention. I had thought that when my *Life of Lucan* was completed, I'd probably have one more book left in me. I'd been thinking of a problem in connection with the Sepoy Rebellion of 1857 in India, something that had been teasing at me for a long time. But now undertaking work of that nature seemed futile, for reasons I didn't care to stop and examine. What I needed was busy work, not real work.

Rudy's papers.

I'd made only a bare start on his papers when the *Times* review had appeared and started me on my insane mission to New York. So I sat down at the little table in the attic and got to work.

Just about the first thing I learned was that my son had specialized in beginnings. Aside from the opening scenes of over a hundred television scripts that never got written, there were countless folders containing anywhere from two to fifty pages of fiction. Novels, short stories—I couldn't always tell which they were meant to be. Some of the ideas were quite good; but after a powerhouse opening, Rudy would run out of steam. He wouldn't know what to do with his ideas once he had them. It was very frustrating reading; I would have liked to know the endings of at least a few. But if it was frustrating for me, it must have been torture for Rudy—all those promising beginnings that never went anywhere.

But the incomplete stories did the trick. They kept me going, they kept me distracted. *They kept me sane.*

Thank you, Rudy. I wish I could repay you. Thank you.

I'd been reading steadily for almost a week when I came to a folder with the promising title "The Town That Loved Mozart" written on it. But instead of the usual typewritten pages inside, I found a clipping from *The Los Angeles Times* and two Polaroid snapshots.

The newspaper clipping was nearly fifteen years old; it told of the death by cyanide poisoning of a woman named Mary Rendell. Her body had been found on the grounds of a Bel Air mansion; the owners hadn't known the woman, but said they'd given a large party the night before and the victim could have come in with one of the invited guests. Police were checking the guest list.

Cyanide poisoning. How ironic that Rudy should have kept this clipping about a woman who'd died the same bizarre way he was to die. I read through the news story again. Mary Rendell, Mary Rendell. Why was that name familiar?

Both Polaroid snaps were of a painting, the same painting. It showed a man and his shadow . . . of course! *Man and Shadow*, the painting that was missing from Rudy's apartment—and it had been painted by a woman named Mary Rendell. I looked at the clipping a third time; it said nothing about her being an artist. But I was sure that was the right name, Mary Rendell. Now why would Rudy have been keeping these snapshots and a fifteen-year-old clipping, and why had he hidden them in a deliberately mislabeled folder?

I studied the snapshots. In the painting the man and his shadow had reversed their traditional positions. The shadow was upright and three-dimensional and dynamic; the man was stretched out on the ground and flat and elongated. The shadow was casting the man, not the other way around.

Even in the snapshots I could tell the detail work was extraordinary. This Mary Rendell was not one of those East Village pretenders who spend twenty minutes slapping paint on a canvas and then display the finished "work" for the tourists to gawk at even before the paint is dry. No, Mary Rendell was painstaking in her work; I wished I could see the original. One of the photographs was a close-up of the man's head—it showed the face had been painted with great care. It was an attractive face, but the eyes didn't seem to have any irises. Intentionally symbolic, or had the photo's color just faded over the years? I couldn't tell.

Well. What was I to make of that? The clipping and the snapshots obviously meant something to Rudy or he wouldn't have kept them. I knew one person who'd be interested—Marian Larch. She'd said right at the start there was some mystery about the painting, this painting of a blank-eyed shadow-man that was still missing as far as I knew. I'd send the snaps and the clipping along to Marian in a few days, the next time I felt up to venturing out of the house. There was a time I wouldn't let anything go without photocopying it first. No more; why bother? I'd just send everything to Marian—let her figure out what it meant.

Not that I expected what I'd found to make any difference. I was fairly well resigned to never knowing who killed Rudy. Even if the police did find out who the murderer was, it would just be a name to me. Someone I didn't know, probably a name I'd never even heard mentioned. But *who* wasn't as important as *why*. Every day it was becoming more important to me to know *why* Rudy was dead.

Why had Rudy been killed? And for that matter, why had Richard Ormsby been killed? Why had I found it so easy to pick up a lethal weapon and use it? Why was I sitting there like a fool in a Washburn, Ohio, attic asking myself impossible questions?

Keep on reading Rudy's papers. Keep busy reading. Keep reading. Read.

14

Marian Larch

We got a court order to put a tap on Nathan Pinking's telephone, but the judge turned down a similar request for Ted Cameron's phone. He said we couldn't tap in on the alleged victim without his consent. Captain Michaels and I talked it over and decided bringing Cameron in on it at that stage would do more harm than good; so we went with just the one bug.

And what do you know—the tech people who installed it found someone had been there before us. Nathan Pinking's phone contained a multi-directional mike of the sort that picked up everything spoken in the room, not just telephone conversations. It was of standard manufacture, nothing there to tell us who had planted it. We left it, in order not to tip off whoever had put it there that the police were now in on the act.

"Who do you think?" Captain Michaels asked.

"Cameron or Leonard Zoff," I said. "The first for self-defense, the second for sheer meanness. But I wouldn't bet on either—it could be someone we don't even know about. Pinking's a man who makes enemies easily."

So we waited; the calls we monitored were for the most part regular business calls. Pinking did call Cameron twice. The tapes made it clear Pinking was coercing Cameron, but there were no open threats and no talk of payoffs. A man named Rothstein from the DA's office listened to the tapes and said they'd be useful as supporting evidence, but they weren't enough for an arrest warrant.

In the meantime I was busy prying information out of the television networks about their fall schedules. I wanted to find out just how deeply involved Cameron Enterprises was with Nathan Pinking productions. This is what I learned had been scheduled:

1. *LeFever*—a one-hour crime/action series sponsored by Cameron Enterprises, Ted Cameron, president. *LeFever's* first-year sponsors had been unwilling to pay the huge increase in advertising rates NBC had decided on (based on the show's steady climb in the ratings). Cameron Enterprises had taken over full sponsorship.

2. *Crossover Valley*—a trash-passion prime-time soap on CBS, running time one hour. Sponsorship was split between Lorelei Cosmetics, a subsidiary of Cameron Enterprises, Augusta Cameron, president; and Ross Insurance Associates, no connection with Cameron Enterprises. Lorelei Cosmetics was a new

sponsor; Ross Insurance was a carry-over from last season.

3. *Down the Pike*—A thirty-minute yokel comedy ABC had planned to cancel until Watercraft, Inc. agreed to pick up the tab. Watercraft was owned by Cameron Enterprises and its president was Roger Cameron.

4. *Gimme an A*—a new half-hour comedy series about high school cheerleaders scheduled to debut on ABC in October. The sponsor was Shakito Electronics, which was owned by Watercraft, which was owned by Cameron Enterprises. The president of Shakito Electronics was Peter B. McKenna, who had married a Cameron and had taken on the presidency of Shakito when his wife died.

5. *On Call*—a made-for-TV movie doubling as a series pilot and starring Kelly Ingram, penciled in for an early December showing on NBC. Three sponsors: Featherlight Footwear, a Cameron Enterprises line of boots and shoes; Mercury Office Machines, a subsidiary of Cameron Enterprises, Robin Cameron, president; and Lorelei Cosmetics.

So, with the exception of Ross Insurance's half-sponsorship of *Crossover Valley*, Ted Cameron's conglomerate was footing the bill for everything that came out of Nathan Pinking's production company. Footing the bill and then some; the networks had to make a profit. The nets bought the shows from the production companies, paying less than what it cost the companies to make them and charging the sponsors as much as traffic would bear. A show had to run at least three years before it could go into syndication, and only then would the production company that made it begin to realize a profit—from the residuals. So by locking Cameron Enterprises into full-time sponsorship, Nathan Pinking had found a way to make sure all his shows eventually reached the syndication stage. He might bankrupt Cameron Enterprises in the process, but his own future was secure.

I felt certain that was what Augusta Cameron and the others were up in arms about. Two one-hour series, two half-hour series, and a movie—that must have made a terrific drain on Cameron Enterprises' resources. Pinking also had two more programs in development; rumor at the networks was that he also had sponsors sewed up for them as well (guess who).

Thus when the call came from Los Angeles, it was more in the nature of confirmation than of providing new information. A Sergeant Finley of the LAPD had, at our request, interviewed Ted Cameron's Aunt Augusta—and Aunt Augusta had talked his ear off.

"She's out to stir up as much trouble as she can," Sergeant Finley said. "She made no bones about that. Augusta Cameron lives in a constant stage of rage—she's furious with her nephew. And all because of the television advertising."

"I think it goes back farther than that," I said, "but it's the TV sponsorship that's got all the Camerons riled up this time. Did she say what her plans were?"

"She got a little coy about that—I think there are still a few Camerons she wants to bring over into her camp. She didn't say so, but I got the impression that if the entire family unites against Ted Cameron, he'll pretty much have to resign. That's what Augusta wants—Ted Cameron's resignation."

"She has a good chance of getting it." Ted Cameron was running close to the edge; he might have to resign to avoid a nervous breakdown.

"Why doesn't Cameron just pull back on the TV advertising?" Sergeant Finley wanted to know. "It can't be worth losing his company over."

"He can't. It's a long story, but he's committed. Four series and a movie this coming season."

"Yeah, I know. Augusta says that will come close to bankrupting them because they're just not that big a conglomerate—they can't put that much money into television."

I thanked him for his help and hung up. Talk about being between a rock and a hard place. Ted Cameron was caught between Nathan Pinking's blackmail on one side and Augusta and her army of Camerons on the other. Pinking's hold over Ted must be herculean to have forced him into a position like that.

What had Ted Cameron done?

The answer came in a brown mailing envelope postmarked Washburn, Ohio.

I looked at the two snapshots of *Man and Shadow* and wondered how Ted Cameron could ever have got himself into such a fix. No question, it was his face in the "man" part of the painting; those strange eyes with their invisible irises were unmistakable. It wasn't too surprising that the New York gallery owners I'd contacted when Rudy Benedict died hadn't known of the painting or the artist: Mary Rendell had been dead for fifteen years, and she hadn't been old enough to have earned a reputation for herself when she died.

CYANIDE POISONING IN BEL AIR DEATH

The body of the woman found on the Bel Air estate of Ted Cameron, a vice president of Cameron Enterprises, has been identified as Mary Rendell, age twenty, of 1175 Costa Mesa Drive, Santa Monica. Dr. James E. Vernon of the Los Angeles Medical Examiner's office says the cause of death was cyanide poisoning.

Miss Rendell's body was discovered late Monday afternoon by Ernesto Garcia, a gardener at the Cameron estate. Neither Mr. nor Mrs. Cameron knew the victim. Identification was established by means of a medical alert bracelet the victim was wearing; Miss Rendell was diabetic.

Cameron suggested the victim may have come on to his estate with a guest at a party the Camerons had given Sunday night. Lt. Joseph Taylor of the LAPD says police are interviewing the party guests in an attempt to find someone who knew Miss Rendell.

So Ted Cameron had not yet been promoted to president of Cameron Enterprises, and he'd still been married to one of his two wives. Probably the first; fifteen years ago he'd have been about thirty, young for a vice president—but then he had the right surname. I called Sergeant Finley in Los Angeles and asked him to look up the results of the fifteen-year-old investigation into the death of Mary Rendell.

When he called me back he said, "Unsolved. The investigating officers didn't even have a suspect. Mary Rendell hadn't been in Los Angeles long enough to make much of an impression—only seven months."

"Where was she from?"

"Little town in Oklahoma called Rushville. She wanted to be an artist, says here."

"She'd made a good start at it," I said, looking at the photo of *Man and Shadow*. "Did the autopsy reveal anything other than cause of death?"

"Like what?"

"Oh, like pregnancy?"

"Nope."

"Drugs?"

"None. Nothing at all out of the ordinary. 'Healthy Caucasian female'—life terminated by ingested cyanide. Now it's your turn. Why are the New York police interested in this old unsolved killing?"

"Because it looks as if Mary Rendell's killer has turned up here. Can't tell you anything officially yet—I have to talk to my boss first." I promised to let him know when we had something concrete and hung up.

Before going to Captain Michaels, I needed to make one more phone call. I dialed the number of Cameron Enterprises' corporate headquarters and asked to speak to the Public Relations Director. PR people can almost always give you what you need, and they never ask why you want to know.

A woman identified herself as Mrs. Sullivan, and I said, "Hello, my name is Marian Larch, and I'm trying to get some information about clothing dyes. I know Cameron Enterprises uses a lot of dye—could you tell me who your supplier is? Or suppliers, plural, if you use more than one?"

"We manufacture our own dyes. We have better quality control that way. And we don't have the headaches of late deliveries and the like that we'd have if we contracted out to vendors."

"I see. And where are your dyes manufactured?"

"We have three laboratories. One here in New York, another in Fort Lauderdale, Florida, and a third in Los Angeles."

"Thank you, Mrs. Sullivan, you've been most helpful." If she only knew.

I sat and thought about it. I thought about it a lot. I looked at it this way and that, from every angle I could think of. A few holes, but structurally sound, as they say. I decided to go with it.

I knocked on Captain Michaels's door and opened it before he could yell *Go away*. He was on the phone; he covered the mouthpiece and barked, "Later, Larch."

"It can't wait. I've got something."

He scowled at me but nodded. He finished his phone conversation and then growled, "This better be good. I got a man up in the twenty-sixth precinct waiting for orders. What's so important it can't—"

"Will you stop snarling and listen? This is important. Ted Cameron killed Rudy Benedict."

He leaned back in his chair and stared at me, blew air out through his lips. "Okay, that's the punchline. What's the lead-in?"

"Rudy Benedict was trying to blackmail Cameron. He had a piece of evidence that linked Cameron to an unsolved murder in Los Angeles fifteen years ago. Unfortunately for Rudy, he didn't have the knowhow to deal with a man as dangerous as Cameron. But even though he killed him, Cameron wasn't able to recover the evidence linking him to the old murder. That passed into the hands of Nathan Pinking, who's much more adept at covering himself in a dirty fight than Rudy Benedict ever was. Pinking undoubtedly knows Cameron killed Benedict as well—whether he can prove it or not, it's an added screw he can turn."

"What was this evidence Benedict had?"

"A painting titled *Man and Shadow*. It was missing from his apartment at the time of his death—the bill of sale was in his safety-deposit box, but the painting was gone. I tried to get a line on it at the time, but nobody had ever heard of the painter. Her name was Mary Rendell and she was only twenty years old when she died. She was the murder victim in Los Angeles fifteen years ago."

"And Cameron?"

"Probably killed her. Cyanide poisoning again, for one thing. For another, Cameron lied to the police at the time— said he didn't know her. But it's Cameron's face that's in Mary Rendell's painting. He knew her all right—he knew her well enough for her to make him the subject of a painting. Cameron was married at the time, and in line for the presidency of Cameron Enterprises. Mary Rendell must have become an embarrassment to him. I checked with the LAPD— the autopsy report made no mention of pregnancy or drugs. Maybe the threat she posed wasn't sexual. First thing you think of with a man like Cameron. But right now I'd have to say his motive for killing her is in the unknown category."

"*If* he killed her. You're doing a lot of supposing there."

"Granted. But Cameron wouldn't be vulnerable to blackmail unless he had some guilty connection with Mary Rendell's death."

"Okay, that'll play. But how did Benedict get the painting in the first place?"

"Probably just bought it in all innocence. The bill of sale's signed by a small California dealer long since gone out of business—Rudy had a few pieces of inexpensive original art, all of it by unknowns. He picked up *Man and Shadow* when he and Mary Rendell and Ted Cameron were all living in California, fifteen years ago." I put the newspaper clipping and the two Polaroid snapshots on Captain Michaels's desk. "Fiona Benedict found these among Rudy's papers." Poor Fiona Benedict, sitting there alone in her attic going through Rudy's legacy of paperwork. She'd actually held a picture of her son's murderer in her hand and hadn't known who it was.

The Captain looked at the photos first and then read the clipping. "Rudy Benedict a blackmailer?" He shook his head doubtfully. "Doesn't fit the profile we got on him. The picture I got was of a cautious man, somebody who didn't believe in taking risks."

I tapped the newspaper clipping with my forefinger. "That's not a photocopy. That's the original newspaper item, from fifteen years ago. Rudy Benedict kept it all this time. It took him fifteen years to work up the nerve to do something about his knowledge that Ted Cameron had lied about Mary Rendell. He'd reached some kind of turning point. Rudy was always talking about quitting television and writing for the stage, but he was never quite willing to take all the risks that involved. But his discontent must have reached the point where once in his life he decided he would take a chance."

The Captain grunted. Not convinced.

"Look," I said. "Even attempting blackmail was in Rudy's case a hedge against risk-taking. He wanted to write a play, but he wasn't willing to risk financial failure. So he tried to put the bite on Ted Cameron, to force him to back his play or come up with grocery money or maybe both. He wanted Cameron to provide insurance against failure, one way or another. Rudy Benedict was an ordinary man who attempted one extraordinary thing in his life, and he got killed for his efforts."

Captain Michaels massaged his chin. "Maybe. So how'd the painting get into the hands of Nathan Pinking?"

"I'm just guessing here. Maybe Pinking saw the painting hanging in Rudy's California house and made the same connection Rudy did—and either stole or bought or 'borrowed' the painting. But I'm more inclined to think a lifetime of playing it safe led Rudy to try covering his back by giving the painting to Pinking for safekeeping. Without telling him why, of course. But when the time for the shakedown came, Benedict didn't handle it right and Cameron killed him—and then, too late, discovered Rudy didn't have the painting. Maybe Rudy had showed him photos of the painting—those two there, or others like them. But the real thing wasn't in Rudy's apartment."

"So Cameron killed him for nothing."

"That's about it. He would have been better off in the long run if he'd just agreed to pay Rudy whatever he asked. Rudy would never have bled him dry the way Nathan Pinking is doing—he wouldn't know how, for one thing. By killing Rudy, Ted Cameron just gave Pinking another hold over him. It's ironic, in a way. Cameron killed off the 'easy' blackmailer only to end up in the hands of a worse one."

"Where did Cameron get the cyanide?"

"Cameron Enterprises itself can supply the raw materials a poisoner would need. They manufacturer their own dyes—and they have laboratories both here and in Los Angeles. Ted Cameron could just help himself, both places. I'm sure we can prove he had access—that's all we'll need, isn't it?"

Michaels shrugged. "Should be." He shifted back to the other man involved. "I wonder how Pinking protected himself—letter with his lawyer, I suppose. And the painting? He wouldn't leave that in any accessible place—I suppose his lawyer could hold that too. Okay, I think we'll hold off on Pinking until we pick up Cameron. Which one is more likely to talk?"

"Cameron," I said. "He's living right on the edge. It shouldn't take much to push him over."

"That's what I'm afraid of," the Captain muttered. "We're gonna have to go careful there. I don't want any psychiatrist up and saying he's not competent to stand trial. Good way to win a little cheap sympathy."

I found it hard to feel any sympathy at all for Ted Cameron, cheap or otherwise. *He* wasn't the one I was worried about. I was worried about somebody else.

How was I going to tell Kelly?

15
Marian Larch

I had to hand it to Captain Michaels; he'd played it just right. After first checking with Cameron Enterprises to make sure the boss was in, the Captain and Ivan Malecki and I paid an unannounced visit to corporate headquarters on Lexington. Three of us to arrest one man—Ivan was along to supply a little extra muscle that nobody really thought would be needed.

What the Captain had done was very simple. He'd put the old *Los Angeles Times* newspaper clipping and the two Polaroïd snapshots on Ted Cameron's desk without saying a word. Then, when Cameron had had time to assimilate what they meant, Captain Michaels said, "We're going to give you a choice. Confess to the murder of Rudy Benedict and stand trial here in New York, where there's no death penalty. Or don't confess, and we'll extradite you to California where you'll be tried for the murder of Mary Rendell. There's no statute of limitations on murder—and California, I need hardly remind you, has the death penalty."

For a moment I thought Ted Cameron had gone into shock. He stared at Captain Michaels with his mouth open, his blank eyes unblinking for so long that even Ivan began to feel uneasy. "Is he all right?" he whispered.

Eventually Ted Cameron closed both his mouth and his eyes, but still he did not move or speak.

"Of course," the Captain went on, "if you're a gambling man you might want to take the chance that the California DA won't prosecute a fifteen-year-old case too vigorously. And all guilty verdicts in capital cases are automatically reviewed by the California Supreme Court—you might get a break there. But you got to balance that against the fact that you're a big shot, and the newspapers always have a heyday whenever a big shot is on trial, you know, speculating whether there's one law for the poor and another for the rich. They always do that. It might make your prosecutors a little prickly, less inclined to ease up. Personally I think you'd do better here. But it's your decision. It's your life."

Cameron licked dry lips and said, "I want my lawyer."

"Of course you do," the Captain said in almost paternal tones. "And you'll get your lawyer, just as soon as we take care of a few little rituals first." He nodded to Ivan and me. I read Cameron his rights while Ivan put the cuffs on him.

It was the cuffs that finally jarred him awake. "Are these necessary?" he asked bitterly. "What am I going to do—shoot it out with you? Run away? Where would I run?"

Michaels walked out of the office without answering. "Let's go," Ivan said, nudging his prisoner forward. I brought up the rear. The cuffs were *not* necessary; but then the Captain was trying to get a confession out of Ted Cameron. Amateur criminals such as those who kill for personal reasons are sometimes intimidated by the accoutrements of the law.

We marched Cameron past his stunned secretaries, one of whom was talking earnestly into the telephone. I wondered whether she'd called Cameron's lawyer or his Aunt Augusta.

I kept waiting for the dam to break, for the bomb to go off. But by the time we got Ted Cameron into an interrogation room at Headquarters, he had an almost beatific expression on his face. His hands were steady, his voice was calm, he had no nervous mannerisms. He was in a state of false euphoria because the impossible battle he'd been waging was at long last over. He'd lost—but the relief of being finished with the struggle was so great that nothing else mattered. The Captain and Ivan and I had seen this before, and we all knew it was a temporary state; if we got anything out of him it was going to have to be quick. So he let him call his lawyer even before we booked him. Confessions signed without the presence of legal counsel had a way of being thrown out of court.

"Tell us about Rudy Benedict," Captain Michaels said.

Cameron didn't answer—looked at me instead. "You're Kelly's friend, aren't you? What are you going to tell her?"

"The truth."

He gave a half-smile. "Are you certain you know the truth?"

"No, I'm not. Why don't you make sure I've got it straight?"

Cameron's attorney arrived, a pale, white-haired man named Trotter whose field was corporate law and who was clearly out of his league. He demanded we postpone the interrogation until he could get a criminal lawyer for his client, but the law didn't require us to await the appearance of specialists so we said no. Trotter did the next best thing and advised his client not to say anything.

"I don't want to see her," Ted Cameron said to me. "I mean, I don't want her to see me like this."

"I'll take her the message," I promised.

Then he talked. Somewhere in the midst of his false euphoria Cameron had decided he was better off with us than facing a probable death sentence in California. Or maybe he just needed to talk, to tell somebody about it. His first instinct had been to protect himself, to call for a lawyer. But then when he had a lawyer, he ignored his advice. It happened all the time (fortunately for us). Trotter protested constantly, practically begged Cameron to shut up, *ordered* him not to sign anything. But the president of Cameron Enterprises had given up. He'd had all he could take; he was through. Two murders, the impending loss of his business, the horrors of being blackmailed—it had all finally caught up with him.

His connection with aspiring artist Mary Rendell turned out to be sexual after all. He said she was "a mistake I once made"—thus casually dismissing a human life in so callous a manner that whatever possible sympathy I had left for him was utterly destroyed. When it was time for their affair to end, twenty-year-old Mary Rendell had been shocked and unbelieving. She wouldn't let go. Cameron himself was only thirty at the time and not as experienced in handling sticky situations as he was later to become. An uncle who was then president of Cameron Enterprises was on the verge of retirement; and Ted, brightest new star in the Cameron firmament, was terrified that an extramarital scandal might queer his chances for the job. Cameron Enterprises was a large conglomerate now, but it was still a *family* business.

So poor, naïve Mary Rendell had to go. Ted Cameron poisoned her, and lived in constant fear of discovery for months afterwards. He became president of Cameron Enterprises over Aunt Augusta's strenuous objections (she'd wanted the job for herself); and as soon as he safely could, he moved the corporate headquarters to New York. A new start in a new place; he even had a new wife by then.

Things went well for him after that; he had years of smooth sailing. Cameron had reconciled himself to the fact that he was a successful murderer. Business was good; he'd turned out to be the right choice for Cameron Enterprises' chief executive—a fact that kept Aunt Augusta at bay. His second marriage failed, but he quickly discovered that the life of a rich, unmarried man in New York City wasn't all that hard to take. No unsurmountable problems in his life.

And then one day a snapshot arrived in the mail, a snapshot of a painting in which Cameron's face was easily recognizable. On the back of the snapshot was written *Man and Shadow, painted by Mary Rendell*. Cameron had not known of the existence of the painting. Mary had probably been saving it as a surprise. "She was like that," he said off-handedly.

I wondered—not for the first time—why Mary Rendell had put her lover in the shadow position in her painting. Perhaps she'd instinctively sensed there was something basically insubstantial about Ted Cameron. Or was it just her way of saying she didn't completely understand this man she was so involved with?

It was Rudy Benedict who'd sent Ted Cameron the photo. When the two men met, Rudy was the nervous one. He told Cameron they'd run into each other in California years ago, that, in fact, he'd been a guest at the party Ted and his first wife had thrown the night Mary Rendell was killed. Ted didn't remember him.

The relationship between would-be blackmailer and blackmailee-elect had been a strange one. Rudy Benedict clearly had never tried anything like that before in his life, and he was *very* uncomfortable. His approach, Ted Cameron said, was that of an insecure job applicant while he himself had been cast in the role of prospective employer. Rudy wanted Ted to understand *why* he was putting the screws on him; that was important to him.

So Ted Cameron had nodded sympathetically and listened to poor, second-rate Rudy Benedict's dreams of theatrical and literary glory. This pretended interest Rudy mistook for sympathy; he began to relax a little. All he wanted, he said, was living expenses until he could get one play written and produced. Just one, that was all. When his play opened, he would hand over *Man and Shadow* to Ted Cameron. Whether the play succeeded or flopped made no difference. Rudy just wanted to be taken care of until he had his foot in the stage door. His blackmailing ambitions were so limited it didn't even occur to him to demand that Ted Cameron put up the money for the production of his unwritten play. All he wanted was an *allowance*.

Ted Cameron had deliberately fostered Rudy's need to believe he was a sympathetic listener. That part made perfect sense to me; his naturally courteous demeanor inspired an easy acceptance of Ted Cameron as a thoroughly civilized man. He and Rudy met several times, and Cameron always carried a bottle of cyanide crystals with him, waiting for an opportunity. They'd sit guzzling beer like a couple of stevedores, talking about the best way to arrange Rudy's new income so as not to invite the unwelcome interest of the Internal Revenue people. Rudy wanted the money to appear as legitimate income on which he would pay taxes, so he suggested Cameron buy up a contract for Rudy's services that Nathan Pinking held and which was about to expire. Businessmen could always use writers.

Who was Nathan Pinking, Ted Cameron wanted to know. Rudy told him. By then they'd progressed to Rudy's apartment, and Ted had stared at the postered walls with unconcealed amusement. Rudy had hastened to explain it was only a temporary living arrangement, that he hadn't even bothered to uncrate his paintings but had simply stored them all in the pantry. *In the pantry*, he'd said. That decided Cameron. When Rudy made a beer-necessitated trip to the bathroom, Cameron had picked up a spare set of keys from the top of Rudy's bureau. When Rudy came back in, Ted had agreed to the proposed way of paying off the blackmail. The two men parted on good terms; they'd even shaken hands, Cameron said. But he'd left his cyanide crystals behind in Rudy's Lysco-Seltzer bottle.

As he was telling us this, Cameron seemed more struck by Rudy's ineptness than by his own perfidy. After Rudy was dead, Cameron had taken his stolen keys and gone back to the apartment. He found the paintings in the pantry, but *Man and Shadow* wasn't among them. It had all been for nothing.

At one point he'd seriously considered paying Rudy the blackmail he'd asked; it wasn't all that much. He'd killed him because he decided he couldn't leave anyone alive who knew his guilty secret.

So double murderer Ted Cameron could do nothing but wait. He had no idea where the painting was; the newspaper stories had made no mention of a missing painting. As the days went by and nothing happened, it was beginning to look as if he'd get away with this one too. Then one day a voice on the phone identified its owner as Nathan Pinking and suggested a meeting.

Ted Cameron knew right away his new blackmailer was no apologetic Rudy Benedict. The first thing Pinking had done was explain that he'd left the painting with one lawyer and a letter of explantion with another. He'd come by the painting because Rudy Benedict had put it in a storage locker on West Thirty-fourth Street and had asked Pinking to hold the key. *Just in case something happens*, Rudy had said. Pinking had thought it a bit peculiar at the time but then had forgotten about it—until Rudy Benedict had been murdered.

Pinking had told Ted Cameron he'd recovered the painting from the storage locker but still didn't know what it meant until he saw a picture of him (Cameron) in the newspaper, in connection with Cameron Enterprises' negotiations for a friendly takeover of some small Florida beachwear company. Now that Pinking had a name to attach to the face in the painting, things began to fall into place. Pinking had been living in Los Angeles at the time Mary Rendell was killed, and he vaguely remembered that Cameron Enterprises was somehow associated with an unsolved murder. He sent his secretary to the library with instructions to track it down; and when she did, Nathan Pinking knew he had the ideal sponsor he'd long been looking for.

He'd started out easy, Ted Cameron said—if you call demanding full sponsorship of *LeFever* at jacked-up rates starting out easy. Even that took some doing, but Cameron managed it. Then the demands increased, and Cameron understood his company was expected to underwrite anything and everything Pinking wanted to put on the air. Cameron was becoming desperate to find the sponsorship money; he started forcing the ancillary companies to assume part of the burden. Unfortunately for him, Lorelei Cosmetics was in the best financial position of all the individual companies under the Cameron umbrella and the logical one to be tapped for the most funds. So Aunt Augusta was the first to sniff trouble, but soon the whole Cameron clan was up in arms. Ted Cameron was in serious trouble. Not only was his guilty secret in the hands of a totally unscrupulous, totally unreliable man, but Cameron was also in danger of losing Cameron Enterprises. Clearly there was only one thing to do. He was going to have to kill Nathan Pinking.

There was the problem of the two lawyers, though. One had the painting, another had a letter that would incriminate Cameron. He would have to find out who the lawyers were, and then hire someone to burglarize them. The two robberies and the murder of Nathan Pinking would all have to be timed to take place simultaneously, otherwise Pinking would guess what was up if the lawyers were taken care of first. Cameron didn't like the idea of bringing hired criminals in on it, but he could see no way around it. It would take very careful planning. He was working on the plan when something happened that made him change his mind.

He met Kelly Ingram.

The way Cameron explained it, he was obsessed with her. He'd never been fixated on a woman before in his life, and he didn't know how to deal with it. He was completely bowled over. Kelly changed everything; Cameron couldn't chance losing her. He didn't want to do anything, anything at all, that was the least bit risky—like committing a third murder. He began to feel as if his illicit luck had suddenly run out. He was *afraid* to kill Nathan Pinking; because this time, the important time, something might go wrong. He couldn't risk it. Without knowing it, Kelly Ingram had saved Nathan Pinking's life.

So Ted Cameron had to put up with Pinking's control over him; he said he felt he was living in a torture chamber. It was Kelly that kept him going. And then Nathan Pinking, who saw only dollar signs when he looked at Kelly Ingram, had commanded Cameron to stop seeing her. But losing Kelly did not revive Cameron's earlier resolution to kill his blackmailer; by then the fear of failure had become too deeply ingrained. Nathan Pinking gave Ted Cameron an order, and Ted Cameron obeyed. He could no longer make decisions. He could no longer *act*, he could only sit back and be acted upon. He was drained, defused, whipped. He was through.

So when Captain Michaels had put the two Polaroid

snapshots on the desk, it had taken Cameron a few minutes to understand it was finally all over. But when he did understand, he was relieved. Nathan Pinking had once speculated that Rudy Benedict might have held back a snapshot or two; but since Rudy's papers had all been shipped to his mother's house in Ohio, there didn't seem to be much danger. Pinking felt sure that the snapshots—if they did indeed exist—posed no threat to the cosy financial arrangement he and Cameron had finally settled on. And that, Cameron said, was all. End of story.

The lawyer Trotter hadn't said anything for a long time. He sat staring at Ted Cameron as if he'd never seen him before.

Cameron had a question. "Did Rudy's mother find the photos? In his papers?"

"That's right," Captain Michaels said.

Cameron made a noise that might have been a laugh. "I have a favor to ask, Captain. When you arrest Pinking, tell him where the photos came from. He was so sure they'd cause no trouble. Will you tell him?"

Ivan Malecki cleared his throat and said, "Did you have a bug planted in Nathan Pinking's office—a listening device?"

Cameron looked mildly surprised and said no. Somebody else, then. Cameron turned invisible irises toward me, looking for all the world like a blind man. "When will you tell her?"

"Now," I said. "Before she has a chance to hear it on the news."

He smiled and thanked me. Politest killer I ever met.

I got up and left.

I'd known it wouldn't be easy, but it was even worse than I'd expected. The words were barely out of my mouth before she started rejecting them.

She didn't take in half of what I said—she didn't want to hear any of it. It was pitiful, the way she kept looking for excuses. She blamed Captain Michaels, she blamed me, she even found a way to blame Fiona Benedict. She was willing to blame the *entire world* before she'd blame Ted Cameron— he meant that much to her. It's hard, admitting you made a mistake that big.

"He's killed two people, Kelly," I said. "He's admitted it."

She refused to believe it, simply *refused*. I decided there was no point in pushing it; she was going to have to have time to accept it. Time by herself, time to ease her way in. Bullying her wouldn't help.

When I left, she looked as if she wanted to kill *me*. I've never felt so bad in my life.

When I got back to Headquarters, the reporters were there. Nathan Pinking had been brought in and charged with blackmail and with being an accessory to murder after the fact (for concealing evidence); Captain Michaels had already made a statement to the press. A blackmailer and a murderer arrested in tandem, and both of them fairly well-known figures. A lurid tale, but even *The Wall Street Journal* was interested in this one.

I sat at my desk waiting for the traffic going in and out of Captain Michaels's office to stop. Ivan Malecki came over, saw the look on my face, and said, "That bad, huh?" When I nodded, he squeezed my shoulder and went away. For which I was grateful; sometimes a pep talk is the last thing you need to hear. It had been a nerve-wracking day and I wanted to go home.

Catching a murderer isn't the cause for celebration you might think. There's no good feeling to it. It's a depressing scene, and the main feeling is one of shame. Shame that we should be like this; you look at a killer and you see a piece of humanity that's failed in its essential nature, that of being *humane*. The last thing in the world you want to do is go out and hoist a few and congratulate yourself for being so clever. Catching killers is just something that has to be done, like carrying out the garbage. They're both disease preventatives.

I felt absolutely rotten about Kelly. I'd have been glad to offer her a shoulder to cry on, but she'd made it clear she didn't want me within ten miles of her. There wasn't anything I could do. I'd just have to rely on her common sense to see her through.

Finally the door to Captain Michaels's office was open and he was in there alone. I went in.

"Good work, Larch," he said. "You stuck with it and you came up with a blackmailer as well as the killer." I must not have had my face rearranged right yet because he said, "Kelly Ingram didn't take it too well, huh?"

"Not well at all."

"Give her time. That's a helluva lot to have to swallow all at once. She'll come round." Back to an easier subject. "You'll get a commendation for this one, you can count on it."

"Then am I right in thinking this is a good time to ask for something?"

He stage-sighed. "Ask."

"Assign me to the Richard Ormsby murder."

He looked surprised. "You still want on that one? It's a dead case, Marian."

"Maybe. It doesn't need to be."

He squinted one eye at me. "You think you know who did that one too?"

I shook my head. "I just have an idea or two I want to follow up. But I can't if you won't assign me to the case."

He told me he thought I was crazy but okayed the assignment. I thanked him and went back to my desk. One more chore to perform before I could call it a day; my role as bearer of bad news wasn't quite finished.

I called Fiona Benedict in Washburn, Ohio, and told her her son had died because he'd made the mistake of trying to blackmail a murderer.

16

Kelly Ingram

It was weird seeing Leonard Zoff sitting at Nathan Pinking's desk in Nathan Pinking's office. Taking care of what used to be Nathan Pinking's business. It was weird thinking of Nathan in jail for blackmail, although I'd done my damnedest to make sure he got there. What it was thinking about Ted, there was no word for.

Leonard looked at me sympathetically. "Wouldn't hurt you to get back to work, darling. Sooner the better."

I nodded listlessly; he was right. What I needed was some sort of set daily routine, the kind of thing where you didn't have to think at all. *LeFever* was just the ticket.

"You feel awright?" Nick Quinlan asked me.

"I feel all right, Nick," I said. "Just not a whole lot of energy, you know?"

"Yeah, I know." He nodded somberly. "Happensa me sometimes. Too bad we doan git to do those three, y'know, the Barbados shows. They'd make ya feel bear. Hey, Leonard, how come we're not goin' to Barbados?"

"Shut up, Nick," Leonard sighed. The connection among producer Nathan Pinking and sponsor Ted Cameron and the promised extra episodes in Barbados that were nothing more than blackmail booty—it was all too much for Nick to grasp. "Sorry, Kelly," Leonard said. "He means well."

I shrugged; it didn't matter. Nick looked puzzled. He did that a lot—look puzzled.

It had taken some getting used to, the idea that my ex-lover, the joy of my life and the light of my existence let the drums roll and the trumpets sound ta-taa (idiot idiot *idiot*)—was in fact a cold-blooded killer. And I mean cold-blooded, that's not just a phrase, it means something. Look at what he did: he killed Rudy Benedict. *Rudy Benedict*. Un-doubtedly the most miscast would-be criminal on the face of the earth—and Ted couldn't find any way of handling him other than killing him? There were a number of things Ted could have done. He could have paid him off. He could have tried to talk him out of it. He could have stolen the painting. He could have threatened to tell Rudy's mother.

"I know it's early to be starting on the new season," Leonard Zoff was saying in his loud voice, "but I'd like to get as much in the can as possible before Kelly's movie airs in December. The network might want us to start taping her new series right away—depends on how fast they can sign up a sponsor. We won't have any trouble there, Kel, I'm sure of it. It's good stuff, a sure-fire series idea. You're lucky you got it finished before Nathan Shithead was arrested."

"Lucky. Yeah."

"Whassamadda with *LeFever*?" Nick said sourly. "Not goodanuff for ya?" Now there he was *pretending* to be dumb. Even he understood about having your own series.

Leonard started stroking Nick and I tuned out. I didn't know Mary Rendell, of course, but Marian Larch said she was only twenty when Ted killed her. A *girl*, for Christ's sake—such a dangerous person that murder was the only answer? Seemed to me Ted Cameron was the big bad successful killer only when he came up against weak opponents like Rudy Benedict and Mary Rendell. But when he faced off against somebody a little slicker, like Nathan Pinking, *Ted* was the one to knuckle under. A lot of married, upwardly mobile types had Mary Rendells in their lives, but they didn't *kill* them for crying out loud. They either handled the situation and got away with it or they didn't handle it and got found out, but they didn't become murderers rather than face a setback in their professional lives. And if Ted hadn't killed Mary Rendell, he wouldn't have had Rudy to worry about. He killed those two people simply because it was the easiest way to solve his problems—he wasn't willing to make the effort to find another way. And if you don't think that's cold-blooded, I'd like to know what the hell is.

And there I was, Little Miss Stars-in-Her-Eyes-and-Rocks-in-Her-Head. I never knew, I never suspected, I never had an *inkling*. Even when I figured out Ted was being blackmailed, I still didn't believe he'd done anything *bad*. I was so besotted with the man I was even able to rationalize away blackmail. I wanted him to be a certain kind of man and I *made* him that kind of man, in my mind, I mean. It was just that I knew what I wanted and I decided he was it and I never saw what he really was. I never knew Ted Cameron at all.

Do you have any idea what it feels like to find out you've slept with a murderer? And not just once, but repeatedly? Try to imagine it—learning your bed partner is a killer. Kinky thrills, a real turn-on? Maybe for some people. Me—it just made me sick. I threw up every day for a week. Finally Leonard Zoff called and insisted I pull out of my "mulligrubs" —whatever they are. When I did, I found some changes had taken place in the world.

"I was thinking of a new car for LeFever," Leonard was saying soothingly to Nick. "One of the flashier sports models. What do you say to that?"

"I get to pick it out?" Nick asked.

"Who else?"

Sure you do, Nick. Don't hold your breath, Nick.

Nathan Pinking's production company was now Leonard Zoff's production company. The way Leonard explained it, Nathan was still a minor partner and his share of the profits would go toward supporting his family while he was in prison. For some reason that Leonard didn't explain, Nathan had had a choice only of either selling to Leonard or shutting down—which wouldn't pay his family's bills while Daddy was a guest of the state. So the long battle between the two had finally come to an end, and Leonard had won. With Nathan locked up for a goodly number of years, Leonard would have it all his own way.

You'd think he'd be on top of the world, wouldn't you? Well, he wasn't. As a matter of fact Leonard was kind of lackadaisical, going at the early taping of *LeFever*'s third season as if it was every bit as exciting as checking over last week's laundry list. Nick was always half asleep anyway, and what with me just coming out of the blues, it wasn't the most scintillating meeting I ever attended. Leonard was businesslike and all that; we were making plans and getting on with it. But Leonard had lost a lot of what my grandmother would have called his spizzerinctum—his special up-and-at-'em kind of drive. Maybe it just wasn't the same without Nathan Pinking to scrap with.

"Kelly, darling, pay attention, please. We're gonna do more out-of-city location shooting this time, so you and Nick will have to keep your calendars clear after the twenty-first. Don't even go making a dental appointment without checking with me first. I'm gonna have enough on my mind without schedule conflicts and all that shit."

All that shit. "Leonard," I said abruptly, "did you once send me a laxative and a carton of toilet paper?"

The color drained right out of his face—and then drained right back in. "Toilet paper, darling? Why should I send you toilet paper?"

But it was no good; he'd given himself away. "Why, Leonard?" I asked. "Do you resent me that much?"

"What are you talking about?"

"You know what I'm talking about. A bottle of Lysco-Seltzer containing a laxative and a carton of toilet paper. You sent them."

Nick said lazily, "Whire we talkin' toilet paper?"

"You're crazy," Leonard said. "I didn't send you that stuff."

"Okay, Leonard," I sighed. "If that's the way you want it."

Things were a bit edgy after that, even though both of us did this big act about how everything was hunkydory again. Don't know why I let it bother me that much, but it got to

me. Hitting on small bad feelings to keep away the big ones,
I guess.

The meeting dragged to a close. Nick had come in a
limo—it was getting harder and harder for either of us to
appear in public without drawing swarms of autograph-hunters.
That was good most of the time, *God*, the years I dreamed
about it!—but you have to be *on* the whole time and I just
wasn't up to performing right then. I asked Nick if he'd drop
me at Police Plaza.

On the elevator down, Nick draped one arm across my
shoulders in that posture he likes best when he's talking to
women. "Doan look so sad, pretty Kelly," he said. "The
hurtin' stops soonsya let it. Let it stop, Kel."

Well, who'd have thought Nick Quinlan had that kind of
compassion in him? He'd said exactly the right thing. I
wondered if I could ever get mad at him again after that.

"Asides, it doan help LeFever's image none, you goan
round lookin', y'know, unsatisfied."

Yep. I could.

I wanted to see Marian Larch—strictly personal sort of
thing, no police business. It had eventually sunk in on me
that I'd been just awful to her when she came with the news
about Ted. I was *blaming her* for what happened—actually I
should have been thanking her, I guess. It was pretty goddamned clear that *I* didn't have enough sense to see through
Ted Cameron. I'd have just gone on drifting along, never
knowing. Nathan Pinking aside, what if things had stopped
being good between Ted and me? Would he have gotten rid
of me the way he did Mary Rendell?

*Put him out of your mind. Just stop thinking about him.
He slips into your mind, force him out by thinking of other
things. It can be done.*

Ivan (I have *got* to find out his last name) said Marian
was down in the Property Department. I decided to go
looking for her rather than wait, because a lot of the good
folks at Police Headquarters were giving me the eye. I was a
different kind of celebrity here; my ex-lover was a murderer.
Think of other things.

Ivan insisted on escorting me because they didn't like
people—"civilians" was Ivan's word—wandering around the
Headquarters building and that may even have been true. (If

we're civilians, then the police are *military?*) Marian was just coming out of the Property Department when we got there.

"I'm sorry!" I hollered at her.

Marian jumped a foot. "For what?" she demanded, alarmed.

"For being so nasty the day you, well, you know, when you brought me the bad news."

Her plain, friendly face crumpled into a smile. "Oh, that's all right," she said generously. "I probably could have found a better way to tell you."

"No, it was my fault. I acted bad or maybe badly and I'm sorry for both of them and I apologize."

"Nothing to worry about. We were all tense, it was a tense situation and—"

"Damn it, Marian, I am *trying* to take the blame. Will you shut up and let me feel guilty?"

Ivan looked worried. "Are you two kidding or are you fighting?"

"I am perfectly content to let you feel as guilty as you like," Marian said to me majestically, "so long as your guilt trip does not interfere with my stance of gracious understanding."

"You're kidding," Ivan said with relief.

"And you were right about something else," I went on. "It was Leonard Zoff who sent me the toilet paper."

"Ah-hah. Did he admit it?"

"No," I said, "but he gave himself away when I asked him. Just now, at a meeting."

"I think it's good that he knows. That *you* know, I mean. It'll make him think twice if he's ever tempted to send out any more toilet paper gifts."

"He seemed honestly surprised when I brought it up. But then he pretended not to know what I was talking about."

"*I* don't know what you're talking about," Ivan complained. "Why are we talking about toilet paper?"

"You're not by any chance related to Nick Quinlan, are you?" I asked him.

"We're talking about an associate of Kelly's who had trouble getting through the anal stage of his development," Marian explained to Ivan. Which didn't really explain anything, come to think of it. Neat trick.

"Are you through for the day?" I asked her.

"Lord, no. Tons of work."

"Then sneak away for a break. You can do that, can't you?"

"I'm almost finished," Ivan said hopefully.

"Sorry, love, I'm all set for this big dramatic scene with Marian and there's no man's role in it."

He grinned. "Is that the actress talking or the woman?"

"Depends on who's asking," I said. "The cop or the man."

He didn't like that much, the implication that cops and men were two different things. (It was okay for him to do the same thing to me, though.) He tried to laugh it off. "Hey, that's not what you're supposed to say."

"I know," I sighed. "I'm supposed to say something like *I was a woman before I was an actress* and then bat my eyes and smile. Sorry, Ivan, I'm just not up to it today, okay?"

"Okay," he said dubiously.

Marian was laughing. "Now, what's got into you? Come on—I think I can sneak a break at that."

"My family always said 'bathroom tissue,'" Ivan called after us by way of goodbye.

We went to a private club on East Fiftieth that I didn't much care for except that it sure as hell was *private*. I didn't have to worry about strangers coming up to me there or even being gawked at. Normally I rather like being gawked at, but circumstances were different now. Our private booth had one-way glass in the window; we could watch the passing parade outside without being seen ourselves.

"This place must cost you an arm and a leg," Marian said in hushed tones. "All I wanted was a cup of coffee."

I explained how lack of privacy had suddenly become a real problem. "I don't even feel comfortable in your office, Marian. People stare there too."

She nodded. "So what's this big dramatic scene you told Ivan you wanted to play?"

"What's his last name?"

"Ivan's? Malecki."

"Malecki, that's right. Couldn't remember it. Did I offend him, do you think?"

"No, but you puzzled him. You sounded out of character."

"I am. Completely out of character. Not sure what my character is anymore."

"Oh Gawd, not the existential miseries."

"No, nothing like that. It's just that everything's shaken

up. Leonard sitting behind Nathan's desk and not looking at all happy about it—"

"Really? That's a surprise."

"Surprised me too. I don't mean he regrets taking over the production company—he's going ahead with everything okay. But he's not getting the kick out of it he should be getting. He should be King of the Hill now, but he's not."

"Maybe he needs Nathan Pinking as an adversary to spark him. Could be it was the fight itself that kept him going."

"That's what I was thinking. He and Nathan have been battling for so long, Leonard must feel something is missing from his life now."

A waiter appeared pushing a trolley laden with about forty fancy finger sandwiches and at least twice that many elaborately iced pastries. That's what you got in that place when you asked for *just coffee*.

When he'd gone, I said, "Marian, I hope you don't mind my dragging you away from your work. No big scene, that was just to keep Ivan Malecki from coming along. There are just some things I don't understand. Like why did Nathan Pinking sell out to an old enemy like Leonard? Why didn't he sell to somebody else?"

"He couldn't. You had no way of knowing it, but Leonard Zoff already owned forty-nine per cent of Pinking's production company."

"*What?*"

"And Pinking owned forty-nine per cent of Zoff's theatrical agency. It was a deal they worked out when they dissolved their earlier company—Pinking and Zoff Productions. You remember, I told you about that."

"Then they were still partners? All this time?"

"They certainly were. And the contract they signed specified that neither partner could sell his share without the permission of the other partner. So once Pinking was arrested, Zoff had him over a barrel. Pinking had to sell to Zoff or see the business fold. If he hadn't been worried about providing for his family, Pinking probably would have just told Zoff to go to hell."

"That's something that's always amazed me," I said, nibbling on a pastry. "How Nathan could be such a monster *and* a good family man at the same time."

"Never heard of the Mafia, huh?" Marian said wryly.

"Anyway, Zoff bought just a big enough percentage from Pinking to give himself majority control of both the production company and the agency. I think he's going to hire somebody to run the agency for him."

"Yes, he's already done that. He promoted one of his own people. Leonard's going to keep on managing a few of his clients, though. Including me." Leonard-the-agent had just negotiated my new *LeFever* contract with himself, Leonard-the-producer. I *think* I came out all right on that one.

"Do you have a new sponsor for *LeFever* yet?"

"Oh God, yes. NBC had to fight 'em off, even though they raised the advertising rate again. It's weird, isn't it? You'd think that once the story became public—well, look. Here's this producer that's been blackmailing somebody into sponsoring his show. The other advertisers *ought* to be thinking that the show has to be a real turkey if that's the only way a sponsor could be found. But no—they're lining up for the privilege of paying for *LeFever*. We're in the news now, and it doesn't matter what that news is. Just so people are talking about us—that's all that counts."

"What about your movie?"

"Same thing. They've even started negotiating about my news series, the one to be based on the movie. In fact, all of Nathan's shows have been covered except *Down the Pike*—ABC cancelled that one. But if things keep going like this, Leonard Zoff is going to end up a rich man."

Marian made a vague gesture with her hand. "Well, that's show biz."

"No, it isn't," I said glumly. "That's the advertising biz."

A silence grew between us. We drank our coffee and looked out the window. There was something I wanted to ask her, but my mouth had grown suddenly dry. I took a drink of water; it didn't help.

I'd forgotten Marian Larch could sometimes read minds. She said, gently and considerately, "He's undergoing psychiatric examination. A whole team of doctors, the Cameron clan got them for him. The police psychiatrist has already declared him competent to stand trial, but the date won't be set until the Cameron psychiatrists are finished."

I nodded; that's what I'd wanted to know. "I've decided to put him out of my mind." My voice sounded strained.

Marian smiled sadly. "Good idea."

And then I was surprised to hear myself saying, "I don't want to do any more *LeFever* episodes."

Marian raised an eyebrow. "Well, well. Now what do you suppose the connection *there* is?"

"I don't know." I tried to think. "I tell you I'm going to put Ted Cameron behind me and I suddenly realize I hate the television show I'm doing. Why would one lead to the other? Ohwowohwow. I don't know, Marian—I told you I was out of character today."

"Maybe that's it," she said. "I'll bet it's the character you're playing that you don't like. Do you see any connection between your television role and the role you were playing with Ted Cameron?"

I was so shocked I couldn't speak. I wanted to yell, I wanted to hit her, I wanted to deny it at the top of my voice. The character I played in *LeFever* was only a human toy, for God's sake, something for the hero to play with. I wasn't like that, I didn't *think* of myself like that, I knew better... at least I thought I knew better. All of a sudden I was filled with doubts, uncertainty. It was an *awful* feeling.

Finally I said, "Fiona Benedict was wrong about me." Somehow that came out sounding too much like a question. I made it more positive. "She was wrong. She had to be."

Marian looked at me a few moments as if trying to make her mind up about something. Then abruptly she said, "Kelly. Don't judge the Miss America contest. Call your lawyer friend Howard and see if he can break the contract for you."

How ironic. How dumb. I started to laugh. It sounded artificial, even to me. "Relax. I'm not going to judge any Miss America contest. It's all been decided. They cancelled *me*." Marian didn't say a word; just sat there with her mouth open. "That's right. Seems my image is no longer wholesome enough for them. What with a killer for my lover and a blackmailer producing my shows, I'm no longer fit to associate with young American virgins. That kind of dirt rubs off, you know." I sounded even more sarcastic than I'd meant.

Marian let out the breath she'd been holding. "If I said I was sorry, I'd be lying and you know it. I'm sorry you didn't have the pleasure of telling *them* where to get off, but you're well out of it, Kelly. You don't need that. *You don't have to play those games*. Now for Pete's sake pull yourself together and get back to being your usual peppy self. You make me nervous, the way you're drooping around. You're well rid of all of them, Cameron and Pinking and even Miss God Bless America. You've had just one fortunate escape after another—what are you so gloomy about? Cheer up, damn it! You don't realize how lucky you are."

She looked and sounded exactly like a sixth-grade teacher I'd once had. "Yes, ma'am," I said in a tiny voice. "Go screw yourself, ma'am."

"That's better," she beamed. "Now I hate like the very devil to leave this sinfully luxurious establishment you've brought me to, but I do have to be getting back. Work awaits."

Belatedly I realized how much of her time I'd taken and signalled to the water. "Thanks for listening, Marian. What are you working on now—or am I allowed to ask?"

"Sure you are. I'm on the Richard Ormsby case now."

"Oh?" The waiter brought the bill and I signed; two coffees, fifty dollars. When he'd left, I said, "That case is still open? It's been a while. Do you really think you'll ever know who killed Richard Ormsby?"

"I already know who killed him," she said bluntly. "I even know why he was killed. What I don't know is how the hell I'm going to prove it."

17

Marian Larch

Ivan Malecki sat on his spine and scowled at his feet stretched out in front of him. "I don't believe it. There's no way that can be right."

I wanted to grab him by the shoulders and give him a good shake. It had taken me the better part of an afternoon to convince Captain Michaels, and now Ivan was being stubborn.

The Captain shifted his considerable weight in the big chair behind his desk. "I'm not totally convinced myself,

Malecki," he said. "But if she's wrong, there's no harm done.
If she's right, we damn well better follow through."

"I just don't believe it," Ivan said mulishly.

One more try. "Look, Ivan," I said, "can you suspend
disbelief about one basic matter, for just a moment? Every
time we investigate a killing, we go in assuming the victim is
dead for a reason that directly involves him. Either he's been
killed in the heat of passion, or he's a threat to somebody, or
he stands between the killer and something the killer wants,
or—"

"Yeah, yeah. This isn't my rookie year, you know."

"Okay, then, can you just forget about all that? Assume,
just for a minute, a man can be killed for reasons that have
nothing at all to do with him personally—all right?"

"Sure." Ivan sat up straight. "Jesus, Marian, you think
I'm dumb or something? The gangs go joyriding and take pot
shots at whoever happens to be standing on the sidewalk.
Shooting up the neighborhood just for the hell of it. Those
people aren't killed for any *personal* reason. Matter of chance."

"Then assume for just a moment that Richard Ormsby
too was killed for reasons that had nothing to do with him."

"Crap."

"Maybe it's not, Malecki," Captain Michaels helped out.
"Scotland Yard turned up a few enemies who wouldn't mind
seeing Ormsby out of the way, but every one of them was in
England at the time he was shot. Ormsby was in New York
only four days before he was killed. Yeah, I know—it's
possible something happened in those four days that made it
necessary for somebody to get rid of him. But it's not very
damn *likely*, is it? Well, is it?"

"No," Ivan muttered reluctantly.

"And we haven't turned up any reason why anyone over
here would want him dead except Dr. Fiona Benedict and
her damned book, and we know she didn't do it because she
was in the lock-up at the time of the killing. So what's left?
Do we tell the Commissioner and the British Ambassador
and maybe even the Queen herself, gee, we're sorry, we can't
find out who killed the visiting celeb so we're going to go
work on other cases now, goodbye and thank you? Look,
Malecki, he didn't get it for any of the usual reasons, so now
we gotta take a look at the *un*usual reasons. And Larch here
has come up with a lulu."

"It's downright weird, Marian," Ivan grumbled.

I couldn't argue with that. "The whole case has been weird. Starting with Fiona Benedict's attempt at murder. The police case against her was weak right from the start. Both of you had trouble believing Fiona was guilty of attempted murder—a lot of people felt that way. But she did try to kill Ormsby. She tried hard. Even though she didn't succeed, her *trying* to kill him is germane to what happened later."

"You know what happened later?" Ivan cocked an eyebrow at me.

"I think so. If you're willing to assume for a moment that Richard Ormsby was killed for reasons that had nothing to do with him personally—then take a look at the aftermath of the shooting. Three things happened. First, there was a big surge in the sales of *Lord Look-on*. Second, the collapse of Ormsby's planned publicity tour caused a lot of trouble for a lot of people. But it's the third thing that's important."

Ivan nodded impatiently. "Fiona Benedict was released from custody. So?"

"So, who benefits from her being out of jail? Who, aside from Fiona Benedict herself, is the one person on this earth *who is better off* because Fiona was released? What did she do when she got out?"

"She went home."

"She went home, to Washburn, Ohio. To her son Rudy's papers. She is the only person alive who was in any way likely to go through those boxes and boxes of papers and read everything in them. We already had our go at them and didn't find anything—I spent several days there reading just the business papers, and they were only a small fraction of the whole lot. No, Fiona's the only one who could be counted on to look at *all* of Rudy's papers, to check every folder. And she did, coming up with the bit of evidence that gave us both a murderer and a blackmailer. You see? That's what made Fiona Benedict so important. *That's* why Richard Ormsby was killed—so we'd have to let Fiona go. She'd be no help locked up in a cell. Ormsby's killer wanted that evidence found. He wanted it so much he was willing to kill to make it happen."

Ivan whistled tunelessly a moment and then said, "You mean one of the Cameron family."

"No, no, Ivan—it wasn't the murderer he wanted caught. He didn't give a hoot about Ted Cameron."

"The blackmailer then? Nathan Pinking?"

"Right. And who is it who's benefited from Pinking's arrest?"

The name had been hanging in the air for a long time; it was Captain Michaels who finally spoke it aloud. "Leonard Zoff." He mulled it over. "Far as we can tell, Zoff didn't even know Ormsby. And he sure as hell didn't move in the same circles as Fiona Benedict. He knew Rudy, but he'd never had any reason to meet Rudy's mother. So that means Zoff killed a man he didn't know, in order to get a woman he didn't know released from jail. If Larch is right."

"It's *weird*," Ivan pronounced emphatically.

Agreed. "Leonard Zoff was losing his battle with Nathan Pinking," I said. "Pinking was successful and showed every sign of becoming more so. Zoff was keeping his head above water, he was doing all right—but he wasn't hitting it as big as his old enemy was. He had to sit there and watch Pinking pulling away from him. That must have hurt bad. Those two men lived for the pleasure of outdoing each other. Anyway, Zoff had one ace in the hole. Kelly Ingram. Kelly was on her way to stardom, and that's all Leonard needed—one really big star."

"She'll make it," Ivan said pontifically. "She's there now as far as I'm concerned."

"But then Pinking put her under personal contract when he gave her her role in *LeFever*," I went on. "He made it a condition of signing, Kelly told me. Pinking was helping with the star build-up, he cast her in a TV movie, he was going ahead with a new series in which Kelly would star. The bigger a success Kelly became, the more money that meant for Pinking—because he'd see to it that she appeared in nothing but Nathan Pinking productions. And Leonard Zoff had to stand there and watch his one chance at Easy Street gradually being taken over by the man he hated most in the world. No wonder he was moved to action."

"Wait a minute, wait a minute," Ivan said. "How would Zoff know there was any evidence that'd lead to Pinking's arrest? How'd he know about those photos? And where they were? He couldn't have known about them unless Rudy Benedict told him. Are you saying Rudy told Zoff what he was doing?"

Captain Michaels fielded that one. "No, Rudy didn't tell Zoff anything. But remember what Ted Cameron said—that Pinking had speculated Rudy might have kept back a couple of photographs of the incriminating painting? Then Cameron said Pinking decided the photos would pose no threat once Rudy's mother had all his papers shipped to Ohio. Even if she did find them, she wouldn't know what they meant. What Pinking didn't know was that Marian here had already shown a lotta curiosity about that missing painting, and Fiona Benedict remembered that and mailed her the photos."

Ivan objected. "But all that talk about the photos, that was between Cameron and Pinking. Zoff wasn't there. How would he know what—oh. The bug."

Michaels nodded. "Zoff would have had Pinking's office bugged just to keep tabs on what his enemy was up to. The blackmail scheme was a bonus he hadn't counted on."

I said, "I had a talk with Leonard Zoff not too long after Rudy Benedict was murdered, and I remember he expressed a kind of mild outrage that we weren't going through everything of Rudy's looking for clues—every file folder, every envelope. At the time I thought it was just the concern of a man who wanted to see a friend's killer caught. But of course that's what I was meant to think. I ended up reassuring him that Rudy's mother was going to check all the papers and she'd let us know if she found something. So Leonard Zoff *knew* Fiona Benedict was going through those files. He knew because I told him."

"So all he had to do was sit back and wait," Captain Michaels said. "Zoff had known Rudy Benedict a long time, and everyone acquainted with the writer knew what a cautious, self-protective man he was. Zoff was sure those photos would be there, and sooner or later Fiona Benedict would find them. She might not know what they meant, but she wouldn't just pass over them the way Pinking thought she would. Zoff knew Dr. Benedict was checking *for the police* as well as for herself—Pinking didn't know that."

"But it didn't work," Ivan said, slowly coming to accept the theory. "Instead of staying in Ohio and reading her son's papers, Dr. Benedict came here and tried to shoot Richard Ormsby. She really did try?"

"She really did try," I nodded. "Ormsby hit her where it hurts. She must have thought she was protecting herself."

"Like mother, like son," Captain Michaels grunted.

True. Those two had been more alike than either one of them had ever realized. "I'd like to know when Zoff first began to understand why Rudy had been killed. Would

Cameron and Pinking have actually used words like *blackmail* and *murder* while they were working out their private financial arrangements? I can't see that. Zoff must have pieced it together slowly over a number of overheard conversations. Captain, do you remember the missing file folder?"

"What missing file folder?"

"The first time I talked to Nathan Pinking, I asked to see the file he kept on Rudy Benedict and it was missing—"

"Yeah, I remember."

"Well, it's back in the filing cabinet now. I went to Leonard Zoff's new office after he took over the production company—Nathan Pinking's old office. Nothing out of the ordinary in Rudy Benedict's folder. Same sort of thing I read in Rudy's business files in Ohio—in fact, I think I remember a few of the letters. But the file is back."

"So why was it missing in the first place?" Ivan asked.

"Zoff probably filched it when he first began to puzzle out what was going on. He may have been looking for evidence that would tie Pinking to the blackmail of Rudy's murderer. I think it's more likely he was just trying to find out whatever he could about the whole Benedict-Cameron-Pinking situation. Zoff *might* have found something in Benedict's folder, but I doubt it. He probably just returned the file intact after he moved into Pinking's office."

"Or the secretary had simply misfiled it all along," Captain Michaels muttered.

"Mimsy?" Ivan grinned.

"I think it was still Tansy at that point," I said, grinning back. "But even without any help from that particular file folder, Leonard Zoff was sitting pretty there for a while. All his problems were going to solve themselves. His enemy had committed a felony and evidence of a kind was just waiting to be uncovered in a dead man's papers in Ohio. Zoff wouldn't have to lift a finger—it'd all take care of itself. Once Pinking was out of the way, Zoff would have everything—the production company, the agency . . . and Kelly Ingram."

"Then one day it all blows up in his face," Captain Michaels said. "The woman he'd counted on to find the evidence for him—she's not sitting quietly in Ohio reading through Rudy's papers at all. She's sitting in a New York detention cell on a charge of attempted murder. Think how he must have felt. To see *everything* he wanted within his grasp—majority ownership of both businesses, a new star in his pocket, the defeat of his enemy. And then to watch it all start to slip away—and why? Because of a book some Englishman wrote. He must have had trouble believing what was happening to him."

"So he wasn't going to be able to sit back and watch it all work out nicely for him," Ivan nodded. "He was going to have to do something to get Fiona Benedict out of jail and back to Ohio. What could he do? Hope her attorney could get her off? Possible, but chancy. And time-consuming. Maybe he felt he was running out of time?"

"Maybe," the Captain nodded. "But whatever he was thinking, he ended up convincing himself that his best chance was to make us believe Fiona Benedict wasn't guilty of trying to kill anybody. And the best way to do that was to go ahead and commit the crime she'd been charged with trying to commit. So he was careful to duplicate her method—the TV studio, the gun." Captain Michaels paused. "Man lives over half a century without resorting to criminal acts to survive and then suddenly turns to the worst crime of them all— pretty good sign of how much he wants a thing."

Ivan stood up and stretched. "Well, it's a good story. What are you going to do with it, sell it to the movies? There's not one bit of evidence that that's the way it happened."

Captain Michaels grinned broadly. "That's where you come in."

"Me?"

"You're going to blackmail Leonard Zoff."

Ivan sat down again, rather quickly. "Blackmail. Now there's an original thought."

"That's the point," Michaels said. "The idea's already planted. Zoff has to be superconscious of the fact that blackmail can follow murder. And the shooting did happen in a public place, remember—he can't be *sure* nobody saw him."

"Jesus, he was hiding in a stairwell behind a door! Only his arm and the hand holding the gun would have been visible. Nobody can identify him from that."

"Is he going to take a chance on that? Would you? Besides, he wasn't firing blind. At least one eye had to be exposed—part of his face must have been showing. For two seconds, maybe, but it had to be showing. There was a moment there when someone could have seen him. Nobody did, but he doesn't know that. And that's where we get 'im."

"Okay, he might go for it," Ivan agreed. "But why me?"

"Because he doesn't know you, Ivan," I said. "He'll be wary of you. If he pays, then that's an admission of guilt. We've got him."

"Yeah, well, this guy's a killer, you know," Ivan scowled. "He might just think of some other little solution, if you know what I mean."

"Don't worry, you'll go in armed and we'll be only seconds away," the Captain said. "We're going to set this up ver-y carefully."

"Yeah, well, about that," Ivan said uneasily. "Isn't that entrapment?"

"Nope," Captain Michaels said happily. "Had a long confab with Rothstein in the DA's office. He says only a set-up that leads to the commission of a crime, a new crime, is entrapment. But our set-up will reveal an old crime, one that's already been committed. We aren't going to lead Zoff into doing anything illegal—*paying* blackmail isn't a crime. So we're okay there."

Ivan had one last objection. "All right, so we're covered on the entrapment angle. But it's been nearly two months now since Richard Ormsby was killed. Why'd I wait so long to start my squeeze?"

"You had to find out who the man with the gun was first," I said. "What you saw at the Ormsby shooting was a face, an unfamiliar face with no name attached to it. But you're good at remembering faces. So you started working backwards from Richard Ormsby. He led you to Fiona Benedict, who led you to Rudy Benedict, who led you to the wonderful world of television and all the magic people in it—especially those gathered under the Nathan Pinking umbrella. So one by one you started checking them out until you came to the face behind the stairwell door. Then you had your man."

"Yeah." Ivan frowned. "An eyewitness who didn't come forward at the time. I suppose it's possible. But will Zoff buy it?"

"He can't afford not to," Captain Michaels said shortly. "If he killed Ormsby, he'll at least agree to a meeting."

Ivan accepted his fate with a big sigh. "Okay. If he tells me to go to hell, we won't be any worse off than we are now."

I said, "And if he doesn't tell you to go to hell, then we can wrap this thing up and go home and *forget* about it. Thank God."

The men grunted agreement.

18
Kelly Ingram

It was that pink dress that finally did it. I went for a costume fitting and they gave me this clingy *pink* thing to wear and I hit the ceiling.

I detest pink. I loathe pink. I hate it so much I embarrass myself, wasting a good strong emotion like hatred on a *color*. The costumers were a brother-sister team called Lesley, they both answered to the same name, no fooling. When we first started *LeFever* I'd made it clear I didn't want to wear pink, ever, and Nathan Pinking (*Pink*ing) had backed me up. But now we had a new producer and Lesley was or were testing the waters, so to speak, indulging in a little muscle-flexing, just what I needed.

"Look," I told them, "I'm not going to start off this way. We both know the game you're playing, and I'm just not going to go along. When you have something I can wear, call me. I'm not even going to try this pink thing on."

"But Kellylove," one word, "it's perfect for you," Leslie-male cooed. "It's so y—"

"Call me when you have something I can wear," I repeated and walked away. I heard him muttering to his sister but the only words I could make out were *prima donna*.

Things had not been going at all well. Nathan Pinking was a blackmailer and a rat and a skunk, but he was also a good organizer. Nathan had delegated a lot of his responsibility, but Leonard Zoff was trying to handle most of the detail work himself and it was too much for him. Once we got rolling he'd probably get the hang of it a little better, but right now things were a bit rough. We were getting ready to start taping the new season of *LeFever*, and the very first script gave me a sour picture of what I had to look forward to.

I had only three scenes, and I was to play all three of them in a horizontal position. On a bed, on a towel beside a pool, and on a sofa. I'd convinced Leonard the sofa scene could be just as suggestive if I played it sitting up, but now I had that damned pink dress of Lesley's to worry about.

But what was really bothering me was my new series. The pilot movie was going to show in December; its title was *On Call*—subtle, huh? If NBC bought it, they were going to want the series to keep on with the kind of thing the movie showed. Nathan Pinking had used the *LeFever* writers, and those guys didn't strain themselves any. They'd written the same kind of story they wrote for *LeFever,* except they just switched the male and female roles—as if a woman were just some sort of reverse man. *I* had the adventures, and they'd hired some good-looking actor to gaze adoringly at *me* while I was involved in all those preposterous goings-on. They'd gone at the whole thing wrong, just taking the easy way. It was my series and I wanted it to be right—but I hadn't really been able to make Leonard understand that.

I'd bugged him mercilessly until he showed me the story treatments Nathan Pinking had assembled; Leonard hadn't yet decided which ones to commission writers to turn into shooting scripts. One of them contained a flashback sequence that was supposed to show me just entering college.

"You get to be a student, darling," Leonard had said loudly. "Won't that be fun? Pot and protest and free love— just the thing to win the college crowd. Maybe even a classroom scene. Don't you worry none, Kel, you can still pass for eighteen, nineteen, whatever the shit it is. We won't hafta do any close-ups—you just squeeze that fabulous butt of yours into a pair of tight jeans and we got it made."

Suddenly I'd had enough. I had played the game; I'd let my thirtieth birthday pass without mention. My reason was financial as well as personal: I belonged to a profession where youth was money in the bank. In television, a woman depreciates in value as she grows older, like a car. Men don't; just the women. So maybe there was something wrong with the profession itself, if it made you feel your right and proper age was something to be ashamed of. And there was Leonard Zoff, glibly assuming I'd be delighted at the chance to play a teenager again.

"I'm thirty years old, Leonard," I said. "My schoolgirl

days are over. I think we can find a better story than this one, don't you?"

He'd argued a little, out of principle; I don't think he really cared one way or the other. But I'd made up my mind right then, I was through pretending to be younger than I was.

That was earlier in the week. But from star of my own (to be) series I'd quickly been bumped back down to mere appurtenance, appendage, accessory, attachment, adjunct to the hero, I did look that one up. My *LeFever* character was more a piece-of-tail role than ever, and the vibes I got from Leonard were telling me my new series would be just more of the same. *Nothing* was right. In short, I was spoiling for a fight. I had to have it out with Leonard.

So on pink-dress day I went charging into his outer office, breathing fire (I hoped). Mimsy looked up from her desk, not at all alarmed. "Is he in?" I growled in my best tough-broad voice.

"He's out looking over location sites," she purred at me. "Anything I can do?"

"Damn it, Mimsy, don't be so friendly—can't you see I'm mad?"

"And you want to stay mad," she nodded understandingly. "Would it help to yell at me a little?"

"Naw," I said, starting to cool down. "Leonard's got to talk to Lesley, for starters. Did he tell you where he was going?"

Mimsy's face took on tragic overtones that would have done Medea proud. "Sorry—he didn't. I asked him three times before he left, but he went out without telling me."

"Did he take his limo?"

She caught on immediately. "Of course—all I have to do is call the driver." She punched out a number on the phone.

Leonard never drove himself anywhere. He claimed New York traffic was the one thing in life he was truly afraid of. Mimsy spoke briefly into the phone and then hung up.

"Well?"

"The driver is on his way back to the garage. He said Mr. Zoff got out at the Eastside Airlines Terminal and told him he wouldn't be needing the car any more today."

"Eastside Terminal? He's not leaving town, is he?"

"No—and I don't think he's meeting anyone. He must just be looking for a shooting site."

One sure way to find out. I went down to the street and stopped a taxi. Rain was threatening and I didn't have an umbrella, but I didn't want to take the time to go back and get one. Leonard Zoff wasn't going to get away from *me*, he wasn't.

19

Marian Larch

"Again," Captain Michaels sniffled. He was catching a cold and his eyes were red and watery.

Ivan cleared his throat. "At the appointed time I proceed to the designated rendezvous point—"

"Jesus, Malecki, you're not in training class, talk English." The Captain's cold was making him cranky.

Ivan managed to keep a straight face and started over. "At five minutes to eleven I go into the Eastside Airlines Terminal. I wait until the last stragglers and latecomers have gotten on the airport buses departing at eleven. Then I approach Zoff."

Two plainclothes officers would already be inside, one of them behind the counter.

"I tell Zoff I'm the one he's waiting for," Ivan went on. "If he wants a name, I tell him Ivan. If he wants to go someplace else to talk, I tell him absolutely not."

We'd picked the Eastside Terminal because first of all it had to be a public place. No blackmailer who intended to go on living would agree to a private meeting with his victim. The Eastside Terminal had people coming and going, but there were never huge crowds of people there who stayed put for any length of time.

"What if he insists?" I asked Ivan. "What if he says he won't talk to you in a place where there's a chance you'll be overheard?"

"Then I remind him he's in no position to insist on anything. I tell him my partner is watching from outside, and if Zoff has brought a weapon to force me to go with him, my partner calls the police the minute she sees us walk out the door."

The "partner" had been Ivan's idea. He'd thrown himself into the role with gusto, trying to think the way a blackmailer would think—a Method cop. He said the only sure way a blackmailer had of protecting himself was to convince the victim that if anything happened to him, the blackmailer, the victim's guilty secret would immediately be revealed to the world. And the best way of doing that, Ivan said, was not the conventional letter-with-a-lawyer gambit; that's what Nathan Pinking had done and Ted Cameron was already figuring a way around that when things came to a head. No, the best way was to produce a partner, one whose existence was established beyond all shadow of a doubt but whose identity was withheld from the mark.

Since the initial contact was to be made by telephone, we decided the caller should be a woman. Otherwise Zoff might think he was dealing with one man pretending to be two, disguising his voice over the phone. We had a police-woman from Narcotics make the call; Zoff might have recognized my voice. She'd told him she certainly was glad to get hold of him, because she'd spent the *longest* time trying to track him down—ever since the day Richard Ormsby had been killed, in fact.

Zoff had bluffed at first, pretending not to know what she was talking about. Stalling for time. *But he had agreed to a meeting.* An innocent man would have told her to stop bothering him or *he* would call the cops. But Leonard Zoff had instead asked her what she wanted. She'd named the time and place for the meeting, and told him to bring ten thousand dollars with him. Then she had informed him she herself would not be there, that all their dealings would be done through an intermediary, her partner. *All* their dealings, she'd stressed. We wanted Zoff to start thinking this was no one-time payoff, that he was on the hook for good. Push him a little.

Ivan, the ostensible intermediary, would be wired as well as armed. Captain Michaels and I would be in an unmarked car around the corner on Thirty-eighth Street, listening to every word that was said. We were there strictly as back-up. If everything went according to plan, we wouldn't move in until the money had actually changed hands. Ivan would make the arrest; the two police officers planted inside would witness the payoff and provide assistance if needed.

Captain Michaels took out a handkerchief and blew his nose. "Then what?"

Ivan said, "Then I ask him for the ten thousand. I tell him my partner and I aren't greedy, we just want enough to live on comfortably."

"And if he asks when's the next payment?"

"I tell him I'll let him know. But I don't bring it up if he doesn't."

I said, "What if he doesn't hand over the money right away and tries to bluff it out instead? What if he says it's only your partner's word against his?"

"I say I'll tell the police I was also present at the Ormsby shooting—that makes *two* eyewitnesses, exactly what the law requires for a positive identification. I'll tell Zoff our story will be that at the time we didn't want to get involved, we didn't know who the killer was anyway. But now that we do know— it's begun to bother us, we feel we should step forward and do our duty, all that stuff. I'll tell him the cops might not believe our reason for keeping quiet so long, but they're sure as hell going to be mighty polite to two people who can ID a killer for them."

"And if he asks who your partner is?"

"I laugh in his face."

"If he doesn't bring the money at all?" Captain Michaels coughed.

"I say I'll give him one more chance. Now that he knows we're serious, he either produces the money or he goes to jail."

"New time and place for the payoff?"

"Noon tomorrow. The fountain at Lincoln Center."

"What if he claims he can't get his hands on ten thousand in twenty-four hours?"

"I laugh in his face again. Then I quote the balance as of this morning in his Chase Manhattan account."

"That should rattle him a little," Captain Michaels grinned. "Have we thought of everything?" Pause. "Yeah, I think so. Okay—any questions?"

I couldn't think of any. Ivan shook his head.

"All right then, let's go," the Captain said. "If we're lucky we can wrap this up before the weather breaks."

20

Kelly Ingram

It was almost eleven o'clock when the taxi let me out at
the Eastside Airlines Terminal. The rain was still holding off,
thank goodness. The terminal isn't very large; I pushed the
door open and spotted Leonard Zoff right off. He was standing back from the counter, a raincoat over his arm, scanning
the faces of the other people there—maybe Mimsy was
wrong, maybe he was meeting someone after all. He seemed
nervous. I walked up and planted myself in front of him.

He was clearly underjoyed to see me. First he gave a
little start, then his features settled into a kind of hounddog
sadness. "It's you," he said dully.

I agreed it was. "Leonard, we've got to talk."

He nodded. "But not here. Too public."

Wasn't he waiting for someone? I looked around. "Don't
you want—"

"No, no, this is no good," he muttered, suddenly in a
great hurry to get out of there. He grabbed my elbow and
steered me out the door. "There's a park about a block from
here—if we don't get rained on."

But we never got there. Two young couples, two *very*
young couples (should have been in school) recognized me
and proceeded to raise a minor fuss, how nice. I was quite
willing to stop for a moment and play the famous television star graciously acknowledging her admiring public,
but Leonard had me bundled into a taxi before I quite
knew what was happening. He seemed angry for some
reason.

He gave the driver the name of a pseudo-Victorian
tavern uptown. When we got there, Leonard tossed his
raincoat on to the seat of the booth and gestured impatiently

to the waiter. It wasn't eleven-thirty yet, but he ordered himself a liquid lunch. I asked for coffee.

When he'd had his first long swallow, he seemed to brace himself. "All right, spell it out."

I said, "First of all, Leonard, we need a basic understanding about where we're going from here. Then we can work out the details as we go along."

He nodded wearily. "Yeah, the details. I can hardly wait. Starting with the money, no doubt."

The budget, he meant. "Well, there's always room for more money. But I meant other things—the *kind* of show we're going to be turning out, primarily."

His face grew longer and sadder than ever. "I was afraid of that. You and your partner won't settle for anything less than total control, will you?"

"My partner?"

"I go through all that shit and come this far only to have a couple of dumb broads take it all away from me, is that it? Who's your partner, Kelly?"

I was stunned. "Are you actually calling me a *dumb broad*?"

"Yeah, I gotta be careful what I call you now, don't I?" he sneered. Then he seemed to think better of it and shook his head and said, "Don't mind me, darling, I'm a bit shook, y'understand. This is the last thing in the world I expected. I don't *deserve* this. Kelly—I'm not like Nathan Shithead, I don't enjoy hurting people."

What on earth? "I know that, Leonard. I never thought you did."

"But it didn't stop you, did it? You're just as grabby as all the rest of them. You see an opportunity, you don't give a shit who it is you walk over."

I was beginning to get mad. "Now look, Leonard, there's something you better understand right now. You simply cannot talk to me any way you please. From now on you will speak to me with courtesy and respect or you will not speak to me at all." Since I had absolutely no way whatsoever of backing up that ultimatum, I was pleasantly surprised to see him pale. "Do you understand me?"

"I understand," he whispered.

Now *that* got to me. The only time in my life I'd ever before heard Leonard Zoff whisper was when he had laryngitis. Something was greatly out of whack. "Are you all right?" I asked him. "Do you feel up to talking now?"

"I'm all right—let's get it settled." He waved a hand dismissively. "It's just that *you* are about the last person I'd have thought . . . Kelly, don't you understand? I did it for you as much as for me. Nathan Shithead would have ruined you, he'd have milked you for all he could get for three, four more years and then *phlooey!* Out in the garbage with Kelly baby. He don't care what happens to nobody. Me, I wouldn't do that to you. I'da nursed you along, paced things right so it would go on as long as you wanted it to go on. I had big plans for you, Kelly!"

This was definitely turning into one of the weirdest conversations I'd ever had. "What do you mean *had*, Leonard? You're still going to do all those wonderful things for me."

"Not if I can't call the shots. How can I? You breathin' down my neck all the time?"

"Breathing down—Leonard, you don't even know what I want yet!"

"Oh, I have a fair idea! Unless you've changed your mind," he said, his voice dripping sarcasm. "Maybe you don't want the money now?"

I slapped at the table in frustration. "I *always* want money, Leonard—who doesn't? I keep telling you that's not the main thing, but since that's what seems to be bothering you—all right, start with money. I don't want my new series to be the quickie, shoddy thing *LeFever* is. And that takes money. Money for good scripts, money for enough time to do the job right—"

"And money for Kelly?" His lip raised in a sneer.

"Why not?" I said hotly. He'd been sneering at me ever since we came in. "Leonard, face it—you're just going to have to shell out. And you might as well start right now."

He stared at me with open contempt on his face. Then he reached to his inside jacket pocket and pulled out an envelope that he dropped on the table. "Count it if you want. It's all there."

Now what? With a sigh I opened the envelope and counted ten one-thousand dollar bills inside. It was an ordinary white envelope, about nine inches wide, no imprinting. I ran the gummed flap across my tongue and sealed the envelope. I sat without speaking for a moment, just holding it in my hand. "Leonard. I am sitting here quietly, making no fuss, trying to understand why you just handed me *ten thousand dollars*."

"Keep your voice down," he muttered. "Because that's how much your partner said bring, that's why. Don't ask for more because I don't have it."

"There's that word *partner* again. What partner, Leonard? What are you talking about?"

He was angry: "What are you trying to pull? Your unidentified sweet-voiced friend on the phone, the one who set up our meeting in the Eastside Terminal. Who'd you think?"

"I still don't know what you're talking about. What meeting? We didn't have a date to meet in the Terminal."

You know how that comes-the-dawn looks spreads so-o-o-o-o slowly over somebody's face? Well, that's what happened to Leonard just then. At least *he* understood something; I was still floundering. Abruptly he shook his head. "No, wait a minute—you didn't just happen to run into me there. You came looking for me, don't tell me you didn't."

"I'm not telling you I didn't."

"So how'd you know where I was?"

"Mimsy called your driver. He said he let you out at the Eastside Terminal."

"Oh my God," he said slowly. "My God. That simple. It *wasn't* you. I shoulda known it wouldn't be you." He gave himself a sort of little shake and reached out and took the envelope back from me. "This was a mistake, Kelly. I thought—well, never mind what I thought. The whole thing was a mistake. Just forget about it, will you?"

But I'd had enough time for a few things to filter through. The symptoms were familiar enough, God knows; I'd seen them once before. "You said the person on the phone who set up the meeting was 'unidentified'—right? Does that mean just anybody can call you up and tell you to take ten thousand dollars to the Eastside Terminal and you'll do it? I never knew you were that free and easy with your money."

"I said forget it, Kelly."

"You're being blackmailed, aren't you, Leonard?" I asked as gently as I could.

He didn't answer; a tic had developed under his left eye.

"Don't pay," I urged him. "I've seen what it can do to a man. Whatever it is your blackmailer has on you, it can't be worse than what's going to happen to you once you give in and start paying. Don't pay."

He laughed humorlessly and put the envelope back in his pocket. "Gee, thanks for the swell advice, Kelly." The tic grew stronger.

"Don't be so quick to dismiss it. You don't know what you're letting yourself in for. Besides, the only blackmail victim I've ever known turned out to be a killer, and you certainly haven't done anything like that." Which of course started me wondering what he *had* done. *I did it as much for you as for me*, he said. What on earth could that be?

Leonard leaned forward and said in that strange new whispery voice of his, "I have this terrible feeling about you, darling. I'm afraid you're turning into a problem."

"Because I made you miss your, er, appointment? You don't know who your blackmailer is, do you? You thought it was me. I. How could you, Leonard? Me, a blackmailer?"

"Yes," he said heavily. "It was a bad mistake."

"Are you worried about what he'll do? Or she. They were probably there all the time and saw what happened. You'll hear from them again."

"No doubt." The tic under his eye seemed to be slowing down.

I did it as much for you as for me. What blackmail-inviting thing could he have done that would have benefited both of us? The only thing that had happened lately that was sheer good news for Leonard was Nathan Pinking's getting himself arrested. From that one event all of Leonard's subsequent blessings flowed. And Leonard was so convinced Nathan Pinking would have ruined my career that his take-over of Nathan's business would have been good for me too, to his way of thinking. (And he may have been right.)

But Leonard didn't have anything to do with Nathan's arrest. What did he *do* that was as much for me as for himself? Nathan was arrested because that horrible Fiona Benedict had found some pictures in Rudy's papers that led Marian Larch to Ted, and Ted blew the whistle on Nathan. None of it would have happened without those photographs Rudy's mother found. And she wouldn't have found them, she would still be sitting here in New York waiting for her trial if somebody hadn't come along and . . . oh. *Oh*.

Oh, goodnessgracioussakesalivemercymeoh.

That was it. That was what he'd done. That had to be it. "You killed Richard Ormsby," I said stupidly, my own voice little more than a whisper.

Leonard gave a little nod—not in confirmation of what I'd just accused him of, it was more like a little I-was-right nod to himself. As if he'd known all along I'd get there eventually if he just waited long enough.

I put both hands on the table, palms down, helping to

steady the room which had suddenly begun to move in a seasick-making kind of way. If he hadn't mistaken me for the blackmailer... I would never have... and he actually... "And you had the gall to say you did it as much for me as for yourself! Leonard, have you lost your mind?"

"It was *entirely* for you, you stupid bitch!" he hissed. "You think I was just gonna stand there and let Nathan Shithead take you away from me? You could have been a big star, Kelly. A *great* star."

I didn't much like that *could have been*. "Don't you go blaming me, you bastard," I hissed back. "You killed one man so you could take another man's business away from him and now you're telling me it was all for *me*? It was all for Leonard Zoff, that's who it was for! Stop kidding yourself."

"Look under the table."

"What?"

"Under the table, look under the table." He jerked his head angrily.

So I looked under the table. What I saw was a gun in Leonard's hand, pointing at me. A gun? Pointing at me?

A *gun*. Pointing at *me*.

I sat back up and said the first thing that came into my head. "All right, all right, I'll *wear* the pink dress!"

He stared at me. "Darling, sometimes you just don't make good sense. Now listen. This is what we're going to do. Keep your hands on the table where I can see them—that's right. Now I'm going to signal the waiter. When he gets here, you are going to pay the bill. You got money? Good. Then we're going to get up and walk out of here and get in a cab."

"And nobody will even notice that you're holding a gun on me?"

"It'll be under my raincoat—nobody'll see it."

I tried to put a brave face on it. "What are you going to do if I make a break for it, Leonard? Shoot me in front of all these people?"

"Richard Ormsby was surrounded by a whole buncha people," he said pointedly.

Oh yeah. I forgot about that.

So we did it the way he said. The waiter brought the bill, and I paid while Leonard *kept me covered* under the table, good heavens. I left a tip on the little tray that was twice the amount of the bill, hoping to catch the waiter's attention. He didn't even deign to look at me.

"Don't try anything," Leonard warned me as we got up to leave.

My problem was I couldn't convince myself I was in real danger. Sure, I understood the man was a murderer and I was a threat to his safety. But balanced against that was the fact that this was *Leonard*. I was having trouble believing Leonard would hurt me. Not because I was a magic princess that bad things never happened to, but because I represented a long-term investment that was just beginning to pay off. Besides, I'd always looked on Leonard as something of a clown; it was hard recasting him as a killer. He was just Leonard, the man who'd been guiding my career for years. The man whose professional advice I'd followed to pretty good results. The man who . . . had sent me toilet paper as a way of telling me what he really thought of me. Ah yes, *that* man.

The rain had started while we were inside and it was coming down hard now. Which meant, of course, there wasn't a taxi to be had. There was no canopy or overhang to stand under and I didn't have an umbrella, so I was soaked to the skin within seconds. I must have looked ridiculous, standing there on the curb sopping wet. But I couldn't have looked as silly as Leonard, who was equally wet while carrying a perfectly good raincoat over his right arm and hand, his gun hand, oh dear.

Finally a cab stopped. The driver glared at us as we climbed in; he'd have to wipe the seat off. I was surprised to hear Leonard give the address of the *LeFever* soundstage and offices. A weight lifted: that place was just crawling with people.

We were separated from the driver by one of those thick plastic shields; he wouldn't hear us if we talked low. "Leonard," I whispered, "what are you going to do?"

"Don't talk."

"You aren't really going to shoot me, are you?"

"*Quiet*," he said.

"I'm whispering," I whispered. "Are you really going to *shoot* me?" I decided to change the emphasis. "Are you really going to shoot *me*? It isn't necessary, you know. If my staying alive depends on keeping my mouth shut, you really think I'm going to talk?"

"Darling, you know I can't risk that."

"What risk? I will gladly become your *accomplice* before I'll do anything to get myself hurt. Besides, I can't prove a thing—Leonard, you know I can't prove anything. You're safe."

"You don't understand. I can't even afford the accusation—you could start the police investigating me just by hollering." He looked at me with something like regret on his face. "Oh Kelly, Kelly! Where'm I gonna find another face and bod like yours? Why didn't you just mind your own business?"

I'd thought I was minding my own business. "I'll say it again. I'll never do anything to get myself hurt. Come on, Leonard—do I strike you as the suicidal type?"

He didn't say anything to that, so I pressed my advantage. "Leonard, I can help you pay off these blackmailers if that's the way you're determined to handle it. I won't say a word to anyone, I certainly won't talk to the police. I'll even stop spleaking to Marian Larch if that'll make you feel better."

"Spleaking?"

"Spleaking, speaking, you know what I mean." Was I nervous? "Leonard—how about it? A kind of partnership?"

"Darling, we both know the minute I let you out of my sight, you'd go screaming to that homely police detective friend of yours."

"Look in the mirror, buster," I snapped, angry for the wrong reason. He just laughed. I think he was beginning to enjoy the situation, once he'd made up his mind I had to go.

Speaking of mirrors. I half-turned my back to him and started mugging, I mean I was making these *terrible* faces, hoping the driver would see me in the rear-view mirror. But no, *that* one kept his eyes on the oncoming traffic. He didn't care what was going on in the back seat.

Just as we got out of the cab Leonard pressed the gun into my side and said, low, "Remember, Kelly, I'll shoot you in front of a witness if I have to. Then I'll shoot the witness."

So we ran through the rain into the building and I said *hello-isn't-this-awful-yes-we-got-caught-in-it* to the guy who ran the newsstand in the small lobby. I turned automatically toward the elevators but Leonard stopped me.

"Back here," he said.

The offices and some of the workrooms were upstairs, but the soundstage holding the *LeFever* sets was on the ground level. It suddenly hit me what he was planning and *then* I believed I was in danger. I had to know the place before it became real.

The *LeFever* sets had been repaired and repainted and refurbished and re-whatever else they needed, and Mimsy had distributed a memo (signed by Leonard F. Zoff) threatening everything short of dismemberment to anyone foolhardy enough to venture on to the sets before shooting actually started. That was to be the following Monday. This was Thursday, naturally; disasters always come on Thursdays. He could shoot me and leave me on the set and nobody would find me for four days. Didn't have to worry about an alibi that way, I guess.

My body would be lying there for four days. Four whole days.

"Leonard," I said, "I'll *smell*."

"What?"

"You leave me lying on the set until Monday, I'm going to stink to high heaven by the time they find me."

He stopped walking and looked at me with a kind of awe. "Kelly, I don't know of another single person who'd think of that at a time like this."

"Hell, lots of people would. You'd think of it yourself. Come on, Leonard—you wouldn't want to be found like that, you know you wouldn't. Figure out some other way."

He just shook his head in amazement and gestured me to go on. He unlocked the outside door to the soundstage and switched on the work lights. These gave barely enough illumination to keep you from tripping over things, and not always then. I shivered; we were both still dripping wet. Leonard put a hand on my shoulder to stop me while he thought about where he wanted to go.

Karate? Kung fu? Aikido? I didn't know any of that stuff. And I couldn't just out-muscle him. *And* I hadn't had any notable success in talking him into or out of anything. About the only thing left I could think of was divine intervention. A lightning bolt to burn him up while missing me altogether. The earth opening up and swallowing him while miraculously leaving me untouched. Any old ordinary Act of God would do. The more scared I am, the weaker the joke.

LeFever had only four permanent sets—LeFever's office, his apartment, a room in a police precinct station, and a plain corridor that changed its fictional location every week. In addition, one or two temporary sets might be needed; one for a gym had been built for the first episode. All the sets were crowded close together; space was at a premium. Leonard took me to the new gym set—because it was the farthest from the outside door?

Speaking of which—it opened! We both heard it; Leonard slapped his free hand over my mouth and pulled me down to the floor. We cowered there in the shadow and listened to a voice say, "Sumby leffa work lights awn."

I'd never heard anything so lovely in my life. It was wonderful beautiful terrific Nick Quinlan, and when a feminine murmur answered him, I knew what he was doing there. Showing her the *LeFever* sets, well, that was the excuse. Nick knew the sets would be deserted.

"This here's LeFever's bedroom," he said.

Feminine murmur.

I felt Leonard tense. If Nick and his lady lingered on the bedroom set, Leonard and I would stay where we were. But if he showed her around the rest of the soundstage, we'd have to move. I was on my knees on the floor with Leonard holding me. I felt around on the floor with my left hand and sure enough it was wet, the floor I mean. Our dripping clothes had made a little puddle there. If Nick turned more lights on and came through and saw the wet floor then maybe—wait, hold it. That meant, first, Nick would have to *notice* the water. Then second, he'd have to *realize* it had no business being there. Then third, he'd have to *investigate*. Forget it.

Nobody was going to come riding to the rescue. If I got out of this, I was going to have to do it myself.

Male and female laughter mingled; they were staying in the bedroom. I'd never have another chance like this one—I was going to have to let them know I was there. I couldn't holler because Leonard's big hand was still covering my mouth, but I could struggle and kick out with my feet and make *some* noise.

So I did. In fact, I almost got away because I caught Leonard by surprise. I kept hitting backwards with my one free elbow and I kicked and squirmed and banged my feet against the floor and made as much racket as I could. Leonard stopped me by turning me over on my front on the floor and laying or lying on top of me, it felt like both. His hand never left my mouth.

"Hey, whazzat?" Nick said from the bedroom set. "Jeer sumpin?"

Feminine murmur.

"Sumby's here. Lezgo."

Rustle of clothing, a piece of furniture scraping on the floor, departing footsteps, silence.

Leonard was laughing as he let me up.

21

Marian Larch

"Judith H. Crist!" Captain Michaels yelled into my ear as Kelly Ingram pushed open the door to the Eastside Airlines Terminal. "What the hell is *she* doing here?"

The radio speaker attached to the tape recorder on the car seat between us came to life at about the same time. "Godalmighty, Kelly Ingram just walked in," came Ivan's voice. "What do I do now?" A sign of how rattled he was—Ivan could send but not receive.

"Want me to go take a look?" I said.

"Hell, no," the Captain barked, his cold making him hoarse. "Stay put, Ivan'll keep us informed."

"They're standing there talking to each other," Ivan's voice said. "He was surprised to see her but she wasn't surprised to see him—it was like she was looking for him. Captain, I hope you're thinking of something fast because people are starting to look at me funny for talking to my shirt."

I glanced at Michaels. His face was drawn into a scowl, giving no sign he'd heard. We waited.

"Captain, they're leaving," Ivan said. "You know what I think? I think he thinks Kelly's the blackmailer."

"Damn, damn, *damn*," Captain Michaels muttered. "Start the car."

I started the car. Kelly and Leonard Zoff came out together—but almost immediately they were stopped by some kids wanting Kelly's autograph. While that was going on, Ivan slipped out the Terminal door and climbed into the back seat of the car. Up ahead, Zoff had flagged a taxi and he and Kelly were getting in.

"What about the plants?" I asked. The police officers inside the Eastside Terminal building.

"Leave 'em," Captain Michaels growled. I pulled into the line of traffic behind the taxi.

The whole set-up was shot to hell, all because Kelly Ingram had put in an unscheduled appearance. The situation just might be salvageable—we could try to reschedule for the next day. That wasn't what was worrying me. What was worrying me was the thought of Kelly in the taxi with Leonard Zoff in those circumstances. "Ivan, you really think Zoff believes she's his blackmailer?"

"Looked that way to me. Remember, we just said 'partner' when we called him—we didn't say whether it was a man or a woman."

Captain Michaels sneezed.

"So what do we do, Captain?" Ivan wanted to know. "Just tail 'em, make sure she's safe?"

"Let's see where they go first," Michaels said.

They went to a chi-chi bar on East Seventy-first. I pulled into a no-parking zone and immediately had a fat man in an apron yelling at me until I flashed my badge.

Ivan did a quick check inside the bar. "There's no other entrance," he said, climbing back in the car. "And there's no good place inside for me to stand and watch. They might see me."

So we sat there without talking for a long time, watching. Finally I said, "If they separate when they come out, then we're okay—we can go ahead and set up another meet tomorrow. But if they stay together, we just might have a problem."

"How do you figure?"

"Well, obviously they're in there clearing the air—Zoff can't go on thinking she's a blackmailer much longer. It all depends on whether he gives himself away before she does. If he tips her off that he's being blackmailed and then finds out she isn't involved, well, then Kelly becomes a problem. Let's see what they do when they come out—whether they stay together or not."

"Mm, maybe. Everything could be okay and they'll just go on back to work together."

"We ought to be able to tell by the way Kelly carries herself. Whether she's willing or unwilling."

It started to rain, those heavy gray sheets of water it's impossible to see through. After a few minutes it slacked off into a steady, heavy downpour. The streets had virtually emptied of people. We waited.

Then Kelly Ingram and Leonard Zoff came out and stood in the pouring rain, looking for a taxi.

Captain Michaels sniffled a question.

"Unwilling," I said.

We all three spotted the raincoat at the same time—the raincoat that was keeping Leonard Zoff's right hand dry while the rest of him got soaking wet. "Jesus, he's got a gun on her," Ivan said unnecessarily. I turned on the ignition.

They finally got a taxi—which took them straight to the *LeFever* soundstage on West Fifty-fourth. Ivan did not repeat his suggestion that they might just be going back to work; Zoff's raincoat had taken care of that.

The taxi double-parked and let them out; they both ran for the building entrance, though I didn't see how they could get any wetter than they already were. There wasn't even a no-parking zone for me to pull into this time, so I stopped only long enough to let the two men out. I drove into an alley and left the car there. I made my own dash for the building entrance; the rain was still coming down, hard.

Inside, the lobby was empty except for a man behind a newsstand counter. I hesitated, not knowing which way to turn.

"If you're looking for a fat man and a skinny man who just came running in here," the newsstand man said, "they went thataway." He jerked his thumb past his right ear.

I called out my thanks and took off in the direction he'd indicated. Towards the soundstage where the sets were, not the elevators.

Captain Michaels was leaning on one hand against the soundstage door, catching his breath. "'S locked," he panted, "Malecki's gone for a key. Tell me what's inside."

Briefly I described the layout of the sets. "It's a lot smaller than it sounds," I said. "They don't waste an inch of space. How do you know they're in there?"

"Guy at the newsstand."

Ivan came back with the building supervisor, who was

grumbling. "Second time I had to do this. What's going on in there?"

"Second time?" Captain Michaels said. "Who'd you let in before—a man and a woman?"

"Yeah, thass right."

"Was the woman Kelly Ingram?" I asked him. "Do you know her?"

"Sure I know her, but it wasn't her. It was some lady friend of his."

"Of whose?"

"Why, Mr. Quinlan's, acourse. Who we talking about?" He unlocked the door.

Nick Quinlan? Ivan, the Captain, and I all exchanged blank looks—and decided to leave it for later.

"Leonard Zoff—does he have a key to this door?" Captain Michaels asked.

"Sure—he's paying the rent now, ain't he?"

Captain Michaels shooed the building supervisor away. "We separate once we're inside," he said. "And we do it quiet. They could be anywhere."

One thing I hadn't counted on was the dimness of the light. I crouched to the right of the door until my eyes had time to adjust. I couldn't hear a thing. Then I started to edge my way around the first set, feeling with my foot for the camera cables I remembered as being all over the floor. The way was relatively clear, though. The cables wouldn't be underfoot until next week, probably, not until they started shooting.

I stopped to listen. Captain Michaels and Ivan were both off to my left, neither one of them making a sound. Ivan, you expected to be quiet; but Michaels always surprised me, a big man like that moving like a cat. I'd no sooner thought that than I heard a slight scraping sound. But it came from directly ahead, not from my left. I eased my gun out of my shoulder bag.

I heard another sound from the same place, close, this time like someone bumping into something. If I remembered right, I was right behind the set of the bedroom of LeFever's apartment. I felt my way along to the last flat of the wall. Then I took a big breath, swung around the flat on to the set, went into my crouch, yelled: "Hold it right there!"—and found myself pointing my gun at a very startled Kelly Ingram.

Who said, peevishly, "Hold *what* right *where*? For heaven's sake, Marian, put that thing down and stand up! You look ridiculous."

Slowly I lowered my gun and stood up straight. Kelly, for some reason, was wearing a bedsheet. "Why," I asked, "are you wearing a bedsheet?"

"My clothes are soaked—I'm just trying to get dry. Oh, by the way—it was Leonard Zoff who killed Richard Ormsby. I've got him locked in a closet over there."

Oh, by the way. Wasn't that overdoing it a bit?

At that moment Captain Michaels and Ivan Malecki erupted around the other end of the set. They too went into a crouch and they both yelled "Freeze!" at exactly the same moment.

"My goodness, you folks do that a lot, don't you?" Kelly said wonderingly. "And *freeze?!*" She turned to me. "You really say that?"

"They do," I said. "I don't."

Captain Michaels decided that was a good time to have a sneezing fit. Ivan was still in his crouch, his arms stretched out holding his gun and his eyes flickering back and forth. Finally he looked at me.

"It's secure," I said. "She has him locked in a closet."

"In a closet." He stood up. "Where?"

"Over there," she flapped a hand vaguely. "Some sort of janitor's closet—mops and buckets and things."

The Captain was finished sneezing. "You locked Leonard Zoff in a closet, you say?"

"Well, he was going to kill me! What else could I do?"

There was this utter silence for the longest moment—and then everyone started talking at once. "You could have run away!" Ivan kept saying. "You could have called the police! You could have screamed!"

Captain Michaels finally yelled for quiet. He threw up his hands and said, "Wonderful. Simply wonderful. Hasn't this been just a *super* day? Not one damned thing has gone the way it was supposed to." He glared at Kelly. "*We* were supposed to catch Leonard Zoff, not you. Has *anything* gone right today? Anything at all? What next?"

Suddenly an unexpected weight dropped across my shoulders, causing my knees to buckle. "Hiya," a familiar voice said in my ear. "Wha'chall doin'?"

I struggled back up to my normal standing position.

"Nothing—we're not doing a thing, Nick," I said, and wished
Kelly Ingram would stop laughing.

22

Kelly Ingram

Leonard was laughing as he let me up, laughing and
smug and a little excited—and careless.

It happened so fast I can truthfully say I didn't *think*
about it; there wasn't time. It was all kind of dumb, really,
more accident than anything else. Leonard stood up and he
was so busy laughing and being pleased with himself that he
didn't pay any particular attention to where he was putting
his feet. Where he put them was right in that big puddle our
dripping clothes had made—the set we were on was supposed to be a gym so there wasn't any carpet on the
floor.

So when Leonard stood up he slipped on the wet place
and I was half up and half down and Leonard threw one
arm out for balance and held on to me with the other and
there wasn't time to think, remember, that's important,
and from my half-and-half position I kicked out one leg
and caught him right behind the knees and Leonard went
down and cracked his head an *awful* thump against the
floor.

I mean, it was a dreadful sound, I thought I'd killed him.
I'm ashamed to say it, but that thought gave me a moment of
absolutely exquisite pleasure. I got over that, though, and
started worrying about what next. I poked him in the chest a
couple of times and he didn't even moan. I felt his wrist for a
pulse and found one, so he was just knocked out and not
dead. Tie him up! Gag him! Handcuff him to the radiator! All
these silly things ran through my head. I didn't have hand-
cuffs *or* a radiator, I couldn't even see anything to tie him up
with—it was only a make-believe gym, remember.

I knew there was a place nearby where the janitor kept

his cleaning supplies and went looking for it, not easy to do in that dim light. I found it, and it had an old lock with a key in it that nobody ever used anymore, I bet. But when I went back to get Leonard I found I couldn't drag him, he was too heavy. So I thought about it a minute and ended up *rolling* him to the closet. He'd wake up with quite a few bumps and bruises from *that* little journey, heh heh heh. The closet was crowded with buckets and things, and when I got Leonard pushed in his head was turned at what looked like a very uncomfortable angle. He'd have a *terribly* stiff neck when he came to. I hoped.

But what if he woke up with some sort of serious injury? Oh wow, guess who'd be in trouble for that! I remember reading about some mugger who was suing because his victim had fought back and permanently damaged some part of his body, the mugger's body, I don't remember what part. What did the law expect me to do when I came up against somebody who wanted to kill me—scream, faint? I decided I'd better tell the police Leonard just slipped and fell. And he did—that was the truth. I just helped him along a little.

I was shivering—from cold, wet, fear, probably all three. The source of the fear was safely locked away, so now I could do something about the cold and the wet. There were no towels in that make-believe gym, I had to find something else. The sheets of LeFever's bed. I'd just gotten my clothes off and wrapped myself up in a sheet when Marian Larch came flying around the corner of the set and scared me out of my wits all over again.

They'd been following all the time, Marian and Ivan Malecki and Captain Michaels. It was the *police* who were Leonard's blackmailers, of all things, and they'd set something up at the Eastside Terminal that I'd spoiled by waltzing in on, at, around, the middle of, whatever, *hate* sentences like that. But when they all came roaring in to save me and I told them I had Leonard locked in a closet, they didn't exactly act as grateful as I thought they should. Ivan Malecki's eyes sort of glazed over and he stood there like a disconnected robot. Marian and Captain Michaels exchanged a quick glance and then looked away. Marian studied the ceiling while the Captain inspected the floor. Then they turned their backs to each other and stared off in opposite directions for a while. Then they looked at each other again—and suddenly everybody started yelling at *me*.

It was easy for Ivan to say I should have done this, that, the other. He wasn't there, he didn't know what it was like. Good thing I didn't tell them I had assisted Leonard in his fall, then they would *really* have let me have it. Nothing I tried on my own had worked—so when Leonard hits the floor with his head I'm just going to walk away and *leave* him there? Hah, yeah, sure I am, don't hold your breath. I was trying to tell them that when Nick Quinlan wandered on to the set and almost drove poor Marian through the floor with that heavy-armed embrace of his.

Seems he'd been there all along. When his lady heard the noise I was making to attract their attention, she got spooked and ran out on him. So Nick just decided to sack out on the set, on the sofa in the living room part of LeFever's apartment. He'd slept through the whole thing.

Anyhow, we eventually got it all straightened out, even though Ivan kept saying *He fell down and bumped his head?* over and over again in this tone of utter disbelief. Marian gave me an *uh-huh* sort of look but just smiled and didn't say anything. Poor Nick—when Marian told him Leonard had tried to kill me, he didn't believe her.

"Naw, he dint," he said. "Y'got it wrong summow. 'S bad enough about Nathan." As if the rules said there could be no more than one rotter among your acquaintances.

"Where's his gun?" Captain Michaels asked me.

"Oh—I guess it's still on the gym set. He had it in his hand when he fell."

"I'll get it," Ivan said and left.

"If it's the same gun that killed Ormsby," the Captain said, "then we've got our case."

Nick was shaking his head, still having trouble taking it all in. He went off with Captain Michaels to get Leonard out of the closet, no doubt hoping Leonard would have some explanation that would make everything all right again.

Really peculiar thing, I can't explain it, but I was feeling pretty damned good. Yeah, I can too explain it: it was just knowing all that nastiness was over. And there had been a hell of a lot of nastiness, and it had been going on for a long time, ever since Rudy Benedict decided blackmail would help him magically turn into a World-Famous Playwright. No—it started even earlier than that. It started with a young girl named Mary Rendell who had trusted Ted Cameron.

My grandmother had always told me to be careful of the

company I kept, and look at the choice specimens I'd ended up with. My lover was a killer. My producer was a blackmailer. My agent was a killer. A friend had tried to be a blackmailer but got himself murdered instead. His mother had tried to be a killer but managed to mess it up royally. The Benedicts weren't cut out to be criminals—but they sure had tried. Nice crowd I'd been running with. But I was through with them now, I was through with all of them.

There were still loose ends dangling that could trip me up. The network would have to find a new producer for my series—as well as for *LeFever* and the other shows Leonard Zoff had "inherited" from Nathan Pinking. That meant a delay that would screw up the shooting schedule. It also meant a lot of publicity, publicity of the kind that could so easily turn sour on us this time. There were still hurdles to get over.

But they were all *do*-able things, they weren't the kind of difficulties that made you lie down and pull the covers over your head and not even *try*. The killing and the blackmail and the hatred and the fear and the sheer ugliness of what had happened—*that* was over. It was over, and I felt good that it was over.

And I felt good because now I could think about Ted Cameron without getting a sharp pain in my side and without starting to sweat all over. The Ted Cameron I'd been so hooked on had never really existed; I'd made him up. So I had awakened from my pretty dream to find the real Ted Cameron was only a blank-eyed shadow man who killed people to get what he wanted. His absence would not leave a gaping hole in my life.

Besides, he never danced.

I could hear the men taking Leonard out of the closet where I'd locked him. Marian Larch was seated on the side of LeFever's bed, looking kind of droopy.

"Hey, what's the matter?" I laughed. "You've got a killer in custody—you should be feeling good."

"That's not the way it works," she muttered.

Wow, she was really *down*. "Marian? What is it?"

She waved a hand. "Don't mind me—I always get like this when we catch a killer. Depresses me."

I sat down next to her. "Some tough cop you are."

She laughed, a strained little laugh. "I know. I'm supposed to be hardened by now."

"It really bothers you, huh?"

"It really bothers me. It bothers me a lot."

"Well." I'd never have expected that—from this cool lady who always knew what to do. "Are you sure you're in the right line of work?"

Big sigh. "Yes, this is what I want to do. Kelly, don't worry about it—I'll be all right in a day or two."

"A *day* or two!" Jeeze. "That's far too long to stay depressed. So cheer up, starting right now."

"Just like that, huh?"

"You once ordered *me* to cheer up, remember? Not long after I'd learned about Ted—we were in my club, having coffee. You said, 'Cheer up, damn it!' Remember that? Well, now it's my turn—so cheer up, damn it."

She managed a smile. "We don't all have your resilience, Kelly."

"Hey, you should be cheering me up, not the other way around. After all, *I'm* the one who had four guns pointed at me today, you didn't."

"*Four* guns?"

"Four, count 'em, four. First, Leonard's. Second, yours—when you were coming on like Supercop. Then two more, in the hands of Captain Michaels and Ivan Malecki. That makes four unless I've forgotten how to count."

Marian looked stricken, which I guess was better than looking depressed. "I didn't realize—Kelly, I'm sorry. We should have found a better way of handling it."

Aha, she was thinking about something else, about me, a good sign. "Therefore, since you owe me a little cheering up—why don't you come home with me? I can put on some dry clothes and you can put your job aside for a while and we can cheer each other up. How about it?"

But she shook her head and slipped back into the droopy look. "Not tonight. But thanks for offering." Damn, I almost had her.

So I just nodded and said, "Sure, you want familiar surroundings, don't you? Very well, then, I accept."

"You accept what?"

"I accept your invitation—to go home with you where you will provide me with a bathrobe and a cup of warm liquid of some sort."

"Uh, well—"

"Come on, Marian, you need company tonight. And I

could do with a spot of company myself. What do you do when you get depressed? Sit alone in the dark? Listen to sad music? Eat? A lot of people eat when they get depressed. What do you do?"

She half-moaned, half-laughed. "I sit alone in the dark listening to sad music while I eat."

"Thought so." Although I hadn't, really; I was just talking. "But tonight we'll turn on every light in the place and tell funny stories and—well, we'll decide about the eating later. I'm getting kind of hungry myself. What do you say? Am I invited?"

She laughed again, and this time it didn't sound strained at all. "Kelly, I'm kind of glad you're incorrigible. Of course you're invited. You're always welcome—any time at all."

Aren't those nice words to end a story with?

Overview-map Key

P9-CCM-970

Five-Star Trails around Lake Tahoe

A Guide to the Most Beautiful Hikes

Other Books of Interest

Five-Star Trails around Lake Tahoe

A Guide to the Most Beautiful Hikes

Jordan Summers

Menasha Ridge Press

DISCLAIMER

This book is meant only as a guide to select trails in the vicinity of Lake Tahoe and does not guarantee your safety in any way—you hike at your own risk. Neither Menasha Ridge Press nor Jordan Summers is liable for property loss or damage, personal injury, or death that may result from accessing or hiking the trails described in the following pages. Please be aware that hikers have been injured in the Lake Tahoe area. Be especially cautious when walking on or near boulders, steep inclines, and drop-offs, and do not attempt to explore terrain that may be beyond your abilities. To help ensure an uneventful hike, please read carefully the introduction to this book, and perhaps get further safety information and guidance from other sources. Familiarize yourself thoroughly with the areas you intend to visit before venturing out. Ask questions and prepare for the unforeseen. Familiarize yourself with current weather reports, maps of the area you intend to visit, and any relevant area regulations.

Copyright © 2009 by Jordan Summers
All rights reserved
Published by Menasha Ridge Press
Printed in the United States of America
Distributed by Publishers Group West
First edition, first printing

Cover design by Scott McGrew
Text design by Ian Szymkowiak/Palace Press International
Cover photograph © Jordan Summers
Author photograph by Karin Connolly
Cartography and elevation profiles by Scott McGrew and Jordan Summers
Indexing by Rich Carlson

Library of Congress Cataloging-in-Publication Data

Summers, Jordan, 1951–
   Five-star trails around Lake Tahoe: a guide to the most beautiful trails/Jordan Summers.
—1st ed.
      p. cm.
   Includes index.
   ISBN-13: 978-0-89732-959-0
   ISBN-10: 0-89732-959-7
   1. Hiking—Tahoe, Lake, Region (Calif. and Nev.)—Guidebooks. 2. Trails—Tahoe, Lake, Region (Calif. and Nev.)—Guidebooks. 3. Tahoe, Lake, Region (Calif. and Nev.)—Guidebooks. I. Title.
   GV199.42.T16S865 2009
   917.94'38—dc22

                              2009006907

Menasha Ridge Press
P.O. Box 43673
Birmingham, Alabama 35243
www.menasharidge.com

Table of Contents

Dedication

This book is dedicated to Karin—smiling at my every predawn departure and listening patiently to my tales on every late-night return. I could not have started or finished this without her.

Acknowledgments

Many people are responsible for the production of this guidebook. I am grateful to Russell Helms, Martha Breedlove, and Molly Merkle at Menasha Ridge Press for their valuable support and guidance. I am so thankful to Ritchey Halphen, Susan Cullen Anderson, and Shelley DeLuca Kolankiewicz for the very difficult task of editing and bringing this book to fruition.

Thanks to the many fellow hikers who told me about their favorite trails, described wildflower blooms, shared maps with me, snapped photos, helped me identify flowers, and (thanks, Heidi and Jim) even checked my car locks after a senior moment miles from the trailhead. And to Jack Coughlin of Diamond Peak who shared his time and knowledge of local trails with me, as well as Lee Murray, who gave me the skinny on the Thunder Mountain Trail.

The hard work that's performed by trail crews—professionals and volunteers—benefits every hiker in the backcountry. Not only do they pour their sweat into the job, but they also know a great deal about regional trails. Kudos to my friend Bill Holt for his generous volunteer work on the Pacific Crest Trail (PCT) and Tahoe Rim Trail (TRT), and for his suggestion of the Eagle Lake Trail and Rubicon Lake. The condition of Tahoe Meadow (and my map of it) has been greatly improved by the work of Jeremy Vlcan in cooperation with the Tahoe Rim Trail Association.

A casual trailhead inquiry turned into a recommendation for what became my favorite hike, the Glen Alpine Loop. Thanks to Bill and Paula Bertram, who not only mapped it out but also refreshed me with cold hopped beverages and hiking tales on my return. If you follow my route, you can thank Raymond Morales and Emily Bullock, who first showed me the way up to my favorite summit, Pyramid Peak. Fellow TRT hiker Wayne McClelland clued me in to a wealth of trail information and local history of the Incline Village area, including the Folsom Camp Loop.

During what I will remember as the Summer of High Gas Prices, I stayed at the Huckleberry House cabin near Lake Audrian, thanks to the generosity of my friends Adam and Davia Weiner. When I met my hiking partners from Reno, Randy and Mary Peterson, at the Freel Peak trailhead, they came with pack stock—Rascal the Jack Russell terrier hung from Mary's shoulder on a homemade terrier carrier. Thanks so much for your hospitality each time I hiked in Nevada.

It seemed like old times and I was so grateful to be able to hike with my daughter, Ashley, on the trail to Loch Leven Lakes; as well, I enjoyed sharing a great day of trailhead surveillance with my son, Jason. The all-time award winner for patience is my partner, Karin, who waited for ten hours at Squaw Valley while I moseyed along the PCT from Donner Pass. And when she couldn't be there for my end-of-hike ride, I relearned the ancient art of hitchhiking. Thanks to two friendly couples, Wesley and Liz plus Jim and Jan, for helping me accomplish that act with some dignity.

I, along with many others, am grateful to the staff and volunteers of the Pacific Crest Trail Association for their continuous efforts to improve and maintain trails in the remote areas of the Lake Tahoe region. And a special thanks to the PCTA's Brenda Murray for her trail support as well as for her encouraging words. No less credit goes to the Tahoe Rim Trail Association for their ambitious and fruitful efforts in creating an environment that invites public use yet manages to lessen the negative impacts to both trails and lake. The TRTA is fortunate to be associated with two outdoor professionals—Emily Williams and Lisa Cashel—both enthusiastically dedicated to helping others enjoy the wilderness. It is an inspiration to see the results of their energetic efforts.

It was only through the help of others, known and unknown alike, that I was able to accomplish the hikes and descriptions in this guidebook. I am grateful to you all.

Preface

I live in the Sacramento area; smack in the middle of the Central Valley; flat land just a few dozen feet above sea level. Most years, I make my weekly trips to Echo Summit or Incline Village and gasp for the fresh air as my lungs adjust to the elevation before I meander along my favorite trails. That's the routine during the no-snow season. During snow season, I keep at it along the foothill trails surrounding the Yuba and American rivers. But, the trails and destinations around Lake Tahoe are special in comparison to every other mountain locale.

Look what happened in this one area of California. Ancient seafloors rose along with their altered sediments to become mountains. Molten rock from beneath the crust rose and cooled to form domes, peaks, and escarpments. Volcanoes released their molten innards across the landscape, covering it with ashfall, mudflows, or lava. And the valleys, cirques, tarns, and moraines scattered across this Sierra landscape are gifts of flowing rivers of ice. This is one incredible place because evidence of all of this geologic activity is so easily visible. We see it today as Fallen Leaf Lake, the Crystal Range, Rockbound Valley, Mount Rose, Thunder Mountain, Velma Lakes, Half Moon Lake, Slide Mountain, and so on.

It is a hiker's great fortune that three renowned long trails converge in the Lake Tahoe vicinity. The famous Tahoe–Yosemite Trail originates here; the 165-mile Tahoe Rim Trail circumnavigates the lake on a backcountry route; and the crown jewel of long trails, the Pacific Crest Trail, merges at times with both of these famous tracks as its course runs north to south on the west side of Lake Tahoe. Compared to other trails in the backcountry, these three are the finest hikers can expect. These premier trails are graded, engineered, and signed for the benefit of hikers. (And equestrians, officially.)

I can't deny an urge to escape from the city in search of some solitude in the mountains. That's a motivator for me, true. But I like to see other hikers getting out, enjoying the same backcountry that I'm able to enjoy. So I have a subtle motivation to share what I experienced or to inform others how they can also have that experience. I hiked these trails at different times of the year, so you may not see exactly what I see. But if I show you some identifiable signs along the way, you should have no trouble following along regardless of whether it's early, middle, or late season.

Despite 2008 being a low-snow year, the snowmelt rate was only 2 inches per day by mid-May. Many of the trailheads were still closed on June 1, when it snowed one last time. But the trailheads had all been opened by the time it rained over Kirkwood in mid-June (for the last time until Halloween). Come spring, melting snow and warm days cause an explosion of color as flowers fly out of the ground, and hikers have so many options of where to go. I went hiking to Winnemucca Lake during an absolute riot of color and perfumed scents. Name the plant and it was there. And do butterflies like nectar? From the peaks to the meadows, these flying flowers were swarming in massive droves whenever I encountered them.

Most years, I could safely predict a thunderstorm by 3 in the afternoon, every afternoon. This year, the rain stayed away but the lightning came in its place with no quenching relief for the newly ignited fires. And fires there were! This was the year of poor vistas and hazy, smoky days. More importantly, the Angora fire of the previous season reduced the black bears' forage area, resulting in several reports of bears harassing campers at Round Lake and Ophir Creek, and even on Marlette Peak. Fortunately there were no serious injuries.

In identifying and describing flora and fauna, I attempted to check myself and leave my lowland brain in the foothills. I expect to hear about it if I identified a Jeffrey pine as its foothill twin, the ponderosa pine. The same applies to incense cedars and western junipers. (Where did I put my glasses?)

The truth in advertising clause dictates that I "reveal all" about my hikes. Sometimes, as geologists say, "chert happens." I smacked my head when I realized that the Amador County high point that I hiked to was not "the" Thunder Mountain after all. It is an easy 2,000-foot hike from Amador's highest peak, where I sat, over to Thunder, where there is a register and a memorial. You'll see. Secondly, I took two hikes to Twin Peaks on which I was unable to summit. The final 150 feet to the peak, covered with large boulders, are similar in every respect to the final distance on Pyramid Peak. Due solely to a cranky knee that would no longer bend, I was unable to ascend the simple Class 3 scramble. Knowing that it was plain unsafe for me on those days, I had to remind myself that there is a lot more to the mountain than the summit.

My sincere goal is that there is a hike or destination in this book that will interest you, that it will guide you there and return you safely, and that your good hike will encourage you to invite others for a similar experience.

To paraphrase George Wharton James from his 1915 descriptive account, *The Lake of the Sky:* **Get out!**

—Jordan Summers
Elk Grove, California

Recommended Hikes

RECOMMENDED HIKES

Hikes by Category

Introduction

About This Book

The Lake Tahoe region is a magnet for outdoor enthusiasts, and we are drawn there by the millions. Despite the abundance of lofty superlatives that inevitably precede a visit, Lake Tahoe's descriptions do not seem to disappoint anyone.

More than 125 trails are in active use around the Tahoe Basin, and a number of the 40 hikes described in these pages represent the region's most popular destinations. Other hikes lead away from the crowds and take an often-more-difficult route. Trails and destinations are so plentiful in the central Sierra Nevada that these hikes are restricted to an area within 25 miles of the lake's shore.

In the 1840s, explorer John C. Fremont described Lake Tahoe as a mountain lake so entirely surrounded by mountains that he could not discover an outlet (although the Washoe Indians had drawn him a map three years earlier). He mapped the area and called the lake, yes—Mountain Lake. (Why was he an engineer, you ask, when he had such a command of the language?) More poetic heads eventually prevailed. By 1870 it had been settled, after ousting a sullied governor's moniker, that the Washoe Indian words for "big water"—*tah-oo*—would be a proper name for the spectacular lake. Afterward, it was just a matter of agreeing on its pronunciation.

Fremont was no quitter, but he missed the lake's only outlet, which is located on its western shore. It's where Tahoe City stands today and where the Truckee River has most often originated when not blocked by ice dams. Current lake level is 6,228 feet, and the Rubicon Trail comes closest to that mark in this book. Freel Peak in California and Nevada's Mount Rose are the geographic high points

1

around the lake. Both summits are at least 4,500 feet above the waves and are among the peaks that you can reach following these notes.

Lake Tahoe's history is brief but by no means uneventful. Within a decade of Lake Tahoe's mapping by Fremont, gold was discovered and exploited in the foothills and California had become a state. Subsequently, silver was discovered in adjacent Nevada, and the settlement and economic exploitation of Lake Tahoe's natural resources went unabated. Today, great emphasis is placed on preserving the natural resources and creating diverse outdoor recreation opportunities.

Many of the notes enclosed refer to geologic processes and geographic features. You'll find clear explanations of these in geology and natural-history guides and texts, which are referenced in Appendix C. If you don't have those available, this simple explainer might suffice: the mountains around Lake Tahoe are a mess. They are a jumble of pieces from several puzzles—and you can see the types of pieces on each of these hikes. No skills necessary.

Basically, Nevada's border (approximately) used to border the Pacific Ocean. Then, beginning a few hundred million years ago, a chunk of land, similar in size and shape to Japan, slammed into that beach. *Voilà,* new property. New mountains were also formed because the land kept coming. It scrunched up the former beaches and slid under older property. This happened two more times. Each event was followed by lots of volcanoes along the line of the new property. Starting about 250 million years ago, some of Earth's crust melted and rose in the form of large granite blobs that are now called batholiths. This happened from time to time over the next 150 million years. Less than 50 million years ago, the Sierra Nevada started uplifting from the west. This uplift set off the erosive force of water, and river channels were cut into the terrain. And more volcanoes grew along the old coast. Their ash, lava, and mudflows covered much of the original terrain. This went on in such volume for so long that Sierran rivers were filled, passes were covered, and terrain buried. Simple erosion took care of most of that soft volcanic material and the rivers reestablished themselves. Then, about 1.5 million years ago, the cleanup crew showed up in the form of ice. Glaciers formed and covered peaks less than 13,000 feet high with a cap of ice stretching from Lake Tahoe to Yosemite. The erosive grinding power of the glaciers that ensued scraped away much of the debris, sometimes forming it into nice, neat piles that we call moraines. Most of the granite was eroded not by the ice itself but the subsequent freeze—the thaw action of water causes the granite to wear away by cracking or exfoliating, and the process continues with each annual cycle. *Et voici!* (as François Matthes might have said), you have a considerable jumble of rocks to play on.

The hikes offered in this guidebook take you all over that playground, leading to tarns, cirques, moraines, and horns. These hikes don't require you to climb mountains to enjoy being on mountains. Some of the hikes are connected to other hikes or can be readjusted by the reader to create a shorter or longer trek. Most of the hikes involve lakes, streams, meadows, or peaks. All of these are created by natural processes that are often interconnected—such as the succession meadow growing at McConnell Lake or the soil building on Tallac's scree slopes. A natural-history guide in your pack will help make these processes come alive on the trail.

Use the overview map to find possibilities for creating your own custom hikes. Several of these hikes were approached in that manner to create an interesting and rewarding trek. Hikers can do many things to increase their enjoyment of the hikes on the following pages. Enter the trailhead waypoints into Google Earth or other mapping software and look for trails in the vicinity. It's not unusual that one trailhead will serve as the embarkation point for several hikes.

How to Use This Book

The Overview Map and Overview-map Key

Use the overview map on the inside front cover to assess the exact locations of each hike's primary trailhead. Hike numbers appear on the overview map, in the key facing the overview map, in the table of contents, at the beginning of each hike profile, and at the top of each trail map.

The book is organized by region, as indicated in the table of contents. The hikes within each region are noted as one-way day hikes, loop day hikes, or overnight loop hikes (see page xxi). A map legend that details the symbols found on trail maps appears on the inside back cover.

Trail Maps

Each hike contains a detailed map that shows the trailhead, the route, significant features, facilities, and topographic landmarks, such as creeks, overlooks, and peaks. The author gathered map data by carrying a GPS unit (Garmin GPS 60CSx series) while hiking. This data was downloaded into a digital mapping program (Topo USA) and processed by expert cartographers to produce the highly accurate maps found in this book. Each trailhead's GPS coordinates are included with each profile (see next page).

Elevation Profiles

Corresponding directly to the trail map, each hike contains a detailed elevation profile. The elevation profile provides a quick look at the trail from the side, enabling you to visualize how the trail rises and falls. Key points along the way are labeled. Note the number of feet between each tick mark on the vertical axis (the height scale). To avoid making flat hikes look steep and steep hikes appear flat, height scales are used throughout the book to provide an accurate image of the hike's climbing difficulty.

GPS Trailhead Coordinates

To collect accurate map data, I hiked each trail with a handheld GPS unit (Garmin GPS 60CSx series). Data collected was then downloaded and plotted onto a digital U.S. Geological Survey topographic map. In addition to rendering a highly specific trail outline, this book also includes the GPS coordinates for each trailhead in two formats: latitude–longitude and Universal Transverse Mercator (UTM). Latitude–longitude coordinates tell you where you are by locating a point west (latitude) of the 0-degree meridian line that passes through Greenwich, England, and north or south of the 0-degree (longitude) line that belts the Earth, aka the equator.

Topographic maps show latitude–longitude as well as UTM grid lines. Known as UTM coordinates, the numbers index a specific point, using a grid method. The survey datum used to arrive at the coordinates in this book is WGS84 (versus NAD 27 or WGS 83). For readers who own a GPS unit, whether handheld or onboard a vehicle, the latitude–longitude or UTM coordinates provided on the first page of each hike may be entered into the GPS unit. Just make sure your GPS unit is set to navigate using WGS84 datum. Now you can navigate directly to the trailhead.

Most trailheads, which begin in parking areas, can be reached by car, but some hikes still require a short walk to reach the trailhead from a parking area. In those cases a handheld unit is necessary to continue the GPS navigation process. That said, readers can easily access all trailheads in this book by using the directions given, the overview map, and the trail map, which shows at least one major road leading into the area. But for those who enjoy using the latest GPS technology to navigate, the necessary data has been provided. A brief explanation of the UTM coordinates from Hike 1, Mount Rose (page 28), follows:

> **UTM Zone (WGS84)** 11S
> **Easting** 0250189
> **Northing** 4355492

The UTM zone number (11) refers to one of the 60 vertical zones of the UTM projection. Each zone is 6 degrees wide. The UTM zone letter (S) refers to one of the 20 horizontal zones that span from 80 degrees south to 84 degrees north. The easting number (0250189) indicates in meters how far east or west a point is from the central meridian of the zone. Increasing easting coordinates on a topo map or on your GPS screen indicate that you are moving east; decreasing easting coordinates indicate that you are moving west. The northing number (4355492) references in meters how far you are from the equator. Above and below the equator, increasing northing coordinates indicate you are traveling north; decreasing northing coordinates indicate you are traveling south.

To learn more about how to enhance your outdoor experiences with GPS technology, refer to *GPS Outdoors: A Practical Guide for Outdoor Enthusiasts* (Menasha Ridge Press).

THE HIKE PROFILE

In addition to maps, each hike contains a concise but informative narrative of the hike from beginning to end. This descriptive text is enhanced with at-a-glance ratings and information, GPS-based trailhead coordinates, and accurate driving directions that lead you from a major road to the parking area most convenient to the trailhead.

At the top of the section for each hike is a box that allows the hiker quick access to pertinent information: quality of scenery, condition of trail, appropriateness for children, difficulty of hike, quality of solitude expected, hike distance, approximate time of hike, and outstanding highlights of the trip. The first five categories are rated using a five-star system. On the next page is an example.

The five stars indicate that the scenery is spectacular. The trail condition is very good (one star would mean the trail is likely to be muddy, rocky, overgrown, or otherwise compromised). The hike is doable for able-bodied children (a one-star rating would denote that only the most gung-ho and physically fit children should go). Four

01 Mount Rose

SCENERY: ✿ ✿ ✿ ✿ ✿
TRAIL CONDITION: ✿ ✿ ✿ ✿
CHILDREN: ✿ ✿
DIFFICULTY: ✿ ✿ ✿ ✿
SOLITUDE: ✿ ✿ ✿
DISTANCE: *10.2 miles round-trip*
HIKING TIME: *5—7 hours*

OUTSTANDING FEATURES: *Pleasant trail through pine forest, plus a waterfall beneath Mount Houghton. A well-defined trail leads to the summit for a 360° view all the way from Stampede Reservoir in the west to the Carson Range in the east, with Lake Tahoe laid out for 22 blue miles below you to the south.*

stars for difficulty indicates it is a challenging hike (five stars would be strenuous). And you can expect to encounter people on the trail (with one star you may well be elbowing your way up the trail).

Distances given are absolute, but hiking times are estimated using an average hiking speed of 2 to 3 miles per hour, with time built in for pauses at overlooks and brief rests. Overnight-hiking times account for the effort of carrying a backpack.

Following each box is a brief italicized description of the hike. A more detailed account follows in which trail junctions, stream crossings, and trailside features are noted, along with their distance from the trailhead. Flip through the book, read the descriptions, and choose a hike that appeals to you.

Climate

Lake Tahoe has some variety in its climate near each of the cardinal points around the region. South Lake Tahoe has different weather than Tahoe City, which is different from Truckee or Incline Village. But it really boils down to the activities that you can undertake around the Lake. Lake Tahoe's weather is either sunny with snow on the ground or sunny with no snow on the ground.

Tahoe seems to have two distinct seasons. First, there is snow-season and then there is hiking, biking, climbing, and anything else

LAKE TAHOE CLIMATE
(at Tahoe City, California)

Month	Precipitation		Snowfall		Maximum		Minimum	
	in	cm	in	cm	F	C	F	C
Jan	6.18	16	43.8	111	36	2	16	-9
Feb	5.50	14	38.0	97	39	4	18	-8
Mar	4.11	10	35.5	90	44	7	21	-6
Apr	2.11	5.4	15.2	39	50	10	26	-3
May	1.19	3.0	3.8	10	60	16	32	0
June	0.69	1.8	0.2	0.5	69	21	37	3
July	0.26	0.7	0.0	0.0	79	26	43	6
Aug	0.31	0.8	0.0	0.0	78	26	42	6
Sept	0.64	1.6	0.3	0.8	70	21	37	3
Oct	1.83	4.6	2.4	6.1	51	11	31	-1
Nov	3.68	9.3	16.2	41	47	8	24	-4
Dec	5.40	14	33.5	85	40	4	20	-7

that doesn't need snow season. Typically beginning in mid-May, the spring–summer–fall season lasts about five months or until the first snows in early November. The snowpack lingers in the Tahoe area later into spring due to the unique pattern of high daytime temperatures followed by freezing temperatures at night. However, spring opens hastily with dozens of plant species eager to get up and get busy. Summer morphs into autumn without notice as every area begins to dry out after putting on an outstanding colorful display. The one type of summertime display that hikers need to avoid is that of lightning. Just about every afternoon the sky brews up a threatening batch of clouds—an atmospheric caution flag to anyone approaching a peak, ridge, or exposed rocky area.

Lake Tahoe gets its moisture-laden air from the same place as it gets its weekend visitors: from the San Francisco Bay Area. Prevailing westerly winds carry moisture right up to Donner Pass and Echo Summit as they blow eastward along the watershed canyons of the Yuba and American rivers. These warm valley winds rise as they run directly into the Sierra Nevada, which blocks their paths. The average annual snowfall of 2 feet in Colfax is eclipsed 46 miles away by that of Donner Summit's 34 feet.

Before every drive to Lake Tahoe to "conduct research," I checked and rechecked the National Weather Service forecasts at the National Oceanographic and Atmospheric Administration's Web site at **wrh.noaa.gov.** This is an essential step in preparing for any day or overnight hike.

— Water

You would think that this would not be a topic of caution, what with some gazillion crystal-clear gallons of it captured in Lake Tahoe. But water is an issue in the Lake Tahoe region just as it is everywhere, possibly more so in fact. Most local bumpers carry a sticker entreating everyone to "Keep Tahoe Blue." Trails around here have been designed or reengineered to specifically abate the effect of runoff water, which can carry huge loads of sediment into the lake.

Few hikes in this guidebook don't come near or cross water in some form. And that water is especially important for hikers, both for recreation and hydration. Throughout these chapters, I have suggested possible fill-up spots for you and your water system (bottles or bags).

Giardia lamblia remains a persistent problem in this region as in all other backcountry areas. Since cattle are no longer prevalent, wildlife biologists have noted a downturn in the levels of this pathogen. But it remains at dangerous levels due to the impact of humans and the animals they bring with them. *Hint:* If you have been following hoof prints or paw prints, you may want to watch where you get water. Chances are that the maker of the prints got water there, too.

For this reason, I strongly caution that all water is suspect, regardless of its clarity. (My microscopic eyesight has diminished slightly, so I can't see the bad guys anyway.) There are a few reliable methods of water treatment specific to giardia and cryptosporidium. Filtering works, as do chlorine dioxide tablets, iodine tablets, chemical mixes, and UV light. In camp, water can be purified by bringing the water to a boil. At the first bubble, it is pure. Just pick the method that suits you both for convenience and taste, and then rigorously use it on any drinking water in the backcountry.

All of these methods work, but they must be used in order to be effective. This is important. A case of giardiasis is not pleasant and it only takes one drink from that "crystal-clear stream."

Clothing

It should be as simple as throwing on a pair of trail runners and a pair of shorts, which is fine, but there are risks to that approach. These risks span the spectrum from merely not enjoying the hike on the not-so-problematic end all the way to death-will-come-within-four-hours on the other end. Some well-chosen duds can mean the difference between a pleasant trip and a dismal search-and-rescue team after-action report.

KILLER COTTON. The Fatal Fabric. These are names for that fabric that is oh-so-comfortable on a hot summer day but lethal when worn in the backcountry. Eliminate it from your hiking closet and use synthetics, silk, or wool for your body-covering needs.

BASE LAYER. This layer is responsible for wicking moisture, that is, perspiration, away from your skin so that it can evaporate without cooling your skin. Undershorts and a shirt of wicking material will keep you dry and warm. Cotton feels great next to your skin until it becomes sweat-soaked.

INSULATION LAYER. A wicking T-shirt isn't enough to insulate your body when the temperatures drop or the wind picks up. A layer of a synthetic fleece or a wool sweater will help hold warm air around your body. Another protective layer, such as a wind jacket, can be used effectively. A soft-shell garment often provides not only insulation, but also water- and wind-repellency.

OUTER LAYER. Quick-drying, durable shorts or convertible pants with lots of pockets are standard trail outerwear. A lightweight, long-sleeved shirt will offer some sun protection on long, exposed stretches, and a lightweight wind shirt can guard against warmth-robbing breezes.

SOFT-SHELL JACKET. Coated with a durable water- and wind-repelling finish, this garment can ward off light rain and also insulate, depending on the lining thickness.

RAIN GEAR. This clothing should shed rain on the outside and allow you to remain dry on the inside. A hooded jacket or an anorak (one zips and one pulls over your head) should have pit zips for ventilation. Pants should have zippered cuffs so you can easily put them on and take them off.

BANDANA. Like a clothing multitool, it is great for swatting at mosquitoes, wiping brows, and acting as an impromptu hat.

BOOTS. Lightweight hiking *boots* rather than trail shoes are my recommendation for every natural trail.

GAITERS. This accessory is almost essential for me to keep dirt, sticks, seeds, and other crud from getting inside my boots and the burrs off my socks.

Maps

Maps are an essential piece of gear that may play a vital role in your safety on even the most tame day hike.

I carried these waterproof maps with me on every hike, and their condition after more than 40 hikes shows their utility and durability.

Lake Tahoe Basin, USDA Forest Service, California/Nevada. Trails Illustrated Map #803. Evergreen, CO: National Geographic Maps, 2006

Lake Tahoe Recreation Map: Tahoe Rim Trail. San Rafael, CA: Tom Harrison Maps, 2007

Lake Tahoe Trail Map. Adventure Maps, Inc., 2007

A Guide to the Desolation Wilderness. Eldorado National Forest and Lake Tahoe Basin Management Unit. San Francisco: USDA Forest Service, Pacific Southwest Region, 2000

Essential Gear

What I decide to carry with me on every outing depends in large part on where I'm headed and what I'll be doing there. (This list won't do much for sailors or Arctic explorers.)

These are the essentials that I carry on every hike in the mountains. Some items I hope I'll never use. The emergency-only items can, however, prevent a simple injury from turning into a life-threatening ordeal. Because I'm unable to predict the outcome of every hike, I prepare to some extent by asking myself, "Which emergency won't happen to me on this trip?"

So I don't have to worry about a long list of items, I use these -*tion* ("shun") words to describe essential gear.

PREPARATION: A plan of your route, your gear, your destination, and your return time to be left with an emergency contact

NAVIGATION: The route description, a trail or topographic map, a simple compass, and the knowledge to use them (a GPS receiver or altimeter for increased precision and speed)

HYDRATION: Full water bottles plus extra; water treatment tablets; or purifying filter

NUTRITION: Nutrition bars, snacks, or meals for the day plus extra

IGNITION: Matches, lighter, fire starter, or stove with full fuel bottle or canister

ILLUMINATION: Headlamp with fresh batteries

RADIATION: Sun hat, sunglasses, sunscreen, lip balm, UV-resistant clothes

INSULATION: Base layer (wicking), insulation layer, rain gear, extra socks, soft-shell jacket, extra (unworn) insulating garment

MEDICATION: Your personal daily medications, first-aid kit with fresh supplies, instructions, and the knowledge to use them

PROTECTION: Space blanket, tarp (to shelter accident victims in sun or rain), survival bivy sack (to warm hypothermic victims)

STABILIZATION: Trekking poles (third leg, monopod, shelter pole, cougar and bear defense, poison oak deflector, general poking and irritating of small creatures)

IN ADDITION: Emergency lists, signal whistle, signal mirror, knife, multitool, cord

Additional Gear

For day hikes I use a 30- to 40-liter pack, and for overnight hikes I carry a 60-liter pack. Aside from the essential gear that I carry on every hike in the mountains, I carry some extra things ("must keep that pack full") that might help make your hikes more enjoyable, too.

Camera
Tripod
GPS device
Extra batteries
Trowel

Monocular
(half of a binocular)
Field guides
Notebook and pencil
Specimen bags

Overnight hikes do not require much more gear. I use various one-man tents and bivy systems.

Sleeping bag (rated to 30°)
Tent or bivy with footprint
Stove and fuel
Mug and pot

Food (1.5 pounds per person
per day)
Down vest
Camp shoes

Without being overly precise about it, the total of my gear for a three-day hike would not exceed 35 pounds. On the other hand, my daypack was never less than 23 pounds. Your needs certainly will vary.

First-aid Kit

A typical first-aid kit may contain more items than you might think necessary. These are just the basics. Prepackaged kits in waterproof bags (Atwater Carey and Adventure Medical make a variety of kits) are available. Even though quite a few items are listed here, they pack down into a small space:

Ace bandages or Spenco joint wraps

Antibiotic ointment (Neosporin or the generic equivalent)

Ibuprofen or acetaminophen

Band-Aids

Insect repellent

Matches or pocket lighter

Sunscreen

Benadryl or the generic equivalent, diphenhydramine (in case of allergic reactions)

Butterfly-closure bandages

Blister kit (like Moleskin/Spenco "Second Skin")

Gauze (one roll)

Gauze compress pads (a half-dozen 4-by-4-inch pads)

Hydrogen peroxide or iodine

Whistle (more effective in signaling rescuers than your voice is)

Epinephrine in a prefilled syringe (for people known to have severe allergic reactions to such things as bee stings, usually by prescription only)

Hiking with Children

No one is too young for a hike. Be mindful, though. Flat, short, and shaded trails are best with an infant. Toddlers who have not quite mastered walking can still tag along, riding on an adult's back in a child carrier. Use common sense to judge a child's capacity to hike a particular trail and always anticipate that the child will tire quickly and need to be carried. A list of hikes suitable for children is provided on page xvii.

General Safety

To some potential mountain enthusiasts, the deep woods seem inordinately dark and perilous. It is the fear of the unknown that causes this anxiety. No doubt, potentially dangerous situations can occur outdoors, but as long as you use sound judgment and prepare yourself before hitting the trail, you'll be much safer in the woods than in most urban areas of the country. It is better to look at a backcountry hike as a fascinating chance to discover the unknown rather than a chance for potential disaster. If you're new to the game, I'd suggest starting out easy and finding a person who knows more to help you out. In addition, here are a few tips to make your trip safer and easier.

- **ALWAYS CARRY FOOD AND WATER**, whether you are planning to go overnight or not. Food will give you energy, help keep you warm, and sustain you in an emergency until help arrives. You never know if you will have a stream nearby when you become thirsty. Bring potable water or treat water before drinking it from a stream. Boil or filter all found water before drinking it.

- **STAY ON DESIGNATED TRAILS.** Most hikers get lost when they leave the path. Even on the most clearly marked trails, there is usually a point where you have to stop and consider in which direction to head. If you become disoriented, don't panic. As soon as you think you may be off track, stop, assess your current direction, then retrace your steps to the point where you went astray. Using a map, a compass, and this book, and keeping in mind what you have passed thus far, reorient yourself, and trust your judgment on which way to continue. If you become absolutely unsure of how to continue, return to your vehicle the way you came in. Should you become completely lost and have no idea how to return to the trailhead, remaining in place along the trail and waiting for help is most often the best option for adults and always the best option for children.

- **BE ESPECIALLY CAREFUL WHEN CROSSING STREAMS.** Whether you are fording the stream or crossing on a log, make every step count. If you have any doubt about maintaining your balance on a log, ford the stream instead: use a trekking pole or stout stick for balance and face upstream as you cross. If a stream seems too deep to ford, turn back. Whatever is on the other side is not worth risking your life.

- **BE CAREFUL AT OVERLOOKS.** While these areas may provide spectacular views, they are potentially hazardous. Stay back from the edge of outcrops and be absolutely sure of your footing; a misstep can mean a nasty and possibly fatal fall.

- **STANDING DEAD TREES** and storm-damaged living trees pose a real hazard to hikers and tent campers. These trees may have loose or broken limbs that could fall at any time. When choosing a spot to rest or a back-country campsite, look up.

- **KNOW THE SYMPTOMS OF HYPOTHERMIA.** Shivering and forgetfulness are the two most common indicators of this stealthy killer. Hypothermia can occur at any elevation, even in the summer, especially when the hiker is wearing lightweight cotton clothing. If symptoms arise, get the victim shelter, hot liquids, and dry clothes or a dry sleeping bag.

- **TAKE ALONG YOUR BRAIN.** A cool, calculating mind is the single most important asset on the trail. Think before you act. Watch your step. Plan ahead. Avoiding accidents before they happen is the best way to ensure a rewarding and relaxing hike.

- **ASK QUESTIONS.** National and state forest and park employees are there to help. It's a lot easier to ask advice beforehand and it will help you avoid a mishap away from civilization when it's too late to amend an error.

Animal and Plant Hazards

MOSQUITOES

You will encounter mosquitoes on most of the hikes described in this book. Insect repellent and/or repellent-impregnated clothing are the only simple methods to ward off these pests. Mosquitoes in California are known to carry the West Nile Virus, so all due caution should be taken to avoid mosquito bites.

BEES AND WASPS

Unless you are allergic to the sting of bees or wasps, these insects should not be considered dangerous to you. Sit next to a batch of wildflowers—right up close—and watch the bees fly in and out as they maul the colorful buds. You are invisible to the bees, which are concentrating on far sweeter treats than you. Enjoy your hike without worrying about these helpful insects.

You may, however, have an opportunity to chance upon a wild hive while following any of these hikes. If you hear a constant buzzing that grows louder with your approach, walk away, as you have likely found a hive or a swarm. Bees will attack if their hive or queen is threatened.

TICKS

A tick is a bloodsucking arachnid (spider family; not an insect) found in almost every outdoor environment, usually in low trees and tall grasses. Of the nine species of ticks found in California, the western black-legged deer tick has been labeled as the vector for Lyme disease. Lyme disease has been reported in the Lake Tahoe region.

These tiny parasites are about the size of a freckle or sesame seed and are hard to stop from landing on your body. You can spray or wear repellent-impregnated clothing. But the best method for dealing with them is to conduct a thorough inspection of your entire body and then remove any found ticks.

POISON OAK

A concern that you can dismiss in the Lake Tahoe region is a rash from poison oak. This three-leaved plant does not grow above 5,000 feet. You will not encounter it in the Lake Tahoe region.

Specific Hazards

Two species of vertebrates living in the Lake Tahoe region are potentially dangerous. Mountain lions and black bears are present in every area hiked for this book. The probability that you'll encounter either of these animals, however, is remote.

Mountain Lions

Mountain lions are important members of the natural community and may be found in this area. Although these animals are seldom seen, they can be unpredictable and have been known to attack humans without warning. It is best to hike with another person and to keep children close when hiking. If you should encounter a mountain lion, wave your arms overhead and make plenty of noise to frighten it away.

These, or words to their effect, are often seen at trailheads or recreation area entrances throughout the region. Mountain lions are a real and potential danger and hikers should be aware of their presence.

Mountain lions are everywhere in California and most abundant where there is a supply of deer and ground cover. The mountain lion is also known as a cougar, puma, or panther. They are tan-coated and have black-tipped ears and tail. They weigh between 75 and 150 pounds and are about seven feet long from nose to tail.

Never approach a mountain lion. If confronted, do anything to make yourself appear larger: raise your outspread arms, wave hiking sticks or tree limbs, gather other hikers (especially children) next to you. Act threatening, but allow the animal a path to escape. Absolutely avoid bending over or turning your back on mountain lions. Do not run. They will mistake these actions for those of a prey animal. Make noise, yell, and throw rocks or anything else at hand without bending over.

If you are attacked, try to remain standing, as lions will try to bite the neck or head. Always try to fight back. In 2006, a woman successfully used a ballpoint pen to fight off the mountain lion that was attacking her husband. Both survived.

California Black Bears

With the possible exception of mountain lions, most animals will be scared of you and will not be a threat as long as you respect the animal's space. California has a large population of black bears, which are actually cinnamon to dark-brown colored. The threat from black bears is that they are very intelligent and always searching for large quantities of food to build their nutrition stores. Despite weighing between 200 and 500 pounds, black bears can run up to 30 miles an hour.

Conflicts between bears and humans usually occur because bears want your food. It's easy pickings, after all. If a bear is successful at nabbing your food, it returns to do the same to someone else. Now the bear is not a wilderness creature; it has become a nuisance bear. A nuisance bear is removed from the area once and then, if it returns to forage for human food (and it will), the bear is destroyed.

For the sake of the bears whose territory we like to hike in, take all precautions to keep food items under your control. Do not leave food out and unattended—not even for a few minutes. If a bear is eating your food or shredding your pack in search of your snacks, *do not* attempt to retrieve any of your food items. In the bear's mind, it is now his food. Let the bear have it. That way, you can walk away with a great story. If you try to reclaim the food, you may not be able to tell any story. Secure your food for the protection of yourself and the bear.

In the unlikely event that you do encounter a black bear on the trail, do not run. Make eye contact but do not stare. Pick up small children to keep them from running. Back away slowly. If a bear approaches, make yourself appear larger by spreading your arms or holding your jacket open. Make as much threatening noise as you can by yelling or banging gear together.

Most bears fear people and will leave when they see you. If a bear woofs, snaps its jaws, slaps the ground or brush, or bluff charges: *you are too close! Back away!*

If a bear is after you and not your food, throw rocks or sticks and make every attempt to frighten it away or fight it off. Don't bother to run; they're very fast.

Rattlesnakes

Northern California's only native pit viper, the Northern Pacific rattlesnake, makes its home in the Sierra Nevada foothills, and its range extends to the Upper Montaine Belt—approximately 5,000 to 7,500 feet elevation in the northern range.

Backcountry Advice

In many cases, a permit is required before entering the backcountry to camp or day-hike. It is a help to other hikers, to the environment, and to yourself when you practice low-impact camping methods. Adhere to the adages "Pack it in, pack it out," and "Take only pictures, leave only footprints." Practicing "Leave no trace" camping ethics while in the backcountry benefits everyone.

Open fires are often not permitted in the backcountry, especially near lakes, in high-use areas, and during dry times when the Forest Service may issue a fire ban. Backpacking stoves are the prescribed method for cooking in the Tahoe region.

Wildlife, and in particular, black bears, learn to associate hikers and backpacks with food. It is up to us all to protect them from becoming dependent on our supplies. The use of a canister to protect your food from being nabbed by a bear is a far superior method than hanging a bear bag. Odor-proof plastic bags, however, are effective in keeping smaller animals out of your food. Use these methods to protect yourself and the wildlife.

Solid human waste must be buried in a hole at least six inches deep and at least 200 feet away from trails and water sources; a trowel is basic backpacking equipment. Paper products should not be buried and never burned. Carry out your used paper products in a doubled plastic bag and dispose of them at home.

Following the above guidelines will increase your chances for a pleasant, safe, and low-impact interaction between humans and nature. The suggestions are intended to enhance your experience in the Sierra Nevada Mountains. Forest regulations can change over time; contact forest ranger stations to confirm the status of any regulations before you enter the backcountry.

Tips for Enjoying the Lake Tahoe Area

You have made the first important decision affecting the successful outcome of your hike by reading this guidebook. Be sure to study the introductory information: the advice there is gained from hiking and climbing in many environments, and can generally be held true across all of those situations.

Prepare by leaving detailed trip information with an emergency contact and by gathering information about the hike from the appropriate agency as listed in Appendix A (page 257). Use the area map to determine the location of alternate hikes and make sure they match your abilities.

These hikes are rated as Easy, Moderate, or Strenuous. These ratings—using a five-star system—are a completely subjective method based on somewhat objective criteria. You should get some satisfaction, however, out of the knowledge that these hikes were rated by someone with no more than average abilities who arrived from sea level without acclimatization for the majority of the hikes.

EASY HIKES. This is Lake Tahoe. There are mountains all around it. Where are you going to find something easy to hike around here? The criteria, hard as they are to find, are just that the trail be groomed, nearly level, and shorter than 2 miles. The Tahoe Meadow Interpretive Trail is an "Easy" hike. Add another star to it, and the rating means a longer, graded trail where you may break a momentary sweat. Lake Margaret seems to fit this description.

MODERATE HIKES. Three stars means you'll be hiking more than 5 miles with some up and down along the way. If you are a nonsmoker in average physical condition, these will seem easy, but they are a bit more involved and may take more time. Bump the action up by one star and enter the "challenging" zone. This could mean more navigation work, a longer trail, steeper inclines, higher elevations, or any combination of those things.

STRENUOUS HIKES. Five stars will be everything you imagined. You can count on some sustained or steep inclines as well as rocky, long, or missing trails. Pyramid Peak is short but vertical. It's strenuous. So is McConnell Lake Loop because it is long, rocky, and vertical. See? Incredibly subjective.

Lake Tahoe and the surrounding Sierra Nevada mountains are special in more ways than their rugged beauty. Follow the various permit processes to the letter and you won't have to retrace your steps prematurely or in the company of a ranger. Having hiked all over the country, it's satisfying to see well-maintained trails resulting from the fees I've paid. Even the day-hike permits, being free, benefit hikers. First, they let potential rescuers know who went where and when. Second, that same information actually helps the U.S. Forest Service determine the priorities for trail and facility improvements and maintenance.

The signage method that the Forest Service uses to identify roads in their domain is fairly simple. And because Lake Tahoe is surrounded by three national forests and borders three wilderness areas, hikers are very familiar with them. However, as a reminder, this can help in navigating to the trailhead.

Main forest roads such as the road to Wrights Lake (Wrights Road) are noted by a small, square, brown-and-white sign with a numerical Forest Road designation, such as, in the case of Wrights Road, FR 4, or simply the number 4, or 04, within the white-bordered square on the brown background.

Signage for secondary forest roads is distinct and more descriptive. The sign itself, still decorated in Forest Service brown, is a vertically oriented, slender rectangle. For example, a secondary forest-road sign at the Wrights Lake Visitor Center is labeled "12N23." Tertiary roads are seen less frequently in this area because they are normally useful only in actively logged areas. None were used in this book to navigate to trailheads.

There are so many locations in the "Tahoe vicinity" that are worth hiking to and writing about that I had to limit my range to a strictly defined area. By drawing a line consistently 25 miles from Lake Tahoe's shore, I defined the area on which to focus my attention. I then divided the resulting amoeba-shaped region into three sections by doing some border-flipping. Mirroring the California–Nevada border yielded three nearly equal areas, placing hikes to the east, west, or south of the lake.

Trail Etiquette

Whether you're on a city, county, state, or national park trail, always remember that great care and resources (from nature as well as from your tax dollars) have gone into creating these trails. Treat the trail, wildlife, and fellow hikers with respect.

- **HIKE ON OPEN TRAILS ONLY.** Respect trail and road closures (ask if not sure), avoid possible trespassing on private land, and obtain permits and authorization as required. Leave gates as you found them or as marked.

- **LEAVE ONLY FOOTPRINTS.** Be sensitive to the ground beneath you. This also means staying on the existing trail and not blazing any new trails. Be sure to pack out what you pack in. No one likes to see the trash someone else has left behind.

- **NEVER SPOOK ANIMALS.** An unannounced approach, a sudden movement, or a loud noise startles most animals. A surprised animal can be dangerous to you, to others, and to itself. Give them plenty of space.

- **OBSERVE THE YIELD SIGNS** that are displayed around the region's trailheads and backcountry. They advise: Hikers yield to horses and bikers yield to both horses and hikers. A common courtesy on hills is that hikers and bikers yield to any uphill traffic.

- **ON ENCOUNTERING MOUNTED RIDERS** or horse packers, hikers can courteously step off the trail, on the downhill side if possible. Speak to the riders before they reach you and do not hide behind trees. You are less spooky if you are able to be seen and heard by the horse. Resist the urge to pet or touch the horses unless you are invited to do so.

- **PLAN AHEAD.** Know your equipment, your ability, and the area in which you are hiking—and prepare accordingly. Be self-sufficient at all times; carry necessary supplies for changes in weather or other conditions. A well-executed trip is a satisfaction to you and to others.

- **BE COURTEOUS** to other hikers, bikers, equestrians, and others you encounter on the trails.

The full moon fades into daylight near Middle Velma Lake.

part one
Lake Tahoe
East Hikes

1

Despite
the
abundance
of
lofty
superlatives
that
inevitably
precede
a visit
to Lake
Tahoe,
descriptions
do not
seem
to
disappoint
anyone

01 Mount Rose

SCENERY: ✪ ✪ ✪ ✪ ✪	HIKING TIME: 5–7 hours
TRAIL CONDITION: ✪ ✪ ✪ ✪	OUTSTANDING FEATURES: *Pleasant trail through*
CHILDREN: ✪ ✪	*pine forest, plus a waterfall beneath Mount Houghton.*
DIFFICULTY: ✪ ✪ ✪ ✪	*A well-defined trail leads to the summit for a 360° view*
SOLITUDE: ✪ ✪ ✪	*all the way from Stampede Reservoir in the west to the*
DISTANCE: *10.2 miles round-trip*	*Carson Range in the east, with Lake Tahoe laid out for*
	22 blue miles below you to the south.

Your trail is very straightforward and pleasant to walk the entire way. You'll use a ridge at the foot of Mount Houghton to gain 200 feet in the first 0.5 miles before crossing that ridge to traverse for the next 2 miles with a zero elevation gain. You'll have great views of Lake Tahoe initially before your destination begins to dominate the vista. The final 2.5 miles to the summit are interrupted only by a few switchbacks up the more than 1,700 feet to the top of this old volcano.

🚶🚶 No one is certain about the origin of Mount Rose's name—even whether it came from a man or a woman. But we do know that Church Peak, the twin summit on this ridge, honors Dr. James Church of the University of Nevada, who established the first high-altitude meteorological observatory here and developed the modern science of snow survey, which is used today. While on Nevada turf, Mount Rose, at 10,776 feet, is the highest point around Lake Tahoe.

Walk past the pit toilets to the trailhead, situated immediately behind them at the kiosk. Less than 100 feet past the trailhead is the hikers' only trailhead for the Tahoe Rim Trail, which leads to the Mount Rose Summit Trail. The Tahoe Rim Trail Association supplies trail maps at the kiosk, where hikers can also read up on preferred wilderness practices.

Head uphill with a sharp turn at the kiosk and immediately take in the views to the south and west, where Lake Tahoe comes into view. In exactly 0.5 miles, the trail will level out. Conveniently enough, you'll

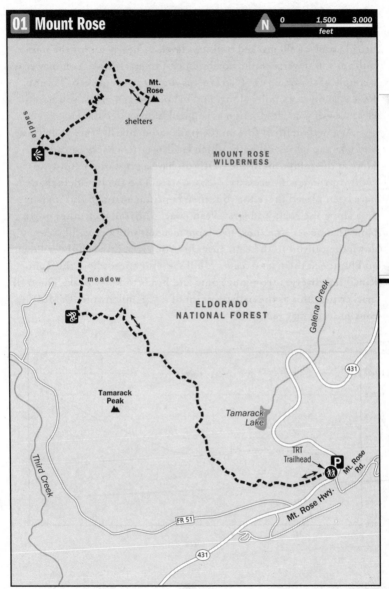

N

0   1,500   3,000
feet

Mt. Rose

shelters

saddle

MOUNT ROSE
WILDERNESS

meadow

ELDORADO
NATIONAL FOREST

Galena Creek

431

Tamarack
Peak

Tamarack
Lake

Third Creek

TRT
Trailhead

Mt. Rose Rd.

Mt. Rose Hwy.

FR 51

431

find a tight formation of boulders shaded by pine, perfect for putting on the sunscreen that you forgot to apply in the parking lot. The broad, sandy, well-marked trail stays level, or nearly so, for the next 2 miles as you traverse to the northwest of Tamarack Peak. You may cross a couple of seasonal runoff streams as you get sneak peeks of Mount Rose at about 1.25 miles along, and in another 0.5 miles, you have a clear view of your destination as you walk along a steep slope.

At a well-defined fork in the trail, momentarily leave your route and take the left-hand path, which leads over to a rocky cascade. Here at the midpoint of the trail, you have a great opportunity to refill your water if necessary. Cross a stream on the boulders that have been placed there for you, then continue through this marshy area along the rock-and-gravel causeway. The trail continues north beneath a power line, next to a large meadow with beautiful views down the canyon to the east. Just after you crash through the willows and lupine at the next stream, you'll see a junction where the Tahoe Rim Trail diverges from our route and heads to Relay Peak. The trail marker pegs this as the halfway point of a 5.3-mile route. (YMMV—your mileage may vary.)

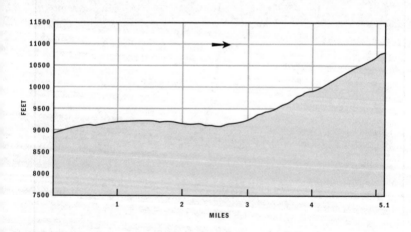

Summer fires cast a haze across Lake Tahoe as seen from Mount Rose.

From this intersection, climb across one of Mount Houghton's eastern flanks and then begin ascending the crease between it and Mount Rose. Climb these tree-covered slopes, then cross to the north side of the ravine and resume hiking up to a saddle 400 feet above. Just before you reach the saddle, you will encounter the boundary sign for the Mount Rose Wilderness. At the saddle, continue to walk around the west to reach the end of a ridge, which you will mount and hike to the northeast. Ignore the blocked-off trail in that saddle leading to the northwest. It is a segment of the Mount Rose Trail leading to Davis Meadow.

Turn uphill to the right. The dirt-and-rock trail becomes somewhat scrabbly as it ascends the prominent ridge in a rather businesslike manner. After reaching the first switchback in 0.5 miles, you may enjoy the chance to take in the scenery (along with some extra oxygen). The switchbacks will lead you to a traverse of the northwest slope, where you will turn southeast on the lower portion of the summit ridge. Three final switchbacks through the rocks carry you up to the ridge and a simple 250-foot walk to the summit.

Some shelters have been erected to protect you from the wind. The thousands of California tortoiseshell butterflies are apparently unaffected by these gusts. From your perch here, you should be able to see Boca, Stampede, and Prosser reservoirs to the northwest. Mount Houghton and Relay Peak are visible to the southwest, and Washoe Lake can be seen to the east.

DIRECTIONS: **From Truckee take Interstate 80 east 2.5 miles to CA 267/CA 89, Exit 188B, toward Lake Tahoe. Drive 11.6 miles and turn left on CA 28. Drive 4.6 miles on CA 28 before turning left onto Mount Rose Highway/NV 431. Drive 8.2 miles uphill to Mount Rose Road, where a large parking lot is on the left.**

From I-80 in Reno, drive 10 miles south on US 395 to Mount Rose Highway/NV 431, and drive 16 miles east to the summit parking lot.

Pit toilets and trash receptacles are available at the top of this year-round pass.

GPS TRAILHEAD COORDINATES	01 MOUNT ROSE
UTM Zone (WGS84)	11S
Easting	0250189
Northing	4355492
Latitude	N 39° 18.768'
Longitude	W 119° 53.849'

02 Tahoe Meadow Trails

SCENERY: ✿ ✿ ✿ ✿	DISTANCE: *1.5–4.5 miles round-trip*
TRAIL CONDITION: ✿ ✿ ✿ ✿ ✿	HIKING TIME: *2–3 hours*
CHILDREN: ✿ ✿ ✿ ✿ ✿	OUTSTANDING FEATURES: *Subalpine meadow*
DIFFICULTY: ✿	*teeming with flowers and wildlife; interpretive trail*
SOLITUDE: ✿ ✿	*describes the flora, fauna, and natural history of the*
	meadows

The paths that meander around Tahoe Meadow are covered with footprints and signs of mammals, the air is filled with songbirds and raptors, and the ground is alive with masses of wildflowers and trees. This hike has no particular destination and it's not going to get you anywhere other than familiar with nature. A natural-history field guide would be a welcome companion on this walk because you will have a chance to use it often.

Begin with a 1.4-mile hike along the Tahoe Meadow Interpretive Loop, which provides hikers of all ages (including hearty wheelchair hikers) a great introduction to this meadow's ecosystem. Finishing this small meadow, it's now time to take in a bit more by hiking along Ophir Creek as it winds through the larger Tahoe Meadow. A combination of natural surfaces and composition boardwalk allows hikers to observe this natural area without disturbing the fragile soils and plants. Hikers are strongly encouraged to keep their pets under control in this sensitive area.

Your journey along the interpretive trail begins at the kiosk next to the trees, directly south of the pit toilets. Head east on the trail as it leaves the shade, and bear right onto the path ahead. You are actually following the Tahoe Rim Trail as it leads to Mount Rose Campground. This grass-surrounded track features several bridges that enable wheelchair access around the loop. The first is just about 400 feet along and spans a tiny stream running out of the copse of trees 50 feet to the north. The broad, sandy trail looks to the left at the meadow that sprouts lodgepole pines as well as willows.

Just ahead is a junction featuring an interpretive display—an overview of the species routinely spotted here. Wildflowers vary throughout

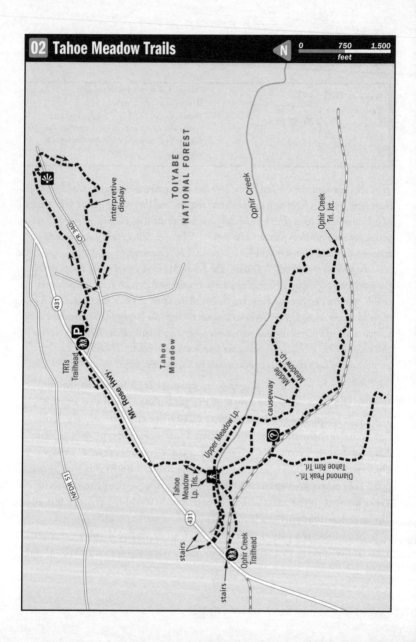

N

0   750   1,500
feet

TOIYABE NATIONAL FOREST

Ophir Creek

interpretive display

CR 840

431

TRTs Trailhead

P

NFDR 51

Mt. Rose Hwy.

Tahoe Meadow

Upper Meadow Lp.

Middle Meadow Lp.

causeway

Ophir Creek Trl. Jct.

Tahoe Meadow Lp. Trls.

stairs

431

Diamond Peak Trl.– Tahoe Rim Trl.

Ophir Creek Trailhead

stairs

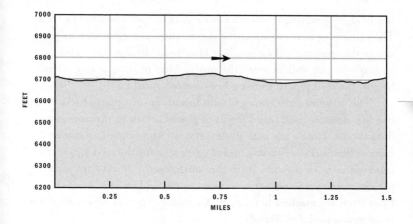

the season, as do migrating birds. This meadow is a favorite area for birders to set up their own perches for observing. The easiest direction on this loop leads straight ahead, past the point where the loop rejoins this path. The boulders to the left of the junction are a good habitat for the Belding ground squirrels that are constantly on the lookout for the red-tailed hawks cruising overhead.

The trail signage points out the trail width, composition, cross-slope, and grade: important information for wheelchair hikers. The next slight grade leads across another small rivulet before the track reveals some of its asphalt past. The trail gains just enough elevation to enable hikers to look down into the meadow to the right. The former roadbed is outlined by pussy paws, paintbrush, and sage and is pleasantly shaded by some magnificent lodgepole pines. A spring keeps the sand ahead somewhat damp, but that also makes it firmer underfoot.

As Mount Rose comes into view, your track bears to the right and leaves the Tahoe Rim Trail. A hundred feet hence is an engineered spur trail leading to a vista point. Next to this overlook is a double lodgepole surrounded on three sides by meadow and facing the tree-spotted knoll to the southwest. Returning to the loop, cross two bridges spanning the creek where you can spot small brook trout. The return leg heads south along the meadow's margin, staying just inside the trees at the foot of Slide Mountain. Bridges span each streamlet as you walk beneath the pines. After pausing at one restful bench, the trail jogs to the west between two small knolls.

The meadow here is ringed with broad, sandy slopes which, like the meadow itself, are a result of glacial action in the not-too-distant past. Follow the path under western white pine and some mature hemlocks as you stay under tree cover for the next 150 yards. Looking into the meadow from the south toward its wet core allows patient observers to see raccoon and coyotes and (at least once that I can attest to) maybe a black bear. Cross the causeway, and a final left returns you to the trailhead.

Now comes a far-larger meadow 0.75 miles to the southwest that offers more trails to explore. Embark from the informational kiosk at the Tahoe Rim Trail trailhead just 200 feet west of the pit toilets. Pick up one of the "green maps" there, provided for your safety by the Tahoe Rim Trail Association. As you walk along, watch for red-tailed hawks soaring above the meadow, usually on their way to a higher perch, but sometimes on a mission, talons poised for lunch. The sand-and-gravel trail is bound by a log fence on the left and Mount Rose Highway on the right. The path veers to the left, angling across the meadow, toward Ophir Creek. This same point can be reached via the stairs along the highway, as well.

To observe the meadow, hikers can walk along the creek and the margins of the open space. To preserve the meadow's plant life and control streamside soil erosion, dedicated conservationists have installed bridges and built causeways and boardwalks. The trails in the meadow are connected to one another but do not have to be followed in any order. However, this is a fragile ecosystem with established trails. Wherever you walk, strictly observe the paths (including controlling your pets and picking up after them).

Starting out from the junction with the boardwalk and bridge crossing Ophir Creek, turn right and ascend the creek on the Upper Meadow Loop. This short loop (0.9 miles, which you are starting in the middle) leads 0.2 miles upstream, giving you views into the meadow and over your shoulder as you walk. Before reaching the log fence, your path crosses a bridge over the creek and returns on the shaded south bank. Follow the trail back the same distance but pass the footbridge and continue to the east along the meadow's border. The loop trail is intersected by the Tahoe Rim Trail close to the bridge.

Traverse along the trees for the next 0.2 miles and just as the trail turns north, look for a junction with the Middle Meadow Trail (also a shortcut to the Ophir Creek Trail). If you want more solitude or a better vantage point, continue along that loop as the posted map illustrates. If you're returning to the trailhead after finishing the Upper Loop, walk to the creek and cross via the boardwalk. This is a great spot to linger, as the trout seem to flash by here as if on cue. Turn northwest and follow the boardwalk back to your starting point. Corn lilies, buttercups, and paintbrush add color and fragrance to the banks of this briskly bubbling creek.

Gain different perspectives by venturing along the 1.7-mile-long Middle Meadow Loop as it heads east down the sloping meadow. The trail stays inside the trees as your route skirts a lightly treed area about 150 yards south of the creek. When you cross an engineered causeway ahead, you pass over a wet area that drains a small meadow 100 yards to the south, which you will pass by on your return leg of the loop.

Vistas into the meadow remain consistently intriguing as you walk eastward to circumnavigate this 150-foot-tall knoll. After you make the turn to the south, cross a stream on some well-placed boulders and stairs and in less than 300 yards, you will intersect the Ophir Creek Trail, your route west, back to the trailhead. Now traveling with the hill on your right, enjoy the shaded trail. The meadow flowers disappear, but the forest is no less brightly colored, thanks

part one

to the brilliant red snow plants. Graze the small meadow to your left and step over its small runoff stream. In just 200 yards, watch for an information kiosk alongside the trail and, 100 yards past the kiosk, you'll reach the intersection with the Tahoe Rim Trail section that leads to Diamond Peak to the south. To get back to the bridge at Ophir Creek, follow your trail straight ahead, to the northwest, about 0.25 miles and then hook a sharp right at the junction that leads you over to the bridge.

DIRECTIONS: Leave Incline Village on Mount Rose Highway/ NV 431, and drive 7.4 miles to the Tahoe Meadow trailhead parking lot, on the east side of the road. Pit toilets are available, but water and garbage service are not.

The trailhead for the Interpretive Loop is across the parking lot, south of the pit toilets. It is marked by an informational kiosk describing the trail.

The Tahoe Rim Trail is marked by a kiosk to the west of the pit toilets.

Additional parking is available on the east side of Mount Rose Highway, with access via stairs at three locations between 0.7 and 0.8 miles southwest of the trailhead parking lot.

GPS TRAILHEAD COORDINATES	02 TAHOE MEADOW TRAIL
UTM Zone (WGS84)	11S
Easting	0249258
Northing	4354920
Latitude	N 39° 18.443'
Longitude	W 119° 54.484'

03 Ophir Creek Trail

SCENERY: ✿ ✿ ✿ ✿
TRAIL CONDITION: ✿ ✿
CHILDREN: ✿
DIFFICULTY: ✿ ✿ ✿ ✿
SOLITUDE: ✿ ✿ ✿ ✿ ✿
DISTANCE: 6.8 miles round-trip

HIKING TIME: 4 hours
OUTSTANDING FEATURES: *Wildflowers, songbirds, mammals, insects, and raptors fill the meadows and sky around Ophir Creek; Slide Mountain looms over your shoulder as you descend to the site of its last catastrophic display.*

From the trailhead beneath Mount Rose, skirt a huge meadow—full of colorful plants and active wildlife—with Slide Mountain over your shoulder. The trail follows the meadow's Ophir Creek partway through the meadow and again steeply downhill to Upper Price Lake. Along the way, stop at vistas where you can observe the hulking slopes of Slide Mountain. The mountain's castoff granite and scree took a toll in human life as recently as 25 years ago.

🚶🚶 While sagebrush stands out brightly throughout the meadow, aspens and willows add color to the fringe and middle of the meadow. Read over the information regarding the Tahoe Rim Trail (TRT) at the trailhead, then strike out along the gravel path bordering the highway. Willows will protect you from the road noise, and the trail will gradually sink and veer southwest away through the meadow. A new causeway completed in September 2008 minimizes the impact of travel through the wet meadow approaching Ophir Creek.

You'll have options upon reaching the creek and the new boardwalk. The alternate route crosses a new bridge here, allowing hikers (and bikers on even days only) to follow the TRT. At the next two junctions, follow the signs by turning left to head south. The TRT will diverge from the Ophir Creek Trail 1,000 feet to the south of that last turn. Keep to the left on the Ophir Creek Trail.

The route turns south, moseying about 400 yards along the boardwalk adjacent to and across the creek until it ends. Then take

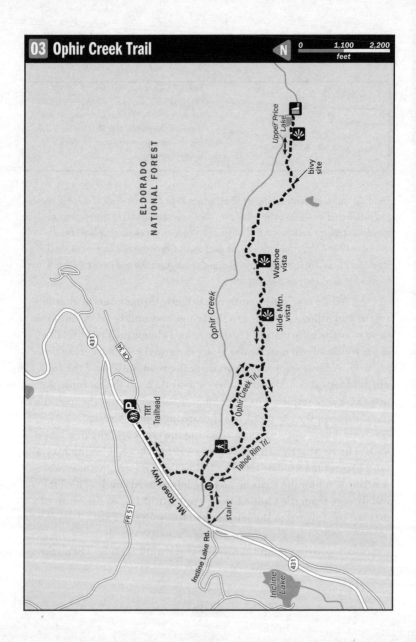

03 Ophir Creek Trail

N

0   1,100   2,200
feet

ELDORADO
NATIONAL FOREST

Upper Price Lake

bivy site

Washoe vista

Slide Mtn. vista

Ophir Creek

Ophir Creek Trl.

TRT Trailhead

Tahoe Rim Trl.

Mt. Rose Hwy.

stairs

Incline Lake Rd.

FR 51

Incline Lake

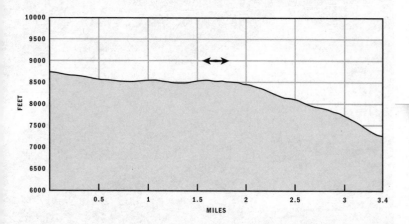

the connector trail off to the left, heading along the margin of the lodgepole pine forest. You will get a nice vista down onto the meadow as you circle above the fragile wet area below. New causeways using recycled synthetic materials keep your feet dry as you walk across this wet hillside. Resume your eastward trek along the fringe of the forest, roughly paralleling the Ophir Creek Trail, 150 feet higher and 1,000 feet to the south.

After you climb a bit, you'll cross a stream with the help of boulders and stairs. Then the trail contours around to the junction with the Ophir Creek Trail. Head to the east here by turning left; the Tahoe Rim Trail is 0.7 miles to the right. The stairs at Mount Rose Highway/NV 431 are 1.2 miles away, and Davis Creek County Park is 6.6 miles east. If you need water, the trail crosses the stream in about 1.25 miles and the lake is about 2 miles away.

Descend the sand-and-rock trail in earnest now through an area thick with willows. Open spots reveal increasingly better views of Slide Mountain. The trail crosses a tiny meadow where thick grasses cover the path and huge views of the Washoe Valley debut to the east. The descent continues, and you must pass by the next side trail,

Slide Mountain's shaky southeast face

regardless of how distinct and tempting it may be. It just goes to the creek—and not conveniently either.

Make a crossing of a cool, willow-clad creek just before reentering the trees. Ahead on the left is a level spot that makes a good bivy site, but only if you have a bear canister for your food. Ahead 100 feet ahead is a trail junction: the path to the right leads to Davis Creek County Park and the path to left, which you take, leads downhill to Upper Price Lake. The cruddy, rocky trail descends more steeply now, but stays well above the creek. You will seem to climb away from the creek as the ravine deepens, more so after Ophir Creek's main stream joins just ahead.

Just about 75 feet above the lake is an opening in the trees that yields an excellent view of the southeast slope of Slide Mountain, looking directly at the face that last released its overburden in 1983. Both Upper and Lower Price lakes were displaced by the resulting avalanche, which destroyed homes and killed one person.

Cross the dam at the lake's outlet and you will find some good campsites on the knoll above the lake. Raccoon, deer, bear and coyote are frequent visitors here. This area is on the margin of the lush Sierra Nevada and the Carson Range, on the cusp of the rain shadow. Mammals of all sizes—voles and ground squirrels, coyotes and raccoons, even deer and bears—seem to be attracted to the regular supply of water that supports this diverse food chain. Songbirds, jays, woodpeckers, turkeys, and raptors are all visible here, possibly for the very same reasons.

The trail is a tough slog for the first 500 feet back uphill to the trail junction and creek crossing. Then it's only a semi-slog for the next 700 feet back to the meadow. Look for signs of raccoon and coyote along the trail, but do not touch any scat with your bare hands. Raccoon feces carries bacteria that attack the brain and are deadly to humans.

DIRECTIONS: From I-80 in Truckee, take Exit 188B south on NV 267. Drive 11.6 miles to NV 28 in King's Beach. Drive 4.5 miles east on NV 28 (Tahoe Boulevard) to Incline Village. From Incline Village, turn left on Mount Rose Highway/NV 431, and drive 7.4 miles to the parking lot on the right side of the highway. The trail begins at the kiosk in the northwest corner of the parking lot.

There are pit toilets located here, but no trash or water services. There's room for a few dozen cars on the pavement and dirt overflow.

Alternatively, park 0.8 miles back along the highway, where stairs lead to the trail at the boardwalk.

GPS Trailhead Coordinates	03 Ophir Creek Trail
UTM Zone (WGS84)	11S
Easting	0249258
Northing	4354920
Latitude	N 39° 18.443'
Longitude	W 119° 54.484'

04 Diamond Peak

SCENERY: ✿ ✿ ✿ ✿ ✿
TRAIL CONDITION: ✿ ✿ ✿ ✿
CHILDREN: ✿ ✿ ✿
DIFFICULTY: ✿ ✿ ✿
SOLITUDE: ✿ ✿ ✿
DISTANCE: *11 miles round-trip*

HIKING TIME: *6 hours*
OUTSTANDING FEATURES: *This hike starts in a flower-filled meadow and just gets better. It features some incredible vistas of Lake Tahoe from secluded outcrops, and the trail, despite short ups and downs, is sandy, level, and pleasantly shaded by firs and pines.*

Tahoe Meadow is a wonderful trailhead—one of the most pleasant around the lake—to embark from on a day hike. The route to Diamond Peak is mostly level, gaining the ridge in about 300 feet and then generally following it south through forests of western white pine, lodgepole pine, red fir, and Jeffrey pine. The high point of the hike is slightly above 8,800 feet, while the destination is at 8,540 feet (and has a chairlift terminus attached to it). For the most solitude, avoid even-numbered days, when mountain bikes have access to this excellent trail.

🚶🚶 Embark from the information kiosk for the Tahoe Rim Trail (TRT) at the northwest corner of the trailhead parking lot. The obvious trail to the southwest parallels Mount Rose Highway and skirts the meadow's border for 0.4 miles. As you approach Ophir Creek, causeways assist your trek across the wet ground and around the fragile plants. A boardwalk extends this protection southeast along the creek. The near future will see a bridge across the creek at this point and a boardwalk to the northwest along the creek, eliminating social trails that relentlessly increase streamside erosion.

Currently, you cross the stream about 100 feet down the board-walk, then return the 100 feet to this point on the opposite side of the stream and follow the signs for the TRT. Shortly after entering the trees, a couple of rapid left turns at the signed intersections will point you southeast on the Tahoe Rim Trail. The next junction to watch for is 1,000 feet ahead, where the Ophir Creek Trail veers to the left and you and the TRT, bound for Tunnel Creek Road, skew right.

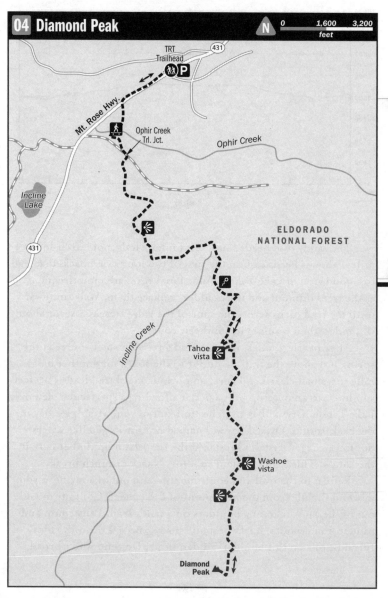

04 Diamond Peak

N   0   1,600   3,200
                    feet

TRT
Trailhead
431

Mt. Rose Hwy.

Ophir Creek
Trl. Jct.

Ophir Creek

Incline
Lake

431

ELDORADO
NATIONAL FOREST

Incline Creek

Tahoe
vista

Washoe
vista

Diamond
Peak

LAKE TAHOE EAST

part one

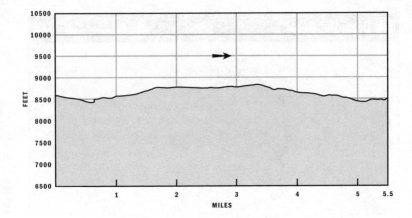

The sandy trail heads southwest under a lodgepole cover for 0.3 miles, when it heads east on the first of two long switchbacks that lead to a good vista of Lake Tahoe. Additional vistas are more frequent as the trees thin out and the boulders replace them. Walk southward until the trail turns across the spur of the ridge, tracks east for about 0.5 miles, then resumes its southerly course.

After nearly 3 miles, you can find a reliable water source at the spring just above the trail. Contour to the south for another half mile to a small clearing. There, an obvious social trail leads 400 feet southwest to an outcrop with a perch affording a spectacular view over Lake Tahoe. Crystal Bay stretches in front of you, with Agate Bay in the background. Crystal Bay was named not for its gemlike waters, but for George Crystal, who staked the first claim on timber here in the 1860s. This is an excellent spot for a snack or lunch break.

Return to the trail and continue into and out of a ravine as you descend slightly from the high point of 8,830 feet. Contour in and out of the canyon among boulders on a sandy trail. Penstemon and pine mat manzanita, buckwheat and pussy paws are the only colorful additions on this boulder-ridden slope. Descend into a broad, flat saddle ringed by lodgepole pine, western white pine, and red fir trees. Hidden from the Tahoe side, vistas into the Washoe Valley and shallow Washoe Lake appear to the east as you descend the sandy trail.

From the next brief vista on the Tahoe side, you can spot the trip's destination, highlighted by the chairlift terminus. Descend to another small, almost circular, saddle, where you will begin to contour along the eastern side of Diamond Peak. A faint trail heads southwest up through the trees (just before they completely peter out) to the peak. Or you can round the curve 400 feet farther south and then, just before entering the saddle, turn uphill on the sandy slope to your destination.

The return to the trailhead is easier, and any missed pictures are still there.

DIRECTIONS: Leave Incline Village on Mount Rose Highway/ NV 431, and drive 7.4 miles to the Tahoe Meadow trailhead parking lot on the east side of the road. Pit toilets are available, but water and garbage service are not. This is about 0.75 miles past the stairs that lead more directly to the trail, but this way you have a pretty meadow to walk in and you can leave your car in the worry-free TRT trailhead parking lots. If the lot is full, park on the south side of the highway 0.75 miles back toward the lake.

GPS Trailhead Coordinates	04 Diamond Peak
UTM Zone (WGS84)	11S
Easting	0249258
Northing	4354919
Latitude	N 39° 18.442'
Longitude	W 119° 54.484'

05 Folsom Camp Loop

SCENERY: ☆ ☆ ☆ ☆ ☆	DISTANCE: 6.2 miles round-trip
TRAIL CONDITION: ☆ ☆ ☆ ☆	HIKING TIME: 3–4 hours
CHILDREN: ☆ ☆ ☆ ☆	OUTSTANDING FEATURES: Historic flume; Tahoe
DIFFICULTY: ☆ ☆ ☆	vistas; wildflower-filled meadows
SOLITUDE: ☆ ☆ ☆	

This loop is easy enough, because the length of the trail runs along an historic flume that formerly delivered cordwood and timber to the Washoe Valley. The route is described in the way I initially hiked it, but it might be even easier to hike in reverse. You'll encounter a few steep spots along the described route, but they're not long, and the total elevation gain is 800 feet over 1.3 miles, or 1.75 miles if done in reverse. The middle 3 miles are essentially flat and shaded.

🚶🚶 Look for the unofficial trailhead near the stairs to the children's ski school, right in front of the lodge at Diamond Peak Resort. Circle past the Crystal Express chairlift and begin gaining elevation along the service road as it winds up to the northeast across moist meadows. Moments after coming abreast of another lift, the road will begin to swing around in the opposite direction, crossing a ski run and a small ridge where you'll have an excellent vista of Lake Tahoe along with an informational display.

When you reach the loading station for Ridge Lift, you could take a short side trip over to Snowflake Lodge, which offers some excellent views over the lake. To get there, walk 0.35 miles to the southwest, past a chairlift and a maintenance garage. This is an excellent destination in and of itself, where you can see the Carolina-blue waters of Crystal Bay, as well as Agate Bay (past Stateline Lookout).

The described hike heads in the opposite direction, to the northeast about 0.4 miles, and the views will be just as stunning. Pass Luggi's Run, named for Diamond Peak founder Luggi Foegger, as the

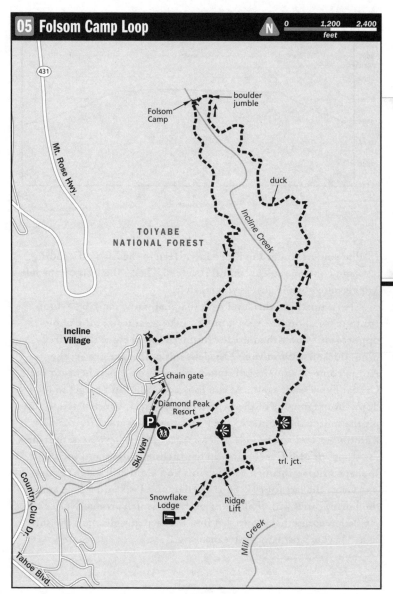

05 Folsom Camp Loop

N 0   1,200   2,400
              feet

431

Mt. Rose Hwy.

Folsom Camp

boulder jumble

duck

TOIYABE
NATIONAL FOREST

Incline Creek

Incline Village

chain gate

Diamond Peak Resort

P

trl. jct.

Snowflake Lodge

Ridge Lift

Ski Way

Country Club Dr.

Tahoe Blvd.

Mill Creek

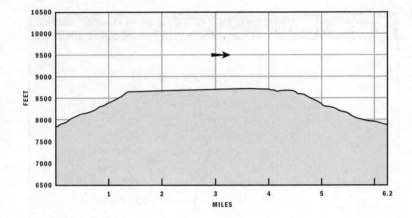

road meanders under the Ridge Lift. Head to the lift's off-loading area and continue steeply uphill 100 feet. There, the trail on the left will become obvious just as you reach it.

Turn north on this level path that maintains the 7,650-foot contour for about the next 3 miles. Take advantage of the photo opportunities over the next few hundred feet, before the Jeffrey pines thicken around you. The views out to the lake are excellent. As you come to a quartet of standing snags, you'll pass beneath the Crystal Express yet again. As you look around, don't forget to look down—for remnants of the original flumeworks, constructed to supply the mines and homes of the Comstock Lode and Virginia City with timber and cordwood. At least 300 cords a day were sent from the slopes of Mill Creek, first up the Incline Railway and then by **V**-shaped flume through the Virginia and Gold Hill water tunnel.

Cross the last four ski runs of Diamond Peak and amble among the Jeffrey pines with their pungent butterscotch aroma. Notice the sap-laden cones that crown red firs; they actually gleam in the sunlight. As you cross runoff streams, you'll see aspens decorated with carvings of past romances and birthdays alongside willows and ferns, all punctuated by the red berries of mountain ash.

Cross a few runoff streams that augmented the old flume and then, as you hike west around a ridge spur, *Duck!* A formerly standing snag has toppled and hangs precipitously above the trail on rocks. Head and neck firmly attached, continue north across a couple of stream crossings employing old flume materials for bridgeworks. The second of these is the nascent Incline Creek.

Another stream just 0.3 miles hence drops from sight beneath a jumble of hefty boulders—almost uniformly 2 meters in diameter—just as it reaches the trail. From this point, your trail turns southwest, crossing an open area that looks broad and flat enough for a large campsite. In fact, this was Folsom Camp, named for the lumberman Gilman Folsom who, in partnership with Sam Marlette, supplied some 40,000 cords of wood per year and employed more than 400 Chinese lumbermen in the enterprise.

Continue past Folsom Camp and cross a wooden footbridge. The trail leading to the northwest continues uphill to Tahoe Meadow. Turn south and meander through the lodgepole and fir on a sandy trail. Soon the path widens somewhat and follows Incline Creek as it descends to the condominium complex near the resort. A footbridge will ease your last crossing, but the creek will keep you company as you turn straight south again after you bump into the condos. A locked chain across the trail is the end of this ride. Step over and walk down the road 0.2 miles to the upper lot.

Crystal and Agate bays

DIRECTIONS: Head east from Incline Village on Tahoe Boulevard for 2 miles. Turn left onto Country Club Drive. In 0.1 miles, turn right onto Ski Way and drive 1.3 miles to the upper lot at Diamond Peak Resort, where hikers are allowed park in the summer. The trailhead is in front of the new lodge below you to the left.

GPS TRAILHEAD COORDINATES	05 FOLSOM CAMP LOOP
UTM Zone (WGS84)	11S
Easting	0247757
Northing	4348999
Latitude	N 39° 15.219'
Longitude	W 119° 55.393'

o6 Marlette Lake

SCENERY: ☆ ☆ ☆ ☆	DISTANCE: *11.6 miles round-trip*
TRAIL CONDITION: ☆ ☆ ☆ ☆	HIKING TIME: *4–6 hours*
CHILDREN: ☆	OUTSTANDING FEATURES: *Gentle grade, wildlife,*
DIFFICULTY: ☆ ☆ ☆	*wildflowers, aspen groves, and lakeside trail*
SOLITUDE: ☆ ☆ ☆	

Watch for this trail to be one of the first to be clear of snow, rewarding early-season hikers with trailside flowers and spectacular views of two lakes that were once part of the famous flume system that supplied water to Virginia City from the 1870s into the 1900s. Deer, owls, goshawks, Stellar's jays, flickers, and chickadees are plentiful on this pleasant and conveniently located hike. First, walk around petite Spooner Lake's north shore to the North Canyon connector trail. Pass Spooner Cabin and Spencer's Cabin on the way to North Canyon Road, which leads to the Marlette Lake trailhead. While the trail initially gains some elevation, the 1,200-foot climb to the saddle above Marlette Lake is one of the gentlest uphill paths on the east side of the lake. A gentle descent leads to the lake's southern inlet stream.

🏃🏃 From the trailhead at Spooner Summit, follow the Tahoe Rim Trail for approximately 100 feet to the Spooner Lake access trail, where you will then head downhill to the left. Follow this shaded path west under lodgepole and Jeffrey pines, then enter the first of many aspen groves as your trail turns to the northwest. The Basque sheepherders would use these smooth-barked trees as canvases for carving their initials, names, and pictures.

While the distance around the lake is approximately equal, the trail on the lake's north side leads directly to the connecting trail to North Canyon Road. But you can park at the Lake Tahoe Nevada State Park parking lot on the east side of CA 28, just before the US 50 junction, for an equally appealing hike on North Canyon Road that is about a mile shorter. Spooner's Summit was the location of Spooner's Hotel, a

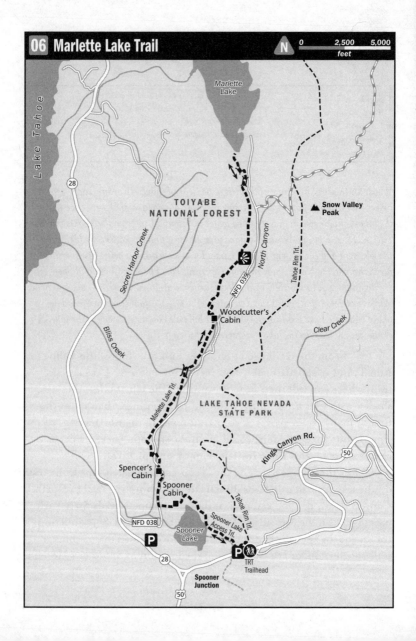

N

0   2,500   5,000

feet

Marlette Lake

Lake Tahoe

28

TOIYABE NATIONAL FOREST

▲ **Snow Valley Peak**

Secret Harbor Creek

North Canyon

Tahoe Rim Trail

NFD 039

Woodcutter's Cabin

Clear Creek

Bliss Creek

Marlette Lake Trail

LAKE TAHOE NEVADA STATE PARK

Kings Canyon Rd.

50

Spencer's Cabin

Spooner Cabin

Tahoe Rim Trail

NFD 038

P

Spooner Lake

Spooner Lake Access Trail

P 🚶

TRT Trailhead

28

Spooner Junction

50

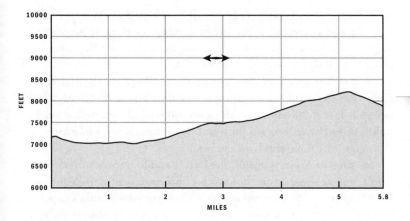

thriving business while the logging and mining industries were hot. By 1915 it had become a collection of ramshackle buildings.

As you descend through the lush foliage, you will pass by the turnoff to Spooner Lake's south trail. The sign will remind you that your dog must be leashed at all times while you are on the Spooner Lake trail. Due to its trout population, Spooner Lake is frequented by anglers of all ages. Comfortable park benches have been placed off the path at frequent intervals around the lake—most have either a lake or mountain vista.

Heading around the north side of the lake, you'll pick up the North Canyon Trail after almost exactly 1 mile. The trail sign on the right, marked NORTH CANYON ROAD, leads off uphill to the north-west. Follow this track toward Spooner Cabin, which you will soon see uphill on your right.

Spooner Cabin is maintained by a private concessionaire for wintertime use by cross-country skiers or snowshoers. Continue downhill to North Canyon Road, then turn right and continue north. In another 0.3 miles, you will see Spencer's Cabin on the left. This cabin was formerly used by the caretaker of the ranch owned in the early 1900s by Charlie Fulstone. It is now used as a summertime rest stop and as a warming hut for wintertime travelers. It is open to all users and has a working woodburning stove. A Leave No Trace attitude is all that is requested by the park.

In another 300 paces you will see the trailhead for the Marlette Lake Trail. As the sign says, this is a moderate hike and your goal will be reached in 3.75 miles. At this point, hikers and equestrians head uphill through the trees on the west side of the canyon, while bicyclists continue their climb on the road.

As your path winds uphill, the Jeffrey and lodgepole pines will help keep you shaded and cool on this duff-and-sand trail. Your track is bordered by fragrant lupine and silvery woolly mule's ears. When the trail turns to sand and the canopy opens up above you, you can't help but notice the wind rattling the aspens on the opposite side of the meadow. Your path will cross North Canyon Creek a few times along the way with the aid of sturdy footbridges.

A good spot to filter water is at the first footbridge, but there are three other decent spots before the lake: 0.5 miles farther on, next to the woodcutter's cabin, or on the other side of the saddle at two or three stream crossings. While this hike is largely shaded, the sun is intense during those times you're exposed. Carry sunscreen and apply it early in this hike. As the sun reflects off of the rock and snow, apply sunscreen to the back of your legs (if you're wearing shorts) and especially to the underside of your chin, ears, and nose.

Your trail switchbacks and points you northeast after you leave the woodcutter's cabin. If you're here early in the day, listen for the sound of flickers hammering at the standing snags in search of yummy grubs. After an hour of hiking, you may begin to interpret the call of the mountain chickadee—the "cheeseburger bird" that flies all around you in aspen or pines. For some excellent views of snow-capped peaks, look back, at about 8,000 feet in elevation, for the vista framed through the trees. If you miss it on the way in, the vista will be framed by the trees and the trail as you return home.

Marlette Lake was named for the man who was surveyor general of both California and Nevada.

If you are intrepid enough to search for higher vistas, look east for the Tahoe Rim Trail heading up to Snow Valley Peak. Six gentle switchbacks carry you up the 1,000 feet to the peak. You can access that trail just before you reach the saddle above Marlette Lake. The hike continues past the saddle about 300 feet downhill to Marlette Lake's inlet.

Douglas-firs add to the shade on this hillside leading down to Marlette Lake. From your uphill vantage point, you'll have a couple of beautiful views of the lake. You will also see the fish ladders for the trout hatchery at the inlet stream on the lake's south end.

Marlette Lake was held in private hands from its inception as a reservoir for the Hobart-Marlette flume system. For decades it has been a popular trout-fishing destination. While the Lahontin cutthroat trout are no longer favored, brook trout and rainbow trout are spawned and raised in these streams.

From this point at the lake's inlet, you can turn left and walk 1.4 miles along the west edge of the lake to the vistas of Lake Tahoe from the dam and the Flume Trail bike path. Explore either side of the lake on the bike path. Return to the trailhead by retracing your steps.

DIRECTIONS: From Carson City, drive south on US 395 to US 50 west, then drive 9 miles to the parking lot on the north side of the highway at Spooner Summit.

From Incline Village, drive 10 miles south on NV 28 to its junction with US 50. Head east on US 50; drive 0.7 miles to the Spooner Summit parking lot.

GPS TRAILHEAD COORDINATES	06 MARLETTE LAKE
UTM Zone (WGS84)	11S
Easting	0249496
Northing	4332385
Latitude	N 39° 06.278'
Longitude	W 119° 53.817'

07 Spooner Lake

SCENERY: ☆ ☆ ☆ ☆	DISTANCE: *3 miles round-trip*
TRAIL CONDITION: ☆ ☆ ☆ ☆ ☆	HIKING TIME: *1–1.5 hours*
CHILDREN: ☆ ☆ ☆ ☆ ☆	OUTSTANDING FEATURES: *Wildlife, wildflowers,*
DIFFICULTY: ☆ ☆	*aspen groves, lakeside trail*
SOLITUDE: ☆ ☆	

Embark from the Tahoe Rim Trail's Spooner Summit trailhead to descend through an aspen grove on the way to the lake loop. If you are in a contemplative mood or hanker to watch birds, there are well-placed benches located around the lake to accommodate you.

🚶🚶 Your slow walk around this former millpond will be rewarded with glimpses of wildlife—both fauna and flora. This trail is off-limits to bikes, but dogs on leashes are welcome.

Spooner Lake is one of those areas around Lake Tahoe that you are just as likely to visit in winter as in any other season due to the popular groomed trails and overnight cabins. If you like to trek on terra firma, though, this happens to be one of the areas that melts out soonest, allowing you to hike in late May or early June. Spooner Lake, along with Marlette Lake and Hobart Reservoir, was part of the famous Hobart-Marlette Water System that supplied Virginia City and the nearby mines. Spooner's former status as a millpond has been erased, and it's now known more for nature observation and winter recreation.

Start at the Tahoe Rim Trail (TRT) trailhead at Spooner Summit. Here at the summit, Spooner's Hotel was a thriving business during the logging and mining heydays. Many wagons and their teamsters gathered here, crowding the narrow road. By 1915, Spooner's Summit had become a collection of ramshackle buildings, evidence of which has been erased from the scene.

Under cover of lodgepole and Jeffrey pines, take a moment to read about the area's natural history and the route of the TRT. For

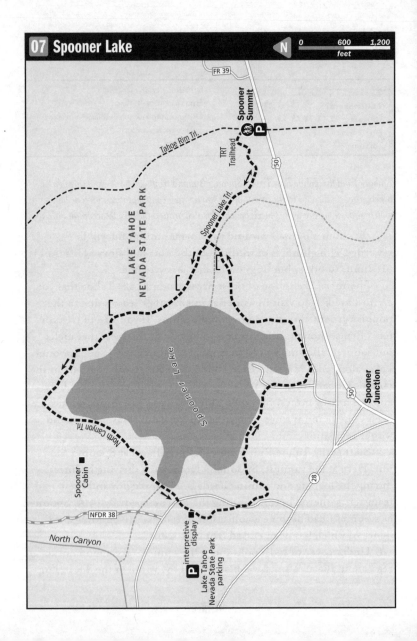

N

0   600   1,200
         feet

FR 39

Spooner
Summit

P

Tahoe Rim Trl.

TRT
Trailhead

50

Spooner Lake Trl.

LAKE TAHOE
NEVADA STATE PARK

Spooner Lake

Spooner
Junction

50

North Canyon Trl.

28

Spooner
Cabin

NFDR 38

North Canyon

P interpretive
   display

Lake Tahoe
Nevada State Park
parking

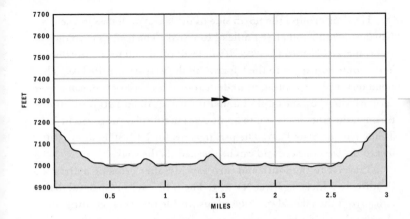

a more intrepid hike, one can leave this trailhead early in the morning and reach Tahoe Meadow by early evening. Pick up a TRT "green map" for some additional details on that route.

A longer hike than Spooner Lake, albeit not as far-reaching as the TRT, is the hike to Marlette Lake described on page 53.

Walk along the Tahoe Rim Trail for approximately 100 feet to the Spooner Lake access trail, then turn downhill to the left. Follow this shaded path west under lodgepole and Jeffrey pines and enter the first of many groves of aspen as your trail turns to the northwest. The Basque sheepherders would use these smooth-barked trees as canvases for carving their initials, names, and pictures. You'll notice that Valentine's Day and birthdays are commemorated quite often (if you get a chance to read a few tree trunks away from the trail).

As you descend through the lush foliage, you will pass by the turn-off to Spooner Lake's south trail to the left. The sign will remind you that your dog must be leashed at all times while you are on the Spooner Lake Trail. Comfortable park benches have been placed off the path at frequent intervals around the lake and offer hikers a spot to relax with either a lake or mountain vista. You will pass anglers of all ages, as Spooner Lake has a healthy population of lake trout.

Heading around the north side of the lake, you'll pass by the North Canyon Trail after 1 mile of footwork. The trail sign on the right, marked NORTH CANYON ROAD, leads off uphill to the northwest. Your route continues to the left around the west side of the lake. The open terrain here is pleasant under sunny skies because you can always cool off when you start uphill under the trees. About 100 yards south through the trees leads you to an interpretive display prepared by Lake Tahoe Nevada State Park. The parking area for LTNSP is about 300 feet to the west of here and can be reached via the trail.

Traverse to the south and turn east just after crossing a dirt road (leading to a locked gate at NV 28). The trail stays a respectful distance from the lake, always tucked just inside the trees, coming too close to the road before veering away. In a matter of minutes, you will reach the junction with the connector trail back uphill. This is a most beautiful section of trail, with several species of ferns, lilies, and an occasional snow plant in early season. In the fall, the aspen glow red and gold in the sunlight.

If you have time to sit and observe the wildlife, arrive very early and take a position on the south side of the lake. From here you may observe goshawks or owls as well as see signs of martens, raccoons, and possibly mountain lions.

DIRECTIONS: From Carson City, drive south on US 395 to US 50 west, then 9 miles to the parking lot on the north side of the highway at Spooner Summit.

From Incline Village, drive 10 miles south on NV 28 to the junction of US 50. Head east on US 50; drive 0.7 miles to the Spooner Summit parking lot.

If the Spooner Summit parking area is full, you can park at the Lake Tahoe Nevada State Park. It is located on the north side of NV 28, 0.65 miles northwest of the US 50–NV 28 junction.

GPS TRAILHEAD COORDINATES	07 SPOONER LAKE
UTM Zone (WGS84)	11S
Easting	0249496
Northing	4332385
Latitude	N 39° 06.278'
Longitude	W 119° 53.817'

2

Despite the abundance of lofty superlatives that inevitably precede a visit to Lake Tahoe, descriptions do not seem to disappoint anyone.

08 Freel Peak

SCENERY: ✪ ✪ ✪ ✪ ✪	DISTANCE: *10.2 miles round-trip*
TRAIL CONDITION: ✪ ✪ ✪ ✪	HIKING TIME: *6–7 hours*
CHILDREN: ✪	OUTSTANDING FEATURES: *This moderately strenuous*
DIFFICULTY: ✪ ✪ ✪ ✪	*hike will reward intrepid hikers with basin-to-range*
SOLITUDE: ✪ ✪ ✪ ✪	*vistas from the highest peak in the Lake Tahoe region.*

Traversing the path of the Tahoe Rim Trail (TRT) from Armstrong Pass to the saddle below Freel Peak is the "moderate" portion of this hike. The final mile to the summit is only moderately strenuous, but the vista is breathtaking. Freel Peak, 10,881 feet above sea level and the highest peak in the Lake Tahoe region, is named for James Freel, who squatted on land at the base of the peak formerly known as Bald Mountain. Freel Peak serves as the easternmost summit of the Sierra. If peak bagging is your thing, Jobs Sister and Jobs Peak are within easy reach of Freel Peak's summit and would make excellent additions to this hike with minimal effort.

🚶🚶 The trail begins on the other side of the bridge crossing Willow Creek, heading west from the clearing where you've parked. The bridge is now blocked by boulders, but this was formerly an OHV (four-wheel-drive) trail, once labeled with a non-bullet-ridden sign as Forest Road 051. Nothing to see here, keep moving. Walk on this track to a point 0.5 miles west of the bridge where, according to the sign, motorized vehicles must be left.

From here, where your single-track begins by following the sign pointing to the TRT, it is less than 0.5 miles to Armstrong Pass. There, the trail from Oneidas Street to the northwest joins the TRT from Big Meadow 9 miles to the southwest. On the way to Armstrong Pass, you'll cross a small runoff stream as you swing around the spur of the ridge. Then your track along the TRT will traverse northward on the west slope of the ridge.

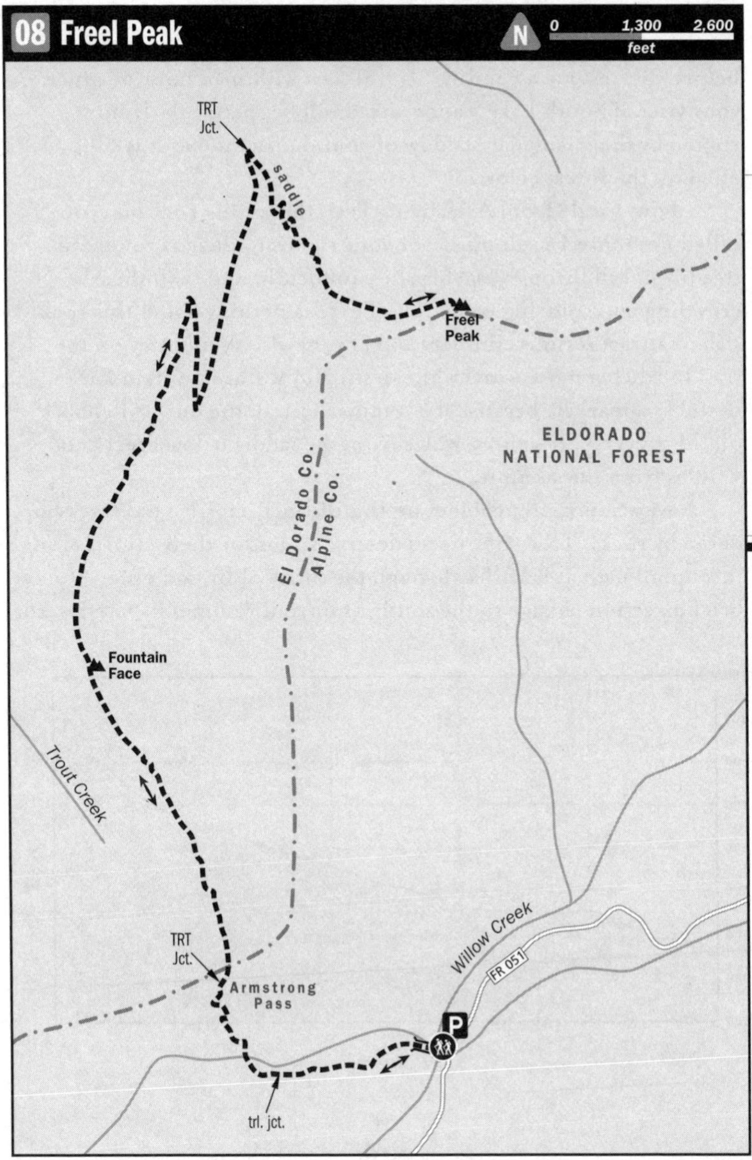

08 Freel Peak
N
0
1,300
2,600
feet
TRT Jct.
saddle
Freel Peak
ELDORADO NATIONAL FOREST
El Dorado Co.
Alpine Co.
Fountain Face
Trout Creek
TRT Jct.
Armstrong Pass
Willow Creek
FR 051
P
trl. jct.

Knowing that your destination is some 2,000 feet above you, there is no comfort in your brief descent through scattered boulders before you resume ascending. If you start within an hour of sunrise, your vista of South Lake Tahoe ahead will be spectacularly interrupted by the triangular shadow of your destination as it is silhouetted on the forest below.

About 1 mile from Armstrong Pass, the jutting rock outcrop called Fountain Face looms over your right shoulder as you tread steadily uphill through sagebrush, paintbrush, and rabbitbrush crowding and coloring your trail. There is nothing about this rock slab to attract serious climbers and anyone else should stay on the trail to reach a more worthwhile destination. But Fountain Face is useful as a marker, because it is 1 mile ahead of the only switchback on this traverse. It's also 2 miles from the saddle below Freel and 3 miles from the summit.

Navigation is no problem on this distinct, mostly sand track bordered by rocks. TRT volunteers deserve kudos for their efforts along this uphill path as it knifes through the shade of fir and pine. After a brief direction change to the south, your trail resumes its northward

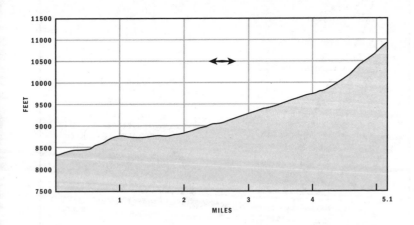

Jobs Sister and Jobs Peak from the windbreaks atop Freel Peak

ascent to the saddle at just over 9,700 feet. On the way, in close succession, you'll cross three runoff streams that create a cool, verdant slope sporting larkspur, lupine, columbine, paintbrush, corn lilies, and assorted white and yellow flowers.

At the saddle, odd-shaped rock outcrops, gnarled trees, and sparse, ground-hugging plant life are part of the interesting landscape, where you can also look out to Lake Tahoe. A sign to the south indicates that you are 1 mile (actually only 1,151 vertical feet) from Freel Peak. Depart the TRT at this point and head south uphill through the trees.

Scree, gravel, and sand bordered by boulders, whitebark pine, and chasms make up the steep but distinct trail to the summit. Plenty of rock steps have been laid to help you up in the steepest sections.

About two dozen switchbacks help you ascend this southerly track to the top. Sensitive plant areas are marked—right next to steep drop-offs. Don't tread on either. After you cross the 10,000-foot mark, the steepness moderates and the trail traverses an open scree slope east-southeast toward the summit.

At the top, a quarter-circle of stacked stone breaks the wind for tired hikers. Look among the rocks for the current peak register, which is now housed in an ammo can. In years past, communications antennas occupied the peak, but they have been removed and only their foundations remain. Vistas into Lake Tahoe and the Carson Basin are interrupted only by Freel's companion peaks, Jobs Sister and Jobs Peak which, as you can see from Freel, are within easy reach.

DIRECTIONS: From the junction with US 50 in Meyers, drive south on CA 89. After the highway makes a looping turn to the east, you will see Big Meadow Trailhead on the left. You will leave the highway on poorly marked Willow Creek Road 4 miles east of Big Meadow trailhead. Willow Creek Road is on the east side of CA 89 about 0.75 miles past Luther Pass. Willow Creek Road/Forest Road 051 heads northeast toward Horse Meadow.

If coming from Carson Pass or Carson City, Willow Creek Road is 1.75 miles north of the junction of CA 88 with CA 89 in Hope Valley.

It is advised that you use a high-clearance vehicle on this road, but careful driving in a wagon will also get you there. Drive 2.5 miles up FR 051 and cross Willow Creek on the bridge, then drive another 1 mile to cross a second bridge. Park in the open area to the east of the creek branch. A small wooden bridge across the creek is blocked by boulders. And so you've reached your parking spot. You'll hike for 0.5 miles to the trailhead.

GPS Trailhead Coordinates	08 Freel Peak
UTM Zone (WGS84)	11S
Easting	0248195
Northing	4301943
Latitude	N 38° 49.818'
Longitude	W 119° 54.047'

09 Round Lake

SCENERY: ✿ ✿ ✿	DISTANCE: *6.2 miles round-trip*
TRAIL CONDITION: ✿ ✿ ✿ ✿	HIKING TIME: *2 hours*
CHILDREN: ✿ ✿	OUTSTANDING FEATURES: *Easy access to a*
DIFFICULTY: ✿ ✿ ✿	*montane meadow and a good fishing lake*
SOLITUDE: ✿ ✿	

This moderate hike along the Tahoe Rim Trail (TRT) leads through a broad, flower-filled meadow to a placid lake reflecting a snowcapped peak in the background. The trail to this popular destination rises swiftly from the trailhead to Big Meadow, which is a destination in itself for many people. Other hikers, bikers, joggers, equestrians, and anglers continue a gentler ascent through this mixed conifer forest to aptly named Round Lake.

🚶🚶 Meiss Country is an area bounded by CA 88 and CA 89, from Echo Summit to Hope Valley. It's named after Benjamin Meiss, who settled on land about 1 mile west of Meiss Lake. Meiss Country includes seven pleasant lakes nestled in a broken and jumbled geology where volcanism and tectonics combine to add to the Sierra stew.

The trailhead is located at the south end of the Big Meadow parking lot. An interpretive sign at the trailhead will give some insight as to the flora and fauna that you can expect to see along the trail. Any alerts or cautionary notices will be placed here. Continue walking south about 500 feet before crossing CA 89 to regain the trail.

A series of switchbacks helps you up the 225 feet that it takes to reach Big Meadow, just 0.5 miles away. The duff-and-granite trail ascends under lodgepole pine and incense cedar, punctuated by displays of lupine and Indian paintbrush. Granite outcrops that surround the trail are used as steps more than once as the trail meanders close to Big Meadow Creek.

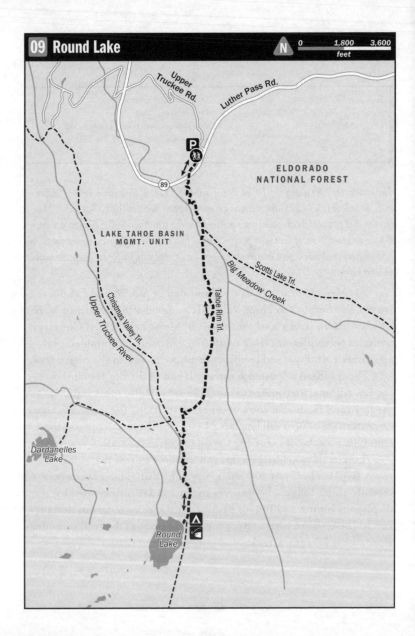

N

0   1,800   3,600
feet

Upper Truckee Rd.

Luther Pass Rd.

P 🚶

89

ELDORADO NATIONAL FOREST

LAKE TAHOE BASIN MGMT. UNIT

Scotts Lake Trl.

Big Meadow Creek

Tahoe Rim Trl.

Christmas Valley Trl.

Upper Truckee River

Dardanelles Lake

Round Lake

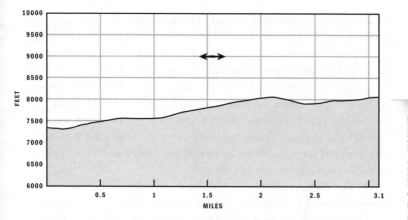

After the trail levels out, you'll encounter a junction where the trail to Scotts Lake leads to the left and our trail, marked to Meiss Meadow, leads to the right. In that direction, the trees part and Big Meadow appears. If you have it with you, this is the last safe point to apply your insect repellent.

A walk in any direction in Big Meadow yields a feast of activity and color from an abundance of sources. The meadow itself is some 2,000 feet long, and perhaps half as wide; it is ringed on three sides by pine and fir forest; the south edge is flanked by rock. A few large erratics dot the landscape and provide small islands of solitude. Buttercups, columbine, and explorer's gentian flash yellow, crimson, and purple in the sun as the shadow of one lone cloud drifts across the meadow. Yellow warblers flash and sing while they dart around the edge of the meadow, probably chasing one of the thousands of butterflies that swarm the flowers. Why they aren't eating any of the millions of mosquitoes isn't in the nature guide.

Under a warm sun and cobalt-blue sky, Big Meadow Creek gurgles through an **S**-curve, its fluid rhythm jamming with the trill of the cheeseburger bird (mountain chickadee) and the hums and clicks of bees, grasshoppers, and crickets. The instantly memorable symphony is recallable on the chilliest winter evening. Hold that thought.

When the trail reaches the trees at the south end of Big Meadow, your trail will narrow and begin ascending for the next mile. Despite some roots and rocks in the trail, the climb is steady and consistently southward. Just about the time that the downed timber becomes noticeable, you'll arrive at a set of 28 wooden stairs to assist you up through the lodgepole pines and white firs. While you are looking down at your feet, glance to the side of the trail to see the red tops of snow plants bursting through the soil.

Presently your ascent will moderate somewhat as the trail turns sandy and you start to skirt an aspen grove that looks as if it has been used as a Valentine's card. While not exactly a meadow, this open area is exposed to the sun, which draws out the corn lilies by the thousands as soon as the snow melts. Insect repellent is a definite plus on this hike, especially along this section next to the creek.

You can enjoy a short break from the climbing for the next 0.25 miles while you descend some easy switchbacks until you reach a junction with the trail to Dardanelles Lake via Lake (also known as Christmas) Valley. If you want to go to Dardanelles, take a 180-degree turn to the north and hike about 1.5 miles to the lake. Your trail continues straight south, climbing gentle switchbacks for about 0.5 miles through boulders of conglomerate rock. The trail walks up to a small rise overlooking Round Lake. Take any of the descending trails along the north end of the lake.

The rock closest to the lake—not friendly for sitting on—is conglomerate that has likely been sloughed off Stevens Peak and blown about in various andesitic eruptions. Despite the lack of smooth granite to relax on, numerous fishing spots dot the north and east shores. The lake's outlet is on the northwest shore and feeds the Upper Truckee River. As you walk over to the outlet, the lodgepole chipmunks will begin following you for the easy meal. As cute as they are, resist the urge to feed them anything, for both their well-being and yours. Squirrels and chipmunks not only can become dependent on handouts, but they also carry the flea that transmits the plague virus. Keep your distance from them despite their cuteness. You will also be harried by Stellar's jays—another famous camp robber, like Clark's nutcracker without the loud caw. With avian flu having been found throughout the foothills, it would be prudent to avoid sharing food with them, as well.

The TRT continues past the eastern margin of the lake for 2.5 miles, south past Meiss Lake, to its junction with the Pacific Crest Trail. There, the TRT turns north toward Echo Summit. Round Lake is well known for its fishing, and that may be reason enough to tarry at this pleasant bowl of water. Retrace your steps for an easy hike out.

DIRECTIONS: From US 50 in Meyers, turn south on CA 89 and drive 5.3 miles to the Big Meadow trailhead parking lot on the left side of the road. There are pit toilets and water spigots, but no trash receptacles, available in this large parking lot. The trailhead is at the south end of the lot.

GPS Trailhead Coordinates	09 Round Lake
UTM Zone (WGS84)	10S
Easting	0760506
Northing	4297594
Latitude	N 38° 47.318'
Longitude	W 120° 00.046'

10 Big Meadow to Daggett Pass

SCENERY: ✿ ✿ ✿ ✿ ✿	HIKING TIME: *12 hours*
TRAIL CONDITION: ✿ ✿ ✿ ✿ ✿	OUTSTANDING FEATURES: *The route traverses lush*
CHILDREN: ✿	*forests of mixed conifers, passes several meadows thick*
DIFFICULTY: ✿ ✿ ✿ ✿ ✿	*with wildflowers, climbs within easy reach of the high-*
SOLITUDE: ✿ ✿ ✿ ✿	*est peak in the Lake Tahoe Basin, and offers incredible*
DISTANCE: *23.8 miles one-way*	*vistas of the basin's peaks and ranges.*

Flat becomes but a memory when you embark from Big Meadow. Gain about 1,500 feet in the first 5 miles. Then the trail turns north and begins to climb up to a high point of about 9,725 feet at the base of 10,881-foot Freel Peak, the highest peak in the Lake Tahoe Basin. Views along the way span from Round Top in the south to the Pyramid Peak and the Crystal Range in the west and Lake Tahoe to the north. East-ern vistas of the Carson Range pop in and out of view as you mostly descend to some degree or other all the way to Heavenly Valley.

🏃 Leave the trailhead kiosk and begin your eastward trek up this serpentine trail. The path is pleasant and nicely shaded by red fir and Jeffrey pine. You gain elevation just to keep above CA 89, which you roughly parallel for about 1.5 miles. Turn north, enter-ing switchbacks, and continue climbing. After 2 miles on the trail, look for the junction with the trail to Grass Lake, 1 mile away. As you snake up this slope, watch for vistas to the south when the trees break. Cross a stream on some well-placed logs in this aspen-flocked glade.

Springwater emerges from beneath a large rockfall of granite boulders in a ravine about halfway up to the vista on the ridge. Your view from this spot is to the east and southeast. Once you make the ridge, just before turning to the east, look for a superb vista over-looking the airport and Lake Tahoe's south shore.

From that vantage point, head southeast and climb to a tiny sad-dle between two small knobs, where you'll find acceptable bivy sites.

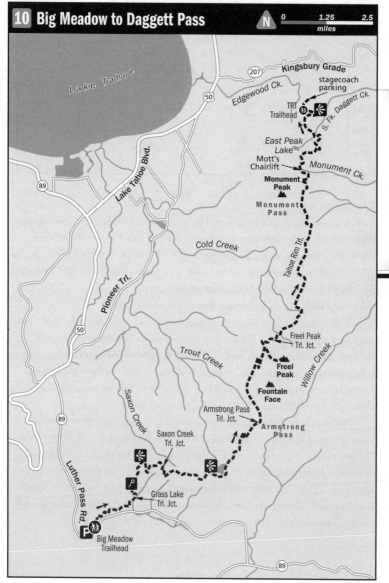

Lake Tahoe

Kingsbury Grade

207

Edgewood Ck.

stagecoach parking

TRT Trailhead

S. Fk. Daggett Ck.

50

East Peak Lake

Mott's Chairlift

Monument Ck.

Monument Peak

Monument Pass

Tahoe Rim Trl.

Cold Creek

Lake Tahoe Blvd.

89

Pioneer Trl.

50

Trout Creek

Freel Peak Trl. Jct.

Freel Peak

Willow Creek

Fountain Face

Armstrong Pass Trl. Jct.

Armstrong Pass

Saxon Creek

Saxon Creek Trl. Jct.

89

Grass Lake Trl. Jct.

Luther Pass Rd.

Big Meadow Trailhead

89

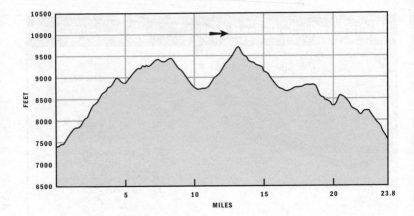

For the first time in about 5 miles, you begin to descend. Switchback down to the junction with the Saxon Creek Trail before you start ascending once again. Climbing to the northeast, look to the right to see a meadow heavy with color. The trail stays away from this one, but climbs to the fringe of a grassy meadow on the far side of the knoll. The trail slides around to the right and heads uphill.

If you need more flowers, Freel Meadows waits for you less than 100 feet uphill. Corn lily, aster, Indian paintbrush, wallflower, lupine, elephant's head, and larkspur display themselves at the height of summer. The sand-and-gravel trail skirts the verdant swale and five minutes later is out of sight as the trail curves away, downhill through the boulders.

Walk uphill through scattered lodgepole to another magnificent vista point. Lake Tahoe spreads out to the northwest and Hell Hole Canyon sits 1,000 feet below your perch. To the south are Round Top and Elephants Back while Freel Peak stands on the northeastern horizon. This view stays with you as you cross the broad, open slope heading east. Swing around the wooded knoll and start tracking high above Willow Creek, north toward Armstrong Pass.

Continue north and the trail emerges from behind its windbreak and makes for the exposed ridgeline. Note the stout lodgepole pine in krummholz configuration. Red fir joins lodgepole and western white pine as you leave this barren landscape and descend toward Armstrong Pass, 700 feet below. Pass the trail marked for the Oneidas Street Trailhead and continue to the northeast toward Freel Peak and then Star Lake, 5 miles ahead.

Begin the assault on the Freel massif by, uh, descending through scattered boulders, then enjoy a slightly uphill traverse to the north. As you walk through sagebrush and rabbitbrush about 1 mile after Armstrong Pass, you'll pass the rock outcrop called Fountain Face. After another mile, you'll reach the only switchback before the saddle, which is yet another mile distant.

Bordered by rocks, the sandy trail uses only these two direction changes on its way to the high point of about 9,725 feet. On the way, you will have a chance to water up at three runoff streams in close proximity to one another. The water and lush foliage here create a cool environment complete with the scents of lupine, larkspur, corn lily, columbine, and assorted white and yellow flowers.

Resume the northward climb along this immaculate trail (kudos to Tahoe Rim Trail Association volunteers) to reach the saddle, where you are only 1,150 vertical feet from Freel Peak which, at 10,881 feet, is the highest point in the basin. Descend to the northwest and sharply adjust to the east, continuing to hike down past Freel to the foot of Jobs Sister. When you are about 0.75 miles past the saddle, watch for a small runoff stream. If you need good campsites, ascend this small stream for bivy options. Lose about 500 feet and cross a rock-filled ravine before making the final descent to Star Lake's outlet stream. The slope offers excellent views of Lake Tahoe in the distance and small meadows below.

The most rewarding aspect of Star Lake is its ice-cold foot soak. But it's a great place to fill up on water, too. Make sure to do your water-getting away from the foot-soaking. The campsites close to the lake are good for a siesta but better choices lie above the lake's northeast corner, away from the trail and lake. After a relaxing break, make a dogleg to the north, then west, to jog over the ridge spur. Then resume the northward descent through pine and hemlock forest and repeat the maneuver in 0.75 miles. Follow the trail as it traverses high above High Meadows on its 3.4-mile leg to Monument Pass.

Though initially steep, the trail's descent moderates some as the trees thin and views to the west open up. Pyramid Peak stands out beyond Tahoe and the Crystal Range. Your vista changes as you reach Monument Pass, where you'll have a vista of Carson Valley and Jobs Sister; it's only fitting as you'll enter Nevada just ten minutes ahead.

Curl-leaf mountain mahogany and buckwheat occupy this dry, boulder-ridden pass. The sandy trail descends steeply toward Mott Canyon. The steep slopes and drastic elevation difference along this narrow, exposed section of trail may induce a case of the mountain willies as you traverse beneath Monument Peak. Enter and exit one canyon and then another. In the second one, you'll find Mott Canyon chairlift hanging motionless above Mott Canyon Creek. This is your first indication of your long approach to Heavenly Valley Nevada ski area.

Climb out of the canyon's shade on a steep, sandy utility road for a gain of 230 feet in 0.5 miles. Traverse to the north across slopes well treed with lodgepole and western white pine. Make a looping descent across a bowl just below East Peak Lake and traverse to a crossing of its outlet, South Fork Daggett Creek. Pass under another chairlift and in about 0.5 miles, your descent to Heavenly will begin in earnest. Round a pointy knob and begin to switchback down to the resort. Watch for a park bench, which is situated nicely for contemplative gazing.

Manzanita and tobacco brush are interspersed with Jeffrey pine and fir as you descend the obvious trail. A trail marker at the end of the second switchback identifies the Tahoe Rim Trail and lists mileages to all the sites you hiked past. Continue downhill for another 0.5 miles to the Stagecoach parking lot and a well-deserved hopped beverage.

DIRECTIONS: To reach the Big Meadow Trailhead from South Lake Tahoe, drive 4.8 miles on US 50 to Meyers. Turn left onto CA 89 and drive 5.3 miles south to the Big Meadow parking lot, on the left. You'll find pit toilets and water, but no garbage services, at this large parking area. Overnight camping is allowed. Turn right at the entrance and drive slowly downhill. The trailhead is to the right of the main parking lot.

Leave another vehicle at Daggett Pass. From South Lake Tahoe, drive 5.6 miles north on US 50, through Stateline, and turn right onto NV 207. Drive 3.1 miles to Tramway Drive and turn right. Drive 1.7 miles to the Heavenly Valley Resort Stagecoach parking area. Leave your ride near the Stagecoach chairlift and look for the Tahoe Rim Trail sign nearby.

GPS Trailhead Coordinates	10 Big Meadow to Daggett Pass
UTM Zone (WGS84)	11S
Easting	0239458
Northing	4297784
Latitude	N 38° 47.419'
Longitude	W 119° 59.983'

11 Pony Express Trail

SCENERY: ✿ ✿ ✿	DISTANCE: 3.8 miles round-trip
TRAIL CONDITION: ✿ ✿ ✿	HIKING TIME: 2–3 hours
CHILDREN: ✿ ✿	OUTSTANDING FEATURES: Historic trail with views
DIFFICULTY: ✿ ✿ ✿	to Lake Tahoe
SOLITUDE: ✿ ✿ ✿	

This short section of the famous Pony Express Trail was used for only a brief time following the inaugural run in April, 1860. For six weeks, riders carried mail over Johnson Pass, down the Hawley Grade, over Luther Pass, and on to Genoa, Nevada. The Kingsbury Grade helped to shorten that route by more than 8 miles, nearly one hour of riding time in those days. While treading on the same track as many brave horsemen, today's foot travelers are treated to spectacular views on this historic trail.

The Hawley Grade Pony Express Trail is an obscure piece of history preserved in dirt and stone. While less than 2 miles long, this brief stretch of trail has seen some heroes who remain largely unknown to history. Regardless of who was riding it, the route from Sacramento to Carson City was the most treacherous of all.

More than two hours after midnight on April 5, 1860, the first eastbound Pony Express rider, Billy (Sam) Hamilton, departed Sacramento's embarcadero in a driving rainstorm with mail satchels bound for St. Louis, Missouri. His destination was past Placerville at Sportsmans Hall, where he would hand over the mail to the next rider, Warren Upson. Speeding off near dawn, Upson had to dismount and pull his horse through chest-high snowdrifts at Johnson Pass and Echo Summit. Using the Hawley Grade Trail, Upson made his destination, Friday's Station at the Nevada border, in eight hours. The mail arrived nine days later in St. Louis.

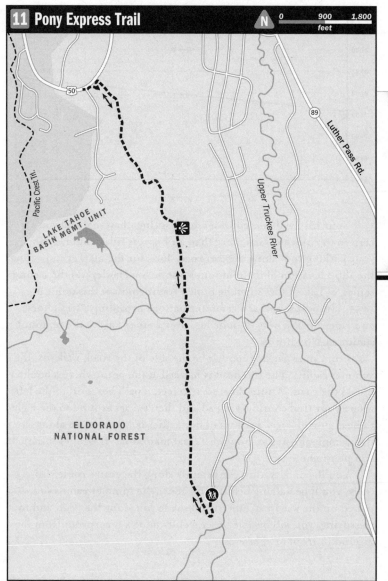

N

0   900   1,800
feet

LAKE TAHOE SOUTH

part two

50

89   Luther Pass Rd.

Pacific Crest Trl.

LAKE TAHOE
BASIN MGMT. UNIT

Upper Truckee River

ELDORADO
NATIONAL FOREST

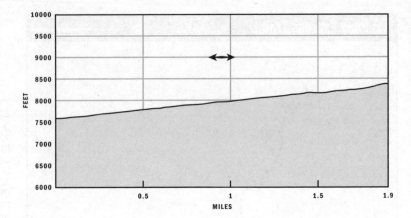

Your hike will take considerably less time than that and you are certain to enjoy the view more than an Express rider could. From your parking spot along the dirt road, look for the marker indicating the 1860 location of the remount station. Asa Hawley was the second settler in Lake Valley when he built a trading post at this point in 1855. His post served as a remount station, providing a fresh horse and rider for the next 10-mile leg, over Luther Pass to the remount station at Woodfords.

From your parking spot along the side of the road, walk past the summer cabins. The trailhead is marked at the point where a boulder blocks the road. Within the next 100 feet, a path bears off to the left where your trail continues ahead and then swings around to the right to head north. Tiger swallowtail butterflies may escort you along as they sample the nectar from white leaf manzanita, fragrant lupine, and penstemon.

You'll gain elevation consistently along the entire route. Initially, you'll be walking behind and above the summer cabins you passed on the way in. White fir will shade you along the trail, and in the spring, you will be able to see woolly mule's ears sprout from the ground in front of your eyes.

Route-finding is simple on this trail. After the turn at the trailhead, you walk north without the interference of switchbacks until a few hundred feet from the summit. Along the way, you'll hear the mountain chickadee and its "cheeseburger" call, and you'll see the cobalt-blue-and-black Stellar's jay. At about the 1-mile point, you will begin hearing the cascading waters of the stream draining Benwood Meadows. The trail does make a very slight direction change as it enters and exits this ravine.

There is a vista point just 0.3 miles ahead where, with a narrow view, you're able to see the south end of Lake Tahoe. There are excellent views down into the Upper Truckee River Canyon along the majority of the trail. While much of the path is shaded, there is little relief from the sun where trees are absent. Wearing sunscreen is advised on this and all trails in the Tahoe region due to the added exposure at high elevations.

Some switchbacks begin within about 500 feet of the summit. In this white fir forest, a grouse stirs and sends me, in one jump, at least 20 feet farther up the trail. Some very large granite steps assist you toward the summit, where you will see a sign commemorating this as a National Recreation Trail. Less than 0.5 miles away is the location where the Pacific Crest Trail crosses Echo Summit.

DIRECTIONS: From Meyers, turn left on CA 89 and drive south for 4 miles, where you'll turn right on Upper Truckee River Road. Follow it downhill 1.1 miles to a left turn onto a dirt road just after crossing the creek. Park along the side of the road without blocking access to any homes.

GPS TRAILHEAD COORDINATES	11 PONY EXPRESS TRAIL
UTM Zone (WGS84)	10S
Easting	0758731
Northing	4298005
Latitude	N 38° 47.571'
Longitude	W 120° 01.261'

SCENERY: ✿ ✿ ✿ ✿ ✿	DISTANCE: *13.5 miles one-way*
TRAIL CONDITION: ✿ ✿ ✿ ✿	HIKING TIME: *8–9 hours*
CHILDREN: ✿	OUTSTANDING FEATURES: *Vistas into the Upper*
DIFFICULTY: ✿ ✿ ✿ ✿	*Truckee River drainage; memorable wildflower displays;*
SOLITUDE: ✿ ✿ ✿ ✿	*volcanic, granitic, glaciated terrain.*

Hiking three trails at once isn't triple the work—in this case, it's the pleasure that is multiplied. The Pacific Crest Trail (PCT) doesn't receive that scenic part for naught. And there just weren't any poor trails used to create either the Tahoe Rim Trail (TRT) or the Tahoe–Yosemite Trail (TYT). Traversing these classic trails is a memorable experience.

Leave historic Carson Pass and travel northwest into the Upper Truckee River basin, which is bound by volcanic ridges from Stevens Peak in the northeast, Red Lake Peak to the southeast, and south to Little Round Top. The basin includes many lakes (remnants of the glaciers that occupied the area): Meiss Lake, Four Lakes, Round Lake, Dardanelles Lake, Showers Lake, and Elbert Lake.

The high elevation point comes as you emerge from the cirque beneath Little Round Top. From there it is downhill, more or less, through small meadows and over steep trail to your goal near the Desolation Wilderness.

The grass-filled meadows and rock-laden hillsides are chockablock full of iris, lupine, larkspur, paintbrush, corn lily, blue flag, bluebell, sulfur flower, Chinese house, mule's ear, elephant's head, buttercup, leopard lily, penstemon, and actually many more still than I could identify.

🏃🏃 Reorganize your gear for the last time at the picnic table and then head southwest on the sandy, lodgepole-clad trail. Keep to the left of the outcrops to round the ridge at the foot of Red Lake Peak. Traffic sounds fade in about 0.5 miles as you hike north and then switchback up to a small pond, where a solitary nearby tree provides much-needed shade after climbing the treeless, south-facing slope.

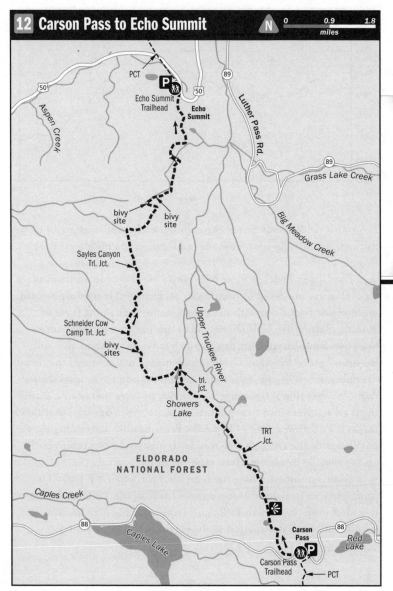

12 Carson Pass to Echo Summit

N 0   0.9   1.8
miles

50

Aspen Creek

PCT

P

Echo Summit
Trailhead

**Echo
Summit**

89

Luther Pass Rd.

Grass Lake Creek

89

Big Meadow Creek

bivy
site

bivy
site

Sayles Canyon
Trl. Jct.

Upper Truckee River

Schneider Cow
Camp Trl. Jct.

bivy
sites

trl.
jct.

*Showers
Lake*

TRT
Jct.

**ELDORADO
NATIONAL FOREST**

Caples Creek

88

Caples Lake

P

**Carson
Pass**

88

*Red
Lake*

Carson Pass
Trailhead

PCT

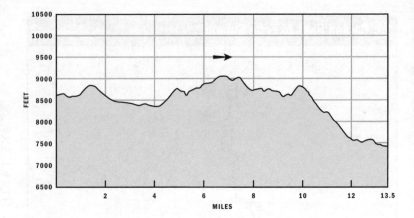

From this saddle, walk north through iris and paintbrush to an obvious vista point 1. 5 miles from the trailhead in the middle of the sloping meadow.

The Upper Truckee River basin and Lake Tahoe lie in front of you. They are bordered by mountains consisting of metamorphic and sedimentary rock along with intrusive igneous rock in the form of granitic plutons like Half Dome. All of this has, from time to time, been overlain with volcanic debris which itself, being somewhat soft, has been eroded by water. Glaciers have occasionally entered the scene, dropping debris of one sort, called erratics, randomly around the terrain. At other times, these rivers of ice tidy up after themselves, pushing their leftovers into neat piles called moraines. Your trail undulates across the northwest foot of Red Lake Peak, steadily descending above but alongside the creek. A side trail leads over to the two cabins built on the river by Benjamin Meiss early in the last century.

To this point, you have been on the PCT and TYT only. The junction 500 feet ahead is the bottom turn on the TRT; to the right, it leads 2 miles to the east to Round Lake, with Big Meadow another 3 miles on. Your destination is ahead, through the meadows;

88

Showers Lake, 2 miles ahead, makes a great lunch spot, while Bryan Meadow, 6 miles on, will slow you down with wildflowers. It's 10 miles from here to Echo Summit.

Moments after joining the TRT, the track widens and makes a few crossings of the nascent waters of the Upper Truckee River. At the final crossing, the trail resumes its normal width and heads through willows up into the pines. After a long, level stretch leading past Meiss Lake and crossing Dixon Canyon, the trail turns into an up-ramp that gains about 375 feet in nearly 0.75 miles. On this hill to Showers Lake, you'll be treated to a walk through many clusters of wildflowers. A fair campsite sits above the lake on the left, with better sites under nice tree cover along the eastern shore, especially at the north end.

A trail junction at the north end of Showers turns you to the right, away from the lake. A downed lodgepole lies 50 feet to the right of the marker. Walk past it about 100 feet and look for the faint trail that steeply descends another 100 feet to cross the lake's outlet stream. A sharp U-turn will send you southwest under an imposing granite wall. A fairly gentle ascent on a sandy trail carries you up to boulder city, where a lupine-dominated meadow follows a copse of lodgepole pines. Heading into the cirque, the northbound trail continues its upward trend and the wildflower viewing becomes more like wading. You will absolutely wallow through dense stands of Sierra willow, giant lupine, larkspur, Indian paintbrush, and plenty more. The color extravaganza starts on the volcanic overhangs above the trail and reaches down to the exposed granite below the trail. With snow lingering on the north-facing slopes beneath an azure sky, the scene is spectacular.

Impromptu bivy sites can be found to the north of Little Round Top, at around 8,900 feet elevation. The vista of the cirque just crossed, from this vantage point, is massive. A rest here is a great idea. A quarter mile hence, your sandy trail skirts a small meadow on its south side. Contour, more or less, to another small, heather-fringed meadow where the PCT intersects the trail to Schneider

Cow Camp. Evidence of cattle operations is all around here. The sandy trail turns to rock when you pass the next meadow, ready to make a 350-foot descent through the lodgepole forest toward Bryan Meadow. In another 1.5 miles, you'll pass the junction for the trail to Sayles Canyon. Bryan Meadow is 0.8 miles past that.

Lodgepoles crowd your trail, which passes Bryan Meadow and then departs the small saddle. From here, you face a tedious traverse across a heavily forested slope, followed by a steep descent to finish the route. When you reach the ridgeline, 0.75 miles from the saddle, your vista is into the canyon that you'll bounce down from ridge to ridge. Drop 150 feet in the next quarter mile into this small cirque, where you'll find an excellent bivy site to the right of the trail just above a flowing creek. Cross the creek and continue on the PCT, which makes tight switchbacks beneath impressive granite outcrops down the west side of the ravine. Use roots and rocks as stairs until you get to the crossing about 0.3 miles past the bivy site. Look for a bivy site on the right, above the creek. The route remains steep and boulder-filled, with cramped switchbacks alongside the steep slant of the ravine's walls. Trekking poles are more than valuable coming down this segment of trail. The slopes are pleasantly shaded by pine and fir, and pileups of boulders as big as Yugos fill the ravine in places.

Finally, when your creek is tame enough to be straddled by a footbridge, you're nearing Benwood Meadow, where scarlet fritillary (*Fritillaria recurva*) grows by the trail. The next stream crossing after the bridge is marked by a lodgepole pine scarred with a blaze. No beeline for the PCT, though. First walk west, then north, then dip east before you're past the meadow, climbing away to the northwest through manzanita and boulders. Continue your downward traverse under cover of mixed conifers.

At the PCT–TRT marker in a clearing, you should be able to see your final destination, which is just beyond the buildings at the snow park. Trail signs will lead you the final half mile, down the west slope of the snow park, keeping above and passing the large parking lot. Continue up the trail, watching for signs for the PCT, TRT, and Pony Express Trail as you walk north.

DIRECTIONS: After coffee at Alpinas in South Lake Tahoe, take US 50 south 4.7 miles to Meyers, then turn left on CA 89 and drive 11.2 miles to CA 88 in Hope Valley. Turn west (right) on CA 88 and drive 8.7 miles to Carson Pass where there is a ranger station and large parking lot with toilets on the south side of the road. Get maps and information here, and most importantly, you can purchase a season-long parking pass for $20—or pay $5 for every night you're parked.

The parking lot for this hike's trailhead is 0.3 miles west, on the north side of CA 88. Equipped with toilets (usually much cleaner than the ones up the road), trash receptacles, and water, this parking area accommodates horse trailers. The trailhead for the PCT at Carson Pass is located at the northwest corner of the parking lot, where a picnic table sits opposite an information kiosk.

The trailhead at the Echo Summit end is 8.8 miles south of South Lake Tahoe on US 50, just 0.2 miles past the highway maintenance station on the right. Turn left at the Echo Summit Snow Park, where there's room for a dozen cars in the trailhead lot. Do not park in the large lot at the snow park. The trail's terminus is on the right, in the trees just above the parking area. There are no facilities at this end.

GPS TRAILHEAD COORDINATES	12 CARSON PASS TO ECHO SUMMIT
UTM Zone (WGS84)	11S
Easting	0239782
Northing	4287374
Latitude	N 38° 41.804'
Longitude	W 119° 59.525'

13 Showers Lake

SCENERY: ☆ ☆ ☆ ☆	DISTANCE: *10 miles round-trip*
TRAIL CONDITION: ☆ ☆ ☆ ☆	HIKING TIME: *8 hours*
CHILDREN: ☆ ☆ ☆	OUTSTANDING FEATURES: *Pacific Crest Trail and*
DIFFICULTY: ☆ ☆ ☆	*Tahoe Rim Trail; flower-filled meadows; granite peaks;*
SOLITUDE: ☆ ☆	*historic cabins; pristine lake; vistas over the Upper*
	Truckee River to Lake Tahoe

Hiking on this section of the Pacific Crest and the Tahoe Rim trails simplifies your day hike, because the path is well maintained and well signed, and the uphills and down-hills are fairly easy. You won't need extensive navigational skills (although you should always carry a map and compass and know how to use them) to find your way along this trail heading north into the Upper Truckee River drainage. Keep your camera ready because there are plenty of vistas and wildflowers along the way. To protect the meadows, stay put to look at the original cabins on the edge of Meiss Meadow; they're easily viewed from the trail. This is a great hike for families with children able to handle a light pack. There is little shade for much of this hike, so take plenty of water (or a method to treat it) and wear appropriate sun protection.

The Meiss Meadow trailhead, a waypoint on the Pacific Crest Trail (PCT), is found at the west end of the parking lot behind the bushes and parking-fee receptacle. Rest your backpack on the picnic table while you read information about the PCT on the kiosk. If you have aspirations for a long hike, you can see that this trail will take you more than 1,000 miles south to Mexico or more than 1,500 miles north to Canada.

This hike is a simple 5 miles to Showers Lake. It begins by head-ing west, climbing at a moderate rate, to round the spur of Red Lake Peak on a sandy and rocky trail. Weary long-distance hikers might find some comfort in a couple of impromptu campsites in the first 0.5 miles of the trail. (The closest water, however, is an intermittent stream another 0.5 miles north.)

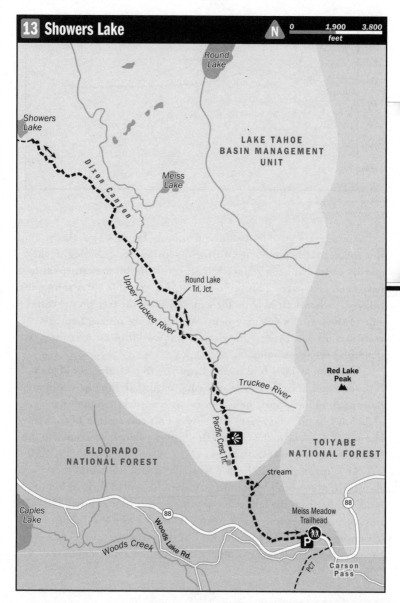

N   0   1,900   3,800
        feet

Round
Lake

Showers
Lake

LAKE TAHOE
BASIN MANAGEMENT
UNIT

Dixon Canyon

Meiss
Lake

Upper Truckee River

Round Lake
Trl. Jct.

Red Lake
Peak

Truckee River

Pacific Crest Trl.

ELDORADO
NATIONAL FOREST

TOIYABE
NATIONAL FOREST

stream

Caples
Lake

88

Woods Lake Rd.

Meiss Meadow
Trailhead

88

Woods Creek

P

PCT

Carson
Pass

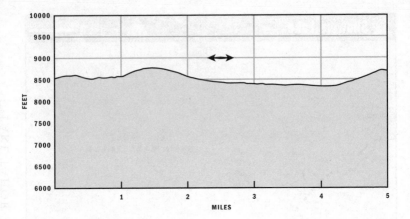

A moderate 300-foot climb up a south-facing slope takes you up to a former cattle pond. According to a forest service biologist, the giardia count has been reduced significantly in this area since cattle have been restricted. This pond is now an acceptable water source for hikers. If you are tired from the exposed hike, the tree on the east side of the trail is a welcome sight. While you are resting here, get your camera out, because the vistas and the wildflowers over the next 0.5 miles are spectacular.

The almost-level trail invites lingering to take pictures of giant lupines, corn lilies, woolly mule's ears, mountain bluebells, Indian paintbrushes, larkspurs, penstemons, asters, sticky cinquefoils, elephant's heads, and Sierra stickseeds. This easy section of trail is about 100 feet above the canyon floor, and gradually descends to the meadow over the next 0.75 miles.

An impromptu trail leads over to the site of the cabins that Benjamin Meiss built in about 1901 when he settled this section of land, 1 mile from the lake that bears his name. (But as noted above, to protect the meadow, don't use it.) The TRT and the Tahoe–Yosemite Trail (TYT) join the PCT at the junction 500 feet to the northwest. This is the southern turn on the TRT, almost the

The Upper Truckee River waits for rain.

beginning of the TYT, and not quite the midpoint of the PCT. If you're glad that yours is just a day hike, just continue to the left on this multi-appellation trail for 2 miles to Showers Lake. The route to the right leads hikers northeast 2 miles to Round Lake, where bears have recently been known to steal hikers' food.

Shortly, the trail turns into a double track while heading across the meadow, which is soggy in early season. You will cross and recross the nascent Upper Truckee River until the double track runs out after your last creek crossing. The trail leads through willows and climbs into white fir trees above the meadow.

Your trail continues on a northwest heading while rising about 400 feet to a point above the southeast corner of the lake. Before you drop down to the lake, notice the wind-protected campsite on the west side of the trail with a view over the lake. There are some highly impacted sites right next to the lake just after you descend to it. Better campsites—and good swimming—can be found among the lodgepole, fir, and hemlock along the east and north sides of the lake. From this vantage point, you have a good view of Little Round Top as it looms just 1 mile to the west.

If you are continuing toward Echo Summit on the PCT, the trail follows the east shore to the lake's outlet, then crosses to the south to navigate around a solid granite wall. Older maps show a trail around the south side of the lake, but this area is marshy and the trail has faded from view.

DIRECTIONS: From the junction of CA 88 and CA 89 in Hope Valley, drive 9 miles west on CA 88 to the parking lot on the north side of the road, 750 feet west of the Carson Pass Ranger Station. From the west, turn left into the lot 3.95 miles east of the Kirkwood Junction on CA 88. This lot and the lot on the south side at Carson Pass are the only legal places to park and the daily fee is $5. (These parking areas have pit toilets, trash receptacles, and often water.) If you are staying overnight, you will need to pay for two days of parking. An annual pass can be purchased at the Carson Pass Ranger Station for $20. This pass can be used at other trailhead parking areas in the Eldorado National Forest and the Lake Tahoe Basin Management Unit, which are described elsewhere in this book.

Hint: If you hike even a few times each season in the Lake Tahoe Basin, this is a good pass to purchase.

GPS TRAILHEAD COORDINATES	13 SHOWERS LAKE
UTM Zone (WGS84)	11S
Easting	0239782
Northing	4287374
Latitude	N 38° 41.804'
Longitude	W 119° 59.525'

14 Fourth of July Lake

SCENERY: ✿ ✿ ✿ ✿	DISTANCE: *11.6 miles round-trip*
TRAIL CONDITION: ✿ ✿ ✿ ✿	HIKING TIME: *8 hours*
CHILDREN: ✿	OUTSTANDING FEATURES: *Botanical displays*
DIFFICULTY: ✿ ✿ ✿	*everywhere; wide vistas in every direction; solitude at*
SOLITUDE: ✿ ✿ ✿ ✿	*camp; huge view down Summit City Creek's canyon.*

Enjoy the massive wildflower displays along the trail to Winnemucca and Round Top lakes, and then leave the crowd behind as you trek to an isolated alpine tarn tucked beneath Fourth of July Peak, almost ready to drop into the Summit City Creek canyon. New trail improvements make this a simple and safe trek downhill.

🚶🚶 Embarking from the trailhead near the ranger station, the lupine-lined trail begins climbing at a nominal rate through lodgepole and fir. Stone stairs help the downhill effort at times and switchbacks at others. After a few stream crossings and just 0.5 miles of easy walking from the trailhead, you'll enter the Mokelumne Wilderness. A tilted meadow where wildflowers begin their display for the senses follows your exit from the treed trail. This is a good time to remember where you packed the sunscreen.

Mingling with sagebrush, woolly mule's ears wave their yellow heads in the wind, accompanied by the crimson of paintbrush and the baby blue of Sierra stickseed. The trail is a visual delight to travel. A few more uphill steps send hikers past Frog Lake, just to the east of the trail. Elephants Back dominates the southern horizon just in front of you. It may not look exactly like a pachyderm from this vantage point, but to the emigrants coming from the east in the mid–19th century, it was accurate down to the ivory tusk made of snow.

Turn from this behemoth, walking toward the more distant giant to the southwest—Round Top. Within 500 feet, the trail splits away from the PCT, which heads southeast to Ebbetts Pass while you traverse across this open slope full of Sierra iris and columbine on

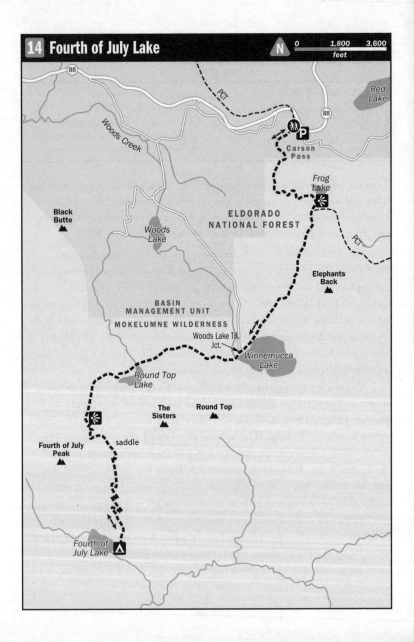

N

0   1,800   3,600
feet

88

Red
Lake

PCT

Woods Creek

88

Carson
Pass

Frog
Lake

Black
Butte

Woods
Lake

ELDORADO
NATIONAL FOREST

PCT

Elephants
Back

BASIN
MANAGEMENT UNIT

MOKELUMNE WILDERNESS

Woods Lake Trl.
Jct.

Winnemucca
Lake

Round Top
Lake

The
Sisters

Round Top

Fourth of July
Peak

saddle

Fourth of
July Lake

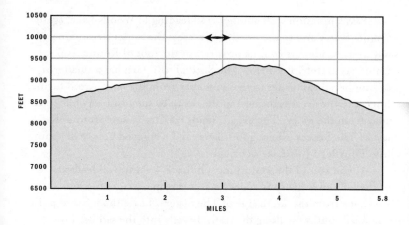

a wide, sandy trail. If you're lucky enough to time your hike with
a recent rainfall, this slope will be packed with Indian paintbrush,
larkspur, shooting stars, sticky cinquefoil, and fragrant lupine.

As you approach rockbound Winnemucca Lake, you'll pass some
campsites on both the left and right. Notice the marker posts indicating the number of the specific campsite. This system of impacting
specific "sacrifice" sites repeatedly is a good way to prevent further
degradation of pristine areas. This same method of campsite identification is followed at Round Top Lake and Fourth of July Lake,
as well. Bypass any trails descending left to the lake; continue to the
south and west for Round Top Lake.

Just before crossing the outlet stream from Winnemucca, walk past
the junction for a trail that leads 2 miles down to Woods Lake, where
there is a campground. Continue past the outlet and climb across
the gnarled feet of Round Top. Take advantage of the runoff stream
crossings where wildflowers species—flax, Sierra primrose, elephant's
head, lavender gilia, and baby blue eyes—tend to congregate. The 300
vertical feet that you see straight ahead takes you about 0.5 miles to the
overlook of Round Top Lake.

Pass a junction with another trail leading to Woods Lake, again 2 miles below and to the north, then cross the outlet stream on your way west. A sideways comma prostrate at the foot of Round Top (more accurately, it is below The Sisters), this tarn has a smattering of numbered campsites in the trees away from the lake. Avoid further impact to the areas right next to the shore by spending any idle time away from the water. The broad, sandy trail leads west around the last of The Sisters, where good views can be enjoyed before dropping into Fourth of July Lake's cirque.

As you round the westernmost hillside, a faint trail leads ahead to the left, and that spur trail comes to a stop overlooking Fourth of July Lake from the south side of The Sisters. Leave the lookout point and head southwest along the trail, directly into the saddle. Five switchbacks lower you about 250 feet before you make an eastward traverse of about 0.3 miles. You'll drop another 200 feet before changing direction midslope. The narrow trail is rocky, but travels through crowds of colorful flowers. After a couple of direction changes, cross a meltwater stream and continue angling downhill. Don't be surprised if your destination looks tantalizingly close from this point. Another 20 to 30 minutes will take care of this downhill.

After the trail's midpoint, five increasingly longer switchbacks control your descent. The lake is right there, but the trail seems to veer away to the east. This new trail avoids the final steep section that posed problems and kept many hikers away from this lake. The older, steeper trail is blocked off where the new trail swings away. Avoid using the closed section of trail. It is not faster, although it may be shorter.

Finally nearing lake level, your trail makes a circuitous approach, first to the southeast and then to the south, until you are even with the middle of the lake. At that point, the trail turns west directly toward the lake for 200 feet, where you begin finding markers for the specific tent sites. At the lake's outlet 200 feet to the south, frigid water dives through the lodgepole and western white pines on its way to Summit City Creek and, eventually, the Mokelumne River. The western shore, or rather the mountain containing it, is graced with some huge Jeffrey pines, sometimes in thick stands, but often standing alone on a precarious mountain perch.

Your hike out is less difficult than it appears. It will take an average hiker about one hour of steady but slow hiking to exit this massive backcountry bowl.

DIRECTIONS: After leaving South Lake Tahoe, drive south on US 50 4.7 miles to Meyers, turn left on CA 89, and drive 11.2 miles to CA 88 in Hope Valley. Turn west (right) on CA 88 and drive 8.7 miles to Carson Pass, where there is a ranger station and large parking lot with toilets on the south side of the road. You can get maps and information here, and most importantly, you can purchase a season-long parking pass for $20—or pay $5 for every night you're parked here. (Big fine!)

The overnight permits for this special-use area of the Mokelumne Wilderness are available only at this ranger station and on a first-come, first-serve basis.

GPS TRAILHEAD COORDINATES	14 FOURTH OF JULY
UTM Zone (WGS84)	11S
Easting	0240008
Northing	4287123
Latitude	N 38° 41.673'
Longitude	W 119° 59.364'

15 Winnemucca and Round Top Lakes

SCENERY: ✿ ✿ ✿ ✿ ✿	HIKING TIME: *4.5 hours*
TRAIL CONDITION: ✿ ✿ ✿ ✿	OUTSTANDING FEATURES: *Two miles south of*
CHILDREN: ✿ ✿ ✿	*Carson Pass, these two subalpine tarns are easily reached*
DIFFICULTY: ✿ ✿ ✿	*by hikers of all ages, and they are great destinations for*
SOLITUDE: ✿ ✿	*family overnights. While this is a popular area for day*
DISTANCE: *7.25 miles round-trip*	*hikes, the only thing crowding this trail will be wildflowers.*

For the first mile to these easily accessible lakes, you will share your trail with Pacific Crest Trail (PCT) thru-hikers. Unfortunately, they will have to hurry on without enjoying the wildflower bonanza that day hikers have ahead of them. Within 2 short miles, you will see and smell colors and scents of more than two dozen varieties of wildflowers. Bring your camera and field guide, along with plenty of insect repellent and sunscreen. Both lakes have several campsites, which are used by permit on a first-come, first-serve basis. While these campsites are "sacrifice" sites meant to minimize further human impact to the area, they are well placed, offering both seclusion and views.

🏃🏃 After you read about Snowshoe Thompson and Kit Carson at the historical monument adjacent to the parking lot, walk to the east end of the lot, where you can gain valuable information inside the ranger station. Your hike starts out at about 8,600 feet elevation in the Eldorado National Forest before quickly passing into the Mokelumne Wilderness and a specially protected zone. If you are camping in this special-use area, ensure that you have received a permit and an assigned camping site from the ranger.

Begin with a short walk from the mileage sign adjacent to the ranger station. Your sandy and boulder-lined trail will start to gain elevation after passing the Carson Pass and PCT trailhead sign. You'll immediately notice lupine adding color to the forested trail.

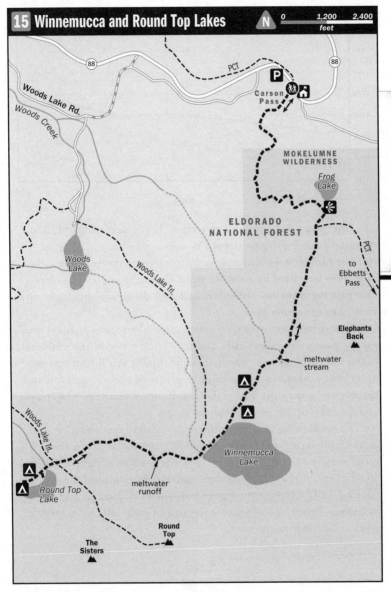

15 Winnemucca and Round Top Lakes

N

0   1,200   2,400
feet

88

Woods Lake Rd.

Woods Creek

PCT

P

Carson Pass

MOKELUMNE WILDERNESS

Frog Lake

ELDORADO NATIONAL FOREST

Woods Lake

Woods Lake Trl.

PCT

to Ebbetts Pass

Elephants Back

meltwater stream

Winnemucca Lake

Woods Lake Trl.

meltwater runoff

Round Top Lake

Round Top

The Sisters

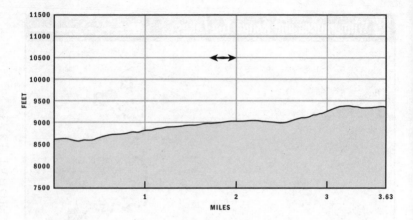

After you cross a rather lazy stream, begin traversing uphill to navigate around a large outcrop. Within 0.5 miles, you will pass into the Mokelumne Wilderness. Your effort to traverse this mass of granite is assisted by steps intended for young knees. The elevation gain turns mellow, however, and even the final switchbacks up to Frog Lake are rather lazy.

After emerging from the forest onto a tilted meadow filled with woolly mule's ears, sagebrush, and Indian paintbrush, the trail rises to the level of Frog Lake where, coincidentally, you'll find a convenient vista point. At your feet will be plenty of sticky cinquefoil and lavender gilia for your macro shots. Off to the south are The Nipple and Round Top for your telephoto shots.

The trail turns away from this vista at 8,870 feet elevation and runs slightly southwest toward Winnemucca Lake, which is about 1.3 miles away and sits at 8,975 feet. If you're looking at the ground and all of its color, it would be understandable if you missed the sign on your left indicating the junction where the PCT diverges and heads to Ebbetts Pass. Unless you're interested in a 22-mile hike, take the right fork to Winnemucca.

Although you're hiking uphill, this sandy and broad trail makes the travel a bit easier. From this point you have a good view of Caples Lake to the west. In a few moments, the trail will become rockier and root-filled, and coincidently, a bit steeper. About this point, you may be glad that you applied sunscreen at the trailhead, because the trail is completely exposed except for scattered trees around the lakes.

As your trail continues to Winnemucca, you'll be astounded by the color flowing downhill from the surrounding rocks: scarlet subalpine paintbrush, Applegate's paintbrush, Torrey's lupine (plus three or four others), meadow penstemon, elephant's head, columbine, Sierra stickseed, mountain bluebell, giant mountain larkspur, meadow larkspur, shooting star, western blue flag iris, western blue flax, and Sierra primrose—and (if this hasn't whetted your appetite) there are more to discover.

Approaching Winnemucca Lake, you will descend from a gentle rise, where you'll see numbered campsites on both sides of the trail. If you are continuing to Round Top Lake, avoid the trails that descend to the left. But Winnemucca is a fine destination in itself. The large boulders (actually glacial erratics) around the lake make excellent wind-protected alcoves, secluded from other hikers, where you can enjoy a picnic.

Bypassing Winnemucca Lake, keep to the left at the trail junction with the Woods Lake Trail just before crossing Winnemucca's outlet stream. Turn due west to begin a 450-foot climb to Round Top Lake, 1 mile away. You will begin by crossing small runoff streams while traversing an alpine meadow sloping beneath Round Top. Mountain heather, Sierra primrose, and little stalks of elephant's head lead you uphill to a level area at the midway point of a steep meltwater runoff, which is crossed easily enough with the assistance of some well-placed rocks. The holdup, as usual, is the profusion of flowers crowding this junction: sky-blue flax, Sierra primrose, larkspur . . . all the usual suspects.

White bark pine, its male cones reddish-purple and swollen with pollen, crowds the ground in its bent and dwarfed krummholz state. Turn to face south and notice the geology of Round Top and The Sisters to its west. Before you is layer upon layer of ancient ocean floor, which has been lifted thousands of feet, altered by heat and pressure, turned, twisted, and carved by tectonic and glacial forces over eons. Round Top Lake, like Winnemucca, is a glacial tarn—the result of glacial meltwater being contained by the lateral or terminal moraines created by the glacier. Before reaching Round Top Lake, you ascend to 9,450 feet elevation, where you stand on a lateral moraine.

A short, steep descent will take you to a trail junction entering from the north. Just next to the trees, this is the trail to Woods Lake, 2 miles away. The shade provided by these trees makes it a popular gathering spot. Cross over the lake's outlet stream and continue to numbered campsites on either side of the trail.

DIRECTIONS: From South Lake Tahoe, drive south on US 50 to Meyers, and then turn left on CA 89. Drive 11.2 miles to CA 88 in Hope Valley, where you will turn west and drive approximately 7.5 miles to Carson Pass. Trailhead parking is on the south side of the highway. A parking permit can be purchased for $5 per day or $20 per season. No permit is required for day hikes, but you must have one for overnight camping.

GPS TRAILHEAD COORDINATES	15 WINNEMUCCA AND ROUND TOP LAKES
UTM Zone (WGS84)	11S
Easting	0240008
Northing	4287123
Latitude	N 38° 41.673'
Longitude	W 119° 59.364'

16 Lake Margaret

SCENERY: ☆ ☆ ☆ ☆	DISTANCE: *4.8 miles round-trip*
TRAIL CONDITION: ☆ ☆ ☆ ☆	HIKING TIME: *2.5 hours*
CHILDREN: ☆ ☆ ☆ ☆ ☆	OUTSTANDING FEATURES: *Pristine, jewel-like*
DIFFICULTY: ☆ ☆	*lake at the end of a well-defined, moderately easy,*
SOLITUDE: ☆ ☆	*picturesque trail*

Lake Margaret is nestled amid a sloped granite field north of Kirkwood Lake. On this 2.4-mile descending traverse, you'll cross Caples Creek twice and will be able to enjoy the flowers that crowd these small, wet meadows. No navigation skills are needed to follow this highly blazed trail, allowing you to concentrate on children's questions along the way. The dirt-and-duff track mostly stays under the lodgepole, with a few short intervals on granite. Rockbound and dainty, Lake Margaret shines in the bright sun, inviting picnickers and swimmers.

🚶🚶 From the trailhead you zigzag downhill, losing 130 feet in 0.4 miles only to regain the majority of it a few thousand feet later. On your gentle descent, the sandy and rocky trail crosses the roots of white fir and lodgepole pine. You may notice a blaze in the form of a small letter *i* on trailside trees. In fact, if you were to start counting the blazes near the trailhead, you would reach 50 well before the lake. From a rocky overlook minutes away from the trailhead, you can hear the sound of Caples Creek below. In another few minutes, you'll cross your first branch of the creek. When the water is low, go straight across on the small log; when the water is over that log, walk downstream to the left about 75 feet to a more substantial log.

As the trail continues north, it is squeezed between the creek on the left and a small, domed outcrop on the right. If the ground is dry, you may find a couple of picnic spots among the lodgepole pines just as you approach this outcrop. You'll notice a casual trail going into the meadow just before your track turns to the east and meets

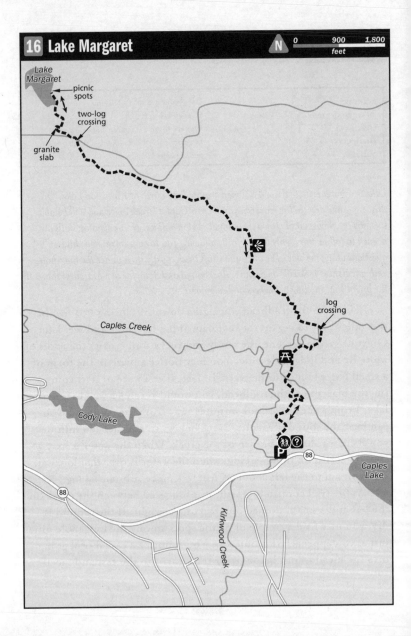

N

0   900   1,800
feet

Lake
Margaret

picnic
spots

two-log
crossing

granite
slab

log
crossing

Caples Creek

Cody Lake

P

88

Caples
Lake

88

Kirkwood Creek

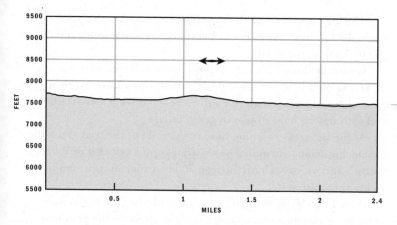

willows lining the granite wall. Corn lilies, plentiful lupine, meadow penstemon, and asters grow among the fresh grass here.

Continue around the dome to the east and parallel Caples Creek to a low, large log that reaches across the wanna-be river. You are now 0.75 miles from the trailhead. After you cross, you'll return to a northwesterly course, again skirting a small meadow where you can look back and see the wall of granite behind you.

Zig to the right and zag to the left at the trail signs that help you up some rocky steps at the end of this meadow. Watch for a directional sign painted on the boulder. There, you'll begin to climb the rocky trail heading northwest. Switchback up through the lodgepole and by about the 1-mile point, your trail will level somewhat as you begin to skirt another outcrop. Pass by the casual trails leading to the little pond and follow the enormous blazes and ducks. Take a moment to look around from the vista point just above the little pond.

Begin descending this outcrop toward the north, where you have a view of pine- and fir-studded granite ahead of you. Follow the ducks through the **S**-curves and continue descending on a dirt path to the west that leads to a rocky chute and a descending sandy trail. Head to the left of the next meltwater pond.

The log causeway near the runoff stream just past the pond marks the 1.5-mile point. A small meadow sits to the south and the granite knob to the north.

Continue downhill on the lupine-lined duff trail adjacent to the creek. Wolf lichen sticks to the trees and aspen leaves rustle in the slightest breeze. Indian rhubarb and corn lilies gather around the stream to make a huge display of green foliage.

At the last creek crossing, head to the right of the trail to use the double-log arrangement that heads straight into a thicket of Indian rhubarb and willows. Crash through and continue on your sandy trail to the northwest.

A trail sign sends you east, up to the wall of a granite outcrop where some well-placed ducks lead straight up across the granite to the north. Descend to Lake Margaret with a slight water view on your way. The trail will lead you around to the lake's east side, which has some nice picnic spots. You'll also find some up on the rock above the lake to the east or to the south.

DIRECTIONS: From the west, take CA 88 from Jackson 56 miles to the Kirkwood ski area. The turn into the Lake Margaret parking lot is 0.5 miles ahead on the left.

From South Lake Tahoe, take US 50 4.8 miles to the CA 89 turnoff in Meyers. Drive 11.2 miles south on CA 89 to CA 88 where you'll turn right, to the west. Lake Margaret's parking lot is 13.8 miles to the west, just past Caples Lake on the right.

The entrance is signed and the parking lot has room for about 20 cars. There are no facilities here, but there is a kiosk with local information posted at the trailhead.

GPS Trailhead Coordinates	16 Lake Margaret
UTM Zone (WGS84)	10S
Easting	0754828
Northing	4288041
Latitude	N 38° 42.258'
Longitude	W 120° 04.175'

SCENERY: ✪ ✪ ✪ ✪ ✪	DISTANCE: *6.6 miles round-trip*
TRAIL CONDITION: ✪ ✪ ✪ ✪	HIKING TIME: *3.5–4 hours*
CHILDREN: ✪ ✪	OUTSTANDING FEATURES: *Wildflowers covering*
DIFFICULTY: ✪ ✪ ✪ ✪	*sloped meadows; volcanic rock formations; wall-to-*
SOLITUDE: ✪ ✪ ✪	*wall vistas from the summit*

Look for a clear day to hike through this volcanic terrain up to spectacular vistas overlooking Silver Lake, the Mokelumne Wilderness, the Desolation Wilderness, and Kirkwood Meadows. The trail winds steadily up about 1,500 feet through huge, sloping meadows full of wildflowers and often thick stands of pine and fir. This trail takes you to Amador County's unnamed high point with the namesake peak as a lower and farther alternate.

🥾🥾 Your easily identified trail embarks on a dirt path under cover of red fir and lodgepole pine. Enjoy their shade along with the lupine blues, paintbrush reds, and mule's ears yellows as you ascend and roughly parallel the road for a bit. Turn away from the road and begin climbing the forested slope. When you break out of the trees, you are greeted by a long, sloping meadow covered with woolly mule's ears accented with asters, lupine, and bright and profuse scarlet gilia. As you traverse the meadow and approach the snow diversion panels atop Carson Spur's ridge, you can see the Two Sentinels ahead to the east and Martin Point to the south, with Martin Meadow and the set-ting moon far to the west.

As you approach the ridge crest, you'll see a unique pair of coni-fers—a Jeffrey pine and a western juniper. Their stunted, misshapen, downhill branches shield their trunks, and their enormous lower branches reach the ground on the uphill slope, bracing themselves against the winds that often scream across this point.

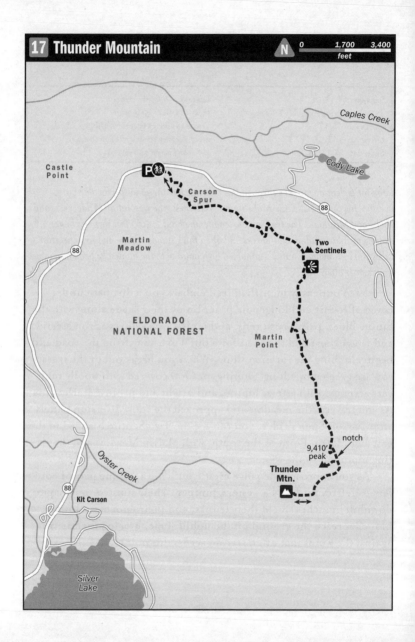

N

0   1,700   3,400
feet

Caples Creek

Cody Lake

Castle
Point

Carson
Spur

88

Martin
Meadow

Two
Sentinels

ELDORADO
NATIONAL FOREST

Martin
Point

88

notch

9,410'
peak

Thunder
Mtn.

Oyster Creek

88

Kit Carson

Silver
Lake

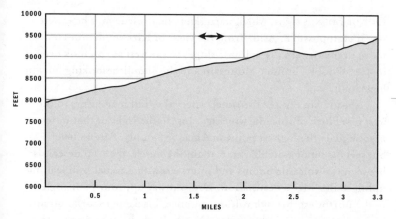

As you quickly pass the avalanche control devices high above the highway, the tree cover thickens and the trail soon resumes its steady uphill trudge. Your eastward march beneath the firs is interrupted by a couple of switchbacks that draw you closer to another avalanche-prone slope and more volcanic detritus. Layered lava on ashfall on lava flow, these remnants of eons of volcanism stand about 900 feet above the highway and tower over hikers on the trail. Turn southwest as you leave the Two Sentinels behind.

A beautiful vista opens both to the east and west after about 1.75 miles of uphill wandering. Silver Lake and Kirkwood Meadows spread beneath you on either side of the ridge. The trailside flowers now include dandelion and pussy paws, and all of them are being mauled by bees. At the next volcanic monster, the trail veers around to the right where blue flax, pink primrose, purple penstemon, yellow wallflower, and red paintbrush are among the trailside color bursts.

Your southbound trail passes beneath Martin Point's eastern twin. Sierra gentian, lupine, and paintbrush join in as you make a beeline along the exposed ridge. The vistas here are, as you may imagine, incredible. But pictures and views may not be on your mind as you hike uphill in the wind past the Kirkwood ski resort's

113

OUT OF BOUNDS signs, which warn skiers that rescue may be expensive if even possible. Aside from the views of Kirkwood, and far more dramatic, are the volcanic slopes to the west as you look over to 4,208-foot Thunder Mountain and the ghoulish-looking terrain beneath it.

Ahead, you can see the notch where the trail maneuvers to the west of a block of volcanic wreckage. Just to the right of that notch is your goal—the highest point in Amador County. After a brief but serious set of switchbacks to attain the notch, the trail descends between two volcanic bombs and intersects with a casual trail leading uphill to this hike's destination. On your way up, your path angles to the northwest through volcanic pumice, blackened scoria, bombs, and agglomerate on a slope of sagebrush, buckwheat, and pussy toes.

Vistas from this summit at 9,410 feet are incredible, even during the fires of 2008. I can't wait for this view on a clear day. An alternate goal is to traverse the slope heading west, following the obvious path from this summit, or by following the Thunder Mountain Trail past the use trail to this summit. Either trail contours around to the west side, approximately 0.5 miles, following the main ridge above lightly scattered hemlock and pine. The trail will curve back to the east following the ridge to attain the summit and its tackle-box register.

DIRECTIONS: Thunder Mountain's trailhead is located 0.4 mile west of the Carson Spur on CA 88. Starting in South Lake Tahoe on US 50, drive 4.7 miles to Meyers, where you'll turn left onto CA 89. Drive 11.2 miles to the junction with CA 88 in Hope Valley. Turn west and drive 8.7 miles to Carson Pass, then continue west another 7.4 miles to the trailhead parking area on the south side of CA 88.

If coming from the west, the trailhead is 3.2 miles east of the Kit Carson Lodge at Silver Lake or 54 miles from Jackson.

The dirt parking area supports about a dozen cars but has no other facilities. An informational kiosk with relative trail locations and distances is posted on the edge of the parking area. From there, you can easily see the trailhead in the southeast corner.

GPS TRAILHEAD COORDINATES	17 THUNDER MOUNTAIN
UTM Zone (WGS84)	10S
Easting	0751541
Northing	4288076
Latitude	N 38° 42.334'
Longitude	W 120° 06.439'

18 Echo Lakes to Lake Aloha

SCENERY: ☆ ☆ ☆ ☆ ☆
TRAIL CONDITION: ☆ ☆ ☆ ☆ ☆
CHILDREN: ☆ ☆ ☆ ☆
DIFFICULTY: ☆ ☆ ☆ ☆
SOLITUDE: ☆ ☆
DISTANCE: 15 miles round-trip
HIKING TIME: 8 hours (overnight)

OUTSTANDING FEATURES: This hike features two famous trails alongside two of the most popular lakes in the Tahoe region. Easy access to a dozen more stunning lakes is eclipsed by the dazzling display of granite presented by the Crystal Range; towering overhead are Pyramid and Ralston, Price and Jacks, Cracked Crag and Echo peaks.

The Desolation Wilderness is one of the most visited backcountry areas in California. Because of its proximity to the Bay Area and Sacramento and its easily accessible trailhead, this entry to the Desolation Wilderness is always highly trafficked, so much so that there are daily quotas for overnight camping. Day hikers are asked to register at the trailhead or at a U.S. Forest Service visitor center at no charge. Overnight campers must secure a permit for a fee.

The trail to Lake Aloha presents no navigation challenges, although a compass and map are essentials. Note that this trail has many intersecting trails. Fortunately, it's part of the Pacific Crest Trail (PCT), Tahoe Rim Trail (TRT), and Tahoe–Yosemite Trail (TYT), and its status means great signage for hikers.

Head to the northeast corner of Lake Aloha for camping among secluded alcoves above the lake—hidden from view, open to the stars.

🚶🚶 Walk directly across the parking lot and over the metal causeway leading across Lower Echo Lake's dam and outlet. Watch for the hooks of anxious anglers as you walk behind them; a polite "excuse me" is always understood (to mean "keep your hooks out of my cheek"). Follow the path to the right at the end of the bridge.

The trailhead is at the information kiosk for the TRT, where you can pick up a map for this section of the trail provided by the Tahoe Rim Trail Association. Climb the path northeast up to a clearing where the trail makes a sharp left, heading west. Walk over to the edge of the clearing and take in the magnificent vista of the South Lake Tahoe basin.

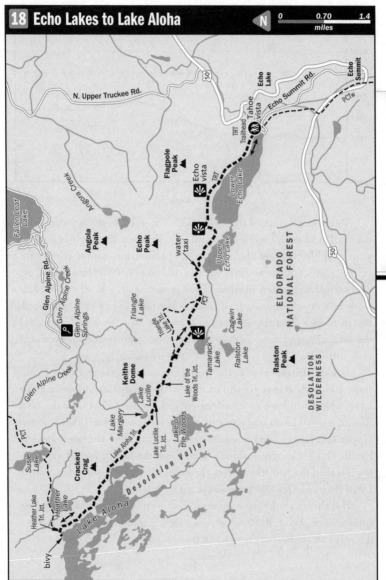

N. Upper Truckee Rd.

50

Echo Lake

Echo Summit Rd.

Echo Summit

PCTw

Tahoe vista

TRT Trailhead

TRT

Lower Echo Lake

PCT

Echo vista

Flagpole Peak

water taxi

Upper Echo Lake

Angora Creek

Fallen Leaf Lake

Angola Peak

Echo Peak

ELDORADO NATIONAL FOREST

50

Glen Alpine Rd.

Glen Alpine Creek

Glen Alpine Springs

Triangle Lake

Triangle Tri. Jct.

Cagwin Lake

Tamarack Lake

Ralston Lake

Ralston Peak

Keiths Dome

Lake of the Woods Tri. Jct.

DESOLATION WILDERNESS

Glen Alpine Creek

Lake Lucille

Lake Margery

Lake Aloha Tri.

Lake Lucille Tri. Jct.

Lake of the Woods

Susie Lake

PCT

Cracked Crag

Heather Lake Tri. Jct.

Heather Lake

Lake Aloha

Desolation Valley

bivy

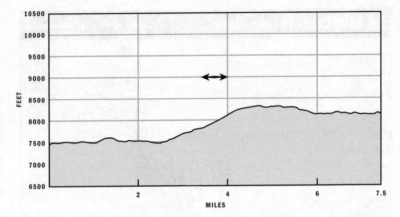

Because it's part of the PCT, TRT, and TYT, it's no wonder that the trail is in such excellent condition. Traverse the slightly rolling path roughly 100 feet above the shore, sometimes under cover of Jeffrey pines and sometimes on sun-baked granite. After a mile of westward travel, when Flagpole Peak is overhead, a brief switchback leads hikers away from a trail that leads straight ahead past the boulder to service the summer cabins along the lake. Now 200 feet above the lake, the trail squeezes beside the warm granite and an excellent vista unfolds.

Under pleasant shade, the trail descends, intersects another cabin trail, and leads across granite in the northwest corner of Lower Echo Lake, where you have an excellent vista of Flagpole Peak over the lake. Round a small knob and you can see the narrow channel that connects Upper and Lower Echo lakes for the majority of the summer. Because Pacific Gas & Electric is able to draw down the top 12 feet of water in the lower of the two, this access for boats disappears late in the season. Until then, a water taxi is available on both lakes.

But this is a hike, so continue your westward traverse along the smaller lake. First, descend across a lightly treed slope, then enter the trees about halfway down the lake. It is 0.6 miles to the water taxi dock from the knob where you first saw the channel. The sign for the water taxi, high in a tree, is easy to miss from either direction. There are three runoff streams just prior to reaching the trail to the dock. If you think you might want to take the boat ride on the way back, mark this spot. The fare is $10 per person, with a $30 minimum.

Climb at a steady pace as you leave the Echo lakes behind. Cross a runoff stream and continue west. In 0.4 miles, you will enter the Desolation Wilderness, a reminder to you that rangers check for both overnight and day-hike permits. Twenty yards on is a signed junction with a trail to Triangle Lake, leading on to Echo Peak. Lodgepole pines shade the trail for another 0.3 miles as you ascend. The stream crossings are well engineered along here.

The uphill dirt-and-duff trail leaves the lodgepoles and crosses a small stone bridge to a spectacular lookout over both Echo lakes and down onto Tamarack, Cagwin, and Ralston lakes, and across to Ralston Peak. Bypass the trail down to Tamarack Lake, and continue uphill at a steady rate—about 450 feet up over the next 0.8 miles. Reach Haypress Meadows just after passing another trail junction leading easily across the sagebrush- and paintbrush-covered slope to Triangle Lake.

Your destination is to the west, across the north boundary of Haypress Meadows. The trail to Lake of the Woods crosses it 0.3 miles ahead in a lush copse of trees. As you hike, another trail heads to the same lake less than 1,000 feet farther on. You are going to meet another pair of trails to the same location when you approach and pass lakes Lucille and Margery. These two small lakes are below the trail to the north. In between them is a signed junction for a trail that veers off to the left leading to the southeastern corner of Lake Aloha.

The described trail descends to intersect Aloha just as the tree cover ends and the granite trail begins. Beneath the Alps-like arêtes of Pyramid, Agassiz, and Price, Aloha greets first-time visitors with a welcoming blast of reflected light. Almost aglow on any day, the shallow waters of this artificial lake glisten above the granite floor. Traverse the sandy or rocky trail beneath Cracked Crag and watch for another faint trail about 0.5 miles from the last trail junction. There you can slip over the shallow ridge down to Lake LeConte and find solitude for your campsite.

Hike about 0.5 miles beyond a small peninsula of rock to reach the next trail junction—east to Heather Lake and west to Mosquito Pass and Clyde Lake. Take the westward trail and begin looking for one of the many possible bivy sites located below the trail but still more than 200 feet from shore. Short hikes from camp will yield some huge vistas for those who choose to rest here beneath Jacks Peak.

DIRECTIONS: From South Lake Tahoe, drive 4.8 miles south on US 50 to Meyers. Stay on US 50 past CA 89 for 5 more miles. Turn right onto Johnson Pass Road. This is a sharp right turn off of a long bend around Echo Summit, so here are some checkpoints: there is a Caltrans maintenance station at the tip of the bend (3.8 miles from Meyers). Your turn is 1.2 miles ahead, just past the renovation-ready Little Norway.

From Placerville, drive 39.8 miles to Strawberry. Johnson Pass Road is 7.4 miles past Strawberry and 1.8 miles past Sierra-at-Tahoe ski resort. Follow the angled road as above.

Drive 0.6 miles along Johnson Pass Road to a left turn onto Echo Lakes Road and stay to the left for 0.9 miles, until you reach the large parking lot above the Echo Lakes store. You can unload packs but not park down below in front of the store near the pit toilets. It's best to park and take the trail and steps down through the trees, behind the pit toilets, to the store.

GPS TRAILHEAD COORDINATES	18 ECHO LAKES TO LAKE ALOHA
UTM Zone (WGS84)	10S
Easting	0756548
Northing	4302664
Latitude	N 38° 50.125'
Longitude	W 120° 02.664'

19 Ralston Peak

SCENERY: ☆ ☆ ☆ ☆ ☆ TRAIL CONDITION: ☆ ☆ ☆ ☆ CHILDREN: ☆ DIFFICULTY: ☆ ☆ ☆ ☆ SOLITUDE: ☆ ☆ ☆ ☆ DISTANCE: 7.6 miles round-trip HIKING TIME: 6.5 hours	OUTSTANDING FEATURES: *Flower-filled meadows brighten the fir-and-hemlock—adorned slopes. Knock-out vistas include Pyramid Peak; Mount Tallac; and the lakes of Desolation Valley, including Aloha and Echo with several others in between. You also have a peek at distant Fallen Leaf Lake and Lake Tahoe.*

Incredible views of a dozen glacial lakes and prominent peaks from a vista point 1,100 feet above Desolation Valley are yours to think about as you begin ascending the lateral moraine forming Pyramid Creek's canyon. The trail climbs at a consistent rate for the first third of the hike, then tests your lungs and legs for just over a mile before resuming a more reasonable slope to the summit.

🚶🚶 Once at the trailhead, take time to fill out a Desolation Wilderness day-hike permit and attach it to your pack. A separate permit, available from forest service ranger stations, is necessary to camp overnight in the Desolation Wilderness.

A few switchbacks send you through the Jeffrey pines and white firs that shade you on the lower portion of this huge lateral moraine. Just as you burst into the sunlight, you'll pass a few cairns marking casual trails from Pinecrest Camp to the east. A beautiful vista point lies less than 1,000 feet ahead. As you stand in this open, sandy spot, Pyramid Creek's canyon spreads out in front of you like a gaping tear in the earth.

Traverse to the northeast for 0.25 miles before some serious switchbacks mark the beginning of about 1,250 feet of elevation gain over the next 1.1 miles. The Desolation Wilderness boundary sign, about 1.25 miles along, will be a reminder that you need a wilderness permit. From this point, about 900 feet above the trailhead, you can glimpse the Sierra at Tahoe ski runs to the south.

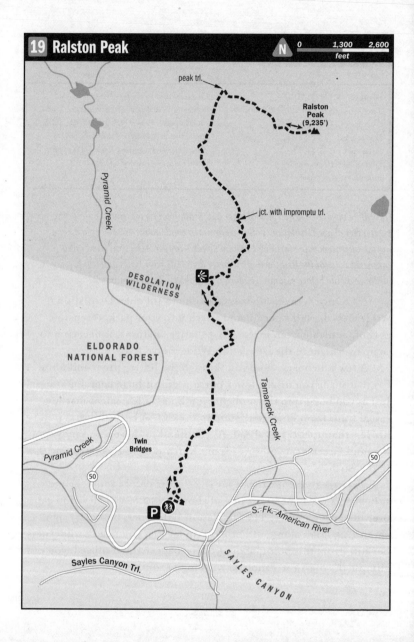

N

0   1,300   2,600
feet

peak trl.

Ralston
Peak
(9,235')

jct. with impromptu trl.

Pyramid Creek

DESOLATION
WILDERNESS

ELDORADO
NATIONAL FOREST

Tamarack Creek

Pyramid Creek

Twin
Bridges

50

50

P

S. Fk. American River

Sayles Canyon Trl.

SAYLES CANYON

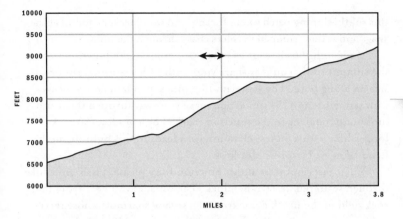

After another 150 feet of elevation gain, you will run into a large boulder blocking the trail, which you will just clamber over to continue on the well-defined, steep, sandy trail. More large boulders sitting 1.5 miles from the trailhead offer a nice location for a quick break, where you can pretend to take pictures while you catch your breath.

The trail will occasionally be tightly bordered by huckleberry oak, manzanita, bush chinquapin, and buck brush ceanothus. Turn away from your view of Pyramid Peak and traverse east across the south-facing slope. In about 300 feet you will step across a stagnant spring seeping water from beneath a boulder. In another 300 feet, your path turns northeast again.

Continue climbing another 200 feet to a pleasant south-facing meadow adorned with pinemat manzanita and buckwheat. Turn northwest and climb another 250 feet to crest a small ridge. An impromptu trail to the summit is marked by a duck near this point, but it has been blocked to wave day hikers away.

A 1,500-foot traverse to the northwest begins with a shallow descent from this ridge crest. About the time that you reach a meadow fed by a seasonal stream, your route will turn to the north. Lupine, corn lilies, Indian paintbrush, asters, and meadow penstemon color this south-sloping patch where flickers and woodpeckers pound at the snags and yellow-rumped warblers chase through the pine.

Your uphill trail leads less than 0.5 miles to the junction with the summit trail. You may share your path with a seasonal runoff stream along here. The western white pines' pendant cones, heavy with sap, glisten in the sun as you make your way through them and mountain hemlock to the junction marked by a modest cairn. A longer hike with a bit less elevation gain leads to this point from the Echo lakes via Haypress Meadows.

Turn east-southeast at this junction for a pleasant half-mile hike through scattered western hemlock. The whistles you hear from the rock field to the north come from the several marmots whose territory you are entering. Watch your trail closely and look back to see where you are coming from (an aim point) so that you do not take an incorrect heading on your return.

The sandy trail leads to the base of the rockfall, just 100 feet below the summit. A brief climb up this talus cap will reward you with 360-degree views—from Lake Tahoe in the distance to Lakes Ralston, Cagwin, and Tamarack beneath you. Your vista includes Lovers Leap, Pyramid Peak, Jacks and Dicks peaks, Cracked Crag and Mount Tallac, and distant Freel Peak. The views of Lake of the Woods, Lake Aloha, and Echo Lakes are spectacular.

If you aren't too busy battling the butterflies on the summit, you may notice the shaggy hawkweed—a fuzzy, yellow-flowered plant glistening in the sun. You will probably also see several golden-mantled ground squirrels darting around looking for handouts. Do them a favor and do not feed them. Before heading down, look for your aim point so you do not inadvertently head too far downhill to the north.

Pyramid Peak and Mount Agassiz from Ralston's flank

DIRECTIONS: The trailhead parking lot in Sayles Flat is on the left side of US 50 just 2.5 miles east of Strawberry (40 miles east of Placerville). Watch for signs for Camp Sacramento.

If coming from the east, the trailhead is on the right past Echo Summit, exactly 2.75 miles west of the Sierra at Tahoe ski area (which is 10.7 miles west of South Lake Tahoe).

The generous parking lot along the broad shoulder of the highway is signed for Ralston Peak and the Our Lady of the Sierra chapel. You can park here or drive about 200 yards up the dirt road, where there is room for four cars to park at the trailhead to the left of the tiny church.

GPS Trailhead Coordinates	19 Ralston Peak
UTM Zone (WGS84)	10S
Easting	0750742
Northing	4299073
Latitude	N 38° 48.291'
Longitude	W 120° 06.936'

20 Pyramid Peak

SCENERY: ✿ ✿ ✿ ✿ ✿	HIKING TIME: *8 hours*
TRAIL CONDITION: ✿ ✿ ✿ ✿	OUTSTANDING FEATURES: *Panoramic vista of the*
CHILDREN: *Not advised for children*	*Crystal Range and the Desolation Wilderness; views*
DIFFICULTY: ✿ ✿ ✿ ✿ ✿	*from Lake Tahoe to Loon Lake, including Lake Aloha,*
SOLITUDE: ✿ ✿ ✿ ✿ ✿	*Echo Lakes, and Fallen Leaf Lake; and clear views to the*
DISTANCE: *7.7 miles round-trip*	*south, including Elephant's Back, Round Top, Thimble*
	Peak, and The Nipple.

Four thousand feet of elevation gain—straight up—had better have an incredibly redeeming quality besides aerobic exercise, and Pyramid Peak via Rocky Canyon dishes it up for hearty hikers only. The views alone are worth the hike up this triangle of granite talus. But the solitude, the adventure, and even the workout will leave you with a feeling of well-being and sense of accomplishment. This is perhaps the hardest hike in the book.

🏃 There are more than a few ways to hike to Pyramid Peak, but the route up Rocky Canyon is definitely the most strenuous. And for every small, strained, uphill step you take, there will be a surprising reward along the trail. Your reward at the top may be more brilliant than you anticipated.

You will not find the trail up Rocky Canyon marked on current maps; nor is it marked at the trailhead. Before crossing to the north side of the road, you should be able to spot one of the two faint trails that ascend the steep bank on large rocks in the dirt. Traffic is very close here, so choose your spot carefully.

Once atop the bank, you will see a large log across the trail. Maneuver around the log and continue uphill for another 100 vertical feet and avoid a false trail to the left. Instead, make sure to go right and stay away from the creek. You will come close to the stream and eventually cross it, but not for a little while. If you are catching your breath after another 125 vertical feet, turn around and take a fresh look at Lovers Leap. From this vantage point, you can clearly

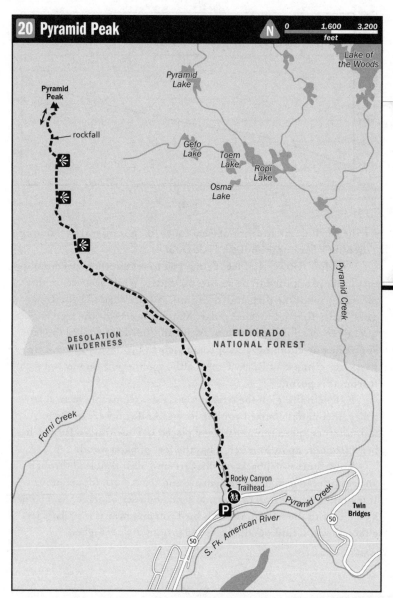

N

| 0 | 1,600 | 3,200 |

feet

Pyramid Peak

rockfall

Pyramid Lake

Lake of the Woods

Gefo Lake

Toem Lake

Ropi Lake

Osma Lake

DESOLATION WILDERNESS

ELDORADO NATIONAL FOREST

Pyramid Creek

Forni Creek

Rocky Canyon Trailhead

P

Pyramid Creek

Twin Bridges

50

S. Fk. American River

50

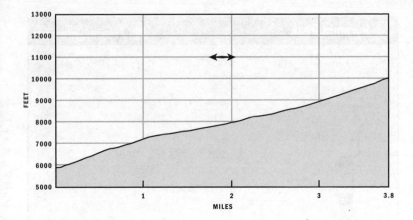

see the small dome in front of what looks like a miniature version of Yosemite's famous monolith, Half Dome.

Another 100 vertical feet brings you to yet another speed bump that looks like it used to be an incense cedar. While you are on this pleasant part of the dirt-and-duff trail, you are shaded by Jeffrey pine, white fir, and incense cedar. Manzanita crowds the trail frequently in this forested section. Avoid another false trail to the left and continue climbing. At approximately 6,350 feet, you get your first clear glimpse of Rocky Creek, although there is no way to reach it from this point.

Keep climbing on the stream's east side, seemingly vertical at times, through the mixed conifer forest. As if you were going too fast, another speed bump has been placed in your trail—a fir that has been trodden upon so much it has the feel of balsa wood.

Your short switchbacks on this dirt-and-duff trail lead through an area littered with deadfall right around the 7,000-foot contour. Intermittently, the trail will turn to sand and rock or scree. As it comes a bit closer to the stream, the only bird you may hear is a Stellar's jay, although you'll find woodpeckers and grouse slightly higher.

If you're here early in the season, you'll find the trail to be a muddy stream nearly everywhere. All of that meltwater carries the seeds that intermittently flow down across the trail, leaving behind a display of lupine, aster, and Indian paintbrush alongside snow plant and pine drop. Within sound of the creek, willows and flowers become quite dense along the sandy trail. A gentle breeze along here will shake the leaves of this grove of aspens.

The crossing at Rocky Creek, about elevation 7,400, is an easy one brightened by mountain bluebells, red and yellow columbine, dense ferns, and paintbrush.

Once on the west side of the stream, you will ascend gradually through lodgepole pine along a huge granite outcrop. Skirt the flank of this outcrop, bouncing between the stream on the right and the outcrop on the left. Duck beneath a fallen lodgepole and then walk around the prone fir. Then resume your climbing among the lupine and pinemat manzanita. Plenty of colorful flowers will greet you when you pass through the next small, sloping meadow.

Right around 8,000 feet elevation, you may find a new meaning in the term *merciless* as you ascend these short, steep switchbacks over the next 250 vertical feet. But of all things, you'll find a nearly flat spot surrounded by willows, asters, corn lilies, and cobalt-blue sky. The little knoll to the left appears as if it would support at least one tent beneath the towering fir. You may see a western white pine with a hollow space at its base, which on closer examination reveals a boulder that the tree swallowed as it grew.

Just as you pass the last little meadow where two or three meltwater streams converge, where another bivy site could be located to the west, you will be able to first spy your destination. Silhouetted against a cloudless sky, Pyramid Peak strikes an imposing figure to a tired hiker at this vantage point of 8,475 feet. Make your way across the jumbled maze of broken rock, where several ducks have been accurately laid out to mark the trail.

A set of absolutely brutal switchbacks help you up the pink granite to the top of this steep rock wall. When you reach the top of that winding course, your trail will be clear—and vertical—in front of you, and although it is a very narrow trail, it is quite distinct. The path traverses to the east side of the slope and then continues on some ridiculously brutal switchbacks, brightened only by the mountain heather growing trailside that guides you straight uphill directly toward the peak.

While you're busy hydrating, turn to the south to get a good view of the Sierra at Tahoe Ski Resort beneath you as well as some distant views of some of the peaks in the Mokelumne Wilderness: Elephants Back, Round Top, The Thimble, and The Nipple.

By 9,500 feet, your well-marked trail switches back and forth through scattered and crippled pines that provide no shade or cover from the sun overhead. Just after another turn, Pyramid's talus slope looms up in front of you. You have only 450 vertical feet until the summit, where some well-constructed circular windbreaks can accommodate lots of hiking companions.

The line in front of you is fairly easy and about as good as there is across the entire south face. This is very easy Class 3 hiking. You may encounter some points where you will need to use your hands to maintain balance on these large granite boulders. Continue straight up to the summit or work your way to the west as you ascend. Pay attention to avoid the steep ascent on the east face and you will be at the top rather quickly.

While you're climbing up you may see a marmot or two. I was greeted at the summit by thousands and thousands of California tortoiseshell butterflies which, once disturbed, flowed from the summit down the path I had ascended. Thirty minutes later, at the base of the rockfall, the flying orange flowers persisted in their downhill deluge.

Linger at the summit to take pictures of this magnificent range that the glaciers sculpted, and of the lakes they left behind. Keep a close eye on changes in the weather as summer thunderstorms are dangerous and can be counted on in the Tahoe area.

Lake of the Woods

DIRECTIONS: This informal trailhead is located on the north shoulder of US 50, halfway between Twin Bridges and Strawberry. A pullout with parking room for six or seven cars sits precisely beneath a programmable highway information sign 43 miles east of Placerville. The sign's silver control box sits at the west end of the pullout. From your parking spot at the 43 milestone, walk 375 feet east along the highway and cross to the steep bank on the opposite side of the road, where two faint trails lead up to a fallen log across the obvious trail. When at the log, the trail is quite visible and leads straight uphill.

GPS TRAILHEAD COORDINATES	20 PYRAMID PEAK
UTM Zone (WGS84)	10S
Easting	0748694
Northing	4299407
Latitude	N 38° 48.501'
Longitude	W 120° 08.156'

21 Half Moon, Alta Morris, and Gilmore Lakes

SCENERY: ✡ ✡ ✡ ✡ ✡	HIKING TIME: *5 hours*
TRAIL CONDITION: ✡ ✡ ✡ ✡	OUTSTANDING FEATURES: *Visit three backcountry*
CHILDREN: ✡ ✡ ✡	*lakes for camping or wildflower photography. Both*
DIFFICULTY: ✡ ✡ ✡	*reports and lies about fish abound. You'll be treated to*
SOLITUDE: ✡ ✡ ✡ ✡	*spectacular views of the 1,300-foot-tall lithic palisades*
DISTANCE: *10 miles round-trip*	*of the largest cirque in the Desolation Wilderness.*

The trail follows Glen Alpine Creek past its namesake spring and resort before making a brief ascent to its source at Gilmore Lake via the Pacific Crest Trail (PCT). The cirque surrounding circular Gilmore certainly is impressive and picturesque, but the crowds that stop here on weekends can be avoided by descending to a massive, deep cirque cradling tiny Alta Morris and aptly named Half Moon lakes. There, campsites and solitude are generous offerings.

🚶🚶 Depart the trailhead and skirt the beaver-inhabited Lily Lake on a forest road surfaced with baseball-sized scree. Follow the road and the trail signs that lead past cabins and waterfalls as described in Hike 22, Glen Alpine Loop (page 137). Pass the resort and springs, where an information kiosk will fill you in on the area's history. The cool, dim light under the pines will not last much longer, as your exposed trail begins at the marker just ahead.

Climb steadily south and then turn to the west for the Desolation Wilderness. Did you remember to get a permit? Fill up your water bottles ahead just prior to a shaded flat with a marker indicating Grass Lake to the left and Mount Tallac, your trail, ahead. Climb slightly through tree cover along the creek's border up to some easy switchbacks that carry you up the face of this slope. After a brief taste of near-horizontal among lodgepole pine, continue an easy uphill on a manzanita-lined trail. Vistas open up on the switchbacks, so have your camera available.

21 Half Moon, Alta Morris, and Gilmore Lakes

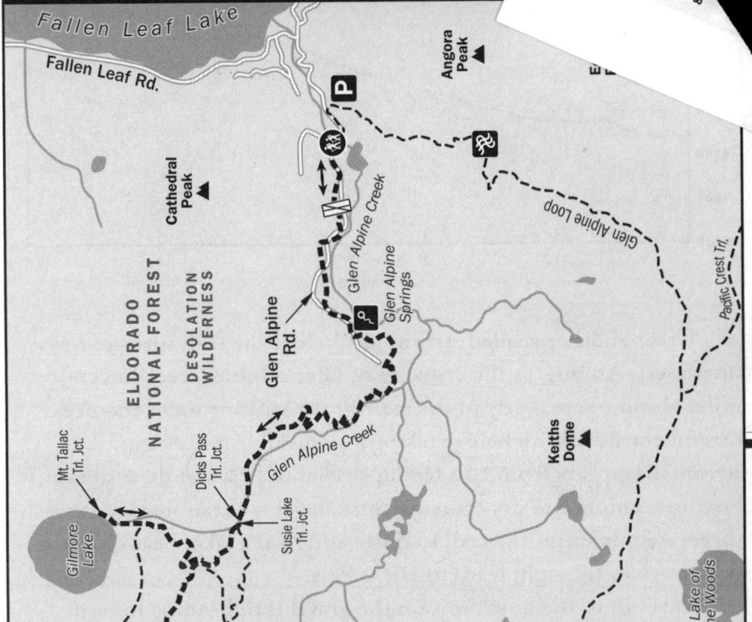

N

9500
9000
850

Fallen Leaf Lake

Fallen Leaf Rd.

Angora Peak

P

Cathedral Peak

ELDORADO NATIONAL FOREST

DESOLATION WILDERNESS

Glen Alpine Creek

Glen Alpine Springs

Glen Alpine Rd.

Glen Alpine Loop

Pacific Crest Trl.

Mt. Tallac Trl. Jct.

Dicks Pass Trl. Jct.

Glen Alpine Creek

Keiths Dome

Gilmore Lake

Susie Lake Trl. Jct.

PCT

Susie Lake

Cracked Crag

Lake of the Woods

PCT

Desolation Valley

alder thicket

Half Moon Lake

Alta Morris Lake

Glen Alpine Loop

Heather Lake

Lake Aloha

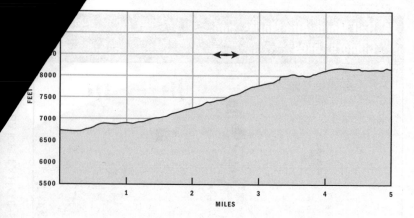

Cross another shaded stream just before the trail turns to the northwest. An interesting crossing of Glen Alpine Creek lies 0.5 miles ahead where, early in the season, the rushing water requires careful consideration before taking a step. After midseason, the stream disappears from 100 feet upstream to 100 feet downstream, leaving a simple and dry crossing. Just ahead is a trail marker for a three-way junction; the trail to Susie and Aloha lakes heads left and your track to the right leads to Dicks Pass.

Take off to the northwest on the gravel trail heading toward the junction with the PCT 0.25 miles ahead. The PCT leads left to Echo Lakes or right to Gilmore Lake. Twenty-five feet up the trail is another junction offering a path to Half Moon and Alta Morris lakes (which you will take later) to the left and a trail to Gilmore to the right. Less than 0.75 miles away, and only slightly uphill, Gilmore Lake (of Glen Alpine Resort fame) squats below a heavily carved cirque. The PCT departs for Dicks Pass off to the west about 300 yards before reaching the lake. Gilmore's shores are tree-splattered on the south and east, where a few social trails lead to some highly impacted campsites that are too close to the shore. To the west and north, the waters are contained by steep, rocky slopes that would send tents sliding into the shallow water. Cross the nascent Glen Alpine Creek to find some good bivy sites and the trail to Mount Tallac. If camping here, a trip up to Tallac is well worth it. Follow the trail uphill from the marker that stands 150 feet northeast of the dam. Hike up to another marker below the summit. For directions from here, turn to the next hike, Mount Tallac (page 145).

Including the trail that you retrace, you will reach Half Moon Lake in about 2 miles. Return to the intersection with the Glen Alpine Trail and turn sharply to the right, heading uphill slightly on broken rock. Your destination is roughly 1 mile ahead. With the massive wall of the cirque to the right, your vistas are limited to southerly views as you ascend and descend this broken rock. Blazes persist in old trees and remain accurate for navigating along here. Pass by a few seasonal puddles on the left and a small, boggy meadow decorated with mountain alder, corn lily, paintbrush, larkspur, and Sierra gentian.

The trail, mostly lined by mountain heather and pussy toes continues traversing northwest beneath a slope filled with a combination of pinemat manzanita, lupine, paintbrush, asters, and chinquapin.

The ridge to the northeast separates this cirque from Gilmore's, and it has dropped a huge load of rock from its flanks. Sagebrush and fireweed add color to the hillside as you pass a large puddle south of the trail. Climb over a small hump and down to a tiny pond fed by a runoff stream with a copse of juniper and lodgepole on its north side.

You can descend to Half Moon and circumnavigate it via your trail. While it does become overgrown and boggy in places on the north side of the lake, the wildflowers here below Dicks Peak are thick late into the season. You can continue around to Alta Morris Lake this way, but it becomes very wet. A better plan, if you want to bivy near Alta Morris (and you should), is to head cross-country after the pond before initially descending to Half Moon.

To do that, head west over the crumbling, undulating terrain, staying between the lake's outlet and a small pond that receives the lake's cascade. Walk above the meltwater puddles toward the tiny land bridge. Acceptable bivy sites are located on the bench above Alta Morris, where the moon will light up the night reflected off this massive granite amphitheater. Dicks Peak, as well as the pass and lake, was named in memory of Captain Richard Barter, "the hermit of Emerald Bay" who drowned there in 1875.

DIRECTIONS: Fallen Leaf Lake Road is located off CA 89, 3.1 miles north of South Lake Tahoe and 24.1 miles south of Tahoe City. Turn from the highway onto Fallen Leaf Lake Road, and in 0.1 mile take the left fork. Drive 4.7 miles along the narrow and winding road circumnavigating Fallen Leaf Lake, past Tahoe Mountain Road, to the marina at the junction of Fallen Leaf Lake Road and Glen Alpine Road. Bear left on Glen Alpine Road and follow it 0.6 miles to the trailhead parking lot.

The lot is equipped with pit toilets, trash receptacles, and plenty of parking. The trailhead kiosk holds a supply of free day hike permits, which are required for travel in the Desolation Wilderness. For an overnight stay in the wilderness, a paid permit is required. These can be secured locally at the USFS Taylor Creek Visitor Center, 150 yards to the west of Fallen Leaf Lake Road on CA 89.

GPS TRAILHEAD COORDINATES	21 HALF MOON, ALTA MORRIS, AND GILMORE LAKES
UTM Zone (WGS84)	10S
Easting	0753240
Northing	4307209
Latitude	N 38° 52.637'
Longitude	W 120° 04.846'

SCENERY: ☆ ☆ ☆ ☆
TRAIL CONDITION: ☆ ☆ ☆
CHILDREN: ☆
DIFFICULTY: ☆ ☆ ☆ ☆ ☆
SOLITUDE: ☆ ☆ ☆ ☆
DISTANCE: 12.7 miles round-trip
HIKING TIME: 8–9 hours

OUTSTANDING FEATURES: *Lakes, peaks, and vistas are in plentiful supply as you hike through thick forest and glaciated terrain. Name your pleasure: waterfalls, cascades, beaver ponds, meadows, polished granite, fragrant wildflowers, or trees. This is one of my favorites because of its varied terrain and vegetation.*

Ready yourself for varied terrain as you climb away from your trailhead, situated between Angora and Cathedral peaks. Pass historic Glen Alpine Springs Resort while ascending its namesake creek to the west. Linger at lightly treed Susie Lake, where Jacks and Dicks peaks loom in the background. Climb to the outlet stream of rockbound Heather Lake's azure waters, brightened by the polished snow-clad Crystal Range. Briefly ascend to Lake Aloha, where your viewfinder will be full of Pyramid, Agassiz, and Price looming overhead. Mosey along Aloha's shore over granite and then take an uphill path away from Lake of the Woods, heading toward Haypress Meadow. Forgo the easy trails down to Echo and view a trio of lakes—Ralston, Cagwin, and Tamarack—from your high route toward Triangle Lake. Return to Lily Lake by descending the steep Tamarack Creek Trail, which is laden with vistas of Tahoe and Fallen Leaf lakes.

🏃 Be certain to pick up a permit from the kiosk located adjacent to the trailhead, which is marked by a locked green gate with the word trail on it. Head out on a double track that skirts the northern margin of Lily Lake. Evidence of beaver activity is present right up to the road overlaid with baseball-sized rock. Within the first 0.5 miles, a U.S. Forest Service sign reminds you to carry a permit into the wilderness, where no fires are allowed. While you're double-checking that you have the permit, ensure that you also have a current map of the Desolation Wilderness. It's a busy area with many trails, and consequently, there are numerous junctions. Two critical junctions on this trip are not satisfactorily marked. This description will guide you, but a map is always an essential piece of gear.

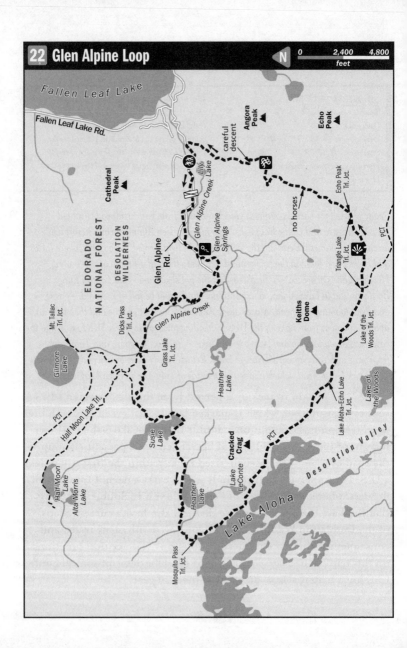

22 Glen Alpine Loop

N

0   2,400   4,800
feet

Fallen Leaf Lake

Fallen Leaf Lake Rd.

Angora Peak

Echo Peak

Cathedral Peak

careful descent

Echo Peak Trl. Jct.

ELDORADO NATIONAL FOREST

DESOLATION WILDERNESS

Glen Alpine Creek Lake

Lily

Glen Alpine Rd.

Glen Alpine Springs

no horses

Triangle Lake Trl. Jct.

PCT

Keiths Dome

Mt. Tallac Trl. Jct.

Dicks Pass Trl. Jct.

Glen Alpine Creek

Grass Lake Trl. Jct.

Gilmore Lake

Lake of the Woods Trl. Jct.

Heather Lake

Lake of the Woods

PCT

Half Moon Lake Trl.

Susie Lake

Cracked Crag

Lake Aloha-Echo Lake Trl. Jct.

Half Moon Lake

Alta Morris Lake

Heather Lake

Lake LeConte

PCT

Desolation Valley

Mosquito Pass Trl. Jct.

Lake Aloha

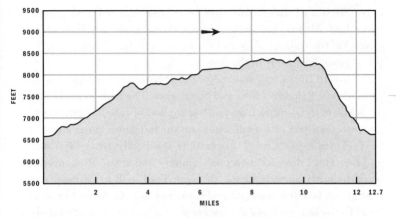

In just minutes, the road begins climbing across granite boulders and outcrops within sight of a short waterfall behind a summer cabin. Walk about 150 yards north, following the signs posted high in the trees. A more impressive and enjoyable waterfall splashes 100 feet south of a large runoff stream that crosses the road, about 150 yards after the road turns to the west. The pools below the falls are suitable for play.

A barn on your left signals your approach to historic Glen Alpine Springs, just 1.1 miles from the trailhead. An information kiosk and the original soda spring mark the trailside site. The trail marker, 200 feet up the forested trail, sends you straight ahead, up the stone steps into the sunlight on a single track. The Desolation Wilderness boundary sign will remind you about the permit requirement about 100 feet before you encounter an easily accessible spot to refill water bottles.

The rock-and-scree trail leads you across a stream, followed by a restful log in a copse of trees where Grass Lake Trail heads left and Mount Tallac–Susie Lake Trail continues straight ahead. Continue straight northwest and climb the switchbacks up the face of a granite slope and into the canyon under Gilmore Lake. Head northwest, cross one runoff stream, and then cross Glen Alpine Creek 3.2 miles from the trailhead. Late in the season, the water disappears underground at the trail crossing and reemerges 100 feet downstream, but is surely wet here early in the season.

Cross to find a trail marker in a shady copse of lodgepole, where you follow the sign to Aloha and Susie lakes. The path to Dicks Pass leads hikers to Gilmore Lake and Mount Tallac as well. Follow the blazes in the form of a small letter *i* on the lodgepole pines along the rocky trail, past a small seasonal lily pond and a trio of seasonal puddles. Head downhill to a small, flower- and grass-filled meadow. Here the junction with the Pacific Crest Trail leads to Gilmore and Half Moon lakes on the right and your trail to Lake Aloha to the left. Head to the left, crossing the stream on the boulder provided there and crashing through the fireweed and corn lily, past the Indian paintbrush, columbine, asters, and clarkia. A **U**-turn between a fir and pine halfway along the meadow marks the beginning of a brief stairway ascent, past a pair of runoff puddles, up to the ridge 30 feet above Susie Lake's rocky shore. Your route continues on this heading on the opposite shore.

With Jacks Peak looming overhead, traverse the eastern margin of the lake, where many backpackers off-load for the weekend (a good reason to come midweek). Cross the lake's outlet stream; a jumble of timber has created a poor dam but caused an attractive cascade here. Mountain heather and pussy toes cling to the shoreline as you swing around the south end and turn north to circumnavigate the lake. A few more acceptable campsites can be found on the western shore across from the small islands. Depart the lake, ascending on timber and granite stairs, and traverse a small slope graced with heather, lupine, and asters. Cross a meltwater stream before descending to the west on timber stairs as you approach Heather Lake's mouth, marked by a live lodgepole and a standing snag.

Traverse westward on this talus-and-boulder slope, remaining well above the northern shoreline. Make sure that no one pulls that

Susie Lake with the Crystal Range in the distance

"one" rock from the jumble next to your right shoulder. A fair siesta site is located at the west end of the lake amid towering western hemlocks and lodgepole pines, surrounded by fragrant larkspur, columbine, yarrow, and Indian paintbrush.

Depart Heather Lake and hike about 250 feet uphill to Lake Aloha. Climb to a meltwater pond, cross a stream, and walk through a willow-clad meadow. Pass under the gray, decaying faces of impressively stout granite outcrops, standing like lithic glaciers. The debris of its terminal moraine shines brightly in the sun at the snout. Rock and timber stairs complete your ascent to the Mosquito Pass Trail junction, which overlooks the northeast corner of Lake Aloha.

Ablaze in light most of the time, Pyramid, Agassiz, and Price peaks shine brilliantly between the Carolina-blue sky and the dazzling waters of Aloha. This is sunglasses territory. Now the route-finding gets easier. With the lake as your handrail on the right, follow the obvious trail across the granite. It sounds implausible that you might go off-route, but just try to walk without constantly staring at the lake and the Crystal Range behind it.

Campsites abound along the lake, and many hikers camp right on the shore and remain somewhat hidden but it is much better to stay at least 200 feet from the shore. Bivy sites are plentiful and secluded on the north shore, well below and out of site of the trail. Excellent sites with incredible vistas can be had around and above Lake LeConte, which is 200 feet or so cross-country to the north-east, over a lip and down into a tiny basin overlooking Heather. If day-hiking, continue southeast toward Lake of the Woods.

The first sketchy junction is nearly 1.5 miles from the Mosquito Pass junction, where the PCT first hit Lake Aloha. Just as you pass the first small copse of lodgepole pine, look for a 4x4 post with no markings in the clearing on the left side of the trail. Heading straight will lead to Lake of the Woods, which does have trails that return to this route, but to follow the described hike, follow the left-hand trail uphill at a slight angle through the lodgepole pines, mistakenly called Tamarack pines by early settlers.

The next 0.5 miles were voted, by a unanimous decision of one, as the most pleasant uphill stretch in the Tahoe area. The trail to lakes Margery and Lucille, followed by one leading down to Aloha, are located within 0.25 miles of each other, followed by another leading to Margery and Lucille again in the same distance. Get ready for more intersections ahead. With many destinations and many people wanting to see them, the Desolation Wilderness is very popular with hikers of all abilities. While day hike permits are free and valid anywhere, over-night permits require a fee and are restricted by quota throughout the wilderness. In another 500 feet, arrive at the top of Haypress Meadows and walk past the junction leading to Lake of the Woods.

Walk about 500 feet farther down trail to an important trail marker, a crux point at the bottom of Haypress Meadow. Just when you get above Tamarack Lake, look for the junction on the uphill side of the trail that directs you upward to the left to Triangle Lake. Downhill leads to the Echo lakes. Leave the PCT here and traverse directly east across this tree-speckled slope occupied by golden-mantled ground squirrels. Just before topping the ridge, a couple of ancient junipers provide some welcome shade. Take advantage of this vista onto Tamarack, Cagwin, and Ralston lakes as well as Upper and Lower Echo lakes.

Descend from the ridge, heading northeast through lodgepole and fir. Pass the trail leading to Triangle Lake at the next junction. The Echo lakes are to the right from here. In 100 yards, be watchful for an unsigned junction. The fork to the right leads to Echo Peak, while your route keeps to the left. The next undulating 0.5 miles of sagebrush and willow take you to the head of the E-ticket ride (where a sign wisely warns equestrians to turn back), before descending 1,700 feet in 2 miles. Excellent advice. You can ponder that here while taking pictures of Fallen Leaf and Tahoe before beginning a steep descent of Tamarack Creek through a grassy hillside sporting sagebrush and lupine.

The slippery duff trail steepens and the ravine squeezes in at a point perfect for filling water bottles. Columbine and paintbrush decorate this cool creek crossing. As you hike beneath Angora Peak and Indian Rock, cross the next stream through the brush very carefully. Unseen to the left, on the downhill side, is a steep drop-off with rushing water cascading over it. Pay close attention after that, as you cross a rockfall. The trail curves back to the west and then to the east, where it follows a few scant ducks across a bare outcrop beneath this immense wall of rock. At a point exactly fifteen minutes downhill from the cascade crossing, the trail may seem to vanish, appearing as if you have to down-climb some rock. Just walk a few feet across the polished rock directly in front of you to pick up your route. No climbing is required on this trail.

When you reach the canyon floor, the track winds past boulders as big as garages, and the vegetation thickens around Lily Lake's inlet streams. Ferns and broadleaf understory make this a pleasantly cool section of trail. The flattening trail and appearance of Cathedral Peak in front of you signals that the road, where you will turn left, is coming up. A few hundred yards lands you in the parking lot again.

DIRECTIONS: Fallen Leaf Lake Road is located on CA 89, 3.1 miles north of South Lake Tahoe and 24.1 miles south of Tahoe City. Turn from the highway on to Fallen Leaf Lake Road, and in 0.1 mile take the left fork. Drive 4.7 miles along the narrow and winding road circumnavigating Fallen Leaf Lake, past Tahoe Mountain Road, to the marina at the junction of Fallen Leaf Lake Road and Glen Alpine Road. Bear left on Glen Alpine Road and follow it 0.6 miles to the trailhead parking lot.

The lot is equipped with pit toilets, trash receptacles, and plenty of parking. The trailhead kiosk holds a supply of free day hike permits, which are required for travel in the Desolation Wilderness. For an overnight stay in the wilderness, a paid permit is required. These can be secured locally at the USFS Taylor Creek Visitor Center, 150 yards to the west of Fallen Leaf Lake Road on CA 89.

GPS TRAILHEAD COORDINATES	22 GLEN ALPINE LOOP
UTM Zone (WGS84)	10S
Easting	0753240
Northing	4307209
Latitude	N 38° 52.637'
Longitude	W 120° 04.846'

23 Mount Tallac

SCENERY: ✪ ✪ ✪ ✪ ✪ TRAIL CONDITION: ✪ ✪ ✪ CHILDREN: ✪ ✪ DIFFICULTY: ✪ ✪ ✪ ✪ SOLITUDE: ✪ ✪ DISTANCE: 9.6 miles round-trip HIKING TIME: 7 hours	OUTSTANDING FEATURES: Mount Tallac is a popular trail for one main reason: it has a magnificent vista of Lake Tahoe, Cascade Lake, Emerald Bay, and Fallen Leaf Lake, as well as a view into the Desolation Wilderness with Pyramid Peak, Freel Peak, and Mount Rose on the horizon.

Your path from the Desolation Wilderness trailhead is a straightforward march to the south along a well-defined ridge that offers excellent vistas over the cobalt-blue waters of Fallen Leaf Lake. The views continue as your trail sidles by tree-lined Floating Island Lake, where your final destination's reflection stands out sharply in the placid waters. But right after Cathedral Lake, the bliss ends. The views will distract you from the tortuous switchbacks, stairs, and straight-ups leading to a veg-etated talus slope capped by Mount Tallac. The memorable photos from the summit are your reward for persisting across windblown slopes and scree-covered trails.

🚶🚶 Once you have filled out your day-hike permit for the Deso-lation Wilderness, start down a forest road behind the information kiosk. A conveniently placed signpost assures you that you are on the route to Mount Tallac and gives two reminders: a wilderness permit is needed and fires are not permitted.

Your trail strikes out to the west, rising quickly in the first five minutes through the manzanita and sagebrush. Enter the tree cover to traverse just beneath the crest of a ridge. When your heading turns firmly south, your hike parallels the shore of Fallen Leaf Lake, even though it remains out of sight for the moment. As you approach the 0.5-mile point, you may begin to notice the unmistakable orange of fire retardant on some of the trees lining the trail, both horizontally and vertically.

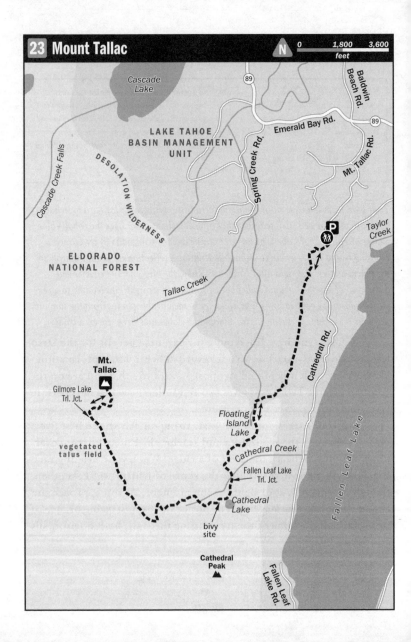

Cascade
Lake

LAKE TAHOE
BASIN MANAGEMENT
UNIT

Emerald Bay Rd.

Baldwin
Beach
Rd.

89

89

Cascade Creek Falls

DESOLATION WILDERNESS

Spring Creek Rd.

Mt. Tallac Rd.

ELDORADO
NATIONAL FOREST

Tallac Creek

P

Taylor
Creek

Cathedral Rd.

Mt.
Tallac

Gilmore Lake
Trl. Jct.

vegetated
talus field

Floating
Island
Lake

Cathedral Creek

Fallen Leaf Lake
Trl. Jct.

Cathedral
Lake

bivy
site

Cathedral
Peak

Fallen Leaf Lake

Fallen Leaf
Lake Rd.

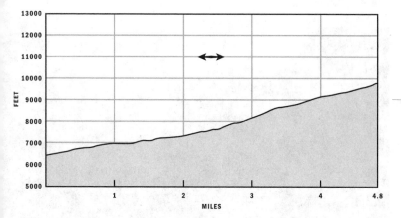

In another 0.25 miles, you'll have an excellent vista of Fallen Leaf Lake, followed by a view of some of the damage from the 2007 Angora fire.

As the Jeffrey pines exposed at the top of this ridge begin to warm up in the sun, they release a wonderful butterscotch scent that fills the air for the next 0.3 miles. Here, the vistas of Fallen Leaf Lake persist, and you may lose some time to camera work unless you wait till your return to get glare-free shots. Tree cover thickens as you leave the open vistas behind and head south along the ridge. At a tight stand of six Jeffreys, the gravel-and-dirt trail turns into rocky steps that descend into the alley between these two ridges. Turn west and south to ascend the parallel ridge on short switchbacks over gravel, then traverse through the pine, fir, and manzanita.

Within an hour of the trailhead and 500 feet after heading south toward Floating Island Lake, you'll cross the Desolation Wilderness boundary. Standing next to a downed Jeffrey pine, the boundary marker reminds hikers about the need for a permit. Watch for the Spring Creek Trail as it joins yours on the right from the northwest.

Mountain maple, mountain ash, and red fir cover the landscape as you approach Floating Island Lake (where no islands currently

Fallen Leaf Lake vista

float). The view into this lake is mesmerizing, but the tread is rock-
and root-encrusted, so watch your step. This oval pond is the perfect
spot to reflect on your day's destination. While you're at it, take pictures of Tallac's jagged peak framed in the mirrorlike surface.

Pass by Floating Island's east shore on the faint, rocky trail. As
you ascend the stone stairs, the flora's red and gold fall wardrobe is
visible among the western hemlock. Head southwest across the talus
slope on this scree-and-gravel trail. A faint trail connecting to Fallen
Leaf Lake Trail intersects your route less than 1,000 feet south of the
lake. Your well-defined trail continues easily across the slope and is
crossed by a seasonal runoff stream just before skirting a small knob.
A larger stream crossing on the south side of the knob is Cathedral
Creek, where logs and rocks assist your crossing.

As you ascend southward under the cover of lodgepole pine, watch for another junction with a connector to Fallen Leaf Lake Trail about 150 paces ahead. About twice that many steps after the junction bring you to touch the corner of little Cathedral Lake. This diminutive tarn, lined with talus and scree and decorated with lodgepole pine, western hemlock, and red fir is the point where the trail turns west and heads uphill into a broad cirque under Tallac. Your climb to the top of the headwall is about 975 feet and should take you about 45 minutes.

The rock stairs are just short of tortuous leading up to a vista point—conveniently located next to a solitary juniper, flattened in its krummholz attire just where you need to catch your breath. The view of Cathedral, Floating Island, Fallen Leaf, and Tahoe lakes is one you may want to recall often. From this photographer's perch, look down to the left for a perfect bivy location: flat, sandy, sheltered, and a picture window. When you leave this bliss, a couple of switchbacks will warm you up before going in and out of tree cover.

Switchbacks get thrown out the window as your trail starts straight up the cirque. As you near the headwall, the trail makes a dramatic traverse to the northwest for about the length of a football field before the uphill torment resumes to the south. Just before reaching the plateau, a group of small hemlocks mark an inconveniently large boulder in midtrail. Remember it for the walk down.

Once atop the cirque, you face a broad, open scree field that stretches to the west. This vast plateau slants dramatically away to the west, not steeply, just an enormous mass diving down as Tallac's summit ascends. The soil, though scant and covered with talus, scree, and gravel, is able to produce light vegetation such as pussy paws, buckwheat, tobacco brush, and fireweed. It also supports woodpeckers and golden-mantled ground squirrels.

Make a sharp **U**-turn to the northwest to begin ascending this massive, tilted block. Traverse the vegetated scree to a small willow-and-sedge-covered meadow. The vista in front of you steepens and the trail remains distinct as your only interruption is to detour around a large, red fir that has obliterated the trail just 800 feet shy of the peak.

Continue your climb up these gentle slopes where, 300 feet below the summit, your path intersects the route to Gilmore Lake. A wooden post marks this junction and arrows indicate that you need to go right for the final 15 uphill minutes. As you head east through the stunted lodgepole, watch for the golden-mantled ground squirrels carrying massive amounts of seeds in their cheeks, digging furiously, disgorging their chow, and running aimlessly away.

The trail approaches the base of the rockfall by edging up next to the east face before turning gradually to the northwest. There are a few braided trails from this point. It is best to look up and pick your route and then see if a trail matches it. The summit of jagged, broken rock affords little room for dallying, as every hiker wants the same view of the lake in his or her picture.

DIRECTIONS: From Truckee, drive 37 miles south on CA 89 to Mount Tallac Road across from Baldwin Beach Road. Turn right and drive 0.4 miles to the first left turn onto an unnamed road; then drive 0.7 miles to the parking area at the trailhead. From South Lake Tahoe, drive 3.9 miles north on CA 89 to Mount Tallac Road. Turn left onto Mount Tallac Road and follow the above directions to the trailhead. There are no facilities at this trailhead. As you select your parking spot, be aware that late in the season, the Jeffrey pine-cones that fall from 75 feet up weigh more than a pound.

GPS TRAILHEAD COORDINATES	23 MOUNT TALLAC
UTM Zone (WGS84)	10S
Easting	0754174
Northing	4312152
Latitude	N 38° 55.290'
Longitude	W 120° 04.092'

Thunder Mountain Trail (see Hike 17, page 111)

part three
Lake Tahoe
West Hikes

3

Despite the abundance of lofty superlatives that inevitably precede a visit to Lake Tahoe, descriptions do not seem to disappoint anyone.

24 Sylvia and Lyons Lakes

SCENERY: ✪ ✪ ✪ ✪ ✪	DISTANCE: *12 miles round-trip*
TRAIL CONDITION: ✪ ✪ ✪ ✪	HIKING TIME: *6 hours*
CHILDREN: ✪ ✪	OUTSTANDING FEATURES: *Massive granite wall at*
DIFFICULTY: ✪ ✪ ✪	*north end of Lyons Lake; shallow pools along the steps*
SOLITUDE: ✪ ✪ ✪	*of Lyons Creek; base camp beneath Pyramid Peak*

At the end of Lyons Creek Trail, the Desolation Wilderness yields up two of its most beautiful tarns. Sylvia Lake sits beneath hidden Pyramid Peak and makes a great staging spot for a climb to the summit. The rewarding climb to Lyons Lake brings you face-to-face with magnificent beauty—from the flowers at your feet to the towering trees growing out of the sheer granite walls. This moderate hike offers wildflowers, lakes, and gentle streamside pools for hikers' pleasure.

🚶🚶 Your trail begins to the left of the information kiosk, where you'll pick up a Desolation Wilderness day-hike permit. After filling out the paperwork and checking distances on the map, head generally northeast along the former four-wheel-drive road, passing by an unused but locked gate.

This parklike trail is guarded by barrel-loads of butterflies and a similar number of mosquitoes. It ends and the singletrack begins after about 0.4 miles, just where a pine on the right has tried to eat a metal sign. After about 20 minutes of hiking, you cross a small creek that feeds into Lyons Creek to your left.

By mid-June, the corn lilies are popping through the soil, and by the first of July, they are joined by columbine, larkspur, lupine, yarrow, elephant's heads, Indian paintbrush, and aster. This colorful display is a needed diversion because the trail has morphed from pleasant dirt to rocks, boulders, roots, and sand.

Lyons Creek is your "handrail" as you navigate a northeasterly course marked by numerous "blazes" on the trailside trees. Formed in the shape of a small letter *i*, these markers are most often found on lodgepole pines and can take on grotesque attributes as the tree ages.

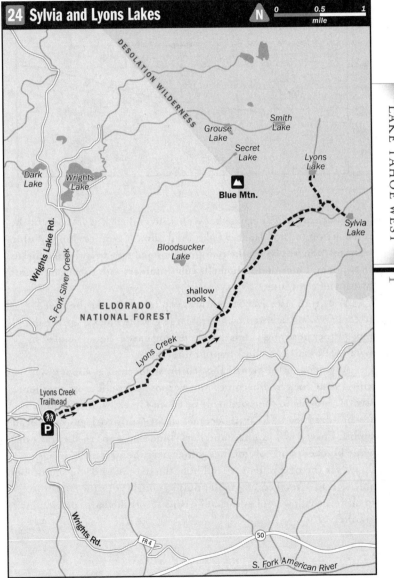

DESOLATION WILDERNESS

Grouse
Lake

Smith
Lake

Secret
Lake

Lyons
Lake

Dark
Lake

Wrights
Lake

Blue Mtn.

Sylvia
Lake

Wrights Lake Rd.

Bloodsucker
Lake

S. Fork Silver Creek

shallow
pools

ELDORADO
NATIONAL FOREST

Lyons Creek

Lyons Creek
Trailhead

P

Wrights Rd.

FR 4

50

S. Fork American River

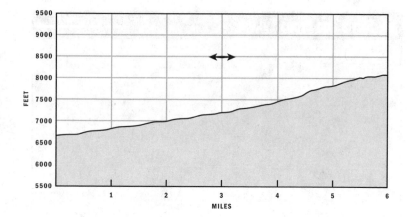

Your trail will alternate between sand and rock as you pass by the intersection to Bloodsucker Lake Trail, almost 2 miles along. Within minutes, you will be on the margin of a small meadow where delicate five spot and mountain bluebells rub shoulders with subalpine paintbrush and corn lilies.

Your trail rises ever so gently as you follow it over the next stream crossing, assisted by several large granite blocks. Ignore the mosquitoes here and watch the wandering daisies being mauled by tiger swallowtail and checkerspot butterflies.

As you enter the signed Desolation Wilderness at about 3.5 miles, your rock trail becomes more exposed. You'll cross another stream, moving to the north side of Lyons Creek, within another few hundred feet. The trail becomes significantly rockier as you head uphill. Pussy paws, lupines, and dark-blue camas adorn the trailside, while bluebells and columbines gather near the stream crossings.

Over the next mile, the trail hugs the stream, and you should be able to find several comfortable spots to dangle your toes in the water or sit in a shallow pool as the creek runs across the bare, polished granite.

Crystal-clear, ice-cold snowmelt flows over ice-polished granite.

While the granite wall to the north steepens as the stream chips away at its base, the rocky trail crosses a wide stream just prior to reaching the Sylvia–Lyons junction. After about 2.5 hours of moderate hiking, spend a few minutes swinging around to the southeast to reach placid Sylvia Lake, bordered by bare granite on its eastern flank. The lake's west side, shaded by lofty pines and firs, has several highly impacted, "sacrifice" campsites that make a great base camp for climbing Pyramid Peak. Use these sites rather than creating even more impacted areas.

Return the half mile to the junction and begin the 500-foot ascent to another glacial tarn, Lyons Lake. This lake has a small, picturesque holding pond beneath its three-foot rock dam. The easiest trail continues on the west side of the outlet stream and crosses the dam to the eastern shore where you can find some suitable campsites on the flat outcrops above the lake.

The shore of Lyons Lake is fringed with a white and pink display of white heather and mountain heather, both of which are abundant in July. Not to be outdone are the Sierra penstemon and pinemat manzanita, and especially not the anemone sequestered among the rocks and boulders on the east side.

While this hike ends here, adventurous hikers can continue around the north end of the lake and up through the notch leading back to the east and Mount Price followed by Mount Agassiz and Pyramid Peak.

As you switchback down the 500 feet to the trail junction, look in the stream for small trout and on the hillside for star tulips, mountain pride penstemon, and Lemmon's drabba.

DIRECTIONS: From US 50, 5 miles west of Kyburz or 4.1 miles east of Strawberry, turn north on Wrights Road/Forest Road 4 and drive 4 miles to the Lyons Creek trailhead, just before the ford of Lyons Creek. You'll find parking for about 15 cars on the right. More parking is available across the road or along the road. The trailhead is behind the sign at the trailhead parking lot.

GPS TRAILHEAD COORDINATES	24 SYLVIA AND LYONS LAKES
UTM Zone (WGS84)	10S
Easting	0739698
Northing	4299362
Latitude	N 38° 48.626'
Longitude	W 120° 14.367'

25 Grouse, Hemlock, and Smith Lakes

SCENERY: ✿ ✿ ✿ ✿ ✿	DISTANCE: *6 miles round-trip*
TRAIL CONDITION: ✿ ✿ ✿	HIKING TIME: *3.5–4.5 hours*
CHILDREN: ✿ ✿	OUTSTANDING FEATURES: *Glacier-polished rock*
DIFFICULTY: ✿ ✿ ✿	*and pristine subalpine lakes.*
SOLITUDE: ✿ ✿ ✿	

The short hike to these three beautiful lakes rewards hikers of all ages with stunning vistas down onto Wrights Lake and the Crystal Basin from up on the edge of the Crystal Range. Your hike begins in a flower-filled meadow and includes cascading streams, glacier-polished granite, and snowcapped peaks. This trek is most often easy but does have some short, strenuous sections to remind you of the elevation.

🏃🏃 Starting at the kiosk at the trailhead, bypass the Loop Trail and cross the swampy area using the footbridge. Watch for the sign for Twin and Grouse lakes off to the right.

This wet meadow is filled with wildflowers in the spring. Unfortunately, the ground is also swollen with snowmelt, and hikers are often busier watching their step. Beneath the cover of Douglas-fir and lodgepole pine you'll pass over a few seasonal streams with the aid of some small footbridges made of either stone or wood. After 100 feet, you'll pass through a DO NOT ENTER stile for horses. After 0.4 miles, the Loop Trail leads off to the left and this hike heads to the right, following the signs to Grouse Lake.

After about 15 minutes of hiking you'll begin to gain some elevation. The trail is slightly sketchy at first, but rock and boulder steps lead you away from the granite terrain for just a short while and into the trees. Some monster stairs made of boulders will help you ascend a set of switchbacks. As you reach the 1-mile mark, look for ducks marking the trail to the north-northeast on this granite slope.

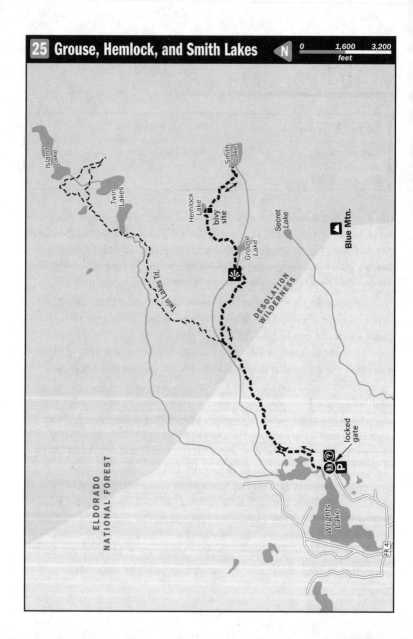

25 Grouse, Hemlock, and Smith Lakes

N

0   1,600   3,200
feet

Island Lake

Twin Lakes

Smith Lake

Hemlock Lake

bivy site

Grouse Lake

Secret Lake

Blue Mtn.

Twin Lakes Trl.

DESOLATION WILDERNESS

ELDORADO NATIONAL FOREST

locked gate

P

Wrights Lake

FR 4

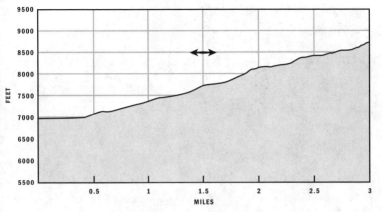

"Ducks" are, most often, three rocks stacked in a prominent place to help indicate a trail. Here, they line the trail like a sidewalk. In any case, avoid following ducks one at a time; pause, look around, then line up two or three ducks ahead so that you get a sense of the trail, a mental map that will allow you to more enjoyably absorb your surroundings. Caution: ducks can sometimes be misleading. After all, you don't know the route-finding skills or the destination of the people who placed them. Hiker beware.

Continuing north-northeast, you'll veer to the right when you reach the end of the granite incline. While the trail is somewhat faint here, you can follow the blazes on the trees, which you may notice as you climb up some exposed roots. In years past, these trail markers (most often a small letter *i*) were scored into the tree bark above eye level. While trail crews no longer create these blazes, they can still be useful for land navigation and route-finding. When you first approach the stream at this point, don't cross it. Rather, continue up the trail to the sign marking the border of the Desolation Wilderness. At this point you have hiked 1.1 miles.

After 1.4 miles, the Grouse Lake Trail splits with the Twin Lakes Trail. Note that you still have not crossed the stream. As you follow the

Ice forms early on Smith Lake.

ducks through this boulder field, notice the weathering of the granite, which exposes these hard, dark inclusions. Ranging from 2 to 12 inches in size, the inclusions were probably the original rock embedded in the magma chamber where this granite pluton cooled.

Continue straight uphill, somewhat angling across the polished granite, and exit at the top right corner through the pinemat manzanita. Keep your eye out for ducks as your trail continues trending to the northeast.

Before the next set of rocky switchbacks, you'll encounter a nice vista point where Wrights Lake and the Crystal Basin are visible. You will recognize the outlet stream for Grouse Lake as it braids out over the trail and cascades downhill to your left. Boulder-hop over this soggy stretch, then climb up through the break on the north side of the lake. If needed, this is a great spot to get out of the wind.

Grouse Lake is rather small, but that allows it to warm up a bit earlier than other lakes. Unfortunately, its rocky shore does not invite much camping. There are a couple of designated camping spots at the northeast edge of the lake, most easily seen as you ascend from the lake on the trail toward tiny Hemlock Lake. If you're inclined to camp, head east-southeast across a low ridge, where you can camp near Secret Lake just beneath you.

Leave the northeast end of Grouse Lake and wind uphill, traversing at an angle toward Hemlock Lake. Notice the very old trail blazes on some very small trees. Despite their small size, these trees have racked up a number of years but have been dwarfed or stunted by the harsh climate (a phenomenon known as the krummholz effect). Without taking a boring from the tree, you would not be able to accurately guess its age.

Winding through some large boulders leads to a wet meadow, where another blaze in front of you points the way to more switchbacks before arriving at a fairly level area. Hemlock Lake has a dramatic wall on its northeast shore. The enormous boulders surrounding the lake exhibit the same weathering pattern as that granite wall. Called exfoliation, the pattern is created when rock is peeled off through a process of repeated freezing and thawing of water, which acts as a lever to pry off layers like an onion. While you are daydreaming about that, the camp robbers (Clark's nutcrackers) know how to recognize a tired and hungry hiker. Beware of them while you're snacking here at Hemlock Lake.

As you head toward Smith Lake, only 0.8 miles away, you'll pass some decent campsites on the right-hand side of the trail. It is a mere 300 vertical feet to the outlet of Smith Lake. The views to the east and north (with the unseen Mount Price in the background) are spectacular. While you won't find much good camping around Smith Lake, there are several areas where boulders will shelter you from the wind so you can fix a hot drink and a snack before heading back down.

Pay particular attention to the ducks while you walk faster on the way down, as some of them can actually be misleading. In fact, at some spots along the trail they can be downright amusing: some ducks are rather complex, with five or six rocks, while others are downright casual, with only two. As you enjoy the luxury of walking downhill, take time to notice the polish on the granite at your feet. Stop. Look around at the hillsides. The reason you don't see all that many trees is that the topsoil was scraped away during the last glacial period and the soil here is fairly new.

DIRECTIONS: From US 50, the road to Wrights Lake is halfway between Kyburz and Twin Bridges. Wrights Road/Forest Road 4 intersects US 50 4.5 miles from Kyburz and 5.5 miles from Twin Bridges. Turn north and drive 4.1 miles, where you will easily ford Lyons Creek and continue for another 4 miles to the lake. You will pass logging pullouts and roads leading to the left to Icehouse and Crystal Basin. When you reach Wrights Lake, pass through a gate and a stop sign, where you'll spot an information kiosk on the left side. Turn right, heading northeast, on Forest Road 12N23. Drive slowly along this one-lane road beneath tall lodgepole pines for 1 mile, passing a group camping area on your right and summer cabins next to the lakeshore on your left. The parking lot is at the end of this road, surrounded by boulders. Your trailhead is past the gate marked OFFICIAL VEHICLES ONLY, which is across from two pit toilets. Walk down that road and head northwest to a gravel path that leads over to the trailhead kiosk.

GPS TRAILHEAD COORDINATES	25 GROUSE, HEMLOCK, AND SMITH LAKES
UTM Zone (WGS84)	10S
Easting	0740711
Northing	4303842
Latitude	N 38° 51.029'
Longitude	W 120° 13.573'

26 Island and Twin Lakes

SCENERY: ☆ ☆ ☆ ☆ ☆	DISTANCE: *8 miles round-trip*
TRAIL CONDITION: ☆ ☆	HIKING TIME: *5–6 hours (overnight)*
CHILDREN: ☆ ☆	OUTSTANDING FEATURES: *Wildflowers scattered*
DIFFICULTY: ☆ ☆ ☆	*across glacially polished granite with peaks above,*
SOLITUDE: ☆ ☆	*views below, and several pristine lakes*

This hike is challenging because of its difficult, flower-lined trail, but its destination is well worth the effort. By continuing past Twin Lakes and ascending to a meltwater lake above it, hikers can escape the crowds and gain fantastic vistas of the Crystal Range, where sunset colors paint the sheer granite walls. Your ascent begins on granite at the edge of a buggy meadow, climbs through a lodgepole pine and white fir forest, follows ducks and blazes across open granite slopes, and crosses streams before ascending a final 200 feet to a pristine bivy site sheltered by a small copse of trees. While descending the 150 feet to Island Lake to regain the trail home past Boomerang Lake and Twin Lakes, you will learn everything there is to know about the lifestyle of marmots.

🏃🏃 This 3.5-mile trail requires good route-finding skills, so prepare yourself with a map, a compass, and sturdy hiking boots. Using the map, familiarize yourself beforehand with the route and the destination.

Leave the parking lot, pass the locked gate across the service road, and head downhill to the signed path that leads to the right to your trailhead. Ignore the arched footbridge in front of you and head to the right on the dirt footpath, which is the Twin Lakes Trail. Small stone footbridges will help you across the wet spots in this meadow, which is festooned with corn lilies. After a wooden footbridge, watch for the junction of the Twin Lakes Trail with the Loop Trail. The Twin Lakes Trail leads to the right, where you will begin skirting a granite outcrop.

Mountain pride penstemon adorns each crack and crevice in these large granite steps. Delicate pink pussy paws surround a granite boulder the size of an 18-wheeler. Splashes of yellow are provided by

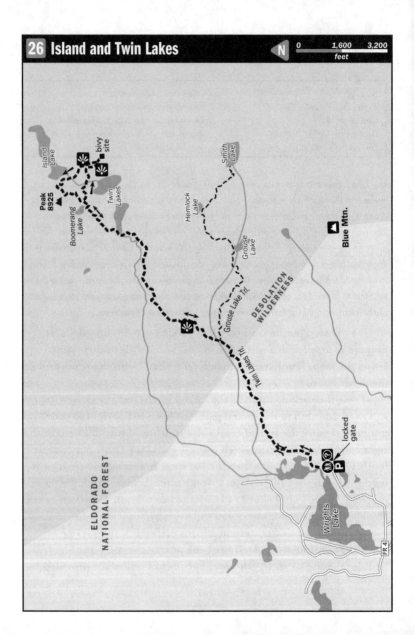

N

| 0 | 1,600 | 3,200 |

feet

Island Lake

bivy site

Peak 8925

Twin Lakes

Boomerang Lake

Smith Lake

Hemlock Lake

Grouse Lake

Blue Mtn.

Grouse Lake Trl.

DESOLATION WILDERNESS

Twin Lakes Trl.

locked gate

P

ELDORADO NATIONAL FOREST

Wrights Lake

FR 4

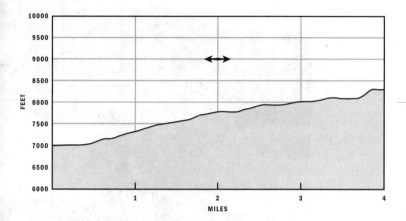

the groundsel, and a handful of star tulips hide among the rocks. At this point, your trail turns from rocky and sandy to forest duff and dirt. Notice the blaze in the shape of the small letter *i* on the lodgepole pine to the left. While this type of blaze is no longer used by the U.S. Forest Service, be alert for it, as the blazes can indicate your correct trail, especially after crossing a stream or granite slope.

Here under the cover of lodgepole pines and white firs, the trail turns from rocky to rooty. Watch your step as you climb through the boulders, rocks, roots, and a granite outcrop on your right. Early in the season, you may find streams where the trail is supposed to be. Continue climbing the large granite steps until your trail angles off through the lodgepole pines. Keep alert for even ancient blazes on the trees. You'll encounter hundreds of ducks marking the trail, which may be helpful at times, but they also mark alternate trails that you may not want to follow.

Your trail steepens as you hear the meltwater crashing through the chasm to the north of the trail. Within a few hundred feet you will encounter the Desolation Wilderness boundary sign. Pass it and continue on the south side of the creek until, in about 300 paces, you arrive at the junction of the Twin Lakes and Grouse Lake trails.

My trekking poles prevent this glacial erratic from rolling away.

Your trail continues beneath pine and fir, zigzagging up until you hit a large granite field. Skirt the bottom of this field as you head to your left, generally northeast. You will cross a small creek just prior to heading across a short granite slope. Your boulder-lined pathway leads to a small creek crossing.

Continue trending generally northeast across vast granite slopes that will reflect the sun so as to cook your body from every direction. Be sure to use plenty of sunscreen on this hike. Keep a sharp eye out for ducks and boulders that have been lined up across the glacially polished granite. The stone was shaped largely by glaciers and later meltwater. The crescent-shaped divots are called "chatter marks"—the result of boulders in the glacier's base sticking as the glacier flows over the bedrock. You will notice some other divots in the stone, this time created by small charges of dynamite. These "petro scars" often mark the correct route when there is no other indicator of the trail.

When your trail levels out at the top of the hill, turn around for a beautiful view of Wrights Lake and the surrounding hills. You will make a couple of direction changes here as the sandy trail winds along and runs into a chaparral-covered hillside where an indistinct trail made of boulders barges uphill. Initially, your boulder-bordered trail is quite distinct.

As the wind whips unhindered across this glacially scoured landscape, the lodgepole pines begin exhibiting the krummholz effect. This "crooked stick" effect is the result of dramatic environmental influences on trees, resulting in their stunted appearance. Groundcover, slope aspect, temperature variation, moisture levels, wind—all have an impact on trees at this elevation.

Your course will head east following the outlet stream from Twin Lakes. Pay close attention to your rock-bordered trail, because it will lead you safely and mostly dryly across the stream. The trail passes through several wet areas before the creek crossing. Approaching the lake, your trail will pass over two narrow, stone dams to reach the north side; there, your trail continues on the way to Boomerang Lake.

Before you traverse the south edge of Boomerang Lake, notice the white blossoms of pinemat manzanita and the delicate pink blossoms of mountain heather draped between the rocks. To the northwest of this little lake is Peak 8925, triangular and pointed in contrast to its rounded companion just to the east.

From this point, you can continue straight ahead to Island Lake. For a more adventurous trip, turn southeast and cross the inlet stream to Twin Lakes. A five-minute climb up the talus on this west-facing slope will lead you to an isolated lake that feeds Twin Lake number two. For a secluded night under the stars surrounded by this enormous cirque, there are two suitable campsites. The first is on the flat granite overlooking the inlet stream just before it takes a dive over the slope.

The second is right next to the lakelet underneath a copse of lodgepole pines.

From here, you can walk to the southern edge of Island Lake and cross on another stone dam. Explore the north side of the lake, where marmots run in herds of 10 to 15 at a time. There is a wonderful vista point on the rise above a bivy spot before you descend to Island Lake. From Island Lake, follow the trail from the north side of the lake back across the stream to Boomerang Lake.

Don't be alarmed if you find yourself occasionally following the wrong set of ducks. They are often confusing unless you keep a sharp eye out. Stay on the south side of the outlet stream until you reach Twin Lakes. Follow the north side of Twin Lake to the south edge of Boomerang Lake, then to the north side of Island Lake.

Whichever lakes you go to, your route out follows the same course from Twin Lakes to the trailhead.

DIRECTIONS: From the **Y** in South Lake Tahoe, drive approximately 4.5 miles to Meyers on US 50 south. Follow US 50 16.5 miles to Wrights Road on the north side of the highway. Wrights Road is exactly 4.1 miles west of Strawberry and 5 miles east of Kyburz. Drive for 8 miles to the Wrights Lake Visitor Center, where you will turn right and drive 1 mile past summer cabins to the end of the road, where the trailhead parking lot is located. If the lot is full, you can use the equestrian parking lot as overflow. Both parking lots have a pit toilet. The equestrian parking lot has water.

GPS Trailhead Coordinates	26 Island and Twin Lakes
UTM Zone (WGS84)	10S
Easting	0740705
Northing	4303841
Latitude	N 38° 51.029'
Longitude	W 120° 13.578'

SCENERY: ✿ ✿ ✿ ✿ ✿	HIKING TIME: *10 hours (overnight)*
TRAIL CONDITION: ✿ ✿ ✿	OUTSTANDING FEATURES: *Meltwater streams*
CHILDREN: ✿	*coursing across glacially polished granite that shines*
DIFFICULTY: ✿ ✿ ✿ ✿ ✿	*even on cloudy days; wildflower displays along every*
SOLITUDE: ✿ ✿ ✿ ✿	*meadow and stream; crossing the Crystal Range to a*
DISTANCE: *15 miles round-trip*	*granite-bound mountain lake.*

"Lake Lois and Lake Schmidell" sounds so friendly and gentle, with a poetic ring to it, but this hike is the opposite of easy. The name of the trail— Rockbound—should be your first clue. Bound on the left, the right, and to the front by granite (more likely, granodiorite), every step is on rock and more rock. Or so it seems. From either trailhead, gain the Rockbound Trail, which raises you from 6,800 feet to 8,600 feet in 6 miles. The shine of the polished granite is interrupted by sluggish erratics, determined conifers, and stealthy wildflowers. Climb to Rockbound Pass and look out over Rockbound Valley from the crest of the Crystal Range. A short descent on the Blakely Trail brings you to beautiful Lake Lois for a peaceful night beneath an open sky.

🚶🚶 Take plenty of deep breaths while you're at the trailhead, because there are several times en route when you are going to audibly gasp at the beauty of the Desolation Wilderness and the Crystal Range. This is a magnificent area and the trail to Lois is exceptional. There are longer hikes than this one—and some steeper—but the trail approaching and climbing to Rockbound Pass has a special degree of difficulty that needs to be taken at a slow, plodding pace.

You are traveling into the Desolation Wilderness, which requires you to pick up a free permit for day hikes or pay a fee for an overnight wilderness camping permit. The permits are available at the U.S. Forest Service Pacific Ranger District visitor center in Fresh Pond (which is east of Placerville) on US 50. Entry and overnight stays in the wilderness are quota-controlled by zone. Because Lake Lois and Lake Schmidell are in different zones but only 1 mile apart,

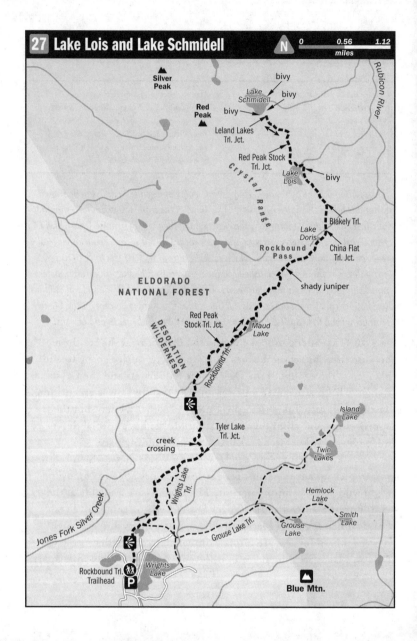

N

0   0.56   1.12
miles

Silver
Peak

Red
Peak

bivy
Lake
Schmidell
bivy

bivy

Leland Lakes
Trl. Jct.

Red Peak Stock
Trl. Jct.

Lake
Lois   bivy

Crystal Range

Blakely Trl.

Lake
Doris

Rockbound
Pass   China Flat
              Trl. Jct.

shady juniper

ELDORADO
NATIONAL FOREST

Red Peak
Stock Trl. Jct.

Maud
Lake

DESOLATION
WILDERNESS

Rockbound Trl.

Island
Lake

Tyler Lake
Trl. Jct.

creek
crossing

Twin
Lakes

Wrights Lake Trl.

Hemlock
Lake

Smith
Lake

Grouse Lake Trl.

Grouse
Lake

Jones Fork Silver Creek

Rockbound Trl.
Trailhead
P

Wrights
Lake

Blue Mtn.

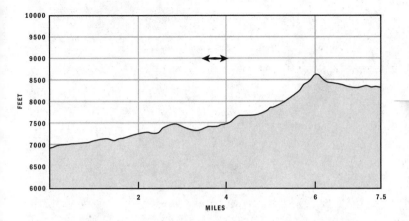

I've included route information to that lake, just in case the zone's quota for one or the other is filled.

Embark from the trailhead to the right of the pit toilets at the Dark Lake parking lot, under cover of mixed conifers. The duff trail soon turns to a premonition of this route—stairs of boulders and stones—which levels out among shoulder-high boulders within the first 0.25 miles. If you get an early start, the warming sun will toast your back as you take a heading on a predominantly northeasterly line. Ignore the connector trail coming from Wrights Lake as you pass Beauty Lake under lodgepole pine and white fir. The standing snags in the dark, shallow water give the pond a strange beauty indeed.

The trail wraps around Beauty at the signed intersection for an OHV trail (which leads off to Barrett Lake), where a NO CAMPING sign leans haphazardly against a stout pine on the right. The trail marker sends you along on duff with ferns brushing against your legs and then uphill on a sandy trail to a junction with the Wrights Lake Trail after an easy 0.9 miles. Walking straight leads to Wrights Lake on the Grouse Lake Trail. The Rockbound Trail continues to the left on a northeasterly track.

Lake Lois and the Rockbound Valley

Hustle around the corner, gain a bit of elevation, and within 0.25 miles you will have a grand vista (one of many) of Pyramid Peak, Mount Agassiz, Mount Price, and the massive walls along the Crystal Range. Around you, the towering firs are crowned with upright cones which, heavy with sap, sparkle like disco balls in the bright sunlight.

You'll encounter another junction just an hour out from the trailhead. This trail, also from Wrights Lake, is the final leg from the Twin Lakes trailhead parking area. If you decide to start there instead, you would initially walk north-northwest from the Twin Lakes trailhead for 0.4 miles and then continue on a paved road for 0.2 miles. At that point you will be on the trail meeting at this junction after about 0.75 miles of legwork.

After you depart this junction heading northeast, watch for rapid direction changes as you cross the bare rock. Manzanita flourishes in the larger crevices while penstemon creeps into tiny—either vertical or horizontal—cracks in the rock. Before you reach the Desolation Wilderness boundary, an enormous panorama opens before you. Enjoy this vista, looking at the cobalt-blue sky wrapped across the polished granite littered with erratics of all sizes (boulders dropped in situ by melting glaciers) adding texture to this living topo map.

But don't get lulled into missing the trail. You will be saying "Huh?" while looking around in a circle if you lose track of the pathway on the rock. Instead, use HUH to your advantage . . . heads-up hiking, that is. Watch for every sign possible by being alert for footprints in the sand, ducks made of three rocks, blazes on trailside trees (particularly at creek crossings), and "handrails" made of rocks or boulders lining the trail. Be cautious about following erroneous tracks and ducks which you won't know are off-track if you go too far, too fast. Slow travel and heads-up hiking will keep you on track.

The junction to Tyler Lake is about 0.5 miles past the last junction. There you tack left and the Tyler Lake trail heads straight. Per the trail marker, Rockbound Pass is only 3 miles on. *Only? Bwa-ha-ha-ha.* The pleasant duff-and-dirt trail beneath the western white and lodgepole pines here leads to a substantial stream crossing five minutes ahead. Roll around the rounded knob of rock to your west before crossing a ravine onto more bare bedrock.

After 3 miles on the trail, your vista is blue sky and hills, granite and conifers. Descend briefly from a small saddle and anticipate yet another humongous vista just around the corner. The sand on the granite creates very slippery footing along here, but blast marks made by trail builders do help you follow the path. Cross a meltwater stream to discover a broad vista—expansive in breadth and height—and glaringly bright with the midmorning sun climbing into a cobalt-blue sky. Make sure you bring along plenty of pixels for this hike. Here it's easy to imagine the routes of the glaciers, as perhaps three of them flowed over top of everything you see in front of you toward this spot.

Descend to the Jones Fork of Silver Creek and cross on either the boulders downstream or on the log upstream. It may not always be windy here, but you might not be surprised to see the bark being blown off the trees. It's time to get set for the next stream, though, as its waters cascade past. Cross on the boulders that have been set up to help you cross safely. Look around for the foot-tall red-orange pine drops that grow beside the trail here. They are a parasite (like snow plants and sugar sticks) which feed, not on plants, but rather on the fungi that feed on other plants. Nature indeed abhors a vacuum.

In another five minutes, about 2.5 hours after embarking, you get a spectacular look at Pyramid Peak. The trail is smartly lined with rocks heading up the side of this glacial escape route. You can see textbook evidence of glacial activity in the polished surfaces on the granite and in the chatter marks, which are the curved smiles on the bedrock where a rock in the ice was stuck on the bedrock and chipped at it. The curve is usually convex in the direction from which the glacier flowed.

Before reaching Willow Flat, you must cross a small hill. Enjoy the moment to be awestruck by the vastness and immensity of the glacially sculpted terrain before you. You can see chatter marks on the granite to the left as you walk down the stairs toward Willow Flat, where you'll find aspen trees, corn lilies, ferns, paintbrush, and leopard lilies. The trail rises 1,325 feet from Silver Creek to the pass over the next 2.75 miles. You are on the easiest part at this point, because 925 feet of that occurs in the last 1.25 miles.

Another couple of runoff streams cross your path, and Lorquin's Admiral butterflies pass going the opposite direction, probably heading to Willow Flat for lunch in their preferred breeding grounds among willows. Your second crossing is next to a large, angular piece of quartz-encrusted granite. Watch the ferns; they hide their roots, which easily grab hikers' ankles.

Back on granite, you start doing a serpentine walk, passing up the turnoff that heads southwest to the Red Peak Stock Trail. Climb a set of stone stairs. The ducks and rocks bordering the trail mark the path well so that you can see the sights. The strange-looking dark spots in the granite are just inclusions of granitelike rock that existed in the magma chamber before the molten pluton rose and the rock simply fell into the molten magma.

Follow boulders, rocks, and drill-holes to keep up with the trail as it winds northeastward. The juniper offers refreshing shade, and the views into Lake Maud's outlet canyon are easy on the eyes as well. Traverse along Maud, which is at about 7,725 feet.

Cross two causeways past Maud's inlet streams and climb across the meadow above the lake, then head for the white pine and the granite stairs. Only 925 feet remain to climb over the next 1.25 miles, and the views are spectacular the entire way. A welcome and venerable-looking juniper shades you at the most appropriate point on your climb to Rockbound Pass. When you reach the pass, you can set your altimeter according to the sign nailed to a red fir atop the pass.

A little display of heather accompanies you down the trail toward Lake Doris, while a verbal greeting from several marmots shouldn't surprise you as descend past chatter marks on the rock beside you. Don't start counting the stairsteps, as they will just make you want to stay out and not go home instead of climbing up them. (I didn't even try to count.) The gray rock is colored by penstemon and paintbrush, and hemlock shades your tread. Step across a few meltwater streams as you approach Doris and its inlet culvert. This moist area is thick with mauve-hued mountain heather. Cross some more meltwater streams as you climb away from the lake on a gravel trail lined with tiny lupine on its margins. From this vantage, it appears as if there could be a fair bivy spot at the southwest corner, close to the pass, or in the trees at the northwest corner.

Within moments, you will pass the trail to China Flat that leads down into Rockbound Valley. At this point, it is time to join the Blakely Trail leading to Lake Lois and Lake Schmidell. Veering to the left side of the canyon, traverse to the northwest across a broad meadow of willow and sedges flanking a small runoff pond. Lake Lois is visible now in the distance.

Before descending to the lake level, look for an excellent bivy site to the left of the trail among the rocks at the northeast edge of the lake. On the chance that the quota here is filled, try for a permit to Lake Schmidell, where there appear to be plenty of fish.

To get to Schmidell, descend to the meadow at the north end of Lois and skirt the marshy land by traversing to the east. Cross the dammed outlet and follow the faint trail across the rocks to its exit from the lake, heading uphill once again. The single-track is easily visible as it leads to Lake Schmidell. Again bypass a junction with the Red Peak Stock Trail halfway to Schmidell. Pass another floral magnet as you head downhill on a pretty chunky trail.

At the junction of the trail to Leland Lakes, the McConnell Lake Loop, turn right to stay on the trail to Schmidell. Leave this view of the lake and descend a bit toward the granite outcrops concealing the waters from sight. Bivy sites can be found at the southwest and southeast corners of the lake on granite; and there are passable tent sites across the outlet dam.

DIRECTIONS: From the **Y** in South Lake Tahoe, drive approximately 21.5 miles west on US 50 to Wrights Road, which is on the north side of the highway, 4.5 miles west of Strawberry.

If you're coming from the west, Wrights Road is 35.8 miles from Placerville and 4.9 miles east of Kyburz via US 50. Be prepared for the turn, as it comes up suddenly at a curve in the road.

Drive for 8 miles to the Wrights Lake visitor center, just past the equestrian parking lot, and then turn left to the Rockbound trailhead at Dark Lake.

Drive 0.4 miles to the trailhead parking area, where there are pit toilets available.

If that lot is full, you can park at the Twin Lakes trailhead by turning right at the visitor center (straight from Dark Lake parking) and drive 1 mile past the summer cabins to the end of the road to the trailhead parking lot. There are pit toilets available there.

If both lots are full, you can use the equestrian parking lot as overflow. The equestrian parking area has water and pit toilets.

GPS TRAILHEAD COORDINATES	27 LAKE LOIS AND LAKE SCHMIDELL
UTM Zone (WGS84)	10S
Easting	0739615
Northing	4303555
Latitude	N 38° 50.892'
Longitude	W 120° 14.336'

28 McConnell Lake Loop

SCENERY: ☆ ☆ ☆ ☆ ☆
TRAIL CONDITION: ☆ ☆ ☆
CHILDREN: ☆
DIFFICULTY: ☆ ☆ ☆ ☆ ☆
SOLITUDE: ☆ ☆ ☆ ☆
DISTANCE: 26 miles round-trip
HIKING TIME: 2 nights

OUTSTANDING FEATURES: *Pass by or visit any one of 13 beautiful mountain lakes; fill every photo card with enormous vistas of the Crystal Range; discover new geologic wonders; and wander past meadows filled with willows, wildflowers, and butterflies. Nights are filled with stars and wind.*

If you have the time and can handle the vertical miles, this may just be one of the most exciting, challenging, and beautiful hikes in the Tahoe region. Depart from Wrights Lake on Rockbound Trail and plan for a night between Lois and Schmidell after turning north on the Blakely Trail. Climb above Schmidell and begin a descending circuit to several inviting lakes on the McConnell Lake Trail, which (I'm certain) was built by, and not improved since, the Spanish conquistadores. Cross the nascent Rubicon River in Camper Flat and ascend the Rubicon Trail to its junction with Rockbound Trail leading up to Lake Doris. Return for a cold beverage at the trailhead.

🚶🚶 Since you are here, you must have made it up and over Rockbound Pass as described in Hike 27, Lake Lois and Lake Schmidell.

Ensure that you have a map and compass and know how to use them before heading out on this loop. At times you will have a grand vista and other times you will be searching for stream crossings under cover of forest or following scant markers over granite outcrops. Aside from that cautionary word, this is one of the best areas for hiking in the Tahoe region.

You have some choices for your first night's campsite. Lake Doris has good sites but my vote is for staying at Lake Lois, just for the vistas across the Rubicon Canyon to Middle Mountain. If you are unable to secure a permit in this zone, then the next logical campsite would be a mile away at Lake Schmidell. Climb away from Lake Lois and descend about 550 feet to its granite-lined southeast

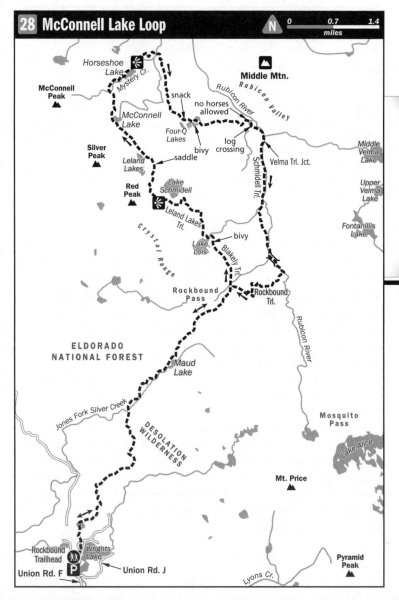

N

0   0.7   1.4
miles

Horseshoe Lake

McConnell Peak ▲

Mystery Cr.

snack

no horses allowed

Rubicon River

Middle Mtn. 🏕

Rubicon Valley

McConnell Lake

Four-Q Lakes

bivy

log crossing

Silver Peak ▲

Leland Lakes

saddle

Velma Trl. Jct.

Lake Schmidell

Schmidell Trl.

Middle Velma Lake

Red Peak ▲ 🏕

Leland Lakes Trl.

Upper Velma Lake

C r y s t a l   R a n g e

bivy

Lake Lois

Blakely Trl.

Fontanillis Lake

ELDORADO NATIONAL FOREST

Rockbound Pass

Rockbound Trl.

Rubicon River

Maud Lake

Jones Fork Silver Creek

DESOLATION WILDERNESS

Mosquito Pass

Lake Alice

Mt. Price ▲

Rockbound Trailhead

🚶🚶 **P**

Union Rd. F

Wrights Lake

Union Rd. J

Lyons Cr.

Pyramid Peak ▲

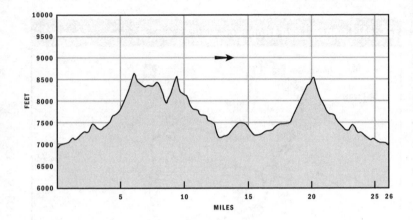

shore. Look for the junction of the trail to Leland Lakes as you near the lake level.

The best sites to set a bivy are on granite at the southeast end of Schmidell. These are best reached by heading to the left when the trail hits the hemlock-shaded outcrops. After a night spent with the winds howling down the east face of Red Peak, regain the trail for a wilderness hike. Head back to the junction leading off to the southwest and traverse about 200 yards to a stream crossing. After using the boulders to get across the cascading water, climb smartly out of the ravine and ascend steeply above the south end of the lake. There's an impressive vista to the north if you need an excuse to catch your breath.

Your track turns uphill and heads northwest for 0.25 miles before it crosses another meltwater stream, which cascades down the steep slope at your left shoulder and resumes its downward plunge to the right of your boot after crossing the narrow trail. Watch and listen uphill for any rocks that might be tumbling down this steep watercourse as it fills Schmidell, then continues to the Rubicon below. Climb out of the ravine, past rangers' buttons and lupine.

A clearing just past a copse of hemlock and pine marks the spot where the trail turns brutally uphill for 100 vertical feet.

This trail may not be all that enjoyable for hikers who have difficulty with exposed heights, but it is not dangerous. You ascend about 450 feet more to the saddle overlooking Leland Lakes, essentially passing behind the cirque that stands above Schmidell. Marmots may watch and verbally pass judgment as you traverse the willow-dotted slope. The trail is mostly visible, but vigilance is key as you sometimes must follow scant (but accurate) ducks.

Cross another stream on your way to the saddle; soon after, the gravel trail leads through willows and pinemat manzanita up to a rockfall. From there, ducks mark the trail as it winds through a meadow to a hemlock-shaded saddle looking down on Leland Lakes. This pair of blue gems is set amid green western hemlocks, which seemingly outline the shores of the twin tarns cut into granite bedrock.

Not to be outdone in steepness, this trail leads impatiently downhill—nicely lined as it leads away from the saddle, then becoming fairly scrabbly before turning seriously steep—requiring near-technical skills to negotiate some of the steps. With granite walls above, the descent abates about 50 feet above the first lake. Walk through some boulders and follow the trail as it turns away from the lake. The trail, spongy in early season, sounds a hollow note after summer heat has sucked all moisture from it. It wanders on a northerly course past the first lake and turns northwest to approach the larger tarn. A surprise is in store as you find a small sandy beach with a nice picnic spot adjacent to it among some trees. Vistas along the lake's wide, sandy trail through the granite are plentiful.

The trail's environs become ravinelike as you descend away from the second of the Leland Lakes. A boggle of downed trees will keep you alert for ducks. The trail maintains a northwest heading along the lake's outlet. Pass a shallow meltwater pond on the left and some garage-sized mountain debris on the right. Lots of rocks

Dawn and dusk are colorful events at the isolated Four-Q Lakes.

assist the next stream crossing before you barge through the willows
and heather and into a large meadow. The lake's southern margin
is fringed by young lodgepole pines, and the trail, now the size of a
rabbit track, edges to the granite wall above the west side of the lake.

With Silver Peak on your left, start out on the half-mile uphill
to McConnell Lake. Your trail is quite indistinct over the granite
and even as it enters the trees, so you need to stay vigilant for ducks
and blazes. Although you are looking for a lake as shown in blue on
the map, McConnell seems less like a lake and more like a succession
meadow despite, or maybe because of, its small marshy area at the
northwest corner. Looking back at the small lodgepole pines moving into the area from the south, it looks as if the meadow first filled
with silt and grasses and then willows before allowing the conifers to
take over. The indistinct trail around McConnell will present a chal-

lenge to anyone not paying strict attention to the trail and its signs. Winding through trees and over fallen logs, it persists northward toward a wall of boulders ahead. One last walk through the lodgepole pines and you start ascending across granite, following the accurately placed ducks. Keep high on the wall and then descend at the north end, following ducks between wet meadow and dry granite.

Crash through the willows that camouflage a drop-off into the next stream and then one more stream before you head across granite to the shade of a short stretch of conifers. Presently, the mystery of the hour is what happens to the stream that bounds down and then disappears beneath your feet. A gradual descent with overwhelming vistas will erase all memories of the next 0.25 miles heading into Horseshoe Lake. Some small ducks lead around and through a gaggle of downed timber. Follow them closely and continue northeast to start around the north end of Horseshoe, passing an interesting lodgepole pine whose trunk emerges from the ground twice. There is a great place to take a nap near the western shore, but it is too close for a camp. Besides, fetching water is difficult here.

Climb away from Horseshoe and soon encounter a junction with the trail to Lake Zitella. You head to Camper Flat on the trail to the right. Notice the lodgepole pine with the blaze—a small letter *i*—carved into its bark. Above the blaze, bolted to the conifer, is a sign declaring HAZARDOUS FOR STOCK TRAVEL. A quick note of thanks for not being a cow or horse and down you go, some 200 feet to Four-Q Lakes. Walk straight across the sandy path and up a granite outcrop, where you have to stop because of the enormous, eye-filling panorama ahead of you.

Follow the ducks as the trail disappears over the hill, staying high on the granite slope, to traverse along the east-facing slope. An amazing vista awaits as you approach a spot overlooking the Rubicon Valley. Marked by three prominent lodgepole pines separated from a venerable juniper by two boulders, the stout limb of the juniper catches you just before you seemingly step over a precipice into the ether.

Your route-finding skills will come into play as you head down-hill to Four-Q Lakes. Look for obvious signs such as ducks, blazes, footprints in sand, dropped bits of trash, and broken sticks or twigs, which can easily keep you on the trail across many types of terrain. You may strain a bit to follow the trail as you make several crossings of the Rubicon's tributaries. On the way to the crossing of Schmidell's outlet, descend about 375 feet, following the trail about 0.4 miles to the east. The route is sketchy here and the ducks plentiful. Many people have laid out their particular route across the wet area leading across this stretch of the young Rubicon. Look for the blaze on a standing snag that leans over a pool and is lined up with an array of ducks leading across the stream. It's hard to say if that was the correct track, but it leads on successfully, so good enough.

The trail, once again outlined with ducks, stretches south on a sandy surface between rock outcrops. Follow the rock piles through the blowdown, even straight uphill. About a mile of traveling to the south, up this tributary of the Rubicon, leads to the first of the Four-Q Lakes. Climb across outcrops and follow the ducks as you pick your way through a stand of lodgepole. A huge wall of granite stands to the west and your trail continues uphill through the trees to the southeast. A brief but serious uphill climb steps you up to the corner of the westernmost lake. There is a nice spot beneath the trees, right off the trail and too close to the lake for camping, to filter water and grab a snack.

Regain the trail, which climbs slightly to overlook this and the next lake from about 50 feet above the shore level. Continue trending east, almost contouring above the lakes. Avoid descending prematurely to the next lake; instead, turn slightly uphill to the northeast, where you'll soon overlook the next two lakes and the granite isthmus between them. When you come abreast of it, turn and walk south to several excellent bivy sites on the granite. These are two of the most secluded and picturesque lakes in the Desolation

Wilderness—according to me. Sunset and stars have nothing on sunrises here. All of them are wonderful, colorful, and memorable. The hiking time from the previous night's bivy was about five hours. (YMMV— your mileage may vary.)

Return to the trail, refreshed and ready for some descending and climbing, then more climbing and more descending, and then home. Zigzag after the ducks and contour along to a rocky crossing of another isthmus between two more Four-Q Lakes. The trail changes direction shortly after leaving the last lake's shore. Continue to pay close attention even though the trail becomes more distinct.

Travel a mile from the second lake's bivy site and you will see a chute carved in granite by rushing water. This is difficult trail to follow but the ducks remain accurate. After more gentle descent, cross another stream on your way to Camper Flat. A sign facing east cautions riders, TRAIL IMPASSABLE TO HORSES 1 MILE BEYOND FOUR-Q LAKES. Equestrians ought to believe that.

Descend a bit more to Camper Flat, where you'll need to watch for a large log on which to cross the Rubicon yet again. Make a sharp left across the creek when your trail is blocked by branches. Cross easily on this large log and turn to the right once on the other side. The path is now a sweet trail—soft, wide, and easily navigated—that roughly parallels the curving stream. Walk past the junction, with the trail leading uphill to Lake Schmidell. Your path leads toward China Flat but ascends to Rockbound Pass before that.

However, in 100 yards or so, the trail to Middle Velma Lake intersects yours. Continue uphill to the right as if you are going to Lake Aloha. Whereas the trail around the loop to the Four-Q Lakes was rather hectic and required full attention, this trail heads south through a conifer forest for the next mile along a placid, well-marked, dirt-and-duff trail lit by the sunlight filtering through the tree crowns. As the trail comes adjacent to the creek, water is easy to filter. A hundred yards south is another junction leading uphill to

Schmidell. Continue ahead, immediately cross the trout-bearing creek, and veer slightly to the southeast under forest cover.

Runoff streams add texture to the trail as you continue south through the broken forest until you take a left jog at a small meadow with a lone pine at its south end. With the Rubicon gaining strength to your left, you will cross a few runoff streams feeding it from your right. First up is a stone bridge, followed by a causeway through a wet meadow of corn lilies, then a quick crossing followed just as fast by another with a dirt-and-stone bridge. After 200 yards you'll encounter another crossing of moderate difficulty followed 100 yards on by one that's much more impressive. Small meadows of corn lilies and lupine push the trees back from the trail on your way to the next junction, 500 feet to the southeast.

Right leads uphill to Rockbound Pass; continuing ahead leads to Lake Aloha. Head right and get ready for your final climb of about 880 feet to the junction of the Rockbound and Blakely trails. White firs provide welcome shade, even at noon, and the many blazes will keep you on route. Cross an open area of broken red, gray, and black rock in the midst of the trees. When the trail comes close to the ravine at a small clearing, look for a passable bivy spot on the left next to the ravine. Wolf lichen adorns even the standing snags and adds a new shade of green to the forest.

The wind plays havoc with trees as they grow here in the Desolation Wilderness, stunting their height, shortening their limbs, exposing roots, and generally making bonsai trees out of any conifer in its path. Just about 500 feet below Lake Doris is a fine example of this krummholz effect—literally "bent wood." Two magnificent firs display the force of the wind here: one has been split in half, and the other so windswept and snow-shaped that its lowest limbs actually wrap around the tree before reaching skyward.

A few runoff streams create the moist, meadowlike open areas that support lupine, asters, paintbrush, corn lilies, and butterflies.

Sometimes a causeway will keep your feet dry crossing these areas. At the last such spot on this uphill, a solitary granite boulder takes a position at the base of the meadow. Fir and hemlock trees sport blazes to guide you across the top of the field and up to the junction with the Blakely Trail, where you will head south to Rockbound Pass.

The stone stairs at the south end of Doris assist you to the pass. On the way in, it seemed as if there were only a few stairs down. Now, the count is several hundred. Make your way up the stairs, no matter how many, and enjoy the vista. Your return path and all of its terrain is laid out ahead of you and all of it (well, almost all) is downhill.

DIRECTIONS: From the **Y** in South Lake Tahoe, drive approximately 21.5 miles west on US 50 to Wrights Road on the north side of the highway, 4.5 miles west of Strawberry.

If coming from the west, Wrights Road is 35.8 miles from Placerville and 4.9 miles east of Kyburz via US 50. Be prepared for the turn, as it comes up suddenly at a curve in the road.

Drive for 8 miles to the Wrights Lake visitor center, just past the equestrian parking lot, then turn left to the Rockbound Trailhead at Dark Lake.

Drive 0.4 miles to the trailhead parking area, where there are pit toilets available.

If that lot is full, you can park at the Twin Lakes trailhead by turning right at the visitor center onto FR 12N23 (straight if coming from Dark Lake parking) and drive 1 mile past the summer cabins to the end of the road to the trailhead parking lot. Pit toilets are available there.

If both lots are full, you can use the equestrian parking lot as overflow. The equestrian parking area has water and pit toilets.

GPS Trailhead Coordinates	28 McConnell Lake Loop
UTM Zone (WGS84)	10S
Easting	0739615
Northing	4303555
Latitude	N 38° 50.892'
Longitude	W 120° 14.336'

SCENERY: ✿ ✿ ✿ ✿	HIKING TIME: 4–5 hours
TRAIL CONDITION: ✿ ✿ ✿ ✿	OUTSTANDING FEATURES: *A lighthouse, an historic*
CHILDREN: ✿ ✿	*mansion amid majestic trees, sandy beaches, and enor-*
DIFFICULTY: ✿ ✿ ✿	*mous vistas of the crystal blue waters of Lake Tahoe and*
SOLITUDE: ✿ ✿ ✿	*Emerald Bay*
DISTANCE: 9.4 miles round-trip	

Hikers on the Rubicon Trail will be treated to spectacular scenery on this fairly mod-erate trail that begins with a short side trip to a historic lighthouse (and a phenomenal vista), and ends with a visit to a renowned residence nestled among magnificent Jeffrey pine. Your trail starts out with a few uphill switchbacks to reach its high point near the historic Rubicon Point Lighthouse, then descends to Emerald Bay, where the highlight is Vikingsholm, a Depression-era mansion. Breathtaking views are com-mon within the first 2 miles, as your trail either looks out on the lake or precipitously down on its shore before entering the cool shade of the Jeffrey-pine forest surrounding Emerald Bay. Curious hikers who brought along binoculars will have clear views of Captain Dick's Tomb on Fannette Island.

🚶🚶 The trailhead begins just past the campgrounds in the day-use parking lot at Calawee Cove. Toilets, water, and trash facilities are available in this parking lot. The trailhead sign is visible at the south end of the lot.

Within the first 100 feet you will have a choice of two trails. Heading straight south will take you along and above the shoreline on the Rubicon Trail. The described hike starts out on the Lighthouse Trail, which makes a **U**-turn heading uphill to the historic Rubicon Point Lighthouse. Ascend a couple of moderate switchbacks, climb-ing above the parking lot through a pine-and-fir forest to reach the monument describing the lighthouse and its role in Lake Tahoe's history. The lighthouse itself is about 75 feet downhill and can be reached by a side trail.

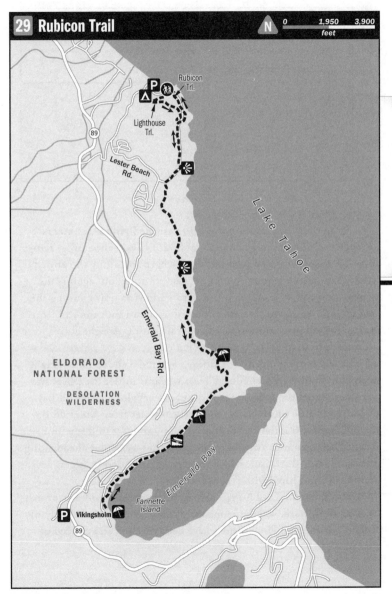

P
△
Rubicon
Trl.

Lighthouse
Trl.

Lester Beach
Rd.

89

Lake Tahoe

Emerald Bay Rd.

ELDORADO
NATIONAL FOREST

DESOLATION
WILDERNESS

Emerald Bay

P
Vikingsholm

Fannette
Island

89

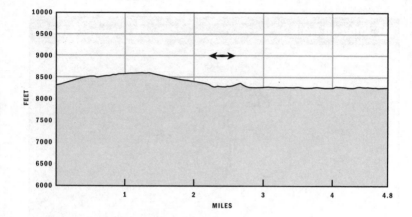

From the vista point on the trail past the lighthouse, hikers
can get a wonderful panorama from South Lake Tahoe up to Kings
Beach with snowcapped peaks in the background along the entire
vista. Genoa, Monument, and East Peak all stand out against the
azure-blue sky. At another intersection and vista point among the
boulders, descend to the left to the intersection with the Rubicon
Trail and follow it south toward Emerald Point. A right at this junction leads back to D. L. Bliss State Park.

June is a great month for flowers around Tahoe. The shady
Rubicon Trail is splotched red by snowplants under the pines and
accented by yellow-capped woolly mule's ears along Emerald Bay.
After just a mile on the trail, you are 2.6 miles from Emerald Bay
Boat Camp, 3.6 miles from Vikingsholm, and 5.2 miles from Eagle
Point Campground. Another vista point lies 0.7 miles ahead along
this sand-and-duff trail, which is often surrounded by green-leaf
manzanita and lined with fragrant lupine.

The Rubicon Trail is regularly maintained, and evidence of that
is clear along here, where the manzanita has been cut back and boulders repositioned. The hillsides have been thinned and cleared of

underbrush and dead and downed trees in order to reduce the forest's vulnerability to catastrophic wildfires such as the Angora Fire of 2007.

Enjoy the gentle slope as you descend nearer to lake level only to climb back up to cross a stream shooting across the trail. More thinning operations are evident as you approach Emerald Point. You will see a broad, flat area—an impromptu beach—just prior to zigzagging through the trees across the point. More tempting beach sites are found within feet of the trail as you turn southwest toward your destination.

The trail becomes somewhat obscure when it passes through the Emerald Point Boat Camp, but careful attention to signs will keep you on track. The trail tends to the lake side just past the boat ramp. Now your level trail is within view of the lake, Fannette Island, and the tour boats that churn around it.

If you have binoculars, you will be able to make out the rock structure near the summit of the island. That is the erstwhile tomb of Captain Richard Barter ("the Hermit of Emerald Bay"), which he built for himself while serving as the caretaker for the cottage owned by Ben Holladay ("the Stagecoach King"). He finally needed to use it in October 1873, when he was outrun by the lake and slipped beneath its surface in 1,400 feet of water off Rubicon Point. The island was referred to as Dead Man's Island before its present name.

Nestled among the big trees is Vikingsholm, a grand home built in 1929 and donated to the state park system a quarter of a century later. The building was designed to fit in its surroundings without disturbing the landscape. You can tour the house and grounds, picnic at one of the many tables, or swim in the ice-cold water. Feeding wildlife is discouraged. Restroom facilities are located on the hillside behind the house. You can reach the Vikingsholm parking lot by climbing the stairs and path beyond the mansion up to the highway, CA 89.

On your return to the trailhead, follow the trail to the junction of the Lighthouse Trail (uphill) and the Rubicon Trail (straight ahead). Whichever one you took on the way in, try the other on the way out. The Rubicon Trail will carefully guide your steps around the face of boulders that are exposed to the water's edge below. (Chain fencing and solid-rock stairs will help you along this section.) Four vista points along the trail are worth every pixel.

DIRECTIONS: Starting at the **Y** in South Lake Tahoe, drive north on CA 89 approximately 11.5 miles to the entrance to D. L. Bliss State Park on the right. Drive past the visitor center to the entrance kiosk, where you can self-pay the $6 day-use fee, then continue to the day-use parking lot.

A reasonable alternative is to park at the Emerald Bay State Park lot, about 2.75 miles before D. L. Bliss State Park. From this direction, your trail would begin with a 0.7-mile descent to Vikingsholm from CA 89 prior to hiking the Rubicon Trail in reverse.

GPS TRAILHEAD COORDINATES	29 RUBICON TRAIL
UTM Zone (WGS84)	10S
Easting	0751435
Northing	4320264
Latitude	N 38° 59.913'
Longitude	W 120° 05.860'

SCENERY: ☆ ☆ ☆ ☆ ☆	HIKING TIME: 5–6 hours
TRAIL CONDITION: ☆ ☆ ☆	OUTSTANDING FEATURES: *Bridge the creek with*
CHILDREN: ☆	*snowmelt water crashing over rocks in a wild cascade,*
DIFFICULTY: ☆ ☆ ☆ ☆	*pass five beautiful lakes with dramatic backdrops,*
SOLITUDE: ☆ ☆ ☆	*travel in lush, mixed-conifer forests, and cross erratic-*
DISTANCE: 10.8 miles round-trip	*ridden granite bedrock polished smooth by glacial mud.*

This is a popular trail despite being incredibly rocky, but even that makes it an interesting trip. Glacial action was an evident agent of geologic change here, and every rock reveals it. The initial 2.5 miles are strenuous in that your elevation gain is about 1,550 feet—almost every bit is vertical without letup.

With the promise of more lakes like it, once Eagle Lake is seen, more must be better. And they are. Velma, Dicks, and Fontanillis lakes are all amenable getaways for a quiet lunch or an overnight bivy. From Dicks Lake, it is downhill almost all the way back to the trailhead.

🚶🚶 Walk past the circle in the parking lot and go up the granite steps to the trailhead kiosk to complete a day-hike permit. Overnight permits are necessary and available at U.S. Forest Service ranger stations. The broad timber-and-sand path leads up and away from the kiosk. A sharp left turn at the outset sends hikers up steps to a junction of the Eagle Lake Loop and Eagle Lake Trail. Follow the trail to the left past buckbrush ceanothus and huckleberry oak, manzanita and willow, where aspens shake in the canyon breeze. You can rest beneath a venerable spreading western juniper, on a bench made for eight overlooking the water crashing down the **V**-shaped ravine.

Continue up the stone stairs to the right, past another vista point, and past the Eagle Loop Trail that again goes off to the right, while this hike takes the trail downhill and to the left toward the bridge and Eagle Lake. A stone causeway precedes the bridge where you cross, and reach a jumble of rock at the other end. Turn south

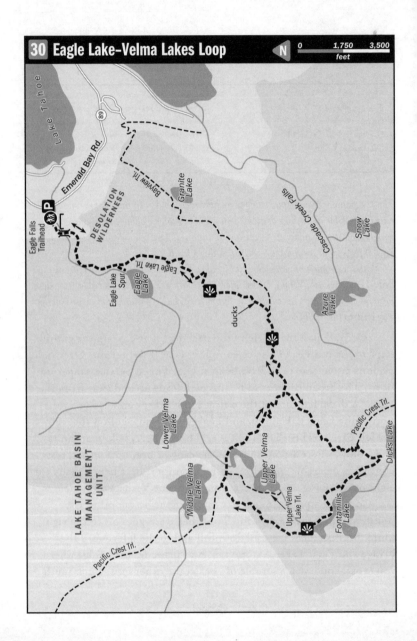

30 Eagle Lake–Velma Lakes Loop

N

0   1,750   3,500
feet

Lake Tahoe

Emerald Bay Rd.

89

DESOLATION WILDERNESS

Bayview Trl.

Granite Lake

Cascade Creek Falls

Snow Lake

Eagle Falls Trailhead

P

Eagle Lake Spur.

Eagle Lake Trl.

Eagle Lake

ducks

Azure Lake

LAKE TAHOE BASIN MANAGEMENT UNIT

Lower Velma Lake

Middle Velma Lake

Upper Velma Lake

Upper Velma Lake Trl.

Fontanillis Lake

Dicks Lake

Pacific Crest Trl.

Pacific Crest Trl.

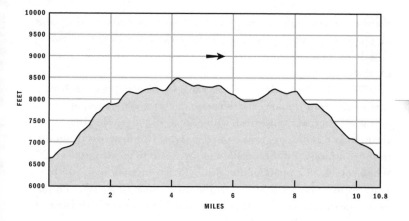

for 100 yards and cross into the Desolation Wilderness. Right in the middle of the rock stairs is your reminder about the permits that rangers always seem to want to see. Turn to the west through the trees to navigate around a small knob for the next 0.25 miles. This uphill traverse crosses a granite slope and then turns to the south and follows the creek uphill.

As you approach the spur trail to Eagle Lake, the air is filled with the crisp melody of aspen and the fragrant butterscotch scent of Jeffrey pine. Take the right fork at the signed junction and walk about 150 yards to an overlook of this pretty tarn, graced with a petite island topped by five firs. The north shore offers some areas to sit and snack or contemplate. There are excellent vistas of the lake and its surrounding monoliths from the trail heading uphill. In fact, these changing vistas actually pull hikers uphill, making the slow-going quite tolerable.

Sierra penstemon liven the trailside rock clusters with their scarlet outbursts. Chinquapin and huckleberry crowd and claw at your knees from time to time. Cross over a small rockfall among some broken Jeffrey pines just short of 7,400 feet of elevation. From a granite outcrop with a scant view of the lake, descend on a duff-and-dirt path, cross a runoff stream, and then switch back to the south. Climb up some boulder stairs that are easy if your knees are four feet off the ground.

Keep aware over the next 200 yards of many short switchbacks, as the scant trail is marked with rocks, ducks, sticks, or not at all. Soon, walk across a sandy trail with a copse of lodgepole pines to your left and polished granite to your right. Climb across the granite to the southwest and then make a loopy ascent to go around a knob. When you reach a small saddle, just before your trail turns south again, your reward will be incredible vistas, including peaks: Phipps to the northwest, Dicks to the south, and Jakes to the north (named for a general, a sailor, and a skier).

Traverse this steep slope about 0.5 miles to the south, losing and gaining a bit on the way. When you reach the decaying granite, be alert for ducks, which will guide your way. Two hundred yards ahead is the junction with Bayview Trail. Turn right, heading west and crossing a spur where another spectacular vista emerges. Dicks Peak and Mount Tallac stand out to the south from this viewpoint. Hike to the west, descending slightly, across the granite slope among lodgepole, western white pine, and western juniper for another 0.5 miles, where you will encounter an important signed junction.

This new junction marker is about 3.2 miles from the trailhead, at approximately 8,200 feet elevation. The trail to Velma Lakes takes a right turn to the northwest and the trail that is described here departs to the left, southwest. On your way to Dicks Lake, you should practice HUH—heads-up hiking—because the trail becomes somewhat indistinct and cruddy going across rocks and roots. A rock-and-sand causeway helps you cross a seasonal wetland or pond, and a little farther downhill, the trail crosses another few small streams draining the larger pond to the left.

Ahead await 300 feet of switchbacks up granite slopes. What better way to start than with stairs made of local material? As you

Along the Eagle Lake Trail

walk along the switchbacks, observe the scratch marks made by rock embedded in the glacier passing over the granite. The smiley-face cuts are chatter marks, where an embedded rock got stuck and plucked out a piece of granite. These marks indicate the direction that the glacier flowed. This area is easy to navigate if you stay on top of it. If you lose track of the trail, stop and regain your bearings, including your last certain location. Then look for ducks or other trail signs: footprints, rocks in a line, blazes, dog prints, and bits of trash, broken sticks, or flowers are all good indicators if you lose your path momentarily.

If you ever feel totally lost, however, have a seat and think about the humor of the situation for five minutes. That should relax you enough to enable you to recall the last known place where you had good trail and then carefully retrace your steps to that point if possible. If not, then relax and think of your plan that you prepared for this event. No sweat. And that won't happen anyway, because you prepared with other navigation tools and this guidebook.

When you reach the saddle, the trail junction marker stands out just 200 feet to the east. Continue east from there if you want to climb across Dicks Pass or go to Dicks Peak, but if you want to go to Dicks Lake, then you must turn to the right at the marker. The trail is clearly defined with shattered granite blocks and erratics the size of Hummers as you walk among lodgepole and hemlock. Six minutes down the trail brings you to Captain Richard Barter's namesake swimming hole, where the trail leads down to the outlet from this junction with the trail to Fontanillis Lake. There are several secluded bivy sites around the north shore. Vistas to the southwest over this lake are fantastic.

From the junction marker beneath the hemlock that lost its twin long ago, follow the trail to the right downhill to Fontanillis Lake. The sandy trail heads northwest and is caught between the bedrock hills overlooking Middle Velma on the right and the erratics littering the area around the shore. The trail passes a stagnant pond on the left, and, after another wet area, slides up adjacent to the lake. Walk along the lake's heather-laced shore past the outlet before you veer away to the north. It was either too wet, or too rocky, or too close for any bivy site to be very good.

As you cross the outlet stream amid stands of larkspur, pause to get a view of Lake Tahoe. Follow the trail as it ascends the ridge in front of you and then descend its west flank to the northeast. The trail is distinct but runs through a debris field of shattered rock and splintered wood. Step across a runoff stream, descending into its ravine and traverse the opposite bank through red fir and hemlock. The trail remains clear despite the blown-down giants all around.

The cones of the fir glisten with sap as they stand erect at the crown. The firs are also decorated with wolf lichen, catching the sun and adding a fresh green to the forest. Continue downhill through massive blow-downs on a very comfortable duff trail. The junction with the Velma Lakes Trail stands in a copse of hemlock and fir.

The marker at this junction states that Phipps Pass heads to the left and Bayview Trail is to the right. This route goes right but there are any number of bivy and tent sites between this junction and 2,000 feet west at the Phipps Pass junction.

Some are within trees and others are on granite and are still secluded. Sunrise on Middle Velma should not be missed. It is a glorious event of color and stillness.

In the middle of the afternoon, a sooty grouse scurries around a hemlock on the duff trail. Woodpeckers hammer and the wind silently lifts butterflies over the trail. The silence is broken by the male sooty grouse vocalizing during its display. The loud thumping echoes all around the open space just before the Upper Velma junction. Pass by that trail and continue eastward, crossing the wide outlet stream from it on a convenient log. Climb away from that and skirt another pond before crossing broken granite to the marshy northern end of that fractured body of water.

Ascend stone stairs to start walking past the shore on a sandy trail across broken granite and shady lodgepole pines. HUH—heads-up hiking again along here. The trail can morph from distinct to not there in a blink. Watch carefully for all of the usual trail signs. Ahead of you is an array of switchbacks and squiggles that haul you about 250 feet uphill across polished and weathered granite. The trail of both stone and timbers is very well constructed. Pass a sandy stretch and it's not yet ready for prime time.

At the next, previously visited, junction, your homeward trail leads to the left rather than returning to Dicks Lake. The next junction, 0.75 miles ahead, returns to the trailhead via Eagle Lake Trail to the left. The Bayview Trail heads to the right and descends 2.8 miles to the Bayview Trailhead. If another car were available, that would make an excellent loop as well. Without an extra vehicle, this might not be practical. CA 89 is not the easiest road to walk, even for that short distance.

Turn left onto the Eagle Lake Trail and begin your descent to the trailhead.

DIRECTIONS: The large trailhead parking lot is located at the large curve in CA 89 directly above Vikingsholm, 8.5 miles north of South Lake Tahoe. If coming from Tahoe City, drive 18.6 miles and turn right at the entrance driveway. Parking is available on the road, but more space and facilities are down the driveway. Pit toilets, a picnic area, and water are available. A $5 fee is required for each day parked. If you're doing an overnight, make certain to enclose the right amount. An annual pass for parking around the lake costs $20 and is available from Lake Tahoe Basin Management Unit facilities. It is very useful if you are hiking more than four times from any of the popular trailheads.

GPS TRAILHEAD COORDINATES	30 EAGLE LAKE–VELMA LAKES LOOP
UTM Zone (WGS84)	10S
Easting	0750137
Northing	4315409
Latitude	N 38° 57.118'
Longitude	W 120° 06.811'

31 Genevieve and Crag Lakes

SCENERY: ✿ ✿ ✿	HIKING TIME: *4–5 hours*
TRAIL CONDITION: ✿ ✿ ✿	OUTSTANDING FEATURES: *Butterflies and hum-*
CHILDREN: ✿ ✿ ✿	*mingbirds will blast from flower to flower as they*
DIFFICULTY: ✿ ✿ ✿	*accompany you up this moderate trail to two scenic*
SOLITUDE: ✿ ✿ ✿	*subalpine lakes.*
DISTANCE: *10 miles round–trip*	

This gentle trail leading to a string of scenic subalpine lakes is part of the Tahoe–Yosemite Trail. With only 1,200 feet of elevation gain over moderate terrain, you don't need to exert a lot of energy to enjoy these backcountry vistas in the Desolation Wilderness. Day hike permits are free and can be obtained at the trailhead. Overnight camping permits are issued for a fee and may be obtained at the Taylor Creek Forest Service Visitor Center.

🥾🥾 From the dirt lot, your path starts on Forest Road 14N42, which begins behind the locked gate marked with the word TRAIL. This dirt double-track is your path for the first 1.5 miles. A single-track begins at the signpost for the Tahoe–Yosemite Trail. A reminder that wood fires are not allowed has been posted in this previously logged area. After a long, exposed initial stretch of uphill trail, you'll sight a refreshing trailside spring nestled in a shady trailside setting.

Over the next mile, your rocky trail will elevate you about 500 feet. The ridgeline that looms about 1,000 feet over your right shoulder separates the General Creek drainage from the Meeks Creek drainage. That ridge is your handrail and you'll follow it southwest until you make the turn southeast farther up Meeks Creek heading to the lakes.

On the way, you'll approach Meeks Creek and find a display of pussy toes, Indian paintbrush, lupine, and Sierra fireweed beneath a canopy of pine and fir. After 2.5 miles of hiking, you'll enter the Desolation Wilderness where your shady, duff-covered trail is

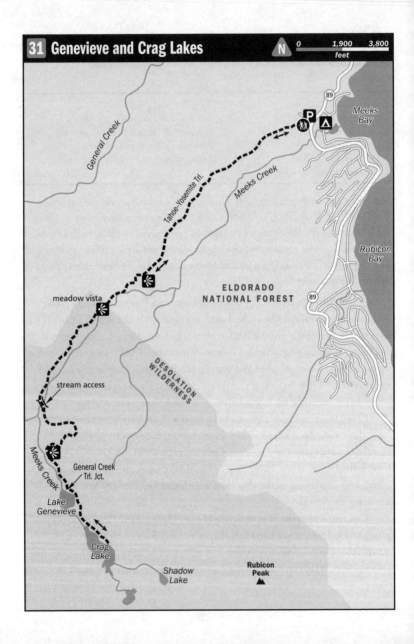

N

0   1,900   3,800
feet

General Creek

89

Meeks
Bay

Tahoe-Yosemite Trl.

Meeks Creek

Rubicon
Bay

ELDORADO
NATIONAL FOREST

89

meadow vista

DESOLATION
WILDERNESS

stream access

Meeks Creek

General Creek
Trl. Jct.

Lake
Genevieve

Crag
Lake

Shadow
Lake

Rubicon
Peak

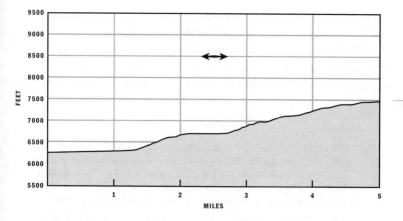

often crowded by ferns, columbine, and asters. The sign is a reminder that you need a paid wilderness permit if you intend to camp overnight and a free day-hike permit otherwise. Before you hit your first switchback, you'll pass a dry meadow on a sandy trail where several of the Ponderosa pines have had their trunks snapped or crowns blown off by wind or snow.

Climb above the creek, where the exposed roots of ponderosa pine and boulder steps help you up the switchback. Pinemat manzanita is colored by Indian paintbrush that's shared by butterflies and hummingbirds. As you round the large knob to your left, red fir trees border this stream where it is level enough for small pools to form. Cross Meeks Creek on a very substantial footbridge before making a detour to the east. Just as your route turns to the southeast approaching Lake Genevieve, you'll have a good vista to Lake Tahoe.

Your sandy trail soon turns rocky, and the last steep uphill before reaching Lake Genevieve has been eased with some steps hammered into the granite. At the top of this little rise, you will have a pleasant vista in front of you, with diminutive Lake Genevieve on the west side of the trail. Some highly impacted sites at the north end of the lake should be used for picnics and conversation points, as they're too close to the lake to be suitable for camping.

The path keeps you high around the unapproachable south end of Genevieve and continues 0.25 miles to Crag Lake. A sandy trail leads you about halfway along Crag Lake's eastern shore. There, you can snap excellent pictures of its pine-dotted western shore.

DIRECTIONS: Meeks Creek trailhead is 11.5 miles south of Tahoe City on CA 89. The trailhead parking lot is on the west side of the road across from the Meeks Bay Campground and Marina. Park in the small dirt lot with room for about ten cars. There are no facilities here. Additional parking can be found along CA 89.

GPS TRAILHEAD COORDINATES	31 GENEVIEVE AND CRAG LAKES
UTM Zone (WGS84)	10S
Easting	0747142
Northing	4323630
Latitude	N 39° 01.608'
Longitude	W 120° 08.704'

32 Rubicon Lake

SCENERY: ✿ ✿ ✿ ✿	HIKING TIME: *4–5 hours (overnight)*
TRAIL CONDITION: ✿ ✿ ✿	OUTSTANDING FEATURES: *Hikers can find seclu-*
CHILDREN: ✿	*sion while visiting five mountain lakes where butterflies*
DIFFICULTY: ✿ ✿ ✿ ✿	*enjoy the all-you-can-eat buffet of wildflowers; the*
SOLITUDE: ✿ ✿ ✿ ✿	*trail is shaded by tall pine and fir.*
DISTANCE: *15.8 miles round-trip*	

The trail to Crag Lake may just whet the appetite of those who want to get past the crowds and set a bivy for a night under the stars. Rubicon fits the bill for solitude. Hike southwest along Meeks Creek, steadily ascending to Genevieve and then Crag lakes. A side trip to Hidden Lake is not unwarranted for those who wish to be, well, hidden. But just a moderate climb past Shadow Lake and Stony Ridge Lake heads you up to the last 500 vertical feet to Rubicon Lake.

This solitude requires a permit. Make sure you have stopped at a U.S. Forest Service or Lake Tahoe Basin Management Unit visitor center to obtain a paid permit. An approved bear canister is required in most areas of the Desolation Wilderness, including Rubicon Lake.

🚶🚶 The trail is cleverly signed TRAIL at the locked green gate. Duck under or go around the barrier and walk nearly 1.5 miles on a dirt road, passing a long meadow, where you will see a marker indicating that your path is part of the Tahoe–Yosemite Trail. In another mile, as you come abreast of a small meadow, watch for the wilderness sign, a reminder that a permit is needed for overnight camping.

Cross some good spots for filling your water bottles, including one crossing on a very stout footbridge, as you ascend Meeks Creek. The trail varies from soft duff to lumpy rock and dirt to tedious sand, along with granite stairs as you climb to petite Lake Genevieve. The General Creek Trail joins from the west near the north shore of this pretty tarn. Just 0.5 miles away is Crag Lake and its long shore,

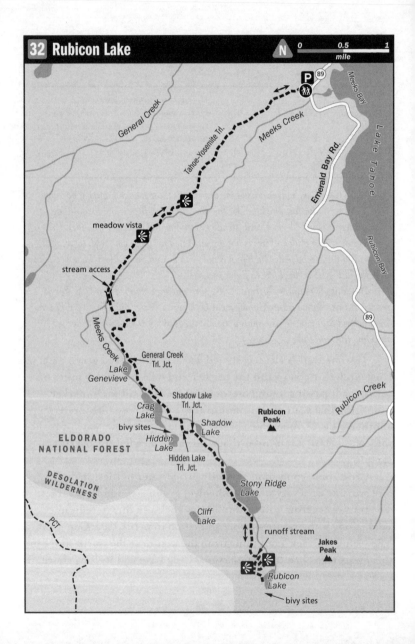

General Creek

Tahoe-Yosemite Trl.

Meeks Creek

P 89

Meeks Bay

Lake Tahoe

Emerald Bay Rd.

Rubicon Bay

meadow vista

stream access

Meeks Creek

89

General Creek
Trl. Jct.

Lake
Genevieve

Shadow Lake
Trl. Jct.

Crag
Lake

Shadow
Lake

Rubicon Creek

Rubicon
Peak

bivy sites

Hidden
Lake

ELDORADO
NATIONAL FOREST

Hidden Lake
Trl. Jct.

DESOLATION
WILDERNESS

Stony Ridge
Lake

PCT

Cliff
Lake

runoff stream

Jakes
Peak

Rubicon
Lake

bivy sites

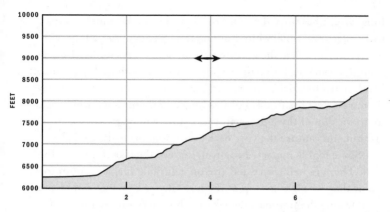

lined with red fir and western white pine over some highly impacted sites good for picnics.

Leave Crag on a sand-and-rock trail, and watch your step as you look at the rock formations across the lake. Climb gently to the south and make a lazy switchback after crossing a stream on boulders. Then look for a social trail (possibly concealed) leading down to Hidden Lake. There are a few bivy spots on the bench above Crag adjacent to Hidden Lake.

Ascend on a gentle, lodgepole-covered slope. Walk past the spur trail to Shadow Lake when you emerge from the trees. Keep above this pond, which is more like a flooded meadow, as the trail heads southeast. Within 20 minutes you will arrive at long Stony Ridge Lake sitting beneath Rubicon Peak. A small trail at the north end of the lake crosses the outlet stream and leads to good bivy sites. The western shore, has many highly impacted sites—too close to the lake and the trail for low-impact camping.

Lupine and mountain ash crowd the base of lodgepole and juniper as the somewhat marshy trail leaves Stony Ridge Lake and continues to ascend 500 feet to Rubicon. Look for surprising displays of Sierra lilies along the spongy path. As the trail leads away from this long lake, it has turned to a bit of a rut. Soon it becomes crowded with sedges and small white flowers, then passes under a huge wall of granite. Traverse the granite outcrop and cross another flower-bound stream—or butterfly magnet, if you will—where lupine, paintbrush, corn lily, daisy, aster, and bumblebees reside. Immediately, then, you start the first leg of five long and three short switchbacks up to the rim of this next tarn. Just before you reach the lake, turn around and capture the vista back down onto Stony Ridge Lake.

Some highly impacted campsites crowd the lake just below the trail. They are well concealed and on a durable surface, but unfortunately they are right on top of the lake. Better bivy sites can be found by following the trail past the lakeside boulders and granite to the saddle overlooking both Rubicon and Grouse lakes. There is also a bivy site among the boulders at the north end of the lake that may keep you out of the wind. Enjoy the stars here and follow the trail downhill mañana.

DIRECTIONS: Meeks Creek trailhead is 11.5 miles south of Tahoe City on CA 89. The trailhead parking lot is found on the west side of the road across from the Meeks Bay Campground and Marina. Park in the small dirt lot with room for about ten cars. There are no facilities here. Additional parking can be found along the highway.

GPS Trailhead Coordinates	32 Rubicon Lake
UTM Zone (WGS84)	10S
Easting	0747142
Northing	4323630
Latitude	N 39° 01.608'
Longitude	W 120° 08.704'

SCENERY: ✰ ✰ ✰ ✰ ✰	DISTANCE: *33.5 miles one-way*
TRAIL CONDITION: ✰ ✰ ✰ ✰	HIKING TIME: *2 nights*
CHILDREN: ✰	OUTSTANDING FEATURES: *Visit 8 sparkling lakes,*
DIFFICULTY: ✰ ✰ ✰ ✰	*traverse wildflower-filled meadows, and enjoy expansive*
SOLITUDE: ✰ ✰ ✰	*vistas of the Desolation Wilderness and the Crystal Range.*

Immerse yourself in the Desolation Wilderness, or at least in one of the eight mountain lakes that you visit on this three-day adventure. You will tread on both the Tahoe Rim Trail (TRT) and the Pacific Crest Trail (PCT), as they follow the same track on this hike. The first day is the longest, yet is still a moderate hike of 15 miles and about 1,000 up-and-down feet, to placid Middle Velma Lake. Day two starts with a brief climb to Fontanillis and Dicks lakes and then begins a switchbacking climb to cross Dicks Pass. One word: vistas. *Descend and pass more liquid gems, dazzlingly bright in the light reflected from the surrounding granite. Camp near Lake Aloha and enjoy an easy day's hike along Aloha, passing three more lakes on your way downhill to Echo Lakes. This hike enters the Desolation Wilderness at Lost Corner Mountain and so requires a wilderness permit stating the location of your first night's camp.*

🏃🏃 Use the picnic table under the trees at the trailhead to recheck and reassemble your gear as well as to affix your permit to your backpack. (Rangers will check for permits and they do escort unpermitted hikers out via the closest trailhead.) If you are missing a map, stop at the trailhead kiosk and pick up one of the "green maps" provided for your safety by the Tahoe Rim Trail Association. This section of the TRT coincides with the PCT, so the grade and track are mellow and well maintained.

Dropping off the road like a skater into a bowl, you begin by circumnavigating the open mouth of the basin, called Cothrin Cove. If only the trail could traverse the upper rim of this snow bowl, then the

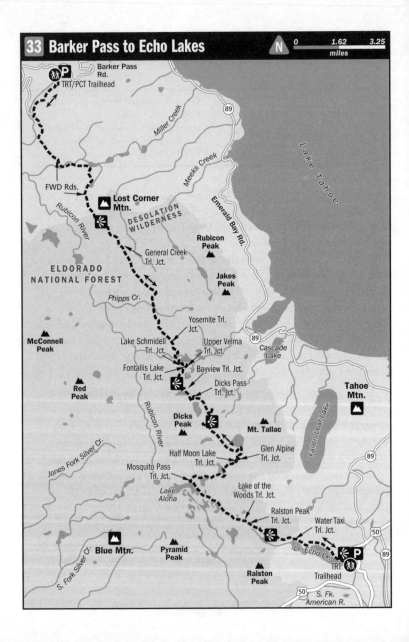

N

0   1.62   3.25
miles

Barker Pass Rd.
TRT/PCT Trailhead

89

Miller Creek

Meeks Creek

Lake Tahoe

FWD Rds.

Rubicon River

Lost Corner Mtn.

DESOLATION WILDERNESS

General Creek Trl. Jct.

Rubicon Peak

Emerald Bay Rd.

ELDORADO NATIONAL FOREST

Jakes Peak

Phipps Cr.

McConnell Peak

Yosemite Trl. Jct.

Lake Schmidell Trl. Jct.

Upper Velma Trl. Jct.

89

Cascade Lake

Fontallis Lake Trl. Jct.

Bayview Trl. Jct.

Dicks Pass Trl. Jct.

Red Peak

Rubicon River

Dicks Peak

Mt. Tallac

Tahoe Mtn.

Glen Alpine Trl. Jct.

Half Moon Lake Trl. Jct.

Fallen Leaf Lake

Jones Fork Silver Cr.

Mosquito Pass Trl. Jct.

Lake Aloha

Lake of the Woods Trl. Jct.

89

Ralston Peak Trl. Jct.

Water Taxi Trl. Jct.

50

S. Fork Silver Cr.

Blue Mtn.

Pyramid Peak

Ralston Peak

Lr. Echo Lk.

TRT Trailhead

50

S. Fk. American R.

89

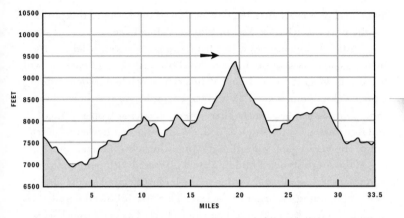

trail would be a straight line south. Alas, the PCT strives to maintain an average trail grade below 10 percent, and so a beeline would ruin the average (and cause a lot of grumbling). So around the horns of this dilemma you go, about 6 miles to Richardson Lake, nestled at the foot of Sourdough Hill. Your track descends about 650 feet and then regains about 450 feet to reach Richardson.

All of the elevation gain will be fully appreciated for, over the next few miles, the vistas of Rockbound Valley are stunning. View Rubicon Reservoir, Rockbound Lake, Buck Island Lake, and the Rubicon River as it builds coming down this lithic trench.

Your trail to the Velma Lakes area is like a roller coaster at a small summer carnival—some up, some down, and some turns but no surprises and nothing frightening. From Richardson, ascend 650 feet over 4 miles and then descend 400 feet in 2 miles. Reclaim that height in the next 1.4 miles, then lose 250 and gain 50 getting to Middle Velma Lake. Now it's cotton candy time. Look around at the plentiful choice of campsites visible above Middle Velma. To remain on the PCT/TRT pathway, this lake is your choice. If you don't mind straying off this described route, there are other options for your bivy site. For a more detailed description of the route to this point, see the next hike, Barker Pass to Middle Velma Lake.

Middle Velma has easy access from two popular trailheads, so it invites small crowds of day hikers to its shores. Although I have not had feet on the ground there, Lower Velma can be reached by descending Upper Velma's outlet creek about 150 feet to the granite shores, where some solitude can be gained. There are other sites at Upper Velma and its unnamed companion as well. So, depending on where you set camp, alternate routes will still keep you ultimately on track.

If the south shore of Middle Velma is arrayed with tents and you don't want to lose elevation going to the lower lake, walk to the junction at the southeast corner of the lake. This hike follows the trail south to Fontanillis Lake and then east to Dicks Lake and over Dicks Pass. To camp in the vicinity of Upper Velma, walk about 200 yards east, following the marker to the Bayview Trail. The next junction marks a trail to your right that leads to Upper Velma Lake, which I have not explored. The trail rounds the lake, crossing the inlet at its south end and then follows the base of the moraine that parallels Fontanillis.

If you want to proceed from the Upper Velma–Bayview junction another 250 yards to explore campsites around the unnamed lake, be assured that you have another alternate route that will not let you miss Dicks Pass. Now on the Bayview Trail, heading east, a large log will help you cross the outlet stream, which has widened into a small pond here. The marshy end of this lake will soon come into view on your right. You can exit the trail as you head around the easternmost node of the lake. Juniper, white pine, lodgepole, and fir are scattered around this secluded lake.

To resume your hike from this unnamed lake, you could always return to the Fontanillis–Bayview junction and continue on the PCT. Or you can continue east on the Bayview Trail to the junction with the trail to Dicks Lake at about 8,240 feet elevation. As you hike to that body of water, you will pass the intersection of the trail coming

Hal Moon and Alta Morris lakes sit beneath Dicks Pass.

around the south end of Upper Velma; 0.25 miles past that point is
the junction with the PCT/TRT heading south across Dicks Pass.

But if you take either of those alternates, you will miss two spectacular lakes and some wonderful vistas. So leave the Velma Lakes
area by way of the trail leading to Fontanillis Lake. The uphill grind
is abated by the pleasant shade of red fir and lodgepole pine above
the mellow switchbacks.

Fontanillis sports no more than a few dozen trees, mostly at the
north end, where one could siesta but not camp. The trail requires
watching as you cross the outlet stream heading into Upper Velma.
But before you continue across the channel, stop for a photo of
the terrain and lakes spread before you, all the way to Lake Tahoe.

Granite reaching out from the flanks of Dicks Peak both intrudes on and encloses Fontanillis' waters. The trail skirts the boggy boulder field around the lake and then heads away on a southeast bearing toward Dicks Lake. A scant half-mile of rocky trail leads you to Dicks Lake, where a junction marker points you north on the trail for Dicks Pass. So, take a left unless you need to filter water, which you could easily do 200 feet over at the lake.

Don't be alarmed by heading northwest away from the lake, as you will hit another junction to Dicks Pass in barely 0.25 miles. This rocky saddle offers a vista onto Lake Tahoe before turning away to the east to begin your zigzag ascent. Views onto the lake from the shaded trail are more awesome with each small elevation gain. The switchbacks are fairly easy and not steep; even so, wooden stairs assist at the hardest spots.

Reaching the open saddle at Dicks Pass, you have vistas to Castle Peak and Sierra Buttes. The sandy trail across the pass heads through hemlock that have been windswept and stunted. This is a great place to take a break—with vistas and sunshine all around, you can look down on Half Moon and Alta Morris lakes, off to Susie Lake, out to Lake Aloha with Pyramid Peak and Mount Price visible beyond it and over to Dicks Peak much closer at hand.

The next 2.3 miles sees your trail dropping about 1,000 feet to the shores of Gilmore Lake. Begin descending from the pass on rocky trail on this scree-covered slope, where switchbacks lead you through hemlock and willow to small, colorful meadows. On this wet, south-facing slope, you will see yellow monkey flower, fireweed, gentian, paintbrush, asters, and yarrow as you find a spot to relax overlooking Half Moon Lake. Level out under the scattered lodge-pole pines as you approach Gilmore Lake from the south. Nathan Gilmore discovered the mineral waters at Glen Alpine Springs and he also pastured his sheep and angora goats in this area. With easy access to filter water and take a dip, this is a fine spot to take lunch.

Retreat from Gilmore by heading south on the trail leading to Glen Alpine, loosely following the outlet stream from this round lake. A couple of junctions ahead will cause some head-scratching, but that's why you have a map. At the first marked junction, a trail leads acutely to the right and heads to Half Moon Lake. About 25 feet down the trail is another marked junction, this time for the Glen Alpine Trail, which goes left where your trail to Lake Aloha heads right.

When you reach the next marker about 200 feet below you, it may seem like déjà-vu, but just follow the marker's arrow to the right for Aloha, Susie, and Heather lakes. Cross the double stream here on the ample boulders provided and begin ascending the moraine on Susie Lake's east side. Your trail continues in its southwesterly direction from the point where you first approach the lake. You just have to walk around this watery obstacle to get to that point just behind those islands. The trail stays above the shore level until after crossing the lake's outlet. You'll spot many shaded spots along the heather-lined shore that are appropriate for filtering water or having a siesta, but they are too close for camping. Round the lake's southern shore and the trail will slide by the island-bearing cove just before heading uphill toward Heather Lake.

A brief climb of less than 150 feet will take you to a traverse under steep slopes to Heather Lake. Approach the lake at the mouth, where a blaze has been long ago carved into the lodgepole standing sentry here. You won't be faulted for looking up twice to the right just to make sure all that talus stays in place. (Don't wiggle that "one" rock.) Ringed by solid and decaying granite, Heather Lake is graced with trees only at its inlets. There is no good camping near Heather, but there are excellent sites on the rock well above its western shore. The ever-popular granite stairs help you ascend the 250 feet to overlook Lake Aloha. The trail to Mosquito Pass traverses the northern shore of Aloha and leads across the pass to Clyde Lake and Rockbound Valley.

This area above the lake but below the trail can offer some private bivy spots, but finding shelter from the wind is another matter. Good bivy sites are available on the granite slopes to the east of the PCT as it parallels the lake. Waking up just as the sun just strikes the peaks that tower over Aloha—Pyramid, Agassiz, and Price—is a memorable moment. Day three begins by roughly paralleling Aloha's shore on a rocky trail.

As you walk beneath Cracked Crag along the rock-lined path to the southeast, you may realize how the permit fees that you paid actually impact the wilderness. Of the many trail junctions, stream crossings, and steep slopes that the PCT and TRT encounter, I have found only one unmarked junction, and that is near the end of Lake Aloha. Immediately after entering trees, look for a junction marked by a blank post. Do not continue along in the trees bordering the lake. Rather, turn uphill on the obvious angled path that leads to Lakes Lucille and Margery. (Continuing straight would have taken you slightly out of the way to Lake of the Woods. There are many intersecting paths in this area, so a mistake in navigation is understandable and not too difficult to recover from.)

This long, gently sloping path was voted as the most pleasant section of trail of the day. Several junctions over the course of the next 0.5 miles offer tempting destinations, but you can just keep going straight toward Echo Lakes. Pass the trails to Lucille, Margery, Aloha, and Lake of the Woods, catching an occasional glimpse of Mount Tallac to the north. This traverse offers you time to slow down, not work so hard, and enjoy the flowers that foretell the upcoming Haypress Meadows. Skirt the top of the meadow just after passing the last Aloha trail, then pass through a copse of conifers surrounding the path to Lake of the Woods.

Cross the meadow and begin a gentle descent, bypassing the left-hand junction of the trail leading across the slope to Triangle Lake. The PCT/TRT now begins descending in earnest, beginning with a well-placed pair of switchbacks. Your views of Tamarack, Cagwin, and Ralston lakes and their surrounding peaks do nothing but improve over the next half-mile. Your superb vista onto Tamarack is eclipsed by a down-canyon view to the east of Upper and Lower Echo lakes. After all cameras are stowed, cross a stone bridge to enter a stand of lodgepole on a dirt-and-duff trail.

Your continued descent crosses more stoneworks and passes another link to Triangle Lake before exiting the Desolation Wilderness. As you approach the north end of Upper Echo Lake, you are able to leave the exposed rock and enjoy the shade of tall lodgepole, to which early settlers mistakenly ascribed the appellation of tamarack. Attached to one of these high above the trail is a small marker signaling the trail down to the small dock and a phone for the Echo Lakes water taxi. This is an easily missed trail, so watch for it if you really want to spring for the $10 fare to save a 5-mile hike. (There is a $30 minimum as well. It's a nice hike.)

Stone culverts contain some of the several runoff streams that sneak down from the left. As you traverse to the east for the next 0.6 miles, the tread remains about 300 feet from the shore and about 100 feet above it. Reaching a high point above the channel separating the upper from the lower, the trail turns to give a view of Flagpole Peak above Lower Echo. The PCT stays above a local path useful only to the cabin owners below. Pass an intersection that leads down to these cabins and stay on the higher trail.

When the trail ascends about as high above lake level as it is going to, your granite path becomes narrower but still safe. In fact, you can see that the safety railings have long ago been cut away. This is a dicey spot during winter travel. About 0.25 miles ahead, almost directly underneath Flagpole Peak, is another pair of descending switchbacks followed by an innocuous junction with the lower trail to the cabins. With the thought of having a cold milkshake at the Echo Lake Chalet firmly in your mind, the last mile to the lake's outlet should be even easier along this level, granite-and-sand path.

Before descending to the lake level, continue ahead to the obvious vista point looking out to Lake Tahoe in the north and Freel Peak in the east. Walk downhill, bypassing any turns until you reach the bottom where the trail passes by the TRT kiosk on the right. Follow the shaded path to the outlet where you can cross on an open metal walkway. The chalet is on the left and cold drinks are served there daily. To reach Echo Summit, follow the signs for the pathway near the pit toilets.

DIRECTIONS: Starting in Tahoe City, drive south on CA 89 for 4.2 miles to Blackwood Canyon Road. Marked with signs for a snow park and the Kaspian Campground, this turn is 0.6 miles north of Tahoe Pines and 22.9 miles from South Lake Tahoe.

Turn west and drive 2.3 miles west. Jog to the left, where Forest Road 15N38 continues straight ahead. Drive across the bridge spanning Blackwood Creek and jog to the right, then 4.7 miles southwest up Barker Pass Road/FR 3. The trailhead parking is ahead on the right, about 0.5 miles after the pavement ends.

There is a small parking lot with room for about a dozen cars, a pit toilet, and a TRT information kiosk with maps, but no trash receptacles. Two picnic tables and a decent area for tents is adjacent for PCT hikers to crash and prepare their packs.

The signed trailhead is across the road from the end of the parking lot driveway.

GPS Trailhead Coordinates	33 Barker Pass to Echo Lakes
UTM Zone (WGS84)	10S
Easting	0739186
Northing	4328913
Latitude	N 39° 04.594'
Longitude	W 120° 14.101'

34 Barker Pass to Middle Velma Lake

SCENERY: ✿ ✿ ✿ ✿ ✿	HIKING TIME: *18 hours (overnight)*
TRAIL CONDITION: ✿ ✿ ✿ ✿	OUTSTANDING FEATURES: *Hike along the Pacific*
CHILDREN: ✿ ✿	*Crest Trail, the Tahoe Rim Trail, and the Tahoe–*
DIFFICULTY: ✿ ✿ ✿ ✿	*Yosemite Trail as they all lead to one of the most*
SOLITUDE: ✿ ✿ ✿ ✿	*beautiful lakes in the Desolation Wilderness.*
DISTANCE: *30.2 miles round-trip*	

Velma Lakes are popular on summer weekends because they are close to Eagle Falls and the trail from Eagle Lake, but if you have a chance to arrive midweek, you may have the waters to yourself. The trail is a long roller coaster through forest and rock with plenty of streams, springs, lakes, and meadows decorated with wildflowers. You will be hiking and camping overnight in the Desolation Wilderness, so you'll need a permit, available at the U.S. Forest Service Taylor Creek Visitor Center. Navigation is easy on this southbound trek, as you never leave the Pacific Crest Trail and there are relatively few distracting junctions.

🚶🚶 Pick up a map provided by the Tahoe Rim Trail Association at the kiosk, tighten your buckles, and step off the edge of dusty Barker Pass Road. Head downhill across the first meadow, where a few springs provoke a word of thanks for Gore-Tex. Larkspur, paintbrush, columbine, and elderberry are prolific in the meadows along this downhill traverse. Turn to the southwest at another small meadow and reenter the forest for a moment until crossing another small meadow. The bright-green mosslike plant adorning the trees is wolf lichen and it grows readily on red firs.

Pass by Barker Meadow just before you come abreast of Barker Creek and, shortly, Bear Lake Road as well. Stay nearly parallel to it for about 0.5 miles as you curve around the northern horn of the basin called Cothrin Cove, below Bear Lake. Cross this same off-highway vehicle (OHV) track after about 2.2 miles from the trailhead. A quick

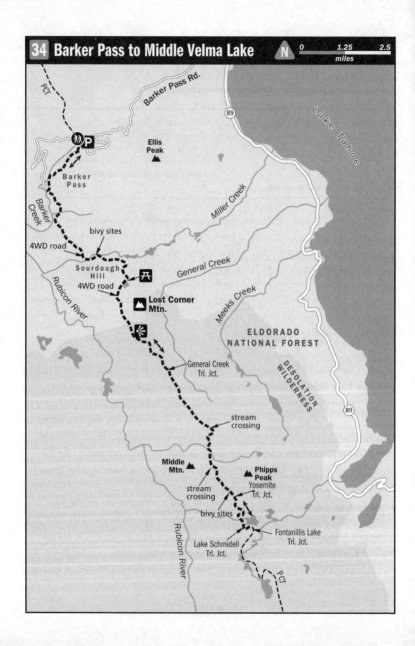

PCT

Barker Pass Rd.

89

Lake Tahoe

P

Ellis Peak

Barker Pass

Barker Creek

bivy sites

4WD road

Sourdough Hill

4WD road

Miller Creek

General Creek

Lost Corner Mtn.

Rubicon River

Meeks Creek

ELDORADO NATIONAL FOREST

General Creek Trl. Jct.

DESOLATION WILDERNESS

89

stream crossing

Middle Mtn.

Phipps Peak Yosemite Trl. Jct.

stream crossing

bivy sites

Fontanillis Lake Trl. Jct.

Rubicon River

Lake Schmidell Trl. Jct.

PCT

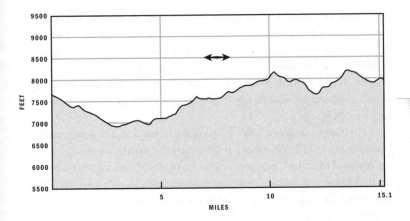

jog left and jag right picks up the trail leading to a crossing of Bear
Lake's outlet 0.4 miles ahead.

The dirt-and-duff trail continues around the southern horn,
heading about 1.5 miles to a crossing of the Rubicon-McKinney
OHV Road, which leads down to Tahoma. It is, according to the
sign, 4 miles back to Barker Pass and 9 miles to Twin Peaks. Go
straight across the road and follow an easterly course on the sandy
trail bordered by boulders. Head southeast 675 feet to a crossing of
Miller Creek, where you will find acceptable bivy spots to the left on
the west side of the creek.

Traverse slightly uphill as you head east, navigating around Sourdough Hill. The trees block any view of it or of Miller Meadows, about
200 yards from the trail. Climb to the south around and over the feet
of Sourdough Hill on the way to a lunchtime break at compact Richardson Lake, about 0.5 miles after the trail turns south away from
Miller Creek. Richardson Lake is accessible by off-highway vehicles,
and the impact here shows heavy traffic but respectful practices.

Depart your poolside café and traverse southwest along the side
of Sourdough again. Cross the OHV road at the signpost in the

middle of the saddle and begin an uphill traverse, gaining about 425 feet over the next 3.25 miles. With Lost Corner Mountain on your left shoulder, you will start to notice good vistas of the Desolation Wilderness at just about the time that you pass the wilderness boundary. Enjoy the views down to Rockbound Lake and Rubicon Reservoir and then to the Crystal Range from Tells and McConnell to Silver and Red Peaks.

The General Creek Trail intersects this track at about 9.2 miles from the trailhead. The sharp left turn to the north can lead 2.4 miles down to Lake Genevieve and then to the Meeks Creek trailhead. This would make a good destination for a shuttle trip day hike. However, the described trail continues about 5.5 miles to Middle Velma Lake.

From this junction, ascend about 1 more mile (how often have you heard that one?). The duff trail will then descend about 1.25 miles to two streams, passing a couple of small meadows on the way. Another 0.75 miles brings you to a fairly businesslike crossing of Phipps Creek followed by a brief, rocky uphill. Then you'll begin an easy southward traverse beneath red fir and lodgepole pine.

Phipps Peak stands above your hat brim as you head southeast on this forested trail. Huge, granite boulders crowd the stream crossing 0.3 miles ahead. From there, the climb is less than 400 feet to some possible bivy sites under the trees. Follow the trail 0.2 miles, where the Tahoe–Yosemite Trail joins from the northeast. Descend almost 275 feet on the winding PCT, going south about 0.85 miles where a causeway assists you across a marshy area with graying standing snags piercing the blue sky.

Ascend slightly and pass the west end of the lake as you head south. Be alert for the signed trail junction leading to Camper Flat and Lake Schmidell. Turn east and head to the south shore of the lake where you'll find numerous sites to set tent or bivy. As tempting as it is, the lakeside areas are highly impacted and generally not sanctioned as campsites. The granite slopes above the shore offer excellent choices.

Return the way you came after a couple of days of midweek solitude. If you have a shuttle car, an alternate exit is to take the Velma Lakes Trail 1 mile to the southeast and 0.7 miles east to a junction with the Eagle Lake Trail and the Bayview Trail. Depending on where you want to leave a shuttle, either route offers an excellent departure from the wilderness.

DIRECTIONS: Starting in Tahoe City, drive south on CA 89 for 4.2 miles to Blackwood Canyon Road. Marked with signs for a snow park and the Kaspian Campground, this turn is 0.6 miles north of Tahoe Pines and 22.9 miles from South Lake Tahoe.

Drive 2.3 miles west and jog to the left where Forest Road 15N38 continues straight ahead. Drive across the bridge spanning Blackwood Creek and jog to the right, then 4.7 miles southwest up Barker Pass Road/FR 3. The trailhead parking is ahead on the right, about 0.5 miles after the pavement ends.

There is a small parking lot with room for about a dozen cars, a pit toilet, and a Tahoe Rim Trail information kiosk with maps, but no trash receptacles. PCT hikers can fiddle with their packs at the two picnic tables near a semi-decent area for tents.

The signed trailhead is across the road from the end of the parking lot driveway.

GPS TRAILHEAD COORDINATES	34 BARKER PASS TO MIDDLE VELMA LAKE
UTM Zone (WGS84)	10S
Easting	0739186
Northing	4328913
Latitude	N 39° 04.594'
Longitude	W 120° 14.101'

35 Ellis Peak

SCENERY: ✿ ✿ ✿	DISTANCE: *6.4 miles round-trip*
TRAIL CONDITION: ✿ ✿ ✿	HIKING TIME: *3.5 hours*
CHILDREN: ✿	OUTSTANDING FEATURES: *Panoramic vistas of Lake*
DIFFICULTY: ✿ ✿ ✿	*Tahoe from Crystal Bay to Pope Beach; awesome vistas*
SOLITUDE: ✿	*into the Desolation Wilderness*

This easily navigated route begins with a stiff half-mile uphill to an open ridge filled with vistas, then traverses across a forested slope before a final easy ascent to the summit. The only distraction on this trail is that it is open to motorbikes.

Your fir-shaded trailhead makes the pathway seem quite inviting, but it quickly gets your attention with switchbacks and boulder stairs that help you gain about 450 feet in the next 0.5 miles. The dirt-and-rock trail levels out momentarily when you emerge from the hemlock and fir. Less than 500 feet to the southeast lies a sloped meadow clad in yellow-capped woolly mule's ears, blue lupine, golden buckwheat, and yellow-eyed asters, all backdropped by the Desolation Wilderness.

Your trail continues climbing another 0.5 miles to the southeast on this ridge above bowl-shaped Cothrin Cove. The dirt-and-scree trail hugs close to several lithic leftovers, close enough to capture digital memories of eerily sheer drops. By the time you reach the 1-mile point, your windblown trail will flatten before, in another 0.25 miles, it begins descending to the southeast through a white pine and red fir forest.

Just shy of the 2-mile mark, you'll cross a broad saddle and pass to the left of a small meadow as the trail assumes a broad tread—probably a logging road—which then traverses the slope. The evidence of past logging is all around, which explains this large stand of single-species conifers.

35 Ellis Peak

N
0
1,000
2,000
feet
Ellis Peak
cairn
Ellis Lake
Ellis Lake Rd.
Blackwood Creek
ELDORADO NATIONAL FOREST
Middle Fork Blackwood Creek
DESOLATION WILDERNESS
Barker Pass Rd.
P

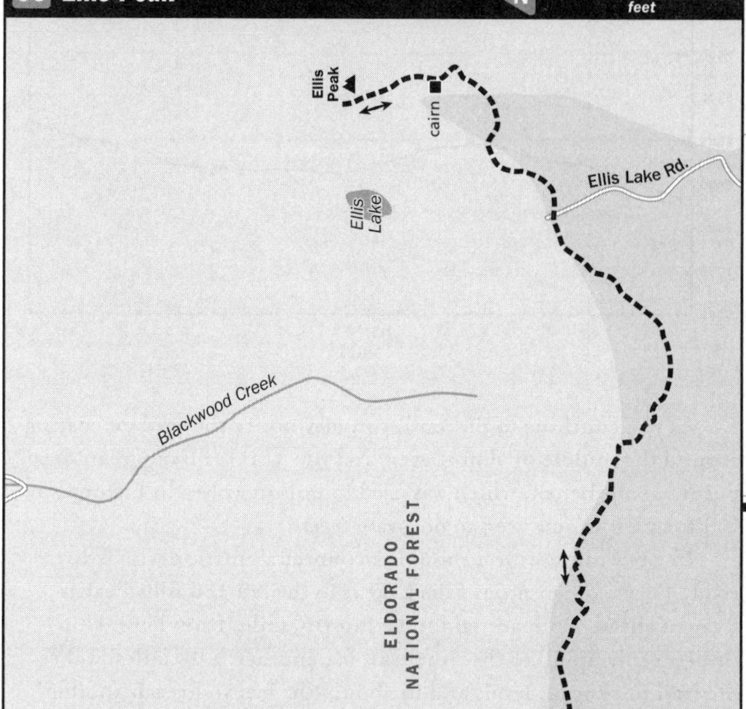

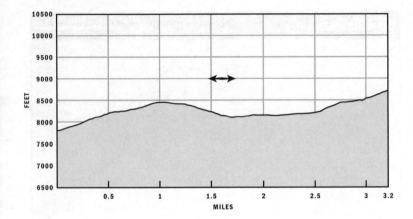

As you continue to descend, you may notice the verdant coating around the middle of almost every red fir. This brilliant green decoration is wolf lichen, which was used to poison wolves in Europe; in California it is now used to decorate trees.

In a few minutes you should encounter a junction with a dirt road. There, a sign notes Ellis Lake is to the left and Ellis Peak is straight ahead. Both are said to be just 0.5 miles from here. Continue steeply uphill to the northeast for another 0.25 miles, where the trail once again levels and in about 500 feet you reach another junction with a dirt road.

Follow the road around to the left; it will lead you to the south end of the Ellis Peak ridge. Look to the right (at about 2 o'clock) for a cairn marking the summit trail, which skirts the east face of the ridge before climbing the rocky trail to the summit.

The lodgepole pine and mountain hemlock clinging to the summit and its slopes testify to the persistent wind direction and ferocity. Tree and slope alike are scoured by the wind over this ridge. Take shelter in one of the rock windbreaks as you snap pictures from above

Homewood. Your view of Lake Tahoe is from north Carnelian and Agate bays to Freel Peak past South Lake Tahoe. Loon Lake is just visible on the western horizon, and tree-ringed Ellis Lake is nestled right below.

DIRECTIONS: From CA 89, turn west onto Blackwood Canyon Road. Marked with signs for a snow park and the Kaspian Campground, this turn is 4.5 miles south of Tahoe City and 0.6 miles north of Tahoe Pines. Drive 2.3 miles west and jog to the left, where Forest Road 15N38 continues straight ahead. Drive across the bridge spanning Blackwood Creek and jog to the right, then 4.7 miles southwest up Barker Pass Road/FR 3. Just after the pavement ends, look for a small dirt parking area above the road to the left. You can park here in front of the trailhead, where there is room for about a dozen cars, or find a spot along the road.

GPS TRAILHEAD COORDINATES	35 ELLIS PEAK
UTM Zone (WGS84)	10S
Easting	0739537
Northing	4328391
Latitude	N 39° 04.307'
Longitude	W 120° 13.869'

36 Barker Pass to Twin Peaks

SCENERY: ☆ ☆ ☆	HIKING TIME: *6 hours*
TRAIL CONDITION: ☆ ☆ ☆	OUTSTANDING FEATURES: *Outstanding vistas of*
CHILDREN: ☆ ☆	*Lake Tahoe, the Desolation Wilderness, and the Granite*
DIFFICULTY: ☆ ☆ ☆	*Chief Wilderness. Meadows are covered with wildflowers*
SOLITUDE: ☆ ☆ ☆	*fed by the many runoff streams.*
DISTANCE: *11.4 miles round-trip*	

This hike follows the Pacific Crest Trail (PCT) and Tahoe Rim Trail (TRT) until they diverge near your destination. It has its ups and downs, literally. For about the first 1.5 miles from the trailhead, gain 600 feet, then lose 475 feet of it over an equivalent distance, only to repeat the first process with another zigzagging 750-foot climb over about 2.3 miles to approach the summit. Then another 200 feet of vertical travel over 500 feet will hoist you to the summit, where the views all around are incredible.

Whether you're day-hiking or camping overnight, a permit is required in the Granite Chief Wilderness.

🏃 After you have re-sorted your gear and snacked at the picnic table, read the interpretive display, picked up a green TRT map, and visited the pit toilet, it's time to hit the trail and head west. Start out overlooking Barker Creek Basin as you head around to the northwest, circling the peak named after a local pioneering rancher.

After 0.8 miles, one stream crossing, and one logging-road crossing, get your cameras ready for a beautiful vista to the east of Lake Tahoe, looking down the tree-filled trough called Blackwood Canyon. Fair campsites can be found nearby, where a social trail intersects the PCT/TRT.

Climb to a tiny meadow on a dirt-and-duff trail leading to a three-section causeway across the wettest area of this flower magnet. Indian paintbrush, corn lily, and lupine color the ground here. The dirt trail soon turns to rock as you climb across a lightly treed scree

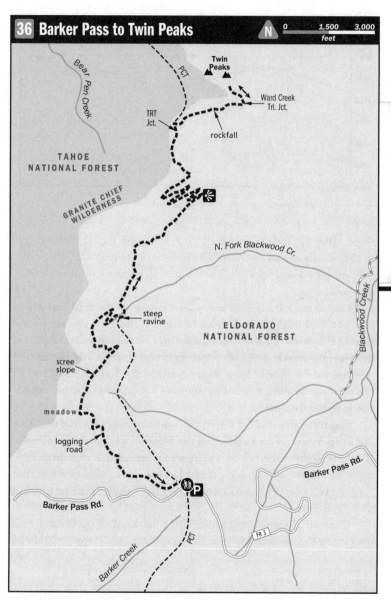

Bear Pen Creek

PCT

Twin Peaks

Ward Creek Trl. Jct.

TRT Jct.

rockfall

TAHOE NATIONAL FOREST

GRANITE CHIEF WILDERNESS

N. Fork Blackwood Cr.

Blackwood Creek

steep ravine

ELDORADO NATIONAL FOREST

scree slope

meadow

logging road

Barker Pass Rd.

Barker Pass Rd.

P

FR 3

Barker Creek

PCT

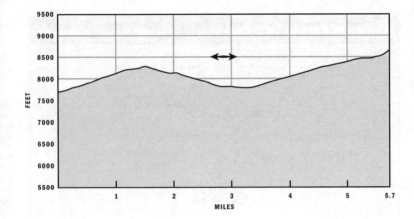

slope. After 1.5 miles, you have a great view onto the lake from right in the middle of this rockfest. The path heads toward a knob of red volcanic scoria and rock. Follow the trail sign to pass to the west of this knob.

Checkerspot butterflies may escort you down the trail along long switchbacks down into and across a ravine. Runoff streams are plentiful in this large, glacially excavated sluice. Fireweed and larkspur decorate the trail at every wet crossing as you descend and recross the meadow on a couple of long, loopy switchbacks. Near the bottom of the meadow, around 2.5 miles, you have a good view of some impressive volcanic structures.

Continue descending until you come skidding to a halt next to the steep-sided ravine containing the North Fork Blackwood Creek. Contour to the north across a steep slope, stepping across three more runoff streams pouring down from the walls of rock above the trail. As you take switchbacks down, vistas of Tahoe continue to tempt photographers.

Contour along without much effort on this duff trail beneath the cover of cone-laden firs for the next 0.5 miles. Cross a rockfall on a steep slope and then ascend a bit to the first of six switchbacks. There is another view of the lake from this first turn. These gently graded switchbacks weave across the slope, staying in the shade of firs up to near the ridge.

Round the corner coming over a ridge of an unnamed peak to, once again, spy your uphill destination. Traverse the north-facing slope and your dirt trail crosses the boundary of the Granite Chief Wilderness. Who has the permit? Within a few hundred feet, you will have another photo opportunity. Follow along as the trail traverses this exposed ridgetop with its vistas to the west. Enter the cover of firs again before the PCT and TRT diverge in 0.2 miles. Keep to the right at the signed trail junction, and head uphill with the dual summits over your left shoulder.

Pass beneath the debris of these two pointed monoliths—summit dandruff—for the next 0.5 miles. The summit trail's junction with the TRT is at the southeastern ridge of the hill. The TRT continues immediately downhill on tight switchbacks while the summit trail turns left through tobacco brush, to the northwest, and climbs across the manzanita-speckled slope to the ridge. Walk steeply up along the edge of the drop-off until the obvious trail disappears.

To gain either summit requires Class 3 climbing skills—basically using hands and feet along with good balance. To reach the east summit, cross to the west through the fir trees. Leave the ridge and head to the talus-and-boulder rockfall below the summit. No trail marks the final ascent to the summit. Serpentine across the rock pile to make your way up. Vistas reach out to Dicks Peak in the Desolation Wilderness and Ward's Peak, Granite Chief, and Squaw Peak as well as the blue water of Lake Tahoe below Homewood across to Freel Peak at the southeast corner of the lake.

DIRECTIONS: Starting in Tahoe City, drive south on CA 89 for 4.2 miles to Blackwood Canyon Road. Marked with signs for a snow park and the Kaspian Campground, this turn is 0.6 miles north of Tahoe Pines and 22.9 miles from South Lake Tahoe.

Drive 2.3 miles west and jog to the left where Forest Road 15N38 continues straight ahead. Drive across the bridge spanning Blackwood Creek and jog to the right, then 4.7 miles southwest up Barker Pass Road/FR 3. The trailhead is ahead on the right, about 0.5 miles after the pavement ends.

The trailhead is adjacent to a small parking lot with room for about a dozen cars. There is a pit toilet and a Tahoe Rim Trail information kiosk with maps, but no trash receptacles. There are two picnic tables that are handy for hikers with last minute gear adjustments.

GPS TRAILHEAD COORDINATES	36 BARKER PASS TO TWIN PEAKS
UTM Zone (WGS84)	10S
Easting	0739171
Northing	4328969
Latitude	N 39° 04.624'
Longitude	W 120° 14.110'

37 Ward Creek to Twin Peaks

SCENERY: ☆ ☆ ☆ ☆	DISTANCE: *12 miles round-trip*
TRAIL CONDITION: ☆ ☆ ☆ ☆	HIKING TIME: *5–6 hours*
CHILDREN: ☆	OUTSTANDING FEATURES: *360-degree vistas of*
DIFFICULTY: ☆ ☆ ☆ ☆	*Granite Chief Wilderness and Lake Tahoe; relatively*
SOLITUDE: ☆ ☆ ☆	*moderate hiking; meadow after meadow of flowers*

This brief segment of the Tahoe Rim Trail (TRT) climbs to the margin of the Granite Chief Wilderness and sneaks breathtaking views of it and Lake Tahoe from above Tahoe Pines and Homewood. A leisurely walk up the old road leads to a trail that continues up Ward Creek Canyon. Cross it and stay above its east bank before leaving it on switchbacks. Approaching the peaks from this direction gives a new perspective on this pair of rocks. Climb to the rim of the forested cirque and navigate around it to the easternmost horn of rock. A Class 3 scramble leads to excellent vistas past Barker Peak to the south and north across Ward Peak.

🚶🚶 This section of the TRT leads back to Tahoe City or forward to join the Pacific Crest Trail (PCT) on the west side of Twin Peaks. Pick up a green map and walk past the locked gate on the dirt-and-gravel road. About 200 feet along is a kiosk with information regarding the Ward Creek riparian zone and stream habitat. Another similar kiosk stands 0.4 miles ahead.

The road passes through a lodgepole and Jeffrey pine forest for about 1.8 miles and bumps into a dirt mound with a marker for Twin Peaks. Cross a stream immediately after this reassuring signpost, which is about 0.45 miles away from a bridge crossing Ward Creek. Just before reaching the bridge, step across another small stream. The bridge is marked with a plaque on the north side and a path down to the creek on the south side.

A direction change to the southwest leads you past a small meadow just as you begin to parallel the creek. Although unseen through the

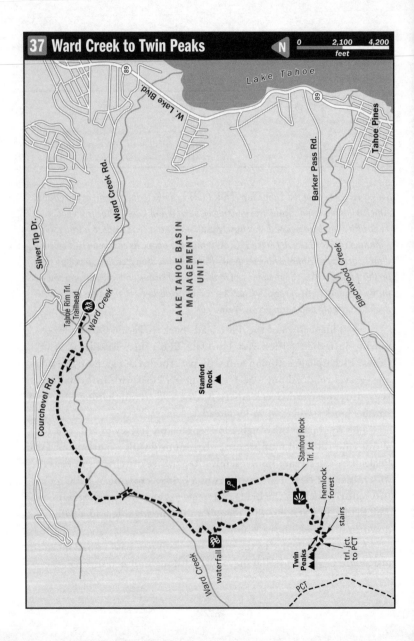

N

0   2,100   4,200
feet

Lake Tahoe

W. Lake Blvd.

89

89

Barker Pass Rd.

Tahoe Pines

Silver Tip Dr.

Ward Creek Rd.

Tahoe Rim Trl. Trailhead

Ward Creek

Courchevel Rd.

LAKE TAHOE BASIN MANAGEMENT UNIT

Blackwood Creek

Stanford Rock

Stanford Rock Trl. Jct

hemlock forest

stairs

Ward Creek

waterfall

Twin Peaks

trl. jct. to PCT

PCT

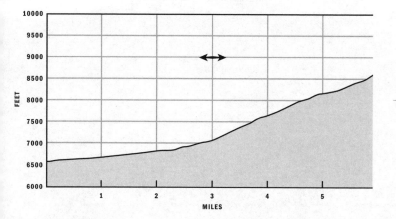

trees, the frogs and birds along the stream make their presence known to hikers. Woolly mule's ears populate the next small meadow, which is made all the more special with its fringe of aspens adding music to the air. Continue southwest among the fir trees.

Cross a couple of streams as you traverse 0.8 miles from the bridge to the first switchback. Enter the cirque and the trail turns away from the creek, beginning to gain meaningful elevation. Look for a small waterfall that can be seen from the stone stairs at the end of the second switchback. Above that, the rocky trail crosses a sloped meadow, thick with mule's ears, aster, and lupine. The trail enters and exits the same meadow at each higher switchback. Repeat the flower displays at each one.

Now, at about 7,300 feet and with your destination in sight, head toward it and then turn on a long, circuitous path away from it. Continue climbing to the south briefly and begin a swing around to the east followed by a lazy turn to the north, climbing across one meadow after another. These meadows all seem to be fed by a spring next to the trail on the next southeast leg, which carries you about

The aptly named Twin Peaks

0.5 miles to the ridge and a junction with the trail to Stanford Rock.
This point is about 5 miles away from the trailhead.

Follow the outline of the cirque, stopping along the way to
take pictures to the north and into the maw of this glacial remnant.
About 500 feet shy of the summit, just after making a sharp right
turn, the hemlocks become so thick that the trail at noon is in
complete shade. That is, however, a real comfort as the trail climbs
and switches back across the slope. Some stone stairs help you up
through a particularly steep section of the forest just before you
reach a brief plateau.

The TRT separates from this route just about 300 feet beneath
the summit, then continues to the left to join the PCT southward.
Your obvious route climbs through the tobacco brush and manzanita

and across the rocky slope littered with random mule's ears. Just after you pass the fallen white pine, Lake Tahoe appears above the trees. Fir and hemlock crowd the way as you edge closer to the north, right up to the rim. The dirt trail climbs a bit on this edge and when it reaches the largest hemlock, you veer to the left to the talus rockfall beneath the summit. Cross the talus to the west and then work back up to the east to gain the windy summit. Pictures taken, this is not a summit for relaxing on, so retreat the way you entered.

DIRECTIONS: From South Lake Tahoe, drive 24.8 miles north on CA 89 to Pineland Drive on the left. Signs on the highway for an RV village are a large landmark. Drive west, by turning left on Pineland, which will soon (0.4 miles) turn into Ward Creek Boulevard. Park in any small pullout on the left, 2.2 miles from the highway. This is hard to see, so watch your odometer closely.

Pineland Drive is 2.3 miles south of Tahoe City. Turn right on Pineland and head west 2.2 miles. The trailhead is just off the road at the Tahoe Rim Trail marker and informational kiosk. Pick up a map here before embarking.

There are no facilities at this trailhead.

GPS TRAILHEAD COORDINATES	37 WARD CREEK TO TWIN PEAKS
UTM Zone (WGS84)	10S
Easting	0742707
Northing	4336120
Latitude	N 39° 08.428'
Longitude	W 120° 11.507'

38 Mount Judah Loop

SCENERY: ✿ ✿ ✿ ✿	DISTANCE: 5.2 miles round-trip
TRAIL CONDITION: ✿ ✿ ✿	HIKING TIME: 3.5 hours
CHILDREN: ✿ ✿ ✿	OUTSTANDING FEATURES: Views over Donner Lake
DIFFICULTY: ✿ ✿ ✿	and Shallenberger Ridge; vistas from Castle Peak to
SOLITUDE: ✿ ✿	Anderson Peak

Mount Judah is one of those rare attractions that seem to have it all for a quick adventure fix: trailhead conveniently close to the highway; a well-tended trail that is only moderately difficult; beautiful vistas of the lakes, mountains, and wilderness terrain; and very little backtracking.

Your route takes you 2.6 miles from the trailhead to the summit, gaining nearly 1,200 feet in elevation.

🚶🚶 After making your way from the parking area to the trailhead, take time to look over the trailhead kiosk. Walking along the combined Pacific Crest Trail (PCT) and Overland Emigrant Trail, you'll be heading generally south for the first half of your trek. This is a moderate hike, but don't let its short length fool you. To stay adequately hydrated, you should carry at least two liters of water.

Leave the rocky trailhead and walk about 200 feet east under the cover of conifers. In about 200 feet you will begin the first of seven switchbacks that help you gain 200 feet to the nose of this ridge above Lake Mary. From the easternmost point of the second switchback, you have a good vista of Donner Pass and the railroad tracks beneath it.

The trail remains quite rocky as the soils here are undeveloped and somewhat scarce.

The end of your switchbacks will bring you across to the west side of this ridge, traversing from north to south along the margin of this lightly forested slope. As you approach a chairlift visible above the ski runs ahead, be on the lookout for a junction with a trail to

38 Mount Judah Loop

N
0
800
1,600
feet
PCT
Donner Pass Rd.
McGlashan Point
Old Donner Summit Rd.
S. Yuba River
P
PCT Trailhead
Lake Mary
Lake Mary Rd.
Donner Peak
Donner Peak Trl. Jct.
Sugar Bowl
ELDORADO NATIONAL FOREST
Mt. Judah
PCT
monument

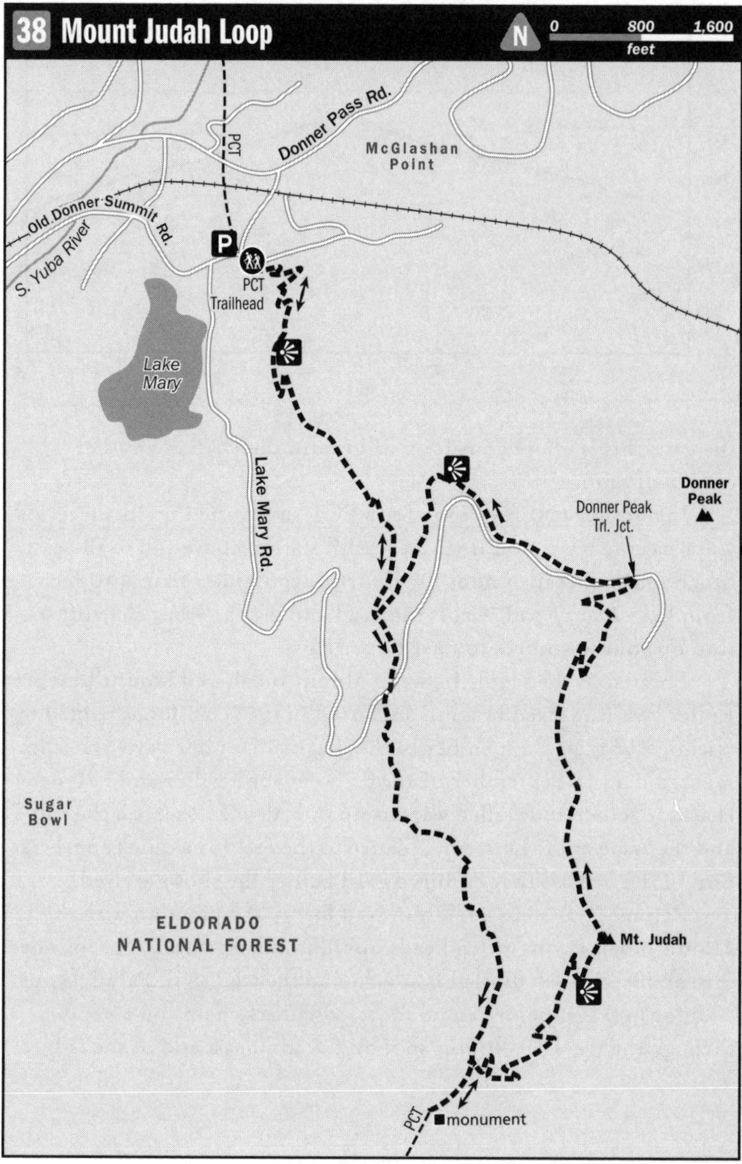

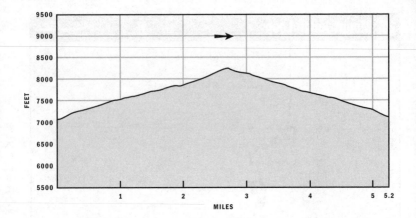

the east; this is where your loop will rejoin the PCT in another couple of hours.

In another 100 feet, look for a PCT sign posted up in a tree. As you clear the trees, you'll see a chairlift station above you to the east. Once you're directly under the chairlift, you're less than 500 feet from Lake Mary Road. Cross the road and pass another chairlift station on your way north toward Roller Pass.

Located in the saddle between Mount Judah and Mount Lincoln, Roller Pass is marked by a rail anchored in the rock. It was named by Nicholas Carriger, a member of the original Donner party. He commented that, in September of 1846, "we made a roller and fastened chains together and pulled wagons up with 12 yoke oxen on the top and the same at the bottom." Glance to the east for a quick appreciation of the ordeals they endured even before the snows arrived.

Retrace your steps a few hundred feet to the junction with the Mount Judah Loop, which heads uphill to the northeast. A reminder that no bicycles are allowed is attached to the trail sign. Parallel your trail for 550 feet before some short switchbacks help you ascend through the trees. From this spot on the southeast end of the ridge, you will climb three sets of switchbacks (two **S**'s and one **Z**) before reaching the summit.

As you wind your way up, you'll notice the frail, clinging vegetation—the pioneer species—that is also responsible for the soil-building that you see in process. Pass by some scarily impressive volcanic "bombs" as you make your way. You'll see more of these massive conglomerates when you leave the summit, which is littered with smaller volcanic debris. Mount Judah's humble summit offers all hikers a well-deserved reward for their uphill efforts. The vista here is 360 degrees and does not disappoint. You can see the PCT as it disappears toward Anderson Peak, or gaze from Mount Lincoln to Mount Disney to Lake Van Norden, and even to Castle Peak. Views from here down to Donner Lake and Shallenberger Ridge can't be beaten.

The route north is obvious as it sticks to the spine of the ridge for the first 0.25 miles, then begins dipping below to the fir and hemlock of the east slope. Stay just beneath the ridgeline for another 0.25 miles where, under the microwave antennas, you descend two easy sets of switchbacks. Follow the track down to a junction with the trail leading off to the right to Donner Peak. A short hike of 0.25 miles gets you on top of that summit. The described hike leads to the left on a tired and faded Lake Mary Road Follow this route by turning left on the Mount Judah loop trail which follows Lake Mary Road, which leads, more or less discernibly, for about 0.4 miles before the trail leaves the road and turns to the southwest. In about 0.25 miles, you'll intersect the PCT again. Turn north and retrace your steps to the trailhead.

DIRECTIONS: Heading east on Interstate 80, exit at Soda Springs and bear right on Donner Pass Road. Drive 3.6 miles and turn right. As you approach this turn, you will see the Sugar Bowl gondola on the right and Donner Ski Ranch on the left. Turn at the next street to the right, Mount Judah Road, signed SUGAR BOWL–MOUNT JUDAH PARKING. If you're coming from Truckee, take the Donner Pass Road exit from I-80 west and drive 7.1 miles to the SUGAR BOWL–MOUNT JUDAH PARKING sign on the left. Drive 0.15 miles and take the first left turn onto Old Donner Summit Road. Follow the road for 0.15 miles to the small parking lot on the left, where there is room for about 20 cars. The trailhead is 250 feet up the road on the right. There are no facilities at the trailhead parking lot.

GPS TRAILHEAD COORDINATES	38 MOUNT JUDAH LOOP
UTM Zone (WGS84)	10S
Easting	0730457
Northing	4355085
Latitude	N 39° 18.870'
Longitude	W 120° 19.614'

39 Donner Pass to Squaw Valley

SCENERY: ☆ ☆ ☆ ☆ ☆
TRAIL CONDITION: ☆ ☆ ☆ ☆
CHILDREN: ☆
DIFFICULTY: ☆ ☆ ☆ ☆
SOLITUDE: ☆ ☆ ☆ ☆
DISTANCE: 15 miles one-way
HIKING TIME: 9 hours

OUTSTANDING FEATURES: *Incredible vistas, including the Royal Gorge of the North Fork of the American River; glacially smoothed and polished granite; fragmented and scorched volcanic debris; alpine meadows full of mule's ears and ringed by fir trees draped with pale-green wolf lichen.*

The Pacific Crest Trail (PCT) stretches from Mexico to Canada for 2,650 miles. The terrain that it covers between Donner Pass and Squaw Valley is among the most beautiful of the journey. Here, where the Sierra begins its slow descent for northbound hikers, southbound day hikers enjoy the reciprocal, an easy ascent into the back-country. An uphill hike across forested ski slopes leads past Donner and Judah before crossing Roller Pass. Western hemlocks block the wind before you reach the apex of another exposed ridgeline, which you will follow to Anderson and on to Tinker. Descend into the upper reaches of the North Fork of the American River canyon, then traverse beneath Billy's Peak. Once across the headwaters of the North Fork, a 500-foot climb toward Granite Chief brings you to the trail descending to Squaw Valley, where you emerge next to the fire station.

🚶🚶 Check the information kiosk at the shared PCT–Overland Emigrant Trail trailhead. The map will give you an overview of the trails' relative locations and distances north and south of Interstate 80. Note that the only means of travel on the PCT is by foot or on horseback. Watch your step on the rocks and roots gracing the trail until the roots are replaced by switchbacks. Here your views will alternate between Donner Lake and Lake Mary. A brief hike up the nose of this ridge leads to a traverse of its western slope.

In about 1 mile, you'll reach the northern junction of the Mount Judah Loop trail and the PCT. Continue toward the chairlift and the

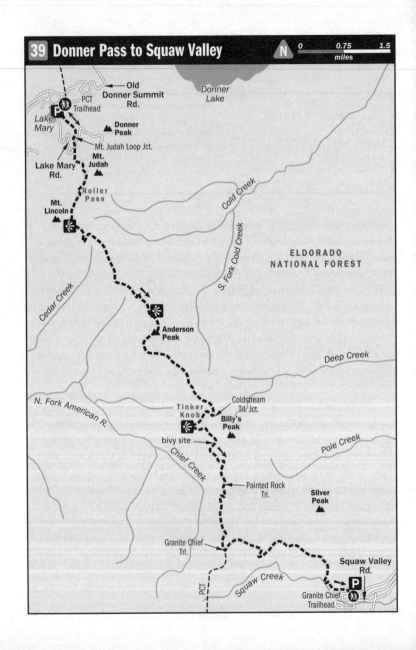

Old Donner Summit Rd.

Donner Lake

PCT Trailhead

P

Lake Mary

▲ **Donner Peak**

Mt. Judah Loop Jct.

Lake Mary Rd.

▲ **Mt. Judah**

R o l l e r   P a s s

▲ **Mt. Lincoln**

Cold Creek

S. Fork Cold Creek

ELDORADO NATIONAL FOREST

Cedar Creek

▲ **Anderson Peak**

Deep Creek

N. Fork American R.

Tinker Knob

Coldstream Trl. Jct.

▲ Billy's Peak

bivy site

Chief Creek

Pole Creek

Painted Rock Trl.

▲ **Silver Peak**

Granite Chief Trl.

Squaw Valley Rd.

P

PCT

Squaw Creek

Granite Chief Trailhead

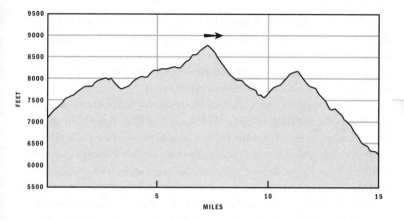

snow-making apparatus on the left, noting the PCT emblems attached to trees on the right. Walk past a beautiful meadow (terrain park) and presently cross Lake Mary Road, where a sign on the red fir reminds bikers not to be here. While the Tahoe Rim Trail permits bikers on most of the trail, they are not allowed on any portion of the PCT, which is reserved for hikers and equestrians.

Continue hiking to the south, in and out of trees and on and off of the rock of Mount Judah's slopes.

As you veer slightly southwest, after little more than an hour on the trail, you will find the marker for the south end of the Mount Judah Ridge. Here you'll have an excellent vista down into Sugar Bowl. Historic Roller Pass commemorates part of the Donner party, which persevered in bringing their wagons over this spot in September of 1846 by laying rails and yoking oxen to their wagons to haul them over this rounded saddle.

Continue on to the right uphill through hemlock, southbound on the east flank of Mount Lincoln toward the distant ridge. Just before you emerge from the hemlocks, you'll see a possible bivy site on the downhill side of the trail.

Once you make it out onto the ridge, you'll be exposed to some ferocious gusts, evidenced by the scant vegetation and clean-swept trail. You will stay on this ridge for about the next 2.75 miles. A conveniently located signpost declares that Anderson Peak is 4 miles south and Tinker Knob, an additional 2 miles.

Vistas to the north now include Mount Judah and Castle Peak. The trail flanks the eroding east slope of Mount Lincoln, where boundary signs warn skiers away from the cliffs. Views to the south include Anderson Peak and Tinker Knob. Vistas to the east include Donner Lake and Shallenberger Ridge. Before you enter the trees again, you can see your trail ahead quite distinctly against the near-naked terrain.

The trail is quite exposed on the left but if you're here in the fall, you may not notice it for the sound made by the profusion of woolly mule's ears. Fuzzy and silent and forming a sea of yellow in the summer, early fall turns them dry and brown, creating a wind song of rustling and rattling leaves. Regardless of their seasonal beauty, they do not make an effective windbreak. Two gentle switchbacks send you downhill briefly through the trees before gaining the ridge again.

Your vistas to the west are magnificent across this landscape of thin and gravelly soils held down by intermittent swaths of conifers that alternate with vast, sloping meadows of mule's ears and lupine. Leave the western white pine and red fir to cross the ridge on the way to Anderson Peak. There is a good deal of exposed trail with sharp drop-offs to the east.

A couple of switchbacks will help you up the next rounded hill before you continue an easy uphill traverse to Anderson Peak. At the next trail junction near the foot of that peak, leave the rustling mule's ears and golden buckwheat behind and follow the PCT as it heads west, to the right, while the trail to Benson Hut continues south, uphill straight ahead. As you head to the southwest on this forested slope, another trail to Benson Hut intersects the PCT at a broken trail sign directly under the summit.

The Pacific Crest Trail, leading south to Anderson Peak, stands in stark contrast on the windswept ridge.

Your course now is to continue—with broken pieces of mountain above you, below you, and under your feet—navigating around decaying Anderson Peak before resuming your southward course about 0.5 miles along the ridgeline toward Tinker Knob. Your path will be interrupted by a sign, decorated with an historic PCT emblem, that confirms the name of this crumbling roadblock that you are rounding and indicates a 4-mile hike back to Mount Lincoln.

Your path follows the windswept ridgeline to Tinker Knob, where it follows the undulating terrain uphill to a junction with the summit trail, which is set squarely in the middle of the North Slope. Follow the PCT by staying to the left; a sign with Tinker's name and elevation is just 100 yards distant.

Descend to the southeast across a broad slope filled with mule's ears and interrupted only by an occasional fir. Your vista to the southwest is one captured from this spot alone: a view into the Royal Gorge—the North Fork of the American River Canyon. Descending through the mule's ears to the junction just ahead brings you to the eastern edge of this ridge for the last time. A sharp left turn would put you on the Coldstream Trail, which would deliver you 7 miles away to Truckee.

Follow the PCT as it traverses along this margin past a PCT signpost. In about 200 yards, 7.5 miles from your trailhead, begin descending a total of 1,050 feet to the headwaters of the North Fork of the American River. Start a businesslike descent on a southerly switchback and take a **U**-turn back to the north before long, undulating switchback down to about 8,100 feet, where you will get a different, but still excellent vista into the Royal Gorge. Here, you'll make an abrupt turn to the east, beginning a long, loopy traverse beneath Billy's Peak. Be on the lookout for a year-round spring 0.25 miles ahead. A second spring feeds the creek that you will cross in another 100 yards. About 300 yards after that you'll spot a suitable campsite in the flat spot a few hundred feet off the trail sheltered by a copse of conifers.

Descend to the south, and shortly after emerging from the trees, enter another field of mule's ears sitting on top of volcanic soil with several runoff drainages. The area also supports a proliferation of firs, which easily take root here. Just before crossing another runoff stream in the apex of this canyon, you will find late-blooming clarkia along with Indian rhubarb and tobacco brush. Cross the stream and head uphill into the western white pines and red firs. Just before the ascent, note a suitable bivy site on the east side of the trail. In a few hundred feet another broad vista opens up to the west for you.

Continue descending next to this huge granite wall, your trail graced by Jeffrey pine and western juniper. If you notice a subliminal craving for butterscotch at this time, blame it on the Jeffrey pine, which emit a butterscotch or vanilla scent from the bark. As the PCT crosses bare granite slopes, follow the ducks or, in some places, the faint blue or red blaze painted on trailside boulders. When you come upon a fractured PCT sign and a seasonal stream, look for good bivy sites near a large meadow about 200 yards to the southeast. In less than 200 feet you'll come upon the Painted Rock Trail, which heads to the northwest. From here, approximately 10 miles from your trailhead, you'll begin a 650-foot ascent to the Granite Chief Trail, just 1.1 miles ahead.

As a side trip from this point, look for the trail about 1,000 feet ahead on the left, which leads up to Mountain Meadow Lake. The unmaintained trail parallels the PCT and meets the PCT at the Granite Chief Trail junction 1.2 miles ahead, so no backtracking would be necessary if you wanted to take that route. On the PCT, ascend the ridge via two sets of **Z**-shaped switchbacks and continue along the ridge until you fall away to the right to skirt this knob above you. Stay just below the ridge until you reach the PCT signpost. Ten paces farther south is the junction of the Granite Chief Trail. If you wanted to bag another peak, it is only 1.5 miles from this junction to Granite Chief.

The described trail turns to the northeast and begins descending the 4 miles to Squaw Valley. In another 500 feet, you get a momentary view of Lake Tahoe in the distance. Descend through the forest on five switchbacks, which are interrupted by a small meadow. Continue losing elevation as you travel east at the foot of Silver Peak's smaller companion. As you approach a much larger alpine meadow, notice the blaze, in the shape of the small letter *i*, on the solitary white pine surrounded by firs. The trail is rather rocky now as it heads through sagebrush and buckbrush into the aspens.

As soon as you hit the polished granite, your destination comes into view. Decay seems to be the word of the moment on this slope. Fallen trees left in place over decades have left their mark on the rock, which is itself splitting, shattering, and crumbling. Follow the ducks past mountain pride penstemon occupying cracks and crevices, soil-packed refuges for seeds. While the trail is easy to follow, pay close attention as it descends at a fair pace. Remember to look for ducks and now gold- or yellow-painted blazes. Three short legs will navigate you around an obstacle near the top of this outcrop—500 feet west, 200 feet south, and 500 feet east—before you descend into a glacially carved ravine.

Your path is a gentle and quiet descent well above Squaw Creek. You have about 700 feet left to descend; look for a spring on the uphill side of the trail while you're still traveling east. Indian paintbrush is a constant trailside partner as you cross small streams about four times over the next 0.5 miles. Follow the ducks closely as you continue heading slightly southeast over the next 150 vertical feet down to the trailhead. The trail terminates at the sign next to the fire station in Squaw Valley.

DIRECTIONS: Heading east on Interstate 80, exit at Soda Springs and bear right on Donner Pass Road. Drive 3.6 miles and turn right. As you approach this turn, you will see the Sugar Bowl gondola on the right and Donner Ski Ranch on the left. Turn at the next street to the right, Mount Judah Road, signed SUGAR BOWL–MOUNT JUDAH PARKING. If you're coming from Truckee, take the Donner Pass Road exit from I-80 west and drive 7.1 miles to the SUGAR BOWL–MOUNT JUDAH PARKING sign on the left. Drive 0.15 miles and take the first left turn onto Old Donner Summit Road. Follow the road for 0.15 miles to the small parking lot on the left, where there is room for about 20 cars. The trailhead is 250 feet up the road on the right. There are no facilities at the trailhead parking lot.

GPS TRAILHEAD COORDINATES	39 DONNER PASS TO SQUAW VALLEY
UTM Zone (WGS84)	10S
Easting	0730460
Northing	4355082
Latitude	N 39° 18.868'
Longitude	W 120° 19.612'

40 Loch Leven Lakes

SCENERY: ☆ ☆ ☆
TRAIL CONDITION: ☆ ☆ ☆
CHILDREN: ☆ ☆ ☆
DIFFICULTY: ☆ ☆ ☆
SOLITUDE: ☆ ☆

DISTANCE: *6.6 miles round-trip*
HIKING TIME: *4 hours*
OUTSTANDING FEATURES: *Three subalpine lakes within easy reach of the trailhead, which is conveniently located close to Big Bend west of Donner Summit*

Loch Leven's convenient trailhead access makes this a popular day hike destination. Hikers are rewarded for their 1,000-foot uphill climb with a selection of subalpine lakes and generous vistas of tree-clad and exposed-granite slopes festooned with flowers of every color.

🏃 Your hike to Loch Leven Lakes begins at approximately 5,800 feet elevation on the south side of Hampshire Rocks Road. While you will navigate generally southwest, you'll need to pay close attention to the obvious trail, often marked by ducks, as it winds around some of the granite outcrops that characterize this terrain. Initially, rocky switchbacks will help you gain a bit of elevation above the road. It seems as if each crack and crevice in every granite step is graced by penstemon in early July. The flat, sandy, gravelly spots are decorated with pale-pink pussy toes. And there is more color to come.

The trail follows the terrain back to the east, crossing a marshy area before ascending on granite-block steps to the west. More switchbacks and changes of direction will bring you up a boulder staircase along a granite slab that ends beneath a large juniper. Ducks will line your path and may sit on top of boulders that form your trail across the granite, leading to a copse of lodgepole pine and a small granite dome on the trail's north side.

A small runoff pond, just large enough to attract a squadron of mosquitoes, crowds the trail as you head west outlining the edge of this rounded granite block. In a moment you will spy railroad

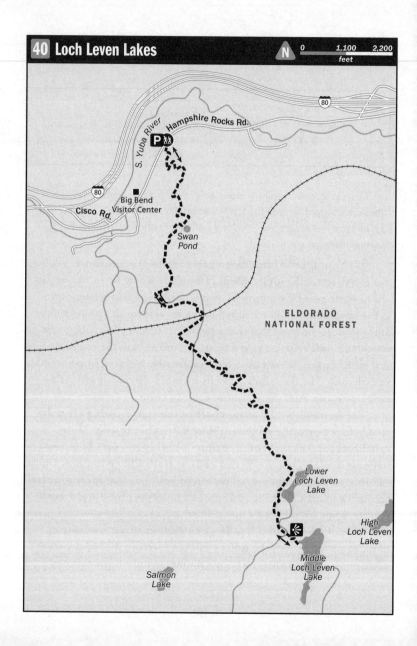

N

0   1,100   2,200
feet

80

Hampshire Rocks Rd.

S. Yuba River

P

Cisco Rd.

80

Big Bend
Visitor Center

Swan
Pond

ELDORADO
NATIONAL FOREST

Lower
Loch Leven
Lake

High
Loch Leven
Lake

Middle
Loch Leven
Lake

Salmon
Lake

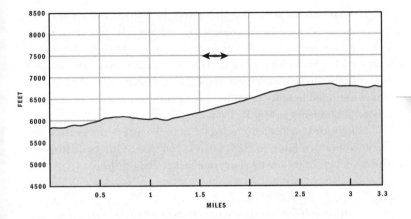

tracks off to the west at the point where they emerge from the tunnels originally built by Chinese laborers for the Central Pacific Railroad. Head south and descend towards the creek, where you will cross on a footbridge that attracts radiant orange and red columbine. From the footbridge, I mile from the trailhead, you will make a short, traversing ascent east to the railroad tracks 0.25 miles away.

The trail reaches the tracks beneath the signal light structure across from a control box sitting next to your trail. Cross the double tracks here and resume ascending the trail. A note of caution: if you see a train just as it emerges from the tunnels, you will probably arrive at the track junction at the same time as the train. Always use caution when crossing: trains run in both directions around the clock.

The first of a baker's dozen of switchbacks up your 800-foot climb begins by heading southwest. Intermittent sunshine breaks through the top of this fir forest, spotlighting the deep-purple larkspur, bright-red Indian paintbrush, subtle-blue lupine, and yellow wallflower. In about 0.75 miles, you will notice the sun shining on you more brightly as the trees thin out and the terrain contours more to reach a notch overlooking lake number one.

Descend on the sand-and-gravel trail to a small clearing adjacent to Lower Loch Leven Lake, where a sign informs: Middle Loch Leven Lake—0.25 miles, Cherry Point Trail—0.5 miles, High Loch Leven Lake—1 mile. You may enjoy a short walk to picturesque Middle Loch Leven Lake, where checkerspot and hairstreak butterflies abound. There are small beaches to lounge on, islands to swim out to, and plenty of campsites at Middle Lake.

Hikers looking for a bit more solitude can ascend fewer than 100 feet in about 0.6 miles to High Loch Leven Lake. Otherwise linger and swim before following your trail back to the trailhead.

DIRECTIONS: Heading east on Interstate 80 from Sacramento, take the Cisco Road exit and turn left under the freeway. Turn right on Hampshire Rocks Road and drive 1.8 miles to a parking area on the north side of the road. Or you can take the next exit, Big Bend, and drive 0.4 miles to the parking area. If driving west from Reno, exit at Donner Pass and cross under the freeway. Turn right on Hampshire Rocks Road and drive 0.9 miles to the trailhead parking. There are pit toilets available at this popular parking area. The signed trailhead is on the south side of the road across from the parking area.

GPS Trailhead Coordinates	40 Loch Leven Lakes
UTM Zone (WGS84)	10S
Easting	0714192
Northing	4354045
Latitude	N 39° 18.559'
Longitude	W 120° 30.854'

Appendix A: Managing Agencies

ELDORADO NATIONAL FOREST
100 Forni Road
Placerville, CA 95667
(530) 622-5061
www.fs.fed.us/r5/eldorado

U.S. FOREST SERVICE
LAKE TAHOE BASIN MANAGEMENT
    UNIT
35 College Drive
South Lake Tahoe, CA 96150
(530) 543-2600
www.fs.fed.us/r5/ltbmu

U.S. FOREST SERVICE
NORTH TAHOE OFFICE
3080 North Lake Boulevard
Tahoe City, CA 96145
(530) 583-3593
www.fs.fed.us/r5/ltbmu

U.S. FOREST SERVICE
TAYLOR CREEK VISITOR CENTER
(530) 543-2674
www.fs.fed.us/r5/ltbmu/
recreation/visitor-center

TAHOE NATIONAL FOREST
631 Coyote Street
Nevada City, CA 95959
(530) 265-4531
www.fs.fed.us/r5/tahoe

TAHOE NATIONAL FOREST
BIG BEND VISITOR CENTER
49685 Hampshire Rocks Road
(old US 40) (at the Big Bend or
Rainbow Road exits off of I-80)
P.O. Box 830
Soda Springs, CA 95728
(530) 426-3609
www.fs.fed.us/r5/tahoe/
recreation/big_bend/index.shtml

TAHOE RIM TRAIL ASSOCIATION
948 Incline Way
Incline Village, NV 89451
(775) 298-0231
www.tahoerimtrail.org

TRUCKEE RANGER DISTRICT
(Donner Pass, Little Truckee
Summit, Truckee River/CA 89
South, NV 267 areas)
9646 Donner Pass Road
Truckee, CA 96161
(530) 587-3558
www.fs.fed.us/r5/tahoe/
contactus/tkrd.shtml

LAKE TAHOE NEVADA STATE PARK
P.O. Box 8867
Incline Village, NV 89452
(775) 831-0494
www.parks.nv.gov/lt.htm
tahoe@parks.nv.gov

Humboldt-Toiyabe National
Forest
1200 Franklin Way
Sparks, NV 89431
(775) 331-6444
www.fs.fed.us/htnf

Humboldt-Toiyabe National
Forest
Carson Ranger District
1536 Carson Street
Carson City, NV 89701
(775) 882-2766
www.fs.fed.us/htnf

Appendix B: Permits

CAMPFIRE PERMIT

You must have a campfire permit to use a stove, lantern, charcoal grill, or wood campfire outside of a developed campground or recreation area. The permit is your agreement to follow the campfire restrictions and regulations in effect.

WILDERNESS PERMITS

The Eldorado National Forest cooperatively manages two wilderness areas with other forests. Both Desolation Wilderness and Mokelumne Wilderness require permits for overnight stays. Desolation Wilderness also requires day permits. Both Desolation and Mokelumne Wilderness Areas require permits year-round.

The permit requirements and processes differ significantly between the two. To learn more about Wilderness areas and to find out how to acquire permits for Desolation and Mokelumne, check out the wilderness page at **www.fs.fed.us/r5/eldorado/recreation/wild**.

CARSON PASS MANAGEMENT AREA

Because of the popularity of the Carson Pass Area, restrictions are now in effect to ensure your opportunities for solitude and a primitive recreational experience, and to protect popular camping destinations from overcrowding and heavy impacts. See the details at **www .fs.fed.us/r5/eldorado/recreation/wild/moke/cpma**.

MOKELUMNE WILDERNESS PERMITS

Permits are mandatory for entry into the Mokelumne Wilderness year round for overnight use.

ANNUAL-USE PASS

This pass allows you to park at six popular trailhead facilities. Parking is normally $5 per day, and the pass costs $20. This is a big savings if you intend to do more than one overnight in these specific areas. These passes are available at the Taylor Creek Visitor Center or the Carson Pass Ranger Station.

The forests appear to cooperate in their management practices. There are exceptions such as the Mokelumne Wilderness near Carson Pass. The ranger station in Jackson cannot issue permits for this special area, even though it is in the same forest; permits can only be obtained at the Carson Pass Ranger Station.

Other cases like this exist, so my advice is to always call ahead to clarify the current permit situation.

In General

Pick up permits for **WEST** side entry at the

Pacific Ranger District

Located 4 miles east of Pollock Pines on Highway 50 near Fresh Pond.

7887 Highway 50

Pollock Pines, CA 95726

(530) 644-6048

Winter: Weekdays only; Monday through Saturday as of late April

Summer: 7 days a week, 8 a.m. to 4:30 p.m. through October

Pick up permit for **EAST** side entry at the

Taylor Creek Visitor Center

Located 3 miles north of the Highway 50/89 junction at South Lake Tahoe, on Highway 89.

Call for hours: (530) 543-2674. Open summer only.

Tahoe Basin Management Unit

Located 2 miles east of the Highway 50/89 junction in South Lake Tahoe on Highway 50. From the highway turn right on Al Tahoe Boulevard, and then turn right at the first signal.

35 College Drive

South Lake Tahoe, CA 96150

(530) 543-2600

Arno, Stephen F. *Discovering Sierra Trees*. Yosemite, CA: Yosemite Association, 1973.

Basey, Harold E. *Discovering Sierra Reptiles and Amphibians*. Yosemite, CA: Yosemite Association, 2004.

Blackwell, Laird R. *Wildflowers of the Sierra Nevada and the Central Valley*. Edmonton, AB, Canada: Lone Pine Press, 1999.

Blackwell, Laird R., *Tahoe Wildflowers: A Month-by-Month Guide to Wildflowers in the Tahoe Basin and Surrounding Areas*. Helena, MT: A Falcon Guide, 2007.

Hill, Mary. *Geology of the Sierra Nevada*. Berkeley: University of California Press, 2006.

Horn, Elizabeth L. *Sierra Nevada Wildflowers*. Missoula, MT: Mountain Press Company, 1998.

James, George Wharton. *The Lake of the Sky—Lake Tahoe*. Boston: L. C. Page & Company, 1915.

Laws, John Muir. *The Laws Field Guide to the Sierra Nevada*. Berkeley: Heyday Books, 2007.

Lekish, Barbara. *Tahoe Place Names*. Lafayette, CA: Great West Books, 1988.

Miller, Millie, and Cyndi Nelson. *Talons: North American Birds of Prey*. Boulder, CO: Johnson Books, 1989.

Murie, Olaus J. *Peterson Field Guide: A Field Guide to Animal Tracks*. Boston: Houghton Mifflin Company, 1974.

Niehaus, Theodore F., and Charles L. Ripper. *Peterson Field Guide: A Field Guide to Pacific States Wildflowers*. Boston: Houghton Mifflin Company, 1976.

APPENDIX C

(Continued on next page)

Powers, Phil. *National Outdoor Leadership School Wilderness Mountaineering.* Mechanicsburg, PA: Stackpole Books, 1993.

Russo, Ron, and Pam Olhausan. *Mammal Finder.* Berkeley: Nature Study Guild, 1987.

Schimelpfenig, Todd, and Linda Lindsey. *National Outdoor Leadership School Wilderness First Aid,* 3rd ed. Mechanicsburg, PA: Stackpole Books, 2000.

Storer, Tracy I., Robert L. Usinger, and David Lukas. *Sierra Nevada Natural History.* Berkeley: University of California Press, 2004.

Thomas, John H., and Dennis R. Parnell. *Native Shrubs of the Sierra Nevada.* Berkeley: University of California Press, 1974.

Underhill, J. E. *Sagebrush Wildflowers.* Blaine, WA: Hancock House, Inc., 1986.

Wells, Darran. *National Outdoor Leadership School Wilderness Navigation.* Mechanicsburg, PA: Stackpole Books, 2005.

Whitman, Ann H., ed. *Audubon Society Guide: Familiar Trees of North America: Western Region.* New York: Alfred A. Knopf, 1988.

Whitney, Stephen. *A Sierra Club Naturalist's Guide: The Sierra Nevada.* San Francisco: Sierra Club Books, 1979.

Index

INDEX

About the Author

JORDAN SUMMERS, a native of North Carolina, grew up near the Smoky Mountains of Tennessee and the Blue Ridge Mountains of Virginia. His teen years in La Jolla, California, introduced him to new terrain and to the Sierra Club.

Summers's undergraduate years at the U.S. Air Force Academy in Colorado exposed him to even more diverse hiking in the Four Corners region—desert, canyon, forest, and mountain.

A high-tech career in Southern California brought him near the mountains for hikes of all kinds—day hikes, ultralight weekends, or weeklong treks. As friends asked him to arrange and lead trips, it became apparent that some new skills were needed. An educational expedition in Wyoming's Wind River Range not only enhanced those skills but also taught Summers how to safely share the outdoor experience using Leave No Trace techniques.

As his daughter and son grew to become more constant hiking partners, Summers had to tackle the problem of how to move their gear into the wilderness. Llamas worked well at this, as it turned out, and by 1991 Summers was leading treks with llamas into wilderness areas of Oregon and California. Summers also served during this time as a local chapter president of the Sierra Club.

Sacramento has been Summers's gateway to the Sierra Nevada and Coast Range for more than a decade.

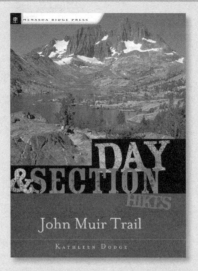

AMERICAN HIKING SOCIETY

Because you
hike.
We're with you
every step of the way

American Hiking Society gives voice to the more than 75 million Americans who hike and is the only national organization that promotes and protects foot trails, the natural areas that surround them and the hiking experience. Our work is inspiring and challenging, and is built on three pillars:

Volunteerism and Stewardship: We organize and coordinate nationally recognized programs – including Volunteer Vacations, National Trails Day® and the National Trails Fund –that help keep our trails open, safe and enjoyable.

Policy and Advocacy: We work with Congress and federal agencies to ensure funding for trails, the preservation of natural areas, and the protection of the hiking experience.

Outreach and Education: We expand and support the national constituency of hikers through outreach and education as well as partnerships with other recreation and conservation organizations.

Join us in our efforts. Become an American Hiking Society member today!

American
Hiking
Society

1422 Fenwick Lane · Silver Spring, MD 20910 · (301) 565-6704
www.AmericanHiking.org · info@AmericanHiking.org

DEAR CUSTOMERS AND FRIENDS,

SUPPORTING YOUR INTEREST IN OUTDOOR ADVENTURE, travel, and an active lifestyle is central to our operations, from the authors we choose to the locations we detail to the way we design our books. Menasha Ridge Press was incorporated in 1982 by a group of veteran outdoorsmen and professional outfitters. For 25 years now, we've specialized in creating books that benefit the outdoors enthusiast.

Almost immediately, Menasha Ridge Press earned a reputation for revolutionizing outdoors- and travel-guidebook publishing. For such activities as canoeing, kayaking, hiking, backpacking, and mountain biking, we established new standards of quality that transformed the whole genre, resulting in outdoor-recreation guides of great sophistication and solid content. Menasha Ridge continues to be outdoor publishing's greatest innovator.

The folks at Menasha Ridge Press are as at home on a white-water river or mountain trail as they are editing a manuscript. The books we build for you are the best they can be, because we're responding to your needs. Plus, we use and depend on them ourselves.

We look forward to seeing you on the river or the trail. If you'd like to contact us directly, join in at www.trekalong.com or visit us at www.menasharidge.com. We thank you for your interest in our books and the natural world around us all.

SAFE TRAVELS,

Bob Sehlinger

BOB SEHLINGER
PUBLISHER